HEAVEN MUST BE
LIKE THIS

Also by Kurt Erkan

Poetry
And Five, Six, Seven, Eight!

HEAVEN MUST BE LIKE THIS

KURT ERKAN

HETSOFF

ISBN: 978-3-00-043556-0
eISBN: 978-3-00-043557-7

Editor: Marissa von Uden
Cover design: Virginie Lamoureux

Printed by CreateSpace, An Amazon.com Company

First paperback edition
First published in 2014

www.hetsoff.com

For my mother and father

Gluttonyday
14 SEPTEMBER

MY FATHER OPENED the door. 'You are the first again, as usual,' he said with warm laughter and grabbed on to me. My father had always clung on to me. A strange feeling. I usually felt confident and strong, independent of any event or person in my personal history. I always loved to be alive, I always loved living. But when he hugged me so, I often felt as if I was actually gaining strength from his being on this world, from him being my father, and from the fact that he was breathing.

I didn't want to think about him ever being absent. As if not thinking about this could save us.

Whenever I saw an article in a newspaper or magazine about a very old man still living, I would instantly gain some hope. I would start to think that it was possible for people to live very long and continue to work. This always made me to refresh my hope about my father living long – longer.

He went to the sitting room, passing through the main hall. He was wearing a striped light-blue shirt and had combed his hair back in a tidy manner. He was expressing his joy for life through his self-care. His fondness for his thinned hair was huge.

He stopped at the dinner table and turned suddenly towards me.

'I missed you. Where have you been for so long?'

'So long? I was here on Saturday, Dad!'

'But you didn't show your face. Okay, I got it, but you might at least call me more often,' he said.

'You're right, old fella. Forgive me. I bought new books. It took a long time to place them all on the shelves. It's not so easy to carry out all these errands on my own, as you know.' I was telling the truth. It was not an excuse.

According to him, I should support him. I was sure he was thinking this again, but this time he didn't mention it and just laughed. I read it in his bluest eyes.

'Your sister is here. We came from the office together. Her husband is still lying low.' He called out towards the kitchen. Lori (*Scorpio*) was very chic as usual. She was dressed and made up as if she was going to an important party, though it was just a small inter-family dinner. I do not know how she finds time to make such preparations. Lori finds time for everything, every time. Time must move particularly slowly for Lori. She must have found a way to persuade the clocks, somehow.

'How are you, kiddo?' she asked. We hugged and kissed each other.

'I am very fine, just a little tired. How are things with you?'

'Can't you see how I am?' she said, and turned around twice, opening her hands to each side. 'It's enough to say "as usual", I think.'

Yes, it was enough. She looked perfect again. Whether her husband was aware of it or not. Anyway, Lori didn't care about her husband being aware of her.

I thought about it all again. I really loved my sister. Her unique, indifferent attitudes towards the world... If I had half the confidence she had, I would not be thirsty for anything in life.

While we were having a quick word, the doorbell rang. Andrew, one of my father's loyal live-in housekeepers, brought in the new guests of the night. Eric (*Sagittarius*) and Danielle (*Pisces*) would also be joining us. They were considered members of the family. Upon seeing Eric, my father put a smile on his face and ran towards him.

'My lad! You came a bit earlier. This is very nice. You have also brought my favourite belle. How gorgeous the night will be with all of you,' he said, starting to distribute his laughs generously even from the beginning of the night.

'Everything is for you, big boss,' Eric said. He was definitely a part of our family; we had known him and his trademark style for a long time, and he knew just what to say and when to say it around us.

I had already become used to his attitudes. He always said these words to my father, but sincerely and without any hidden agendas. He was not just sincere to my father but also to anyone in our family.

While my father was happily welcoming Danielle, treating her like she was a candy apple that had been offered to him as a gift, I managed to interrupt him, with some difficulty, and said 'Welcome!' to Danielle.

Winking at me, Eric turned towards my sister and kissed her cheek, saying, 'How is it possible to become more and more beautiful every day?'

Though Lori was used to getting many compliments, it was apparent in her eyes that this time she internalised the compliment and carried it with honour. Because it had come from Eric.

She was on the verge of replying to his compliment when Eric turned to me. We grabbed on to each other, and he whispered, 'I am very bored, bro.'

I had no time to ask him why, because my father called to us.

'With this outstanding beauty—'

'Oh, Mr Kushner..., don't do it...,' Danielle said.

'Why? I'm just stating the obvious. Anyway, we will drink some cold spirits in the garden. In fact, we do not "want" any of you, do we, Danielle, but out of courtesy, we should ask whether anyone wishes to accompany us?'

'No, Mr Kushner, we don't want 'em,' Danielle said with laughter.

The offer guaranteed such comfort, peace and joy that no one could refuse it. As Eric and I followed them outside, Lori left the group, saying that she was going to check on Andrew in the kitchen.

The garden was very fresh with all the colours and smells it hosted. The four of us stood and talked, enjoying the cold cherry cocktails that were cooling us all down. We were peaceful; life seemed good.

This garden had something that always gave me peace. Only here did I not feel the pessimism that invaded me in autumn evenings at sunset. Or maybe I should say, I felt the pessimism every now and then, but even that feeling could not disturb me when I was in that garden.

Actually, this house and garden had many possibilities for upsetting me. My mother died here one summer evening in the garden. How strange that I feel ashamed of saying that I was peaceful here. I could utter the following words to justify my feelings: maybe my mother's soul wanders around the garden; maybe that's the thing which gives me peace, even though I am not aware of its presence.

Like every moment when my father can find or create the opportunity, he began to ask Eric questions.

'What happened with that man I told you to call? Did you evaluate his proposal? I care for him a lot. I will be very glad if you can support him. And there's another subject I want to ask you about, but this is a personal issue. Will you be available for me alone for a couple of hours tomorrow?'

'Unfortunately, boss, I will be out of the city tomorrow,' Eric said. 'What's the matter? If you wish, I can come and visit you early the next day.'

'All right, then. I want to make a decision on this matter as soon as possible. After dinner tonight, we can talk a little before you leave. If, of course, this beautiful woman allows us to do so.'

Danielle smiled at my father, which meant, "Of course, boss."

'How can she say no to you?' Eric said.

The quick footsteps of Andrew passing through the hall meant that the doorbell had rung again.

'Our big braggart might have come,' said my father. 'I wonder how quarrelling with everybody leaves him any time to run the restaurant...'

'I think the restaurant runs itself,' Eric said, 'so I don't believe he needs to put much effort into it – unless you count watching the customers, and especially the women.'

My father added, 'That stupid bastard will still make a hash of it, no doubt!'

By this time, James (*Gemini*) had already passed through the garden gate and was walking towards us.

'Hello, Father. Hello, V,' he said, shaking our hands, and then turned to Danielle who he had never met before 'Hello, I'm James.'

'Hi,' Danielle said.

Finally, he shook Eric's hand without uttering his name. Though they smiled at each other, they seemed so tense they might have been in a pre-boxing-match press conference. Their hands met roughly, briefly, and released.

'You surprised me by coming this early,' my father said.

'Half past seven, Lori told me.'

'Yes, I'm surprised that you made it on time. You must have a hell of a lot of work on at the restaurant,' my father said, and looked first at me and then at Eric, raising his eyebrows.

I bowed my head to hide my smile, while Eric laughed, looking directly at James.

It was a little chilly outside. The garden was filled with the scents of different flowers and trees. Though we were very close to the city, we were somehow isolated from the big-city noise. We could hear the birds singing. This moment of peace felt great for me after the last couple of tiring days.

Lori came out to the garden and kissed James, saying, 'Welcome, honey!' just like a happy couple do. They put their hands on each other's waists.

James looked at me. 'Yesterday, Gary stopped by the restaurant and waited for you for ages. Why didn't you come? We wanted very much to knock back a drink together. We three brothers together, I mean.'

The expression "brothers" was not a valid term for the three of us, but still I replied, 'A large delivery of books arrived at the store and I was busy processing them. But I'd already told Gary that I might not be able to make it. Why did he still wait for me?'

My father answered, 'Son, when is your brother ever reasonable, huh?'

The evening gained its rhythm as more people arrived. All our favourite faces – and the ones we merely tolerated – would be there that night.

This get-together was very important for my father. His company, which he had worked his ass off for, was sixty-five years old today, and he was celebrating this together with all those he considered family.

I wish I could call it "our company." I had tried to for a while, a very long time ago, but I soon understood that it was not and never would be "mine". In time, I gave up the desire to call it mine.

The only people we were still waiting for were my brother Gary and his wife Amy. We continued to horse around until they arrived. We chatted and gossiped. My father whispered to Eric, while Lori and James talked together, trying not to reflect their nervousness. Danielle told me she wanted to see the new titles that had arrived at my bookstore and would visit me there as soon as possible.

'It's been a long time since I stopped by,' she said. 'Maybe I can help you as well – with the errands I mean. How's that sound?'

'Of course, whenever you want.'

I didn't actually take so much pleasure from spending time with Danielle. Especially not in recent times. This displeasure wasn't because I couldn't get along with her or didn't like her, but because when we spent time together, I often felt that I was walking on a high wire. I was afraid of falling.

The small chatting groups we formed quickly exchanged their members, and time passed. Nancy, Andrew's wife, spotted the late couple approaching the garden gate.

'Mr Kushner, Gary and Amy have arrived. Shall we start serving dinner?'

My father gave his approval with a nod, and Nancy hurried inside at once. As she disappeared, my brother and his wife entered the garden.

'At last, at last! The artistic bohemian approaches... Do you always have to be the last one?' This reproach was my father's welcome to Gary.

'Father, please forgive me. I left my wallet and car keys at the atelier. We had to go back and—'

'Okay, it doesn't matter. Enjoy a drink out here, and then we'll have the meal. I am very hungry. Welcome, Amy.'

My father accepted Amy (*Leo*) as his real daughter. If it had been possible, if my mother's life had not come to an end, I am sure he would have had more children. Instead, he filled this hole with others, like Eric and Amy. He loved all of us and would certainly continue to do so. I'd never had any doubt about it. Except in the case of James. Unfortunately, he treated James as if he were just a naughty stranger who he didn't love and never would. And if you asked me whether James deserved it or not, I'd say he didn't even deserve to be a stranger around this family.

Again, there were handshakes, hugs, chats about weight loss and nice shirts, very smart shoes. Gary (*Aquarius*), like James, was meeting Danielle for the first time that evening. It happened to be my duty to introduce them to each other.

'I seem to know you, but I can't quite place where from,' said Gary.

Without losing time, Amy cut in: 'From TV commercials. She trots her gorgeous legs around every night in our house. You should remember her from there.'

'Oh come on, don't do that to me; it's an embarrassing thing – a very old campaign. They're using it for the second time this year. They say "the target audience likes it a lot." But, good news: I don't do commercials anymore.'

'Bad news,' James said, smiling. Nobody laughed.

'Why not?' Amy asked Danielle.

'I am planning to become the wife of my prince.' This answer attracted all the party's attention to Danielle in an instant. She took

Eric's arm and leaned her head on his shoulder.

My father beat Eric's shoulder and burst into laughter, but Eric didn't seem pleased about the "news coverage". He tried to behave as calmly as he could and accepted the congratulations with what appeared to be an involuntary smile. Though their reasons were different from each other's, Eric, Lori and Amy all reacted to the new information as best as they could, all with similar calmness, all taking sips from their beverages.

'We are still thinking about it; we will see,' Eric said with a tone of voice that seemed to persuade neither himself nor any others. 'Nothing's concrete yet.'

When Nancy invited us inside to the dinner table, my father began to give a speech to Eric about how good it was that Eric and Danielle would be married. Danielle and I led the rest of the group inside for dinner. I was congratulating her and making meaningless jokes to help her regain her pleasure, as she seemed out of spirits due to Eric's attitude – she had given the good news about her marriage plans, and her heart had been injured immediately after. If a painter were to see Danielle's face, he or she could not help but draw this sorrow. My father was walking with Eric, and although they were at the back of the group, I could still clearly hear my father's excited chatter and questions; he had opinions on every subject for Eric. He was like a child meeting his best friend after a long while – that cheerful.

The table had been elaborated as usual by Andrew, a man who never missed a detail. Whenever you sat at Andrew's table, you always asked yourself whether you deserved that much. I could not understand how my father had, despite his severe illnesses, persuaded Nancy to prepare such diversified and delicious (meaning, mostly hazardous to my father) dishes. It is irrational to think "He's her boss, so it's easy," because there didn't exist a boss-personnel relationship between them. Nancy had refused this idea from the beginning.

Her strange thought-systematic might be attributed to a confidence gained after living in the same house with him for more than forty years, but my father always said she'd had the last word on household issues ever since the very first day. She had adopted this role of being the "biggest boss of the house" so well that no one ever wanted to say anything about it. After my mother passed away, she had filled the vacant "mother role" in this same way – without making us realise it, and maybe even without recognising it herself; it was in her blood. Nancy was always right. She had an inborn wisdom. It was something of which she made the best and never cast off. She was in a way one of the observable versions of the word "gifted."

If it had been up to her, she would have prepared different kinds of boiled vegetables and salads and maybe one or two (at most) dishes that included fish – salmon, probably. But that night, she had prepared an incredible menu for my father. Just seeing such a table, let alone eating something from it, could be dangerous for a diabetic old man with high blood pressure.

From the moment I first saw the beauties on the table, I felt that I needed to keep my father away from the inevitable battle of the wills that would unfold.

My father showed each of us to our seats, starting with me. I sat at one end of the table, and he sat at the other end. Lori took her seat on the right side of my father, as usual, Gary on the left. James and Amy took the seats next to their spouses. My left and right side were for Danielle and Eric, respectively.

This frame in which we took our seats created a happy picture in spite of our pasts, our ever-lasting small conflicts, and our differences in core worldviews. Could disparity evolve into happiness?

'I thank all of you for being here tonight,' my father said. 'You know why we have gathered together. I will not beat around the bush like a boring old man. All the people around this table are the most valuable to me: the ones I like most and with whom I want to share my happiness and sorrow. You are all my children. Together, you form the most valuable crowd in the world for me.

'The company I founded exactly sixty-five years ago became what it is today thanks to all your support and sacrifice. Therefore, this is not a celebration, but a thanksgiving dinner. Cheers!'

After the toast, he continued to talk a little more sincerely, sometimes with his blue eyes swimming in a lake of tears. He talked about how he started the business, how he developed it each and every day of his life, and how he wished my mother could have seen it now.

However, he didn't mean everyone at the table with his moving and honourable words of gratitude, and we all knew this. For instance, my brother and I had not supported him as much as he'd wished during his long journey. We had not stood by him like the girls had – Lori and Amy had taken our places. Therefore, they deserved his thanks the most. Naturally, Danielle and James accepted the credit, even though they had almost nothing to do with the company. But Eric could feel proud and share my father's happiness sincerely. In fact, Eric had put in more effort for the company than me and Gary. He was like a counselling centre for Mr Kushner, providing his service 24/7.

My father had always been in charge of the company over the last sixty-five years, through hard times, war times and economic crises. If I was to define his dedication to his company in the shortest way, I would say the company was like his fifth child (his fourth child was Eric).

My father had loved my mother very much, and after she died, he didn't marry again, though he had many opportunities. 'You are already grown-up men. From now on, I do not want to bear listening to a woman's grumbling,' he said, closing this subject even before it was opened. But we were not so grown-up at the time; he just wanted us to believe that we were.

My mother's untimely and unexpected death made him dedicate himself heavily to his work, to continuously dealing with and developing the company – it was an escape from this pain. On the other hand, he never quit investing a lot of time to his favourite books. He spent all his holidays – I mean, the rare holidays he had – at second-hand bookstores in different parts of the world, trying to collect valuable and old books. The books were in languages he didn't understand and were about people he didn't know but who had left their marks in life.

My father was a purely self-made man. He had not attended university but had learned French on his own efforts by going on private courses. He tried to compensate for his knowledge deficiency by reading a lot – a hell of a lot. 'Do you consider yourselves "wise" men just because you got some grades?' my father would always bark at me and Eric. 'I am much more of a graduate than you bastards. Go and read some books – more books – instead of gadding around.'

Though he was a very disciplined man, the one thing he could not restrain himself from was eating. He'd had two heart attacks and two operations in the last two years. The results of the blood tests carried out by various doctors showed that his cholesterol and blood pressure were always at the upper limits of what was considered safe. Diabetes occurring later made his life more difficult. He had to pay too much attention to all his actions and to what he ate. However, he didn't give his life the same importance he gave his job. Whenever we warned him about his health, he said, 'Well, maybe I have a reason, huh? What can I do, my son? Maybe I miss your mum without being aware of it.' Thereupon, we always just remained silent.

I'm sure my father would have preferred it if Gary and I had dealt with the company while Lori gave birth to his grandchildren. However, since my brother and I were not involved in the company, all the burden was on Lori's shoulders. Yet it is wrong for me to define it as a burden, because Lori was very satisfied both with her role in the company and with being such a successful businesswoman. She was fond of power and strength. If she had the opportunity, she could have given birth to her babies and afterwards found a more relaxed position for herself in the company – and the position she'd find for herself would still certainly be above mine or Gary's.

According to Gary, there was a balancing element to his lack of interest in the company. His wife, Amy, provided to the company and to my father what Gary could not provide them in a lifetime. Maybe she even gave so much that it was enough to disturb Lori.

Amy's diligence and wisdom were fully appreciated by my father. He was even glad to know that Amy's success was indirectly useful for Gary. In addition, Amy had a huge value in my father's eyes, because he had known her long before she married Gary – from when she'd been together with Eric. My father trusted in Eric very much with respect to Amy, just as he did with every other subject. If Eric thought Amy was worth being in love with, then Amy was always gonna be a plus for my father. If Amy had first been introduced to my father as Gary's girlfriend, I'm sure my father wouldn't have formed such an intimate relationship with her and would never have thought to offer her a position at his company.

My father was unlucky about grandchildren on the other side of the equation, too. He wished to have a grandchild from Gary and Amy, and probably even would have preferred this to Amy's business-life success. But, it seemed obvious that they had no plans to give him a grandchild.

Regardless of my father's desire to have a grandchild, he would not want Lori and James to have one. For him, James was an incorrigible and bodacious bastard. My father even thought that Lori should end their marriage. But he didn't comment on this at all, as he had respect for his daughter's choices.

My father might have considered us all from the same galaxy, but he surely thought that James was a creature from some other world, spending time among us humans. My father went to James' restaurant just once before he married Lori, but he only had a coffee. It happened after Lori begged him to go there and meet James. That was the first and the last visit. James' success in his business (which my father questioned anyway and did not accept easily) or the fact that he was appreciated a lot in the jet-set community meant nothing to my father, who simply made evaluations and decisions in accordance with his own thoughts and experiences. What others thought about the subject didn't have any importance for him. And nor did James.

My father also didn't care about Gary's artistic creations or pictures, because he believed that being an artist was an instinct, but that Gary's fervour for art was neither a reflection of an artistic nature nor an involuntary choice. He believed that Gary had a lazy nature and that this had led him to decide being an artist was an easy way to live. Mr Kushner considered this attitude disrespectful towards art, and he often became angry at Gary – sometimes inwardly and sometimes openly.

However, in spite of all these thoughts, he did not try to prevent Gary from what he wanted to do, whether art or anything else. He tried his best to stand by Gary and his dreams, though the result according to my father was generally "works of below-average and a life wasted in vain."

For him, at that table, the only person not wasting his life and whose every action was correct was Eric. I'm sure that if Eric were his son, my father would secretly love him most, even while saying, 'I love each of my children equally.' He might still feel this way anyway.

Eric is an ideal human being, according to my father's view on life. He is an active, quick-minded and dynamic person with a work-oriented mind. And he is successful in human relations. Because he had always been near my father, ever since his childhood, my father knew that his character was as beautiful as his looks. The reasons why my father had a strong liking for him and reliance on him were very obvious to me.

Since my father respected and took on whatever Eric decided, he also liked Danielle, not only because she was acquainted with Eric but also because she was his girlfriend – and possibly his future wife.

And I can honestly feel that I also took my share from the eternal and endless love my father had in his heart. There was always a different affection between us. The peace we felt when we were together was unique. What we talked about and shared always had a fresh nature. Maybe because I was the youngest child of the family, or because I had to get over my mother's death with such a little heart, my father had always been an invisible shield for me.

If we think like a devil's advocate and swim in suspicious waters, we may doubt whether my choosing Eric as a friend cemented my father's love for me or not. If I had a friend like Eric, this meant that I had a hidden potential in me that was waiting to be brought out of the woodwork. Perhaps one day I could become a businessman (which means an active soul) as my father desired.

However, when I left the company and started to run my own bookstore, he didn't cause me to feel any shame or incompetency. He did not suppress me with a feeling of debt. He did not show disappointment in me but made me believe that he would always be on my side – whatever I did.

He told me so himself. He said that the world I created with books went well with me and that he felt proud of me. He was aware of the fact that what I did was not for fun. What my father attached most importance to was that one should behave consciously as a human, and not flap one's gums, nor do business recklessly or (in short) live recklessly.

In order not to make the ambiance more emotional, the dinner started with my father's "order."

While passing the salad plate to Danielle, James said, 'Come on, tell us something: is that *Vanity Fair* world really as entertaining as it appears from the outside?'

After this initiation, jokes were made, and everyone said they wanted to be a part of that world, and then they changed their minds and concluded that "it was just as good" not to become involved in it. Everyone was curious about the people Danielle worked with, so she was asked many questions. Danielle answered some of them, and surprised people with the answers, but to other questions she simply replied, "No comment."

The thing at which I laughed the most was James' continual focus on Danielle's cleavage. He didn't miss any opportunity to see more, and tried everything to get another chance, including overdosing on the salad and bread offerings, and asking unnecessary questions.

Noticing his odd behaviour, Eric could not help himself and uttered the joke that had been maintained between us for a long time.

'When one sees a beautiful girl, he cannot keep himself away from her, V. You want to look at her more and more without a break and internalize her.'

I could not help launching forth. 'Sometimes you can't help but wanna see her passport... if you know what I mean.'

Seeing her passport was a code-phrase we used for beautiful big booties, which goes all the way to beautiful Brazilian women. We had been using these words for Danielle before she became acquainted with Eric. Lori, knowing very well what all these words and laughs meant, smiled and then tried to shoot warning looks at James, who was unaware of what was happening.

We laughed and mocked him, but Eric, who didn't want to be the person creating disturbance on such a night, attempted to change the subject.

'Boss, you said that more investment was needed for R & D. But what would the outcome be? Could you allocate some resources there?'

'Those are very meaningful questions for a day like today, Eric,' I said. 'I thank you on behalf of everyone. You could not have depressed us more.'

Eric never got tired of carrying on business issues everywhere he went; he lived business and talked about it all the time. Especially when he was around "da boss."

Lori was ready to answer before my father: 'We could not allocate as much as we wished. Do you want to help us?'

Eric smiled. 'I am not a boss like you, lady. I am just a lawyer working for my humble salary. Unfortunately, I do not have enough money to make an investment. However, if I had any money, I would certainly invest in your firm. Especially if there was an invaluable person like you among the executives....'

The magic of the compliment disappeared with the laughs that came right after it.

My father intervened in this flirtatious question-answer session: 'I am not sure about these new endeavours. In my opinion, it is enough to carry out our own work well so that the company can be sustained in a balanced way. We cannot take any risks. I mean, we should not take risks. I know that these are fast times, when everything changes so quickly, but then again our situation has also changed a lot. Lori always talks about growth and new targets, but this is not right. Times have changed, my son, and things are not on our side. There are big companies controlling big amounts of money. We can't compete with them. We need to know our place; we need to play safe and humble.'

Amy watched for an opportunity to intervene in the speech, and then she found a void: 'I agree with the boss. Everyone wants to put his nose into our biz. If we make any mistake, even the slightest one, they will swarm around us like hungry dogs. As you know, we're already starting to hear about their greedy plans, aren't we?

'Dad, if we know our place, we will have to content ourselves with what we have,' Lori said, ignoring what Amy had said as if it was of no importance. She even didn't look at Amy.

'What we have at our disposal will be enough for everyone, so don't worry about it,' he said. 'I agree with Amy on this. You know very well that we have tried hard to maintain the company for all these years. I do not want to make it fall prey to others by behaving hastily. Okay, talking about business this much will cause me to lose my appetite soon. Can we close the topic? Come on, guys. This is our little fraction of paradise here. Let's enjoy the good company and delicious food we have tonight. Stop talking and start biting. Come on, let's eat!'

Service was carried out and plates were distributed from hand to hand. People praised the meals and tried to guess the secret ingredients added to the recipes to bring each dish to such a mind-blowing result. Before identifying one flavour, another was there to try. All together, we revived old memories and burst into gales of laughter.

I always thanked God at such times for all our blessings and for our togetherness. And for my father being alive. Seeing him so happy and peaceful always gave me strength. We had come through hard times together, and I always felt guilty in some part of my mind for not working with him, and for leaving him alone. But I don't know whether I would have been happy if I had remained with him, or whether I could have made him happier than he is now. My inner voice has always whispered to me that the way I chose was better. For both him and me.

While the feast was going on, I regularly controlled what my father was eating; this had become a kind of reflex for all of us. I was afraid he would exceed his limits. Though the time was passing very enjoyably, my heart sank every time I saw what he was deeply enjoying eating in that moment. I soon lost my appetite. While my plate remained full of untouched delicious meat, sauce and cheese, his was emptied and filled again with various tastes.

'Dad, haven't you eaten a little too much? Let's give a break.'

'I have permission tonight. I stayed almost hungry for four days preparing for this; I managed to sustain, dreaming what I would enjoy tonight. I've made self-denial a habit for years. Nothing will happen to me just because of one night. Don't worry, Dr Miller knows I'm indulging myself tonight. Come on, taste this meat. Its sauce is a little sugary-sour, but I like it very much.' He was determined not to accept any prohibition.

James interrupted, though it was not his business. 'V, a life protected from everything "good" is not so good at all.' Without knowing about anything related to a "good life," James continued to talk: 'People should just behave naturally. Don't worry about it; the boss is a mature man.'

Eric heard the idiotic statements James was making, and he let loose his lawyer instincts to deal a blow to James. 'Yes, we understand that you very much enjoy natural living; that's why you always let your animal instincts free....'

A wave of contagious smiles passed around the table.

Before James could reply, Amy said, 'Don't hit below the belt. He doesn't always live by natural laws; he just likes to behave naturally in some ways.'

Everyone knew what she meant by this, and we all tried to hide our smiles, except my father. He didn't hesitate to burst into laughter.

James appeared to be on the verge of losing his temper. Struggling to control his tone, he said, 'I don't understand what you're trying to say, Amy. Maybe you can express it more clearly?' Without waiting for a reply to his question, he went on: 'I'm sure you also use your animal instincts from time to time, though not very often. But it must happen sometimes. Probably? Isn't that true, Eric?'

It was obvious that if we let this to go on like this, things would get very tense in no time, because James was the kind of man who never knew where to stop.

Taking responsibility, I turned to Danielle. 'Are you ready to eat such amounts of food and become a part of these feasts regularly? If the dishes are as good and various as tonight – and indeed, I will ensure that they are not gonna be – I must warn you that your modelling career will become a beautiful memory in a very short time. I think each and every one of us have put at least four pounds tonight....'

'Four pounds and counting,' Danielle said, helping me to decrease the tension by making everyone laugh. At least she had made an effort.

While laughing at her own joke, she put her hand over mine, and didn't move it for about half a minute. I couldn't make any sense out of it, and as the seconds passed, I started to feel a bit uneasy. Despite the wide open space and the people all around, being this close to her, my chair next to her chair, was starting to feel dangerous. While her hand was touching mine, I felt as if I were connected to a bomb whose fuse was lit and slowly burning. She must have felt my nervousness, for she removed her hand suddenly. I concentrated on an imaginary Ping-Pong ball moving between the meat and puree on my dish.

Whenever we had family reunions, we also often had minor tensions; the reason for this I truly do not know. We all had different lives but all, except for Eric, fed ourselves from the same resource: our father. It was his money we would all share after his death. At one point or another, we would inherit some money, and we'd need to share it. (Our wives and husbands were, of course, going be a part of this process, either indirectly or, if they could manage it, directly). How it would be divided would most probably be determined by my father, but possibly this was what caused the tension that sometimes came between us (for some of us without us even realising it was there, and for the rest consciously). Even though I did not have any concrete evidence to make me feel this way, I could not help feeling that I was right. Where there's money there are problems.

But of course, money was not the only source for tension. Everyone was involved in my father's business in a different way and to a different degree. Some worked their asses off for the business while others were merely relatives of people who were involved. Regardless, they all thought their investment was worth more than the next person's. We had thousands of doubts and plans in mind, and they all touched upon each other at some point, which became clear when we gathered together and talked about them. At those times, long story short, heated disputes arose.

Once, at another family repast, Lori and my father had a serious dispute. I have never seen my father treat her so viciously, not before and not after that night.

The group had been composed of me, Gary, Lori, Eric, Amy and my father. James was not in the picture yet. Danielle was probably at the very early stage of her modelling career, unaware of our group; our lives had not intersected yet. Amy's chair was again located between Gary and Eric, but with a slight difference: her hand was not on Gary's hand but on Eric's. This was in the time when she had only recently started to work with Mr Kushner's company, and when Gary was living with a singer woman whom we had never met, not even once. He preferred not to introduce her to the family.

Eric and Amy were happy, and, as a couple, they were part of the family. Nobody could have guessed that one day they would be sitting on the same chairs at the same table but waking up next to different faces each morning. Life always prepares breathtaking and delicate stories and surprises for us, and we chose not to see them coming. Try visiting your own five-years-ago self at a café, reading your then-favourite book and sipping a mocha, and tell yourself about your today. Would you (I mean, then-you) believe anything?

The night the dispute broke out, Lori had been very nervous. I can't remember why very clearly, but she didn't agree with my father and his right-hand man about a very important strategic issue related to the company's future. Lori brought this topic up at the table from time to time that night, trying to incline my father toward making a decision in a way she desired, but it was an issue that had to be discussed by three people. After a while, my father warned Lori not to talk about business at the dinner table, and we returned to our normal state and light conversations and laughs. Eric and Amy revealed that they might marry in the near future. We talked about this and that, but after a short while, Lori attempted to link the subject to business again. My father warned her more directly this time.

'We are not at the office now. What you want to do is settle a business decision and bypass one of the decision makers, and I do not like it at all. We need to decide on this all together, the three of us. Please do not utter another word about it as now I am starting to get angry.' My father had the ability to slap anyone with a couple of words.

Disturbed at getting such a warning in front of all of us, Lori didn't want to be outdone. 'The company belongs to you and me. I don't understand why we have to wait for a third person's decision.'

'Watch your words, Lori. Tony is not just a "third person".'

'Who's Tony anyway? Someone who wants—'

'The company is mine!' my father said. 'I can give importance to the decisions of whomever I want. This table is also mine, Lori. I will say with whom I want to be together and with whom I do not. Now, I want you to leave the table.'

Every one of us was stunned by these words. My father was too serious to have said this lightly. A single teardrop ran down Lori's cheek. Wiping it with her index finger, she left the table without uttering a word. When I started to go after her, my father stopped me with a harsh rebuke.

When my father lost his temper, he could do anything. But Lori's nature does not allow her to remain silent against any kinds of words – where they come from is not important. Instead of apologising to my father and handling him tactfully, she left the table and then didn't go to work during the following week. My father was the one who eventually approached her to apologize, and then they were on good terms again.

Today there were eight of us at the table, and together we gobbled up everything. Big service plates lay over the table in a miserable way, like abandoned lovers. Laughter coming right out of our hearts filled the air inside with cheer, and togetherness gave birth to a warm ambiance around us.

'Let's see the bottom of this last bottle of wine, and then continue with the desserts,' my father said with his deep voice.

'No, no..., let's stop it here, please, Dad,' said Lori, putting her hands over my father's. 'I agree with V. We have overindulged a bit tonight; we've crossed the line.'

'No! Stop complaining about it,' he said. 'I know what I am doing. The dessert is nothing to be afraid of. It's special. I thought ahead and had them prepare a milky one. I knew that you would bother me; you do it every day. But I am prepared!'

I felt uneasy. All the tiredness of eighty-two years was over his shoulders, in his heart and veins. I didn't want him to force himself anymore.

'Okay, we'll have some dessert,' I said. 'But please come with me and take some fresh air in the garden before dessert. Let's breathe some fresh air, and then we will continue eating.'

Gary agreed with me. 'Come on, I'm dying for a smoke,' he said. 'Let's give up this eating spree just for five minutes.'

Me, my father, Gary, James and Danielle all went out into the garden to smoke and take in some fresh air. The air was cool, and we snuggled deeper into our coats. But Danielle, with her thin and delicate body, soon started to feel chilly. I put my jacket over her shoulders. She smiled and thanked me. Whenever I took care of her, even these tiny bits, I felt that she liked it very much. She always smiled quite sincerely at me. Her smiles sometimes made me forget she was the forbidden fruit.

'Do you think Nico will be busy this winter?' Gary asked James.

'We'll see. I'm trying my best to make it happen. I do PR, man. I have eyes and ears everywhere; an upscale restaurant needs it…. If you wanna earn money, you need it. Always. People are everything. We have upscale clients – very important. If you attract them, the rest will follow. That's how it goes, man. These are the rules.'

'I need to cut in, "man",' Mr Kushner said. 'The problem with that place is actually the fops you define as your customer mass. If a really decent man went there, you would not accept him. I know it. He would not belong there. Being an age-old enterprise requires a different mind-set, James. Also, people expect good service and a good chef, not youngster pricks making rubbish dishes. Your chefs do not provide, is what I mean.'

'If you allow me, boss—'

'Don't call me boss, James. I'm not your boss.'

'Okay, Mr Kushner. Let me offer you a delicious meal from our cuisine one day, and you'll change your mind, I'm sure.'

'I know your place very well. In order not to become more disappointed, I had better not come. At least that way I can still console myself by thinking it might be good or that the chefs are getting better at it. Do not take this hope from me.'

My father and Eric enjoyed this conversation very much, as become clear from their laughter. James knocked down his whisky at once.

It was obvious that my father didn't like James. James was aware of this, but he was helpless. If he loved Lori, he must bear her "asshole father." He even had to agree with all Mr Kushner's opinions, unconditionally.

Growing bored with giving life lessons to James, my father turned his interest to Danielle. He asked her what she was doing and whether she had any interest in books. My brother and I talked about my store and the exhibition he would attend. All this talking about books and exhibitions appeared to make James so bored that for a moment I thought he would explode.

Eric came out to the garden and joined us. He sat on the armrest of the patio sofa where my father sat, talking to Danielle.

'Do not lose this girl,' my father told him. 'She knows what a good book is, and she's as beautiful as a woman can be. Oh boy, if I were younger... I'd duel with you for this girl, you can bet on it. Listen, this girl must be the mother of your children. Take my advice, and be happy for the rest of your life. Do you hear me, boy?'

Eric didn't reply and just smiled. His sudden change in attitudes whenever this subject was raised caused Danielle to feel a bit worse each time; I could see it in her eyes.

Lori came over and asked my father whether he still wanted some dessert.

'Of course I do. But first, I need to go to the toilet. Wait for me!'

He stood up from the sofa slowly, most probably because of the heavy meal he had eaten, and walked towards the house with small steps. Lori and James were talking in a nervous way. It was getting colder; I decided to go inside.

When I steered for the door opening into the garden, I realised that my father had not even made it half of the way; he was still walking slowly. Going up to him, I asked whether he was okay.

'Am I okay? Huh... I'm an old dog, you homeboy. You mind your own business.'

'Oh Dad, come on...'

'What now? Should I get a permission from you to go to the toilet?'

I was snubbed. Leaving him in the garden, I went to the kitchen.

After that gorgeous repast, the kitchen was a wreck. However, Andrew and Nancy were trying to clean it up quickly. If it was required again, they could lay out another rich table in no time. They were always prepared.

I sat on one of the pub stools placed around the bank in the middle and gazed at all the desserts yet to be served. Next to the milky desserts my father had mentioned, there were four other types of dessert and two types of cake, one with fruit and the other with dark chocolate. That night, there was more than enough for eight people; twenty-eight more could have been hosted there.

'How do you manage to make so many different dishes in one night?' I asked Andrew.

He just shrugged and carried on cleaning.

I felt a kind of guilt passing through my heart. It was clear that we could not eat all the desserts that had been prepared. Especially not after having already eaten so much.

This feeling of guilt reminded me of another time, sitting in this same kitchen with the same feeling. She had been with me – my beautiful M. We were attending another family repast, and she had argued with me, and then with my father, after seeing all the leftovers that would be thrown away. In fact, we are not a thriftless family – we do not fritter anything away – but it had been another special day for my father. Out of hospitality, too many dishes were unduly prepared. At least ten more people could have been fed with the food we were throwing away. She had become very angry. If I had belaboured the point, a serious quarrel might have broken out between us. I had chosen to remain silent.

Maybe it would have been better if I had not. Maybe then she would be with me at this repast, too. I didn't know it at that time, but now I know it for certain. There were situations like this when I remained silent even though I should not have. If I had spoken up, my life could be very different. If I had not remained silent, she would not have shouted at me when she was leaving; she would not have uttered, 'It is not even possible to quarrel with you. It's always like I am speaking to a wall! Give me an answer, you fucking idiot!'

My calm nature would give everyone peace, my mother had said when I was a child. 'This boy is very tender-minded. His wife will be very lucky. They won't have any brawls at their home.' Unfortunately, I could not have a family because of my nature, and my mother had not foreseen this.

I was sitting among the colourful desserts and dreaming of old memories when my sister's shriek wrenched my heart. 'Father! Father!' she screamed at the top of her lungs.

Eric, Danielle and James ran towards the bathroom. I followed them.

My father was lying on the ground. Near the toilet. His trousers were loosened and dropped down to his knees. His mouth was open, tongue lolling out; his eyes were half-open and motionless. Suddenly, everyone was gathered around him, shouting at each other desperately, ordering each other to do something. Coming last, Gary shouted to everyone to back up. There was a short silence. Everyone stepped aside. My sense of time broke.

Gary knelt down and leaned over him, saying, 'Father' calmly. He checked his pulse and turned to us. 'Not beating!'

My father's pulse is not beating, my father's pulse is not beating. This voice was rolling in my mind. Every time it hit my skull, it left a burning trace in my heart. I could not move, but stood in the middle, watching what was happening. Lori ran to search for her phone. Amy and Danielle went after her.

Words and questions echoed throughout the house. 'Is it a heart attack? What is happening? It is an attack. His heart...'

Eric leaned towards my father's head, trying to hear him breathe. Did he still have any life to breathe?

He started to carry out the heart-massage he knew from the first-aid lessons at high school. Two strokes and breathe once into the mouth. Two strokes and breathe once into the mouth. He was trying his best, but my father showed no signs of life. Suddenly, I experienced an epiphany: I had come to myself and knew I had to do something. I felt as if I'd woken up from a frozen dream.

Pushing Eric aside, I grabbed my father's shoulders and started to shake him. His head hit the ground, but I didn't care. Thinking that he might wake up because of the pain, I continued to shake him. Then suddenly Eric grasped me from my waist and, with huge strength and anger, threw me aside. I crashed into the bathroom wall back-first. He resumed the heart-massage again. I slid down the wall slowly until at last I was sitting on the ground. I became motionless. My legs sticking out in front of me. Gary was standing between me and my father's body. I didn't want him to move.

Eric's whole body was shaking as he hit my father's chest, his head leaning towards my father. He shouted, 'It's not working! It's not working!' Two strokes and breathe once into the mouth. A more vigorous yell: 'It's not working! Come on!' Two strokes and breathe once into the mouth. 'It's not working!'

Eric started to shout out between his hits on my father's chest. 'Come back... Come back...' This is the last thing I remember from that moment before my vision went black.

When I came back to myself, I was lying on the sofa in the living room. Danielle was sitting at the far end of the sofa. Feeling that I had to stand up, I suddenly made a move, but my head spun dizzily, as if it didn't have any connection to my body, and I fell off the sofa and landed on my hands. Danielle moved at once to help me back onto the sofa.

Lori was in the far corner of the room, talking on the phone. Amy was sitting silently at the dinner table. I could not see Eric, James or Gary. I asked Danielle where they were.

'They went to the hospital,' she said.

For a moment, I felt on the top of the world. I felt an indescribable joy in my heart. It meant that Eric managed to bring my father back to life. It meant that my father hadn't died; he simply needed meticulous care at the hospital.

I sat up. 'Which one? Which hospital? Is he okay? Where are they...?'

Danielle looked at me but could not answer. Lori came over and stood in front of me. She seemed emotionless, like a robot.

'V, calm down,' she said. 'There is nothing you can do anymore. Father is dead. I'm sorry to say this but get used to it. He died of a stroke.'

I didn't know how to react. 'Stroke?' I didn't want to believe what I had heard. I wished it was not real but a nightmare, curse or whatever. I could not speak. 'But, the hospital...,' I wanted to say. I do not know whether I did, but Lori was already answering me.

'They brought him to the mortuary. The boys.'

When I heard those words, I blacked out again. I remember seeing Lori's legs turning around up and down in my mind.

This time when I came to, it was Gary sitting next to me. He had grabbed a chair and was acting like an attendant. I felt better this time; I wasn't dizzy. I straightened myself up and looked around. Danielle was sleeping on the other sofa. Lori and Eric were smoking in the garden. James was standing motionless with his head leaning over the dinner table. Amy was standing, looking out of the window.

'Why is everyone here? Why did you leave him alone? What the fuck are all of you doing here, you idiots? Hey!'

Gary looked at me, but he didn't say a word.

'Why, Gary, WHY?' I asked him.

'Because it is no longer necessary to be with him,' James said.

'What the fuck you're talking about? Gary, what's this fuck saying? How is Father? Where is he now?'

'Calm down, V. We can't do anything anymore,' Gary said.

'It's that easy, huh? In an instant, the blink of an eye – nothing we can do? Is he gone now?'

I could not understand the calmness in the room. I could not believe that my father had been going to the toilet and then had died before our eyes, without any reason. I didn't want to believe it. It was like a bad dream. I wanted to cry, but as I didn't believe that he was really dead, I could not cry. I felt that if I cried, I would have to accept this reality; and if by any chance he had survived somewhere, at the very instant I accepted his death, he would really die.

I started to laugh. My laughter was broken; it sounded more like I was crying, deeply. Amy turned to me. It was clear that she couldn't make any sense out of it either. Gary was also looking at me. As my crying became louder, Lori and Eric, still standing in the garden, turned to look at me.

I could not stop myself. 'It is very strange,' I said. Because what we lived through was meaningless. The man with whom we had been having a perfect time only a couple of hours ago was now dead. Suddenly, and without any reason. Five minutes after I had passed by him on my way to the kitchen. The last words he had uttered were related to his going to the toilet. It could not be real.

I stood up. So did Gary. 'Sit down, V!' he said.

I didn't feel dizzy, but I had a terrible headache. I tried to walk to the bathroom, getting some help from the walls. Eric came and stopped me.

'Stop, V, come on,' he said. 'Come with me. Let's go outside. Let's take some fresh air.'

'This can't be, man, not like this...,' I said. 'Not suddenly like this, not in an instant... I cannot...'

'Come on! Look, I am here....'

Eric took my arm and led me out to the garden. Lori walked towards me and clung to me. She started to cry silently. I felt her tears on my shoulder.

She began sobbing aloud. It was the first time I had seen her cry in a long while. Gary followed me to the garden and hugged me and Lori. The three of us clung to each other tightly. We were shaking. Lori cried on behalf of three of us. I could not help laughing intermittently.

The leaves on the big tree, reviving themselves that morning, swung side to side in the breeze, as if to tell me to stop laughing. I heard them but did not obey.

Greedday
15 SEPTEMBER

WE LAID MY father to rest. I still couldn't understand completely whether all these things were real: all the people who had come, their condolences, that bleak air of sorrow. I felt as if it were too complicated an issue to understand, and that my father would come after a while and settle everything on our behalf, saying, 'Get out of my way, you crooks. You couldn't come through on a task,' and then all these strange things would disappear. Life would be ours again.

My father did show up in the end – inside a coffin.

I like how everyone hides their axes at funerals. I don't want to contemplate whether they bury them or just hide them, but at every funeral I have ever attended, up to that of my own father's, I deemed everyone I saw as my friend. We didn't know each other, but the reason we were all there and our main purpose was apparent: it was our desire to be near someone we loved – to feel sorrow. This is seen as unnecessary by some people, while others truly and deeply feel it. It's the difference between a fair-weather friend and a foul-weather friend.

I was bored. I had not slept at all. After our emotional outburst in the garden, everyone went to prepare for the funeral. I stayed at my father's house for a while. Maybe I wanted to reflect on what had happened, to go back to correct some points if required and bring my father back to life. I'm aware this sounds bizarre, but maybe for the first time in my life, I felt desperate. I could sacrifice everything I had at my disposal, all my material and non-material belongings on this morning. I was ready to start my life from the very beginning and to re-enter into the house by knocking on the door again, erasing what I had experienced during the last eight hours.

For a moment my internal organs didn't fit into my body; I was about to explode. I felt as if I would die of boredom, and so I left the home quickly. I passed by my car and continued on. I intended to walk as far as I could.

The artificial lake that I had thought was near the house was in fact very far away. For me, however, concepts like tiredness and energy had been erased from the world. I took quick steps without stopping. Not with the intention of escaping, but perhaps of finding. Maybe I would see my father on the way, walking slowly. I would put my hand over his shoulder and say, 'Come on, old man. That's enough time to spend alone. Let's go back home....'

Afterward, I couldn't remember all the details about my walk. I just knew that it had lasted a very long time. When I reached a highway close to the house, I realized that I needed to get to the funeral. I tried to thumb a lift, but it seemed no one wanted to pick up a tired, lone wreck of a man whose father had just died. After walking along the highway for about ten minutes, I finally flagged down a cab.

I gave the driver my address, and then watched the view passing by outside, but I couldn't really see anything. It was as if the things moving beyond the window created a background colour, and I was watching the events of the previous night in the foreground. I started to laugh, because I couldn't make sense out of the things that had happened. Was this what death was like, sudden and easy? Or desperate – with the sense of being undeserved? Could it happen so fluidly and quickly and without a struggle? Without the chance to say goodbye – maybe without being able to say it?

But throughout his life, my father had always struggled for everything he had accomplished. He wouldn't yield so easily. There must be some unreasonable things, but I couldn't figure them out. He wasn't one who would accept death that easy. However, I was open to accept everything when my mother died. My father had called us in, and, as he began to speak, he started to cry.

'Fellas, unfortunately, we are alone from now on. Your mother, my wife...' He was biting his fist. I stood up and hugged him. I took his fist out of his mouth, and we grabbed on to each other. Then Lori and Gary joined us. The four of us hugged each other. Just as we had this morning, but with one more missing.

I entered my apartment. More silently than ever. I looked at my belongings and became angry with them. As if they were to blame for my father's death. As if they hadn't done their best, and had brought him death.

After a short while, the phone rang. Gary was calling. He would be there in one hour, and we would go to the funeral together. Before that, Eric and Gary would pick up my father from the hospital. They were not discharging him but were 'picking him up from the hospital.' I smiled at the difference. (You should not say that anything is impossible.)

I took a bath and shaved myself. Like a robot. I embraced normality, like a man whose father had not just passed away. Things were happening, but I couldn't fully take part in them. I just breathed in, breathed out.

I looked through the window in the hall, out at the road. Gary stopped at the traffic lights on the corner. I went downstairs and met him as he pulled up in front of the building. 'How are you?' Gary asked as I got into the car. 'Have you recovered a bit?'

'I think I'm fine,' I said. 'I just don't know how it could have happened. I still haven't figured it out. I'm not even sure it's real.' Can someone whose father has just died utter these words? Are these considered illegal among the laws of death?

'Haven't you slept at all?'

'Have you?'

'Not much. Anyway, it doesn't matter. Let's go now.'

As he drove, Gary sometimes looked at me. He must have been afraid that I was losing my mind.

But it was not as he feared. I was, on the contrary, in the opinion that I was *compos mentis*. The problem was my life in general. It had changed into a very strange condition in the last couple of hours, and now it seemed completely out of control. My life had completely slipped out of my hands.

Eric and Gary had dealt with all the "technical" details of the funeral. In fact, I found Gary's support a little bizarre, as he was far more interested in this task than I would have expected. I would have expected Eric to take on so much responsibility for our family on such a day, but not Gary. I hadn't considered this situation before, but even if I had, I would have reached the same conclusion.

Their behaviour could be seen as normal and expected, I might admit, but what was strange was James' disappearance, and his indifference to what had happened. Of course, he wasn't obliged to do anything at all for us, but how couldn't he feel a bit responsible (or human)?

Together with my brother, I went to the graveyard where the funeral would take place. Eric and Danielle were already there, chatting with Amy. I saw Andrew and Nancy, but I couldn't bear to speak to them just yet. They both seemed very tired, exhausted and sad – at least as much as we were.

James appeared at the very last minute, but he didn't approach us.

'I can't see Lori,' I said to Gary. 'Where is she?'

'I don't know. She said she would get here on time. I called her before I came to pick you up, and then I called her again after we arrived, but her phone is off. I know she'll make it though.'

But there was a problem regarding this point. Why had James felt obliged to come? Because of his wife? But if Lori didn't feel obliged, why would James? Of course, he wouldn't. Did they think that if Lori didn't show up to the funeral, James' appearance would be enough for us? The fact that he hadn't helped to deal with any of our needs or errands, nor even deigned to ask if he could help, could be considered natural for him.

Amy heard us talking. 'I think Lori is at the company,' she said.

'What?! How could she be there at a time like this? What is she doing there?' I said.

'She said there were things she had to do.'

'Come on, don't bullshit me! What can be more important than being here today?'

'Instead of me, you should ask her, the one who is now holding a meeting at the company in order to see how Mr Kushner's shares will be distributed.'

'What are you talking about, Amy? What shares? Please cut this nonsense for God's sake!'

'Gary, why are you silent?' she asked. 'Tell him!'

Gary stared at her angrily.

'Whatever you have to say to me, Gary, please say it,' I said.

Gary glanced over his shoulder and then said, 'Amy's right. The lawyers phoned while you were lying on the couch. Lori didn't think we overheard her call, but we did. She was organising a very urgent meeting for this morning.'

While we were breaking with our father forever, my sister was not with us; she was meeting with lawyers at the company.

The fact that I didn't believe what I had been told didn't change the truth: Lori was not with us, and James had arrived at the last minute and was acting like a stranger who didn't even consider it necessary to stand with us.

I didn't know what to do with this seemingly unreal fact or with the anger and disappointment I felt, because the funeral was starting. We had to go to be with our father, and thus I had no more opportunity to think about Lori or to get angry with her.

As soon as the funeral ended, I immediately approached James.

'Why didn't you come and stand with us? Where is Lori?'

'Calm down. I'm here with you now, don't you see? I still haven't managed to get over the shock. I thought it would be better if I stayed in a corner, without stepping on your feet.'

'Where is Lori?'

'I'm not totally sure where she is—'

'I will find her, and I will ask her about this, do you understand?' I said. 'If what I heard is true, she will fall victim to my wrath for the first time. If you see her, please let her know.'

'What you heard...? V, what did you hear?'

I walked away. I didn't want to listen to James beating about the bush.

'What did you hear?' he continued to call me after, but I had no time to deal with his stupid questions and remarks. I had to find Lori at once.

Eric was waiting for me outside the cemetery with his car. Amy had left to head directly to the company, and my brother had gone to his atelier to get some sleep. Eric and I took Danielle to a taxi station and then headed towards the company. I was very impatient about seeing Lori. I wished I could teleport there.

On the way, we were more silent than our normal selves.

'I'm very upset,' Eric said finally. 'I feel as if my own father died.'

'I know. But why was the woman whose real father died not with us?'

'I can't understand that, and I can't know what Lori is thinking. Maybe it's a female thing? I dunno. Maybe she had to escape because she couldn't bear it – I mean, the pain. You remember what happened at your mother's funeral.'

There is no emotional burden Lori can't bear. She can bear anything. Strong nerves, always under control. Even at my father's funeral, she would have stood on her two feet, and powerfully. If what Amy and Gary said was true – that she was planning something and already taking steps with my father's will in her mind – and if she was too obsessed with money to stand by her father for the last time, I didn't know whether I would call her my sister any more. This meant I could lose two people from my family on the same day.

I had to know what she wanted and what she was going after. I wanted to understand her – if the things she was doing could be understood.

Eric, in fact, thought it was not a good idea to go to the company to talk to Lori. Though he very much trusted in Amy, he warned me that there could be female jealousy or misunderstandings between them, and that this could misdirect me, causing me to fall out with my sister.

'And it would really be too much to have two dead people in just two days,' he said.

'No matter. I want to talk to her face to face and learn the truth. In any case, she has to explain to me why she was not at the funeral.'

When we arrived at the company, Lori was not in her office, and her phone was still off. I called James and asked him whether he had received any news from Lori. He told me that Lori had stayed at home all morning as she didn't feel good. She had planned to drop by the restaurant later that day, but in the end she hadn't felt up to that either, and for some reason had left her phone turned off.

I found this entire story simpler and more stupid than it should be. It had been prepared in a careless way. I knew that Lori didn't need to lie, but I decided to stop by Nico in order to learn the truth.

Eric said he wanted to come with me. Maybe he thought that the special emotions he and Lori had harboured for each other since old times would help us get through to Lori.

Eric was my only friend with whom I had never broken away since primary school. However, 'friend' is a word I don't like to use to describe the relationship between us. What we share is basically like being brothers. Over time, the impression he left on all of us was that he belonged to our family. He occasionally stayed at our house and even joined in our family vacations. His father had died when he was a little boy, and his mother had married again. Though Eric's stepfather never treated Eric badly, Eric had always put my father in his real father's place and loved him accordingly. It was not unrequited love, as my father loved Eric like he was his own child and didn't discriminate him from his own.

In such a way, we grew up before Lori's eyes, as she's six years older than us. Time passed, and we all grew up and matured. Our first youthful excitement, our first loves, and our first sexual affairs all occurred when Lori was around. Whenever we came across a problem that we couldn't solve, or a situation regarding girls that we couldn't decide on, understand or solve, we consulted Lori. She became our insider about girls and affairs. She always showed us the right way and told us what girls expected from us, and how we could get the desired results. Like a spy, she provided us with the correct answers to questions we could never have answered ourselves, even if we had contemplated them a lot.

But in potential quarrels with girls, she was never on our side. She always supported the girls and became their invisible protective angel, ensuring that we couldn't upset or hurt them. She threatened us to punish us and deprive us of her knowledge if we ever broke any one of their hearts. For this reason, we always tried our best to be well behaved and good. We never broke the heart of any girl on purpose. Really. Lori was an ultimate guide for us on the bumpy roads for girls. She was like a guide to a treasure map in which the treasure never runs out.

As time passed, Eric and I became mature young men in all aspects. By then, Lori had already become a woman. Though there were a lot of skirt-hunters admiring her, she never behaved like a spoilt teenager, changing lovers all the time and not knowing what she was looking for. She had boyfriends, and some of them had even been invited to the house to be approved by Mr Kushner himself. We all had nice time when Lori had visitors around. There were even some who I also liked very much.

But one day Lori fell in love with someone who I liked more than any other candidate on earth.

At that time, Eric had only recently started to date Amy. I was seeing Amy's excitement and happiness with my own eyes. They were more friends than lovers, and they took great pleasure in spending time together. Eric was then twenty-nine years old and was a very ambitious lawyer. He was new in the law firm and was working day and night in order to show his talent and dedication. Amy was one year older and was a beautiful and prosperous young businesswoman who had just returned back from an international working position. I don't know who fell for who first, Eric or Amy, but the result seemed as perfect as anyone could desire, so none of us obsessed over the details.

I spent much time with them both together and, as a result, there grew a sincere friendship between Amy and me, and the things we shared increased as time passed. To tell you the truth, I got along well with all of Eric's girlfriends, but I didn't like this at all. The fact that women so easily became friends with me had disturbed me ever since I was a teenager. But I could do nothing about it. Saying 'I don't want to be friends with you, but I'm dying to have sex with you' to someone who had registered me in her friend list would be too rude. And so I always kept those awful wishes to myself.

One evening during those days when Eric was dating Amy, I received a phone call from him. He sounded frantic and said he wanted to meet me. When I met him and first heard his news, I understood why he was so worked up, and I didn't know what to do.

Lori had told him that she'd fallen in love with him, and she wanted them to be together. Just hearing this perplexed me. I mean, Lori was not only my sister, she was considered Eric's sister, too. This "love" seemed impossible to me from the very beginning.

I also found Lori's attitude very strange. I would never have expected her to ask someone to love her. Lori would usually always get what she desired. If she wanted someone, the man must surrender, and the subject would be dropped. It was doubly surprising that she had made such a request knowing the truth: that Amy and Eric had just started dating. How had she dared to ask? I couldn't understand at all how she could just ignore Amy in such a way. But when I reconsidered all of this from the love angle, I gave up searching for reasons. One must always have a respect for love. Love is what we live for. Love is what makes us live.

For a couple of days, I walked around with this subject weighing on my mind. I tried my best not to come eye to eye with Lori. Avoiding her was meaningless, I knew, but I didn't know what else to do. Lori had probably guessed that Eric had been talking to me about her revelation. When she noticed that I was disturbed – or perhaps saw my confusion over the situation – she took steps to talk to me.

She told me that I didn't need to be nervous about this "thing" and that love was the most natural feeling that belonged to humans, and it was not in her power to prevent herself from falling in love with Eric. She also said it was natural for me to feel perplexed about her love for him at the beginning, but, above all, I needed to understand and respect it. She told me she had acted as she wished and didn't have to explain it to anyone, nor did she feel at all guilty – 'Not one bit.'

I didn't think that falling in love with Eric was something for which she should feel guilty either. But how about Amy? What would she feel? Shouldn't Lori have thought about her, too?

'She has nothing to do with this. If everything flows as I've planned it, then she should return to her own world,' Lori said.

That was senseless, like a stone. Lori was very determined and sure about herself and her plan. She didn't accept the possibility that Eric would reject her and stick to his love. I was accustomed to Lori's excessive self-confidence, so I didn't find it odd, but this kind of talk was the first time I had seen female mercilessness in Lori. From that day on, Lori was not only my sister but a woman who could behave too boldly in order to get what she desired.

The love triangle didn't work out in the way Lori expected it to. Eric took Lori out to dinner, and they talked. I never asked Eric about that night, but it was surprising and worrisome for me to imagine Eric and Lori talking about love at the same table. These same feelings (but maybe stronger than what I felt) were surely valid for Eric too. I didn't care about the details or how intense it got, but Eric insisted on telling me much of what happened. At the dinner, he'd explained to Lori that he was in a relationship with Amy, and that he was very happy and didn't want to break up with her. In fact, he wished it would last forever. He also added that even if he had been thinking of breaking up with her (for Lori or another woman), he wouldn't do it in such a way, this suddenly or harshly.

I don't know what she felt during that talk or what passed through her mind, but I was sure that Lori would never forget (or forgive) that night. Lori and I talked about her and Eric just once afterwards, and that was because she wanted us to. Except for that one time, I never asked her any questions regarding her relationship with Eric.

After her rejection, Lori resumed her life as if nothing had happened. She behaved in a calm and normal way, without showing any scars from the incident; it was as if she had never fallen in love with Eric – and as if she had never confessed this to Eric or to me.

However, the subject didn't seem to have been dropped. Since Eric and Amy were a couple, naturally they came to our house together. During these visits, my father had the opportunity to become well acquainted with Amy. As he got to know her more, he started to like her more – with the flame of his affection fed by his trust in Eric. One day, my father decided that Amy would be beneficial for the company, and he offered her a job.

We were having dinner at my father's when he suddenly turned to Amy and said, 'Would you like to work with us?' At that moment, I felt as if time stopped, I glanced at each of the faces around the table, and then at Amy. We all waited for her answer to his unexpected offer, trying to guess what she would say and of course what the consequences would be. I was probably among the first to recover from the shock. I first saw the surprise on Eric's face, and then, at the very same instant, saw Lori's shock. She was looking at both my father and particularly at Eric.

It wouldn't be all correct to define the expression in Lori's eyes as only surprise. It was obvious that she considered this offer a kind of defeat in her own field, in addition to the one she had suffered in the love field, and she was now experiencing a female jealousy. Also, my father had made his offer without asking Lori's thoughts on the matter beforehand, which could only have made her angrier.

Over time, we would all come to know that what I had interpreted as Lori's "defeat" was instead her refuelling for a war that would last for years, and, indeed, one that it seemed would never end.

While Eric was parking the car, I walked towards the entrance to the restaurant. Amy called me.

'Amy, please be quick,' I said. 'It's not a very good time right now.'

'Okay then, I'll cut to the chase. Lori has just fired me.'

'What?? She fired you? What do you mean "fired"? How could she do that?'

'I busted her holding a meeting with Mr Kushner's lawyers. I stumbled upon their meeting by accident. I didn't even know they were in the meeting room until I saw them all there. She was holding your father's will. I mean, it was probably the will. When I asked her whether you and Gary should not be there too, she told me it was none of my business and that I needed to get out of the room right away. When I insisted on staying, she called the security guard and had me escorted out. I'm still shaking with anger. What she's done is very serious and reproachful. I can't still believe it. It is also my company, V, isn't it?!'

What I had been hearing about Lori was getting on my nerves. First, I had difficulty understanding why Eric and I hadn't been able to find Lori at the company. She must have hidden from us, which made it even more likely that there were things going on undercover. Then Lori's bossy attitude towards Amy felt like a pain to my lungs, and this was amplified with a deep disappointment and anger that was difficult to define.

'All right. Look, Amy, I will see Lori soon. Relax for now, okay? Trust me. I will do whatever it takes to make this right.'

After parking the car, Eric had approached and overheard my heated and anxious phone call. He'd stopped before me and riveted his gaze on me. I ended the call with Amy and told him what I'd just learned.

'What the fuck?!' he said. 'What's she doing, man? I can't figure it out or accept any of it on reasonable grounds any longer. This is not Lori; we both know it. But what's happening? Is it because of the shock? Can it be that? Maybe she really doesn't know what she's doing.'

We both felt as if we were hurtling down a snow-slide. It was certain that wherever we stopped, or most likely crashed, there was going to be trouble.

When we went into the restaurant, we found James sitting alone at a table at the far side of the wide room. His bottle of vodka was in his hand as it usually was (independent of the time of day). Surprisingly, he seemed to want to smile, but he didn't succeed.

'Welcome,' he said.

We sat at his table.

'James, we don't want to beat a dead horse,' I said. 'What's going on? When will Lori be here? My father is dead and I'm very sad... now where is she? I called her office but they said she wasn't there. You told me she was at home but now I've heard differently. So where is she?'

'Relax, man, okay. She must be on her way. Wait a little. She'll be here soon. Are you hungry? Do you wanna grab a bite, huh?'

'Do we wanna grab a bite?'

Though I had not eaten anything for a long time, and this could actually be considered as a kind-hearted question if asked by an understanding person in a different place at a different time, I wanted to throw a punch at James' face.

We didn't answer his inappropriate offer.

'You probably have to get to work,' I said to Eric. 'I'll talk to Lori when she arrives, and then I'll go home. You can leave now if you want and deal with your own shit. I'm okay.'

He refused. He might have thought that leaving me alone with James would result in a disaster, but he didn't know that staying with us was no guarantee that there wouldn't be one. James had the potential to make us both mad at the same time (James could bullshit enough to make any number of people mad.)

We waited in complete silence. I had a coffee, and Eric had a glass of mineral water. James continued to drink his beloved whisky. Even for someone watching us from a distance, it would be easy to understand how different we were from James. I watched the people around us. I thought that most of them, or even all of them, should thank God for their moment. They were smiling and eating good food, and seemed to be enjoying themselves. They were beautiful, handsome and wealthy. None of them were acting as if they had lost their father recently or been disappointed by their sister (twice) that morning. They should give up their eating, laughing and flirting for a moment to thank

God at once.

I had ants in my pants as I waited to vomit up my anger, and so the time didn't fly. Every second walked by as if it were carrying a ton of weight on its shoulders. One and a half hours later, Lori came in the front door of Nico. She was not surprised to find me and Eric there, thanks to James' spy moves.

She approached our table and greeted us with a "smile." She stopped next to me and put her hand on my shoulder, waiting for me to stand up and kiss her. I didn't. I didn't want the anger I had been harbouring for the last one and a half hours to be softened at all.

'Where were you?' I said. 'I have been trying to reach you since this morning. Today was the FUNERAL. Are you aware of that? Are you aware of the fact that you MISSED our father's funeral? I want to know. Say it!'

'V, please calm down. I'm aware of it, okay? Is that what you wanna know? You can be sure that, for me, it's been as hard as it was for you. Stop behaving like a child and get a hold of yourself.'

She was insolently serious. I couldn't believe what she had just said. I couldn't stand her disrespectful attitude or her protective shields. She was behaving as if I didn't have any authority, as if everything was under her control; she would answer whichever questions she liked and avoid the ones she didn't, as if she was sure she would be the boss of any place.

I hit my fist on the table. 'WHERE WERE YOU?!'

No one expected such an explosion from me – including me. I couldn't control myself. My hand and voice were behaving independently, without asking my approval. All heads turned towards me. It was obvious that Lori was suddenly afraid and surprised, but she did not step back. She gave up waiting for my hugs and kisses and sat down, hiding her anger.

I fixed my eyes on her, demanding an answer. I felt an unfamiliar wave of numbness and excitement in myself. I experienced micro-vibrations everywhere, on my skin and soul.

'I suppose what you have been through has worn you out a lot,' she said. 'But I need to warn you about not losing your temper.'

'Shut up, shut up, shut up, shut the fuck UP! Where have you been? Just answer me!'

'Behave yourself, V! Everyone is looking at us!'

'What is your excuse for not being at your own father's funeral this morning? Say it?'

'I was busy defending Gary's and your rights, little kid!'

'Defending? What rights? Who said I wanted to be defended? You're saying it's true that you met with the lawyers, is that it? This is disgusting, Lori. Don't you see? Are you so blinded by your selfishness and desires?'

At that moment, the hope I had been harbouring within me from the beginning – that Lori might have a meaningful reason and explanation for not showing up at the funeral, and that everything was an illusion – blew away. It seemed to chip off my heart with a "click" sound and drop away, into the emptiness within me.

She smiled.

'You got the news from the rat that penetrated our family, right? Huh, why am I not surprised? But don't worry; she was treated as she deserved. She had her lesson about not being arrogant to me.'

'Lori, listen to me. I really wanna learn what happened, what you were involved in, and what took place between you and Amy. And immediately. Don't talk in circles. Be reasonable and open, and tell me everything. Please.'

That might have been the first time Lori had ever heard such direct and harsh words from anybody, words that she could consider a threat. Excluding our childhood days, I had never shouted at her before.

From that moment on, because of the events of that day and the strange events that would follow, I lost all my kindness and respect towards Lori. I was no longer interested in how the others felt; I simply wanted to understand what Lori wanted to do, and whether her motives were going to decay and eventually destroy the love, bonds, respect and joy we had all shared for so many years. I didn't want to believe that our family had already started to crack and collapse.

Lori told me how, by coincidence, she had seen the draft of my father's will. It was then just a piece of paper, yet to be officialised by the lawyers. He had left it on his desk and Lori, who'd been working late, had found it and gone over it. So, before my father died, Lori had learned how he would distribute his assets. Though what she learned didn't surprise her, it was the reason for her anger. She would have talked to him and convinced him to change his mind, to make what Lori considered the reasonable and "necessary" alterations to his will, but his sudden death spoilt these plans.

'Look, V, over the years, I've gone into combat with my father on the frontlines during all the hard times of the company. We endured the difficult times and storms together. We had real rivals, tough guys who put us through the wringer. We resisted them. They hit us everywhere, but especially in our weak points. They came after us with vicious words and plans, but we repelled them all. We resisted. While you were busy with your "books" and Gary was "struggling" with his art, we were living the real life, boy. The reason we carried out this battle so sincerely and wholeheartedly was because we were family. We were father and daughter. It is a different thing, you know. Not everybody can easily understand our sincerity. You may not understand it because you were not involved in it. Why weren't you with us? I don't care why Gary wasn't with us. Don't take us off topic by misunderstanding me, but you were not with us during those hard times; therefore, you have to believe what I say. You have to accept what I say.'

Lori was adamantly taking steps in order to achieve what she desired, and she didn't hesitate nor seem to feel any regret about it. I knew her: she would never make any decision without planning it very thoroughly and contemplating the many alternatives. She was no back-stepper. The reason I had wanted to talk to her face to face was to understand what she had done and why, and to stand up to her if necessary. I had never been scared of Lori. And from then on, I never would be, either.

From my father's notes, which were destined to be his will, Lori had happened to learn how his shares would be distributed after his death: Before, seventy percent of the company shares had belonged to my father, and the remaining thirty percent was distributed equally among Lori, Gary and me. But my father had not planned for his seventy percent to be distributed among only the three of us upon his death; we would now have shareholders among us, and this made Lori furious. My father wanted to leave 20 percent to Lori, and 17.5 percent each to me and Gary. That small 2.5 percent extra for Lori must have been her compensation for fighting all those wars by his side.

This might have been somehow acceptable to Lori, except for who the remaining shares went to. Things had become complicated with a 5 percent share left to Amy and 10 percent share left to the Andrew and Nancy. According to Lori, the fruits of all her efforts, time and maybe her life should not be passed on to people who she thought were already earning what they deserved by working at the firm or at home. In her mind, they should not expect any more than their current income, and it certainly was not their right to inherit shares; thus, my father had made a big mistake and then died without having enough time to correct it. It was first Lori's duty and then mine to correct this "big – very big – mistake."

'Hey, wait..., just a sec,' I said. 'Are you aware of what you're saying, Lori? First, how dare you question Father's decisions? It's his money, for God's sake—'

'It was.'

'Bullshit! He gave away his money to the people as he liked, as he desired. It's out of order for you to comment on it, let alone try to change his written decision. Oh, Lori, I really wonder what drives you so far from thinking reasonably. What's more, none of this explains your absence from the funeral. That is to say, "money", if I may summarize the explanations you've made so far, is not a valid reason for your absence. I don't wanna accept this. Tell me something else, Lori, I'm begging you.'

'V, you are really very stupid. I thought you were smarter than Gary, but now I see I was mistaken. Don't you understand that having stranger shareholders at the company would weaken us against our enemies, and to a great extent? Amy is twisting Gary around her little finger. I'm sure that after hearing this news, she'll win over Andrew and Nancy in two minutes. She is very stupid and ignorant and has no idea about the values of the company or what it means for our family. She can sell the shares under her control to whomever she wants. The rivals against whom Father and I have struggled for ages can, in one day, change into people with whom we have to sit down at the same table, and to whom we must explain our decisions about the future of our company. But you and Gary are too stupid and too spoilt to listen seriously to what I say. One of you is playing with his art and the other is playing with his books. You live a childish life, trapped in a cube, far away from reality.'

'Cut that nonsense, Lori! You're talking bull. There are no such enemies around you or around us; you made them up in your mind. All you want is more money and more power.'

'Don't cry like a little girl, V. Be a man! With or without you, I'll do whatever is necessary to take care of the company. If I must, I'll even fight with you. But the company is mine and will stay mine. The earlier you wake up from your childish dream, the better, but I won't lose time waiting for you to make up your idiot mind.'

As the conversation carried on, the rudeness increased and discreetness decreased. The situation seemed absurd, and it was playing out in front of one person who appeared baffled, unable to believe what he was hearing and not knowing what to do (Eric), and another who was more like a rough copy of a human being, one who couldn't comprehend the world in any delicate way (James). As our volume increased, people around us – strangers – were pricking up their ears, listening to the cracks of a family break wide open.

In order to put an end to our argument, Lori stood up and glared at me with eyes of fury. She snatched up her bag from the table, acting as if it might become tainted from sharing the same environment with me, and turned her back to leave Nico.

'You don't behave properly, Lori,' said Eric. 'What I've just heard and seen is not you. No, definitely not you. I can't believe you're really thinking what you're telling us.'

Lori turned back and took two slow steps towards our table.

'Be careful what you say, Eric. You don't know me, and you won't get to know me, either. You had the opportunity once, and you missed it.'

A new dimension and a new front had been added to the fight. Had her declaration of love for Eric once been part of her scheme to win his unconditional support? But he'd always supported her unconditionally. Maybe it was a warning for her dog – named James – not to bark at us. Her words hurt me more than angered me.

Eric seemed at least as surprised as me. When we looked in each other's eyes, we were aware of it. But poor James looked first at Eric and then at me, apparently without understanding anything, with his perplexed mind. This bulky Rottweiler was held by a leash, and when its master pulled it, saying 'Come on, James!' he obeyed, following in her footsteps as they left the restaurant together.

'What was that?' I asked Eric.

'Could it be possible that I never knew her at all?' he said. 'Or that neither of us has ever known her? I don't wanna believe it, V. No way!'

'How well I know her does not matter to me at all right now, even though she is my sister. It makes no difference, because either way she has hurt a lot of people today, and she will continue to do so. I need to stop her. We have enough pain in our hearts; I will not allow her to add more. I have to do something.'

'Don't forget that with this last move, everything has become a little complicated,' Eric said. 'James is her trump card. Now he's her sniper, and he's gonna look for any opportunity to take me down. By the way, I suppose I won't be allowed into this restaurant again. If you like, we can escape without paying the bill. I wanna pull a fast one on this fuck-face.'

We paid the bill and left the table.

Eric went to his office, although I didn't believe he would get much work done. He was probably just trying to escape to a place where he could be by himself, and where he could rest his head. He had also gotten his share from Lori, who had battled him on all fronts. Seeing that a subject he thought was 'dropped' a long while ago was in fact still fresh in her mind confused and perplexed him.

As far as I was concerned, my sister had so disappointed me with her actions that her comment to Eric was just one more thing to add to what had happened. The other things had upset me so much more that revealing her bitterness over Eric's rejection hadn't affected me that deeply. But its results might be interesting in some sense. From now on, James was also involved in the business.

Did I really not know Lori...? Was it possible? I didn't think so. She was my sister. We had spent so much time together, and we used to talk a lot. We didn't have a very intimate relationship, but it certainly wasn't remote either. I'd never thought that one day we'd become strangers or hide anything from each other. I'd always had an infinite trust in her, and in her words. I believed in the peace and trust she provided.

Slowly, I began to lose my ability to make sense of anything that had happened. I couldn't make up my mind. I didn't know where to start. The idea that money was the only thing triggering this turn of events seemed too simple to me – I wondered if there was something else. If the matter was just money, then everything could have been solved easily. But it hadn't been. What made it so complicated? What made it necessary to have secret plans, intrigues and harsh words?

I couldn't think properly, and the deep pain resulting from my father's death, which I still hadn't been able to acknowledge thoroughly, was increasing in me. I was only just starting to understand that my father was dead. One thing I was glad of was that he did not have to see what we were experiencing now, or what we would experience from then on, as a "family."

Lori, a woman obsessed with working, didn't have many friends. She had one or two intimate friends she'd known since very old times. Apart from them, she didn't allow anyone to approach her, especially not anyone she'd recently become acquainted with. The only big love she'd experienced was with a man she dated on-and-off for four years during university. When he went abroad after graduation, their relationship came to an end. I suspected Lori had wanted to go after him, but I don't know why she didn't: perhaps she was not allowed by my father, or perhaps her conscience didn't allow her. Whatever her reason, I sensed (although I was never sure) that they continued to contact each other for years.

Lori and I never gave evasive answers to each other's questions or hid anything, but neither of us liked to speak about our private issues either – not with each other or with anyone. It was not that we found intimacy unnatural but that we both preferred to experience our emotions by ourselves. Even if we wanted to have somebody around us, I had Eric and she... she didn't have anyone.

What Lori harboured in her heart regarding Eric was much more than I could have predicted. Responding to Eric in such a way while James was around showed how bold she was – unless it had been purely involuntary. She had not hesitated to reveal that clearly she had a kind of female hatred towards Eric.

I didn't know the details of how James became a part of Lori's life. If I'd liked James and took pleasure from spending time with him, I would have desired to learn every detail regarding their past. But I'd never even wondered about it.

As far as I knew, Lori had been planning a party for one of her friends at James' restaurant. James, taking advantage of this opportunity, succeeded in breaking through her shields and hence became a member of her life. I didn't expect this relationship, having started in such a way, to continue for long or to bring happiness or children. I didn't think Lori would have a kid with him, not even if two Sundays came together. I suspected she'd married James so quickly partly to take revenge on Eric. James had acted as a kind of sticking plaster for Lori, although he had not known anything about it... until this morning.

I'd known that Lori had some anger and unpleasant feelings towards Amy, but she'd always controlled it and behaved in a professional manner. She revealed it *quantum sufficit* and kept the rest hidden.

In fact, I'd always thought that if they'd met at another time, in another place, Lori might have liked Amy, because Amy was a smart woman doing her job very well, and Lori liked those kinds of people. What had triggered Lori to take steps regarding my father's will, causing her to lose herself, was her knowledge that the person she considered a rival was also a smart person.

Lori had always had a perfect relationship with my father. She had always supported and cared for him. While my mother wasn't there, she listened and understood my father better than the rest of us did. In fact, Gary had always kept himself distant. I had tried to understand and stand by my father as much as I could. Nevertheless, I could see that his relationship with Lori relaxed him more than his relationship with me. He spent most of his time with her because of the company, and naturally this had a positive effect on their relationship. My father loved and protected her very much, although he hadn't hesitated to hurt her from time to time, and Lori had always kept on the right side of him and shown him a lot of respect. (Exceptions don't break the rules.)

Gary and Lori were like two people who barely knew each other, and no more than that. They would never share their secrets or hug each other when they met. I don't think they hated each other, but I couldn't understand why these blood-connected souls maintained such a cold relationship.

Though I sometimes wondered about how Lori felt about Gary's marriage to Eric's ex-girlfriend, I never wanted to ask about it. However, I had some ideas, based on the impressions I got from them when we socialized together. After Eric ended his relationship with Amy, Lori might have hoped or thought (maybe even planned) that Amy would leave the company. However, Gary's marriage with Amy meant that would never happen. She had strengthened her position at the company, and she'd even been able to stand up against Lori – at least until today.

I didn't attribute any wrongdoing to Lori and Gary, and I liked them – sometimes from a distance, and sometimes very closely. I had never hesitated to show my love towards them. My father had always been in favour of showing his love openly, and thanks to him I got used to the idea.

I'd always loved Lori; she was always special. Our love was mutual, I was sure of it. We had always trusted and stood by one another. I'd never thought that one day I'd have so much conflict with her or that we would think so differently and not understand each other.

The moment we'd come into conflict had been an unexpected one, when our sorrow was too fresh to bear. If it had been at a different time, we could have settled all this tension in one or two minutes. We had enough love, respect and happy moments carved into our hearts to manage it. But none of that would help us now that this Amazon was making her first attacks.

All of these love-and-hate matrixes, money problems and potential troubles of the near future were on my mind as I walked around aimlessly. I didn't want to go to work at all. The weather was cloudy. A grey September day on the brink of bringing rain.

Suddenly, M crossed my mind. With her curly hair, shining smile and her reassurances that life can be beautiful, singing *"Dance Little Sister."* I wanted to call her. I wanted to tell her that my father was dead, and that intrigues of the kind you'd normally only see in movies had come out as soon as he'd died. I desired to ask her what she thought about all this. I wanted to confess that I'd missed her.

I didn't do it. I gave up the idea. I decided there was no point in going back. She'd said what she wanted to say, and it would do no good to make a crusted scab bleed again.

I walked without knowing where I was going until I saw a bookstore. I couldn't remember whether I'd ever entered it before, so I took a chance on it and wandered inside. I realised that since opening my own bookstore, I hadn't visited any other one for a long time.

At first I felt a tightness in my chest, but wandering around the bookshelves felt like a meditation to me. I relaxed. I touched the spines of some books while gazing at others. I took one of them into my hand. It was a book I'd read before and liked very much. It felt like meeting an old friend at an unexpected place. If we didn't have a quick talk, memories could be tainted. I opened one of its pages randomly and read the first line that grabbed my attention: *"... and I felt as badly for Holly, every iota, as she could feel for herself."*

Was it a coincidence, or was it M who wanted me to utter these words? I couldn't read any other line. I closed the book and put it down on its place on the shelf.

I had wanted very much to pour out my grief to M at that moment; maybe life prepared a nice surprise for me and made her speak to me in the voice of the book I chose. Would she become as upset as me after hearing all those words been said between us – among our family? I didn't want to predict an answer that would suddenly torture my mind. I walked towards the road with quick steps.

A few hours after our talk at the restaurant, I thought it would be good to meet with Lori again. Whatever I'd said at Nico, it had been said in anger. And I had not been alone in my fury at Lori. However, now that all that frustration had been released, I thought we should meet again and have a more relaxed and reasonable discussion.

I called her, but she didn't answer. I continued my lazy walking, and a short while later my phone rang. I hoped that it was Lori, but it wasn't.

'How is it going, V? Where have you been?'

'Hey, Amy. I'm walking aimlessly to nowhere. What are you doing?'

'Nothing. I'm very perplexed. Just sitting.'

'Look, we talked to Lori. Actually, it was not really a talk. Quarrelling didn't leave us enough time to touch the core issues. In other words, I couldn't find out what things she was involved in. I'll meet her once more, and this time I'll try to talk wisely and learn what the fuck she's into.'

'I know,' she said. 'Eric told me about it.'

Was this a sign that whatever they'd had between them would remain unharmed until they died?

'I need to talk to you,' she said. 'I can't comprehend what I've lived through this morning. I've kept quiet just because I don't want to upset Gary and I don't want to make anything worse, but I can't assure myself that it's right to remain silent. I'm chomping at the bit. I want to tell Gary everything and let the subject go wherever it will go. Because I feel that Lori is trying to trick us, and that if I continue to remain silent, whatever she's up to could become irremediable.'

'Keep calm, and don't confuse Gary's mind. Like the rest of us, he's probably still very upset after the funeral. Let's meet, okay?'

An hour later, Amy picked me up and drove us to one of the museum cafes downtown.

She kept repeating that she still couldn't get over or accept what

Lori had done to her. She didn't even know whether she should go to work the following day, as not only did Lori have no right to treat her this way, Amy did not deserve it. Even if Amy wasn't to be made a partner of the company, she should still be involved in the business as she was Gary's wife.

All she had put on the table was reasonable and right.

'V, it's not just me. If none of us protect our rights, you and Gary will also be harmed because of this situation. Someone who is willing to take my share could "steal" yours just as easily.'

'Your share?' I asked. I couldn't understand how Amy had learnt this information. Only Lori had seen my father's notes regarding his heritage, and she had shared this with only those of us who met her at Nico.

'Eric told me, but I already knew about it. Mr Kushner once told me that what I was doing at the company was worth more than I earned and that one day he would pay me back by giving me a share. He even joked and said, "In case I die suddenly, I'll put it down in my will; don't worry." Those words, which were a sweet joke at that time, are now reality. And if I know Mr Kushner, he would have done what he said. I have no doubt about it. What's more, Lori will do anything to make me suffer; you know the grudge she's nursing against me isn't because of business only.'

Of course I knew it. I felt naïve as I realised that Amy and Lori were both more ambitious than they seemed, which alienated them from me. It meant that I didn't know their true characters, despite all we had shared during the good times we'd spent together. Did I know these people at all? They had hidden so many things from me. I couldn't help wondering where and when their real characters would reveal themselves, and what kind of trouble they would cause for us.

Had I become a person who lived outside the world, far away from its realities, without foreseeing or feeling what was really going on? Had my obsession with books prevented me from connecting with my immediate surroundings, or knowing the people living in my immediate vicinity in a real sense? Was the imaginary world of books so different from the real world? I didn't think so. But one should really understand the cosmos of books and decode the "reality" in them to discern a meaning for his own life. It was my foolishness not to see that conflicts, ambitions, hidden agendas, games and cunningness were not just things to read about in books but actually the realities of life – my life. All the most inhumane and barbarian attitudes, words and secret plans I had avoided attributing to the people in my immediate surroundings were in fact there. I just hadn't seen them. Did that make me a part of the mess we were living?

'You shouldn't tell Gary anything for the time being,' I said. 'Let's try to find a solution. We may solve it before it gets worse. Lori isn't being reasonable right now, because my father's death has affected her very badly, just as it has for all of us. In fact, all her actions are probably due to her experiencing shock; she is not behaving reasonably. I will talk to her face to face again and try to understand what she's thinking.'

'Why are you so naïve, V?' Amy asked. 'Couldn't we take a concrete and positive step? I've known you for a long time, and I like you very much. You know it. I've liked you since the very beginning, since I was with Eric. But now I'll say something I've always held back in order not to hurt you: you are the most naïve man I've ever met. You are good-willed, but naïve. When you have these two features, life becomes merciless, V. You haven't experienced it much until now because your father has always stood by you, even when you didn't realise it. But he doesn't exist any longer, V. There is no very strong person behind you to always protect you. Understand this, because you don't have the right to be so naïve. If you remain this way, life will cause you much trouble. Believe me.'

Hearing advice at this age? When I was wounded? When my dreams and the trust I had in people had just been weakened? Instinctively, I tried to ignore what Amy had said. But a voice from within said that I needed to listen to her. I recognised some reasonable points in her words. Maybe I needed someone to say those things directly to my face. Maybe I needed to be slapped. I had to contemplate what she'd said. I thought about the times I'd been most upset and disappointed. Had these instances happened because of my naivety? Was I really always so naïve? Or was I, maybe even more than that, just a stupid fool?

What was in the past was in the past. Thinking about it would provide me no solutions for the current problems, so I removed these thoughts from my mind. There were much more important issues I had to deal with. Besides, could stupidity and naivety be stopped in just an instant, with a snap-like decision?

Amy agreed that she would stay calm and wait. She wouldn't take any steps without informing me, nor would she act impulsively. Not for a couple of days, at least.

Or at least that's what she said.

'Where do you want to go?' she asked. 'To the bookstore? I'll drop you there.'

'Thank you, but I'll walk a bit,' I said.

'It's gonna rain heavily. Come on, you'll get wet.'

I didn't accept her offer. With everything in my life already unravelling, it couldn't possibly rain on me while I didn't have an umbrella. In a film, the protagonist might have all kinds of trouble and then a downpour without an umbrella would be the deepest point of the black humour, but I couldn't be that out of luck.

Five or so minutes after I got out of the car, it started to rain heavily. I took shelter in a bus station and watched the people passing me by: so many lives, passing me hastily. At that moment, I started to feel angry with myself. It was high time to take a step. I didn't have any right to be so inert – so very passive. While we were experiencing interfamilial erosion, and after experiencing such intense pain, leaving the decisions to "passive Gary", "arrogant Lori" and "wounded Amy" – three clashing points on a triangle – would be too stupid. (Naïve, stupid and foolish. Could I be all three together?) I needed to do something.

I tried to contact Lori once more. She answered.

'I don't have the will or energy to fight with you, V,' she said.

'I don't want to fight with you, Lori,' I said. 'I just want to talk. I want to understand you. Let's be dignified and solve what needs to be solved – together. These days will pass over.'

We agreed to meet towards the evening. I decided to drop by the store to catch my breath and have a little calm time. I thought that doing some errands would be a good way to settle my mind. I managed to find a taxi in the downpour.

At the bookstore, I picked up the post that had accumulated in a pile inside the door, and then pushed aside the small boxes of books that had yet to be unpacked and put away in their correct places. When I reached my small office at the end of the long corridor, I sat at my chair, leaned my elbows on the table, and put my head between my hands. The thought that I might not be able to find peace anywhere else but in this room crossed my mind. Indistinctly.

When I woke up, I had just half an hour left before my meeting with Lori. I rushed out. We were meeting at a wine house that Lori liked very much. It was a little touristic, but an enjoyable place.

By the time I arrived, she was already there and had already started to drink.

'Where have you been?' she asked.

'I fell asleep at the store. Forgive me.'

Lori seemed relaxed and calmer. This was a relief, because I wanted to talk to her openly, understand her and learn what she aimed at.

'What are you thinking about?' I said.

She didn't answer at once. She took a sip of wine and looked at me.

'I'm thinking of what my father would feel if he could see me right now. I'm listening to music and drinking wine on the day he was buried and left alone in cold soil. Is this injustice or ingratitude? Not knowing his worth?'

She took another sip. 'Doesn't matter. He could simply say, "Lori is in shock! She is trying to bear the pain. She is alone." He would find something to say.

'Aside from that, I'm also thinking about what to do. Should I keep the company going, or start a new life? This event has turned me upside down. It's made me question my life in general terms. But I don't want such questioning. You know me: if I start such a questioning, I won't give up until I find the answers. I won't stop until I clean my slate off all my sorrows and regrets. This could cause trouble for so many people, and of course it may upset me too. I can't tolerate such radical changes right now. Father's death has deeply affected me. It's also very recent. None of us have completely accepted the fact that he has passed away yet. We haven't felt the real blow yet – the real pain. Therefore, I need to calm down a bit. To do that, I need to remove the questions disturbing my mind; and to do that, I need a good wine.'

Lori was talking very differently from how she had at our previous meeting. My inner-voice said that we were on the same frequency this time. Every minute that passed, my trust that I did indeed know Lori increased.

'What's disturbing you?' I said. 'Can I help you? Let's solve these things together, Lori. You shouldn't shoulder all the problems by yourself, all alone. I wanna help you.'

She started to laugh silently, and then burst into loud laughter. I was pleased because of her smiles and happiness, but her reaction also meant she wasn't taking what I said seriously. I didn't like that.

'Why are you laughing?' I asked.

'Nothing, but... thank you, but I don't need your help, little boy. The last thing you and I need is mercy. If I include you in the loop, you'll likely show mercy—'

'Mercy to whom?'

'To those who don't deserve it. Anyways, this would make it difficult to solve your problems, and my problems, as well. But still, I thank you for your offer. Look, not even Gary has asked if he can help me.'

My first impression in thinking Lori was calmer now seemed wrong. As far as I could see, she was burning with hatred and still holding a grudge – but perhaps trying to hide it. The only way she could get rid of the heat of her feelings was to know others agreed with her decisions and would act on them. I was determined to learn what she wanted to do, and then hinder her if necessary. Her style of speaking, as if no one could stand in her way, was starting to make me angry.

'I won't allow you to just do anything you want with the company,

Lori. You can be sure of that,' I said.

'What do I want to do?' she said. She still seemed calm.

'For instance, being unfair to others. Hurting someone. Behaving independently on matters that interest all of us...'

'Okay, if you want to talk together about the matters that interest "all" of us, call Gary. That's "all" of us. Call him and we'll all talk together. Now. At once.'

'No, we're a family, Lori. And in this family, we also have Amy. Unfortunately, we have James, too. If we're making any decisions, we must all talk together and decide. In fact, there is no need to meet right now, because there isn't a subject on which we should decide. Father noted down his wishes and left the rest to us, meaning, do what the note says. You saw it. What more is there to talk about? We have no other choice but to comply with his wishes.'

'First of all, James is not a part of this family. Nor is Amy. I don't care about either of them. They can both leave and get out of our lives tomorrow – no, now. Right away. When you say "family," I think only of you and Gary. If it was possible, I wouldn't consider that sluggish man either, but I can't say anything as he resembles my mum. A stubborn man who is the puppet of his wife...'

'Lori, please. Aren't you aware of how cutting your words are? We are talking about your husband and your brother. And the wife of your brother. No one deserves to be spoken about in that way.'

She didn't listen to me. We talked about the same things over and over. She had shaped everything in her mind just as she liked, and what I said had no effect on her.

We were flogging a dead horse. Time flew, but we were going nowhere fast. While Lori talked, I looked outside for a moment and became disgusted with our current situation. We seemed to be bargaining for something. For what? For the rights of the people we liked(?). For money, even if implicitly.

We were mature people, though. As a result, whatever we did or however we behaved, we were responsible for our choices. I believed that I was doing my best. At least, for that day. I had twice tried to talk to Lori and understand what she wanted, but I could neither learn what she wanted to do nor destroy her plans. We would all just have to wait and see what happened.

We were both tired of flapping our jaws. We dropped the subject without finding anything to agree on. Then, we started to talk about my father.

'I couldn't understand what had happened,' I said. 'It was so sudden. We were all so unprepared. I still can't believe it. It's a very strange feeling. I don't remember feeling so surprised when Mother died. That doesn't mean that I wasn't upset or extremely sad. I mean something different. For some reason, Father always seemed very powerful to me, as if he would never die. I realised when he died that he wasn't immortal after all. In fact, he had diseases, and he was plump and old. Most of his friends were dead. And yet I never thought he'd die before me. I couldn't feel it coming. I don't know what made me feel so. But it was like that.'

'Because of love, V. You both loved each other very much. You resembled each other in most ways. Books were your common interest, but also Father had so much respect for your efforts to shape your life in accordance with your wishes, with your heart. You, at least, tried to be with him for some time, but when you saw you couldn't do it you chose to go on in your own way. You continued on in a very determined and reasonable way. And, most importantly for him, you showed you were making an effort. You didn't have your head in the clouds. What you were doing was reasonable; it could be understood. Not like what Gary did.

'What's more, you were the youngest child of the family. That was an innate advantage. Mothers and fathers love their youngest child more. I don't know, maybe from their point of view the youngest child seems more delicate and unprotected in life. Therefore, for them, their parents' love and protection never die out. Whenever we were alone at the company, Father would ask about you. We would talk about you. Even though you were not aware of it, he always thought of you and protected you. He would question whether you needed money or other things. He would also ask for help from me. I worked for him as a spy a lot. I brought him information about you. It made him happy. He was both happy and honoured, because you were standing on your own two feet and managing what you wanted to do.'

'How about Gary?'

'He only asked about him very rarely. I don't know how often he contacted him directly, but I'm sure he talked to Amy more often than to Gary. I know that Father didn't like what Gary was doing, or his lazy and unambitious character. He always wished he could "bring him to his senses."

In my opinion, my father had done Gary an injustice by thinking this way about him. Gary had chosen to proceed in a particular way and, like me, in his own way. 'Even though Gary was not the most unsuccessful man in the world,' I said, 'he was his son. He should not have ignored him.'

'He didn't ignore him. He gave Gary some support. If he'd just ignored him, he wouldn't have given Gary any share of the company. And don't forget, V, if Father had not supported him, Gary would never have found enough money to survive.'

I wondered whether she would continue to work at the company or 'start a new life', as she had suggested at the beginning of the night. I had never imagined Lori working anywhere else other than the company. I couldn't imagine it. Her words were like a puzzle I couldn't solve (yet).

'So, can we conclude that you'd like to start "everything" from scratch? I mean, shaping your life anew? Come on, Lori....'

'I might. Why not? You and Gary don't care about the company. Maybe I want to listen to my inner voice and do something else. Isn't that possible? Maybe I want to live other lives?'

'Did you decide on this last night, or is this something you had in your mind before?'

Was it necessary for my father to die before Lori could surprise me? How had we become so distant from each other while thinking we were close? Why hadn't we talked about our plans, wishes, expectations and dreams before? We were talking now, but my father's coffin cast a shadow over every word we uttered. As I listened to the dreams I hadn't even known Lori was holding all this time, I became more and more surprised, but I couldn't rejoice in the moment. If I'd heard her dreams at another time, I would have offered her some encouraging words; but now I just looked at her, listened, and sometimes smiled. I couldn't smile from my heart or say motivating words. There was something hindering me.

Lori was telling me she thought it was too late for her to give birth but not too late for her to adopt a child. She said it could be the right time for her to fulfil this desire, which she had been postponing for a long time. Now that she had lost someone close to her, the desire to add another member to her family was even stronger.

'But James isn't leaning towards my idea. He already has a daughter whom he loves. He thinks his daughter won't find this idea suitable – that she's gonna get jealous and grow more emotionally distant. In my opinion, he's just putting the blame on his daughter because he doesn't want to shoulder the responsibility of another child. But I don't care what he thinks. I can do it all by myself. I don't need him. Maybe his existence will be helpful for the process of adopting the child, but after that we can get divorced. I don't know whether I must be married in order to keep the child, but it isn't important. I'll find a way, somehow. I want to stand on my own feet and help someone in real sense – maybe catch a soul who's gonna lose her light and care for her with all my heart, change that baby's fate in all the positive ways that I can. Nothing is more meaningful for me. It's something I've been thinking of for a long time.

'After last night, I decided for certain that the only important thing in the world is to make a positive contribution to someone's life. Aside from that, everything else seems meaningless to me now.'

In front of me was a very different person to the one I had talked to at our previous meeting. This was someone I hadn't met before.

'I don't know what to say. I never expected to hear these kinds of things from you. But, good – very good.... Although, I still don't understand how you can be so tough in terms of the inheritance and also have such positive feelings like these. One side of you is like a glass of sweet wine, while the other is like a poison. I can't predict which side of you I'll meet when I talk to you.'

She smiled again. As far as she was concerned, she told me, the issue was dropped and she would not quarrel with me over it any more. I realised that, when I first confronted her today, I had not considered how effectively she could deactivate me and make me passive while she carried on with her own path.

We drank a little more and talked about ordinary things. Then, we left together. It was cool outside. She didn't seem to notice the cold; perhaps the wine had warmed her. She asked me whether I had arrived by car or taxi, and when I told her by taxi, she said she would take me home.

We walked together to the parking lot. The night was quiet, except for the crackling of small stones crushed under our shoes.

'I don't wanna die in a car accident tonight, Lori,' I said.

'You won't, little boy,' she said and then put her hand on my shoulder and leaned her head towards mine. We walked like long-lost friends meeting after a decade.

'You're always talking about the inheritance issue,' she said. 'Did you know you can benefit from my efforts, too – even more than you've imagined?'

'Sorry, what?'

'Just as I will prevent anyone from outside the family gaining shares, I can also do you a favour. According to Father's notes, the house will be inherited by Andrew and Nancy – and as it's not stated otherwise, and as the library is located in the house, they will get that, too. But Father once told me that he wanted to leave his library to you. So, I'll take care of this, and make sure you get the library.'

I couldn't believe my ears. This was another instance of Dr Jekyll and Ms Hyde.

'Lori, are you insane? Do you know that what you're saying is a crime? Does Father have a will? And if he does, where is it now? When will we learn about its contents? Do you really want to change the existing will? Oh my gosh – in other words, will you commit a crime? I admit, I can't even imagine the perfectness of having that library, but your words are almost making me speechless. Your determination scares me. Please, stop. Don't do anything about the will. Don't do anything, I'm begging you, Lori!'

She smiled. 'Don't worry, kiddo. Father wanted it this way. I'm just fine-tuning it, that's all.'

We came up to her car. She winked at me and got into the car.

I took a deep breath and also got in.

'We don't need to drive,' I said. 'You've been drinking. I don't wanna have an accident and become disabled, or die.'

'We're always doing what we need to do,' she said, 'and we always will. It's off the record. We'll forget that we are driving drunkenly. Only for this one time.' Then, she smiled and put the car in gear.

While she was driving, I looked at her face from time to time. She did not look at me at all; she just concentrated on what she was doing. Was the determined expression on her face a prediction of what we would experience in the following days? Would watching her be my only reaction to whatever she was going to do? Would she go on her way no matter what? Was a fortune teller shedding light on our future condition? The road was empty. I tried to find something outside that would keep me busy and free my mind from these thoughts. But I couldn't find anything. Life was making me think of the same issues over and over.

Instead of taking me home, she decided to host me at her place – their place. When we arrived, James was still awake. He pretended to welcome Lori very sincerely.

'Did you two play "fellow feeling"?' he said to us.

I don't know how I would have responded to such a stupid remark if I hadn't already been relaxed after those glasses of wine. I just smiled, and Lori didn't answer him.

James started to tell us what he had been busy with that day. He told us that he'd had dinner with his daughter that evening, and that the restaurant had been very crowded, and that a journalist he met on the run had promised him some positive PR news. None of these subjects attracted my interest or Lori's at all, especially considering the current issues on our minds.

Apparently unable to stand her husband any longer, Lori excused herself and went to bed. Actually, I very much wanted to sleep too. It had been a very tiresome day, and I didn't want to stay up alone with James. My mind was very busy with my father. After getting past the initial shock, the pain had started to affect me, slowly and deeply.

'Hey, V, stay a little longer.' James said. 'Let's drink a glass of something. Let's... let's spare a few words for Pap.... Then you can go to sleep. Come on.'

He was referring to my father as "Pap" for the first time. It was very dishonourable of him to utter that word now; he wouldn't have dared while my father was still alive. He had become a rascal, behaving as he wished. I tried to tell him it was bad manners to call my father Pap now. Realising that I wouldn't tolerate any argument at all, he stepped back and didn't insist on his wording.

'Okay, man, relax,' he said. 'Don't take offence. I'm joking, just to loosen you up. You know I don't harbour ill-will towards Mr Kushner and would never disrespect him. He was like my own father.'

He was right about joking, because he began to sound funny.

'Actually, I wanna talk to you about a subject that's been keeping my mind busy recently,' he said. 'Do you remember when we were all at the restaurant, and Lori said something to Eric about missing an opportunity?'

Nice. Had the night just started? It was very strange that he had hidden this subject from Lori but wanted to talk about it with me. Apart from the answer I would give him, what interested me and made me smile inwardly was his beating around the bush instead of being direct.

'Are you serious?' I asked.

'Don't I seem so?'

'Look, James, if you want, we can make a short summary of recent events: my father died yesterday – and suddenly. In addition, I had some very heated discussions with my sister, as you know. Tell me, how can you now ask me this stupid question? I'm not the right person to talk to about this issue, you know? Lori is your wife, and she's the one who made the comment, isn't she? Why don't you talk to her?'

Though James pretended to be cheerful and relaxed, I could see he was quite nervous. I felt that he and Lori had problems, and it was probably worse than I assumed. It was pitiful for him to try to talk about such an issue with me and not with his wife. He should never want to be put in a situation where he was depending on me to help him sort out his problems with my sister.

'V, you know how much I like you and Gary. [*What?*] I've always got along well with you. [*We got along well?*] We've had a respectful and discreet relationship, and maintained it without doing any injustices to each other. [*Respect? No injustices?*] I don't think our relationship will be harmed in any way in the future, even without presence of our father. But, there is an important subject that leaves me perplexed: it's Eric. He isn't a member of our family. I know, V, that he is your friend, okay, and that he's been around the family for a long time. Father [*Father?*] liked him very much because he benefited from his work. I accept all this. But Father [*Did he just say 'Father' again?*] isn't here anymore. He has left us [*Us?*], and so now we form the family. And in my opinion, we don't need a lawyer like him working for us even if he doesn't require payment. [*Enough!*] We want a real lawyer man; we don't need Eric anymore. We can deal with our work by ourselves. He must leave our family alone from now on. I mean, as a lawyer and... you know. We don't need him, V.'

James' stupid words didn't come to an end. It was obvious that he would keep going until I got angry. It was pointless to try to stay calm. 'Finished?' I asked.

'No, but you can speak, of course. C'mon, I'm listening to you, man.'

I'd longed to get away from the depressing atmosphere I'd been experiencing all day, so I could be alone to think about my father, but James kept trying to pull me into his own darkness by giving me a hard time.

I told him again that Eric was not only important and precious to me, but that everyone else also considered him as a member of "our family." My father didn't "exploit" him for his work but respected his thoughts and worldview, and believed that he was competent in his own business. Hence why my father had consulted him on every subject he regarded as important.

As I spoke, what James' own wife thought about him crossed my mind, and I realized that no one considered James a member of the family, and that no one cared about his existence or his absence.

I tried to tell him that Eric was much more than just a friend to the family and would therefore always be a part of the "family," despite James' wishes. Eric would always stay with us.

But James resisted understanding what I meant.

'V, I see your point, but I wish that you would write off this conceit, and this stupid spectacled man. I wish you would do it for me, V, so that our relationship could become stronger. But if you don't, I can also understand it, at least for the time being.

'Anyway, V, there are some other things confusing me. You should help me understand them, man. At least do that. I have some doubts and questions in my mind – questions that I can't answer. I can't manage all alone.'

James was much drunker than I had first thought. There was no sign of the calm and cautious manner that had been apparent ten minutes ago. As he explained his thoughts and feelings, the alcohol's effects on him increased. Or maybe his sorrows and the alcohol created a synergy that harmed his "strong character." I was sure that if I repeated back to him on the following day what he was saying then, he would feel like thirty cents. A very "strong," "enduring" and "unconquerable" man like him...

'Look, James, you need to understand that what you're referring to as our "family" existed before my father died, but you were not so interested in the family then, so I don't understand why you are obsessed with it now. Your reason doesn't interest me right now anyway. Secondly, you will have to change your view of Eric. What you wanted me to do is something we should never speak of again. Think about it. I can't believe you even said that to me. You had better get used to the idea that Eric will always be with us. I don't want to talk about these issues with you ever again. Do you understand me? Actually, I have my doubts whether you'll even remember this conversation, because you are so drunk. Anyway, I don't have any other choice but to believe that you will. I'm going to bed now.'

I stood up, and so did he. I started to walk around the table on my way to the guest room so I could avoid passing in front of him, but he took two quick steps and confronted me.

'If it's necessary, I can put him in his place, V. I'll do it. There are still things I haven't been able to solve, I feel it, but I'll solve them. In a short time. I'll happily do what I'm meant to do, despite your rejection.'

He started to act sober – and became a complete asshole – in ten seconds. What he said did not herald good news. James was an unreasonable person who could easily cause problems for every matter he worried himself about. He stood before me, staring me boldly in the eye. I walked away.

At that moment, I felt that more bad things were going to happen. They were just waiting for their turn. Worse than that, it wasn't apparent who was going into combat with whom on the war fields.

The only way to escape from this disturbance was to sleep.

I lay on the bed, my mind busy with the crudeness of being a human, and my heart filled only with my father.

Envyday
16 SEPTEMBER

WHEN I WOKE up in the morning, it was quiet in the house. I wandered down the hall into the living room but found neither Lori nor James. It was almost 10 a.m. I hadn't woken up so late for a long time. The previous night's tiredness caused pain in every part of me. I tasted the sourness that had accumulated in my mouth. Moving my tongue over my palate and cheeks, I tried to clean away this sour taste as I switched on my phone. As soon as it turned on, a message appeared on the screen, notifying me that I had received four new short text messages. They had all been sent by Amy.

'*What did you do, V? Could you talk to Lori? Kisses.*'
'*Hi, V, you haven't called me yet. Is everything okay?*'

'V, your phone is still off. I'm sleeping now. Call me even if it's late.'
'V, where are you, I'm wondering what happened. Call me asap.'

Amy's insistent attitude in these hard times left me breathless. I remembered how, when she had been together with Eric a long time ago, her most annoying feature had been her insistence.

I sent her a message: *'I will call you later.'* I didn't have enough energy or desire to give her a detailed report right away.

As soon as my message was sent, she called me.

'V, what did you do? Have you talked to her?'

'Amy, I told you I would call you later. I just woke up. Can we talk later, please? I beg you.'

'V, this is very important. There's no time to wait. Please, tell me what you've learned. We need to act quickly. We need to take precautions as Lori will move faster than us.'

'Amy, it isn't a war; calm down. There's nothing to worry about. I talked to Lori. We'll talk again. We'll find a golden mean in the end.'

'V, I can't be calm. You don't understand. You're not aware of what's gonna happen. Lori is more insidious and organised than us – way more.'

'We'll talk and find a solution. Okay?'

'I'll help. Where are you now? I'm near your place. I'll come and pick you up. How long will it take for you to get ready?'

'Amy, don't talk nonsense. I'm not at home right now. I stayed at Lori's last night. Also, there are things I need to do. Please, be calm and behave accordingly.'

'You stayed at Lori's? Why?'

I was surprised at the improperness of the question, but I didn't answer her in the rude manner she deserved. Without belabouring the issue, I ended the call. Due to Amy's hasty and insistent attitude, I had started the day in a nervous and uneasy way.

In my opinion, Amy had started to lose her talent for thinking when she began to worry about losing what she owned. She had been out of line asking – as if she were my wife or girlfriend – why I had not slept at home. And where was the fault in sleeping at my sister's home? If I were to consider too deeply the deviations in the behaviours of the people closest to me, everything would become harder day by day. Everyone was complaining and entering into crises of uneasiness and jealousy.

Then life suddenly became beautiful when I prepared a cup of coffee for myself. I gazed outside. It was cool, but luminous. The weather I liked most.

I immediately went outside and inhaled the cool air deeply, hoping that my anger would decrease a bit. School children were walking to school with their untouched smiles on, teasing each other and enjoying themselves. I could barely restrain myself from uttering, 'These are the easiest days for you. Enjoy!' But I held myself back, because I didn't want to provoke anger and disappointment in a life they had not yet lived; they were the ones who should understand their own lives.

I left Lori's. While walking, I thought of what I should do. Should I start the day by talking to Lori again about the same issues, over and over; or should I go to work and deal with the errands like a responsible person? These reasonable questions, and thoughts of my father, were passing through my mind when the ringing of my phone woke me back up to the real world.

It was Gary calling. He asked first how I was and then whether I had learned why Lori hadn't come to the funeral.

Pardon me, and you thought your wife was the anxious person? 'Yes, I have. As Amy said, she was with the lawyers,' I said.

'Bitch!'

Bitch? I'd never assumed that Gary was even aware of this word. 'Gary, what was that? Watch what you're saying, man.... Please, get a hold of yourself, and don't say such things while everyone else is already losing it. If you act stupid like everybody else, then what? Please don't lose your grip. Control your anger.'

'Who are you talking about?'

'What? What you mean? Don't you see what's happening around you? Lori, Amy and James... everyone is slowly losing their self-control. I'm trying to tidy up everything – and everyone. I wanna see that my family is a "real" one.'

'Hey, wait, wait.... Amy just called me and told me what dirty things Lori did. She said that in order not to upset me, she had first asked for your support, and that you agreed to help her. But last night stayed at Lori's. Did Lori decide to include you in her master plan? V, tell me, why did you leave Amy in the lurch after saying you'd help her? What's Lori into? What does she want?'

For a moment, I felt as if I was looking down on myself from above. I couldn't walk any more. I was standing in the middle of the pavement with my head down. Gary's words flashed in my mind like lightning. I couldn't understand why he was being so unreasonable. What's more, Amy going to Gary to kick up a fuss about me was a childish attitude that I had difficulty comprehending. I couldn't understand how a group of people who had seemed so intelligent and clever had changed into primary school kids. I didn't want to believe it was happening.

'We need to talk. I'm coming to you,' I said and hung up.

I looked up at the sky and, for the hundredth time in the last forty-eight hours, questioned the reality of all the things I was going through. The changes I had observed in my vicinity made me angry and upset. Worse still, they caused me to question my everlasting belief in hope.

I wanted to gather everyone around a table at that moment and talk directly from my gut. I wanted to shout at them all and say, 'You assholes, this is real! What you're fucking up is a "real" family, you idiots!'

Looking at the blue relaxed me a bit – again. Some unpredicted hope rained on me. *Clouds have all the answers*: this thought cut through my heart like a hot but delicate knife. It didn't hurt me; it woke me up instead.

I had neither eaten breakfast nor taken a relaxing shower. I felt both dirty and hungry. I decided to drop by home, take a bath and grab a bite before meeting Gary.

I took a cab. My phone began dancing in my pocket with its stupid melody. I didn't care.

It started its second dance, but I didn't care about that one either. There was a short silence, followed by another round – and I gave up.

'Have you gone crazy too, or are you checking whether I have?' I asked.

'Option B,' said Danielle with a smile in her voice. 'I think I called just in time. It's obvious from your tone that if you haven't already gone crazy, it's gonna happen soon. What are you up to? Are you at the bookshop?'

'No, it's a long story. I'll tell you about it later. I need to go home, take a bath and eat something. Then I'm going to Gary's atelier.'

'Oh, super nice!' she said. 'Hey, let's have breakfast together. Okay, the plan is, I'll stop by somewhere to get some sandwiches, and then come to your place to enjoy our little breakfast. I'll be there in around twenty minutes. Kiss you!'

Was my luck starting to turn? On a day like this, a beautiful woman was going to come to my place with sandwiches, without me even asking her to? But then again, this attractive packet (Danielle and her sandwiches) also had another name: high-potential-pain-in-the-ass. That Danielle had showed me so much affection recently, even if it was for the sake of friendship, had started to disturb me, because she was a very (VERY) attractive woman. On the other hand, she was also the woman Eric was going to marry.

Either way, it made me uneasy to be near such a beautiful woman after the fresh break-up I'd just lived through. Danielle's perfume, the dark-red shade of her lipstick, her bony hands: they all reminded me of M. It caused me to find Danielle even more desirable than I might perceive her under normal conditions.

I was in the middle of a situation that was creating its own complexity. If Danielle hadn't been such a beautiful and caring woman, I wouldn't have thought about M at such an inappropriate time. Danielle's femininity wouldn't have attracted me this strongly. Despite suffering such a harsh break-up, I had been coping well – till Danielle began hanging around more often. What I feared was that, on top of all the other crazy things going on, I would lose my way, and my problems would only get bigger and bigger.

I was worried not because I had doubts about me or Danielle, or because I was afraid of letting Eric down, but because of the fact that in a complex situation like this one, even a very tiny problem (let's call it a misunderstanding even) could cause me to lose my mind, in the real sense. At least, having survived the last couple of days, I knew that my mind was much stronger and resistant to going crazy than I'd assumed.

My home was silent, just as it had been when I left it, and my stuff was still orderly, having obeyed the rules of universe while I'd been away. I'd missed everything in there.

As I was taking off my clothes in order to have a shower, the doorbell rang. Very untimely, as if the doorbell was trying to tell me something.

'Who's there?'

'Who else are you waiting for, you silly? Open it, I'm starving,' Danielle said.

Though I felt uneasy – she had turned up earlier than I had expected – I ran to the intercom, pressed the button to let her into the building, and ran back to the bathroom, leaving my apartment door open for her. When she reached to my apartment, she shouted inside.

'C'mon in,' I called out. 'I'll be with you in a moment.'

'Okay, I'll get everything ready for you,' she said.

I'd been alone with Danielle a couple of times before, but this was the first time that I was naked – even though in another room – while she was wandering in my house. I had to admit that, apart from being strange and exciting, there was also some element of sinful delight. Still though, I tried to behave with decency (except in my mind).

As I passed the hall between my room and bathroom as quickly as possible, she called out, 'Hey, I bought a chocolate cake. Would you like some as an intro?'

It was pointless of her to ask such a question now. What would change if she learned whether I'd like some chocolate cake now or five minutes later? At times like these, one can't control everything passing through his mind – all the evidence we need are in novels. Was she genuinely flirting with me, or just wondering how I would react to flirting? Did she just want to see whether one more filthy human would be affected by her? Or maybe she was behaving in the most proper and normal way that she could, and I was off my head.

I couldn't make sense out of her presence or behaviour at that moment. 'Yes, please,' I said, and then closed the door.

I became more and more nervous as I couldn't find the reason for her unnecessary intimacy, or my indecent daydreaming. Worst of all, I was secretly pleased with this ambiguous affection. I took off the towel and gazed at my naked body in the mirror. The situation exactly was this: I had cracked a fat because a very beautiful woman had asked me whether I'd like to eat some cake. I felt ashamed of myself but also enjoyed the tension the moment carried, which was difficult to define.

I sat at the edge of the bed and thought of the answer I'd need to provide if Danielle, Eric and I might one day watch this moment together in heaven (if there's a heaven and if I got there). My inability to think up a sensitive answer for my absurd scenario, plus the idea of heaven, made me remember my father again. As if I'd forgotten him for even a second. He was on my mind all the time, but I realised that while I fantasised about Danielle, he has appeared in the centre of my silly brain. Even then, I still hadn't realised how much I would miss him. I felt that my first visit at his new home would make me understand that he had really gone somewhere where I wouldn't be able to reach him, and then, at that very moment, I'd start to perceive the real pain of his loss. I turned myself inside out, thinking about the concept of death. I stood up, put on my jeans and a white shirt, and went into the living room.

Danielle was sitting at the table, smiling at me. She pulled out the chair next to her, and I sat down, letting our chairs form an L-shape.

'Welcome,' I said.

'Oh, you had a shower and made yourself very clean, the freshest smelling man on earth, for this moment. Come, gimme a kiss,' she said.

The heaven scene I had imagined continued to play out in my mind, and I tried not to laugh aloud at my own dark humour. She kissed me on my cheeks. Her perfume was intense, as usual, and seemed to fill my lungs.

'Tell me, how are you after, you know...?' She became serious when she mentioned my father, making me ashamed of my perverted thoughts.

I told her I was very confused and tired, and explained how devastating it was to see my family, which I had always considered strong and tightly knit, and one of the most important sources of my support in life, starting to tear itself apart only two days after the first blow of real life. I was trying – and would always try – my best to ensure that my family wouldn't be knocked out. I wanted to believe that together we were like a very strong building made of concrete and steel, not a palace made of matchsticks.

'Couldn't you be mistaken?' she asked. 'Maybe not all of your inter-familial relationships are now weak or superficial. As far as I've heard from Eric, the issue is about shares or money, or whatever. Lori and Amy are clashing regarding this. Okay, so there's mistrust between them, and they will, I dunno, fight... maybe till they each get what they want. But you shouldn't forget that we are all only human and we all have desires, fears, faults and sins. We must accept everyone with their cons too, right? Our bad sides don't make us totally bad, just as our good sides don't make us angels. Am I wrong?'

That we had humanly desires, "sins" that wouldn't make us bad people... I shouldn't be reading between the lines. Was she writing between the lines?

'You may be right. If I contemplate it too much, my mind might enter into a vicious cycle. In order to make good decisions and take proper actions, I need to keep myself away from all these problems and relax a bit. What we're all living through is enormously painful, though I'm not yet aware of how painful it will get. We still haven't fully processed what has happened.'

I wanted to change the subject at that instant, because the last thing I wanted to do then was to open up to someone. Plus, Eric informing everyone of what we had talked about was starting to make me a bit angry. It might not be a good idea to talk to Danielle, because she might repeat everything to Eric, and Eric would then tell God knows who.

During our brunch, as we talked of this and that, I sometimes recalled what Amy had said to Gary, and the way Gary had relayed her words to me. Sometimes my mind became busy with these thoughts, and in those instances Danielle would touch my arm and give me a heart-warming smile, and we continued to eat. Whenever she touched my arm, I could see how tightly her shirt clung to her elbow. This was not good at all. Not the tightness, but my focus on it.

Then, somehow, we started to talk about M. She asked whether I'd recently heard from her. I hadn't. She began to give me "friendly advice offered within the framework of someone's ex-girlfriend," and I started to feel bored and remembered that I needed to meet Gary.

'If you want, I can drive you to the atelier,' she said. 'I will be passing it on my way.'

I didn't accept her offer. I didn't want to be with her any longer. I thanked her and saw her off with a friendly but superficial hug.

I came back to the living room and lay down on the couch. I realised that I missed my mum. Suddenly. I'd assumed that the scar left by her death had almost healed, but now my heart ached, as if the wound was fresh. I wanted very much to have her near me, and to cry while hugging her. My father had just died, but my eyes became wet for my mother, who had died so many long years ago.

I wasn't feeling well. While the initial shock of my father's death was coming to an end, the real pain of losing him was slowly rising to the surface.

Uncontrolled thoughts ran through my mind from one side to another. I began to feel upset at not having visited my shop much over the last two days. I felt as if I was an irresponsible person. The foolish claim that the show must go on, whatever happens, might not be foolish after all. Perhaps such a psyche was one of the results of being a truly responsible person.

While thinking about whether I should go and deal with my own work instead of visiting Gary at his atelier just to talk about the same issues over again, he called to ask where I was. I told him I was about to leave, and he suggested that instead of meeting at the atelier, we could drink something at Nico.

I refused. 'Wait there, Gary. I'm coming to the atelier.'

This time I took my car, because staring out the window of a taxi didn't help me relax, and I thought driving might be a good distraction from my problems. I turned on the radio, and then realised that I hadn't listened to any music since my father had passed away. Trying not to think about anything, I listened to the words of the songs playing. I let myself be in the now. I felt very irresponsible though, as if I shouldn't be steering my mind away from our inter-familial issues about money – but then again, a five-minute dose of poison between my thoughts felt very good.

Six songs later, I reached the building where Gary's atelier was located. I parked my car and looked up towards the front window. Maybe, in about ten minutes, I'd be entering into a heated quarrel with Gary behind those windows. Or maybe we'd find and apply a magical remedy that would solve all of our problems, and then my life, which had been hell for two days, would heal a little. It couldn't be the same as it was before, but it might be stronger than its previous condition. Who knows. Hope always finds its way, somehow.

I waited in front of the elevator. Out of the blue, I started gazing at my surroundings in a different way. I imagined that the things around me were also living creatures and hence had thoughts and feelings. For instance, I imagined that when Amy had been here this morning and called for the elevator so she could go up to Gary and hastily tell him her perspective, the metal stair-rails on the left side of the elevator had condemned her for her ill-mannered and unnecessary attitude. I liked it. I felt that I wasn't all alone any more. The stair-rails before me had given Amy the stink eye and maybe caused her to feel a little ashamed.

This dream came to an abrupt end when I remembered that Gary had told me Amy called him rather than visited the atelier. The elevator doors opened, and I said goodbye to the metal rails, my potential friends, and then stepped into the elevator.

The atelier's door was no different: the same old. I rang the bell, and Gary opened the door. If he'd planned to behave as if he was angry at me, when we came face to face he must have decided he couldn't manage it, because he simply smiled and gave me a hug. He wasn't the kind of person who could make plans beforehand and apply them later in a professional manner anyway. He couldn't have managed that even if he'd tried. Within any family, only one person could carry out such tasks; and in our family, that position had already been filled.

We sat at the big table by the window.

'So, what's up,' he said.

'Gary, we need to do something and stop all the wagging tongues. The gossip only makes things harder. Everyone thinks of himself first and ignores the rest, and then we end up with very silly misunderstandings. For instance, what did Amy tell you? We'd agreed that she would wait for me to talk to Lori. We wanted to find a solution by ourselves, and we left you out to save you the headache. I don't understand why she turned her back on our agreement and dumped everything onto you.'

Gary explained how Amy had turned up at the atelier that morning and told him that I'd demanded she give me time to talk to Lori but later refused to tell her what Lori and I had talked about. Amy thought that, since I'd even stayed at Lori's house, it could mean I'd decided to join her in a move against Amy. Lori and V together against Gary and Amy.

'Are you insane, Gary?' I asked. 'What reason would I have for behaving in such a stupid way? And what would Lori's reason be? C'mon, don't we all know each other? Are we enemies? Why do we say such things? How strange to suddenly reach this conclusion. It was very late last night, and I was drunk, so I stayed at my sister's house. So what? What's wrong with that? Do I have to account for everything I do to you or Amy? Anyway, earlier you said Amy had called you on the phone. Did she come here in the morning?'

'Yes, she did. But why is that important?'

Metal rails..., you were my friends.

'Look, V, the following days are very critical. Lori is going to do "whatever is required" at once. She might want to keep you busy and out of her way; therefore, you have to keep your eyes open. You shouldn't readily believe in what Lori said. You have to listen to me a bit.'

'Gary, is it really you? Are you saying all this to me? Where are all these things coming from? I think Amy is creating conspiracy theories and you are being influenced by her. You know Lori isn't a bad person. I accept that she's an ambitious woman, but she is not so single-minded or so worshipful of money that she would hurt her own family. Please, don't think such nonsense things or behave so unfairly towards her. I accept that there's a problem and that we must all negotiate in order to solve it, but please don't blame Lori for awful things that she hasn't done, or even thought about. Everybody else might blame her, but please, not you, at least.'

'V, Lori isn't alone. You're aware of this, right? James is her husband. And if someone has a husband like James, we can assume she has enough boldness to do anything.'

I couldn't help laughing at last. With my chair leaning back, I looked outside. It was a muggy and rainy day. The weather was helping me become more and more depressed.

In my opinion, Gary was the person among us who was most intimate with James and who got along with him the best. Someone outside the family could even suppose that James and Gary were close friends. Even my father, blamed for not showing enough attention to James, would have said that Gary was friends enough with James for all of us. Gary would often go to Nico where he and James would eat and drink and enjoy their time together. I always wondered what they talked about, or could talk about.

But things weren't as they seemed. It turned out that Gary also thought that James was a trashy man.

'Why do you behave as if you are close to him then, if you don't like him?' I asked.

'It's not an emotional type of intimacy that we share,' he said. 'It's a physical intimacy — his restaurant is nearby, so I sometimes drop by there to drink some spirits. Does that mean that we're close friends? Not necessarily. I think James presents our relationship to you in an exaggerated way. Like you, I have never been very sympathetic to him either, but I've never found it necessary to correct what he says because I don't care about him or what he says, or what you think about my relationship with him. It's that simple for me.'

How can it be so simple if you don't appear as you are or behave as you feel? Why do you have to meet up with someone you don't like or perhaps even hate? How can that be an unimportant detail for someone? How can it be "that" simple...?

It was just one of Gary's many silly choices of behaviour. I didn't want to wander off-topic or contemplate it anymore. Instead, I told Gary what Lori had said: that she was trying to behave cautiously because she didn't trust Amy: she thought Amy could manipulate and control Gary (and hence his emotions), and that she might sell her shares to a rival, which was what scared Lori the most.

My father hadn't written about issues related to our inheritance before he died so suddenly, but he and Lori had often talked about it, and so Lori just wanted to take care of the details and address the concerns my father had expressed before he died. Amy was Gary's wife and therefore already owned a part of the company, indirectly. Lori didn't think she needed to have any extra shares. Andrew and Nancy were gonna get the exact amount of cash that the shares my father had planned to bestow to them were worth, and they were gonna get the house too; Lori thought that all of this would suffice for the old couple.

'Okay,' I continued, 'I don't accept all of her claims. If it was up to me, I would in fact agree with none of them. I think we have to comply with how my father wanted it to be. On the other hand, it was Lori who devoted her life to the company and who had a close relationship with my father every day. I think we must trust her. She may be right about her worries. It's not because I think Amy will definitely behave improperly, but Lori wants to take precautions. I see her point. At least the money will stay in our family, and this is good. Amy is your wife and therefore a member of the family and the company already. Also, Lori promised me that there would be no unfair changes to Andrew and Nancy's rights. Actually, we can settle this subject without any problems, which seemed impossible before. I do trust Lori, Gary; why don't you try the same?'

'Do I also have to trust her just because you do? That this all seems reasonable from Lori's point of view doesn't guarantee that it's correct, V. What you said about Lori's "arrangements" isn't correct. In fact, I do trust Lori, but it isn't right to change the draft of the will, or my father's notes, or, I dunno, whatever they're called.'

'Actually, Father had made some remarks in accordance with the points Lori is raising at the moment, but as they aren't in writing, there may be some problems, and Lori knows this. She's trying to solve the problems that might result. Lori isn't a bad person. She's our sister. She's putting in some effort for our good. If she can manage it without being unfair to the rights of others, what's wrong with that?'

After uttering these words, I stopped talking for a while. How had I become someone who was standing up for what she was doing and trying to defend her? When had I changed? Had I become encircled by her arguments without even realising it?

'Okay, I trust you,' Gary said. 'Please talk to her and ask her to inform us about what she is going to do. I don't want any problems or tension. I don't want to be the meat in the sandwich.'

I hid the thoughts coming to my mind after hearing him. At least Gary was relaxing a bit. I needed to find answers for the questions perplexing my mind and not confuse myself with the thoughts of others. After persuading and consoling Gary, I shouldn't have misled him again.

I felt well to have come to terms with Gary without much conflict. Taking strength from that, I decided to talk to Amy and prevent her from making a hash of everything. On one hand, I just wanted to talk openly with her. On the other hand, I was angry with her for complaining about me to Gary, which had resulted in his anxiety.

I left the atelier and called Amy.

'Oh, at last,' she said. 'I thought you'd never call me again.'

'Why are you so impatient, Amy? Calm down a bit, please. This aggressive attitude won't help us to solve our problems.'

'Don't worry, V. I figured out that I have to solve what you call "our problems" all by myself. I'm losing time while I wait for you. I could lose everything if I continue to wait any longer.'

'What does that mean?'

'I'm going to the company to talk to Lori face to face and take the share I deserve,' she said.

The meeting of Lori and Amy at the company would most probably make heavy weather of the things. There was a chance they would find some agreement together, but that was against all odds – and either way, I should not let them clash all by themselves; there might be a need for a referee. So, I headed towards the company.

When I reached there, Lori was alone.

'Hey, Lori, you got five minutes for me?'

'Hey, V, of course, c'mon in. Why are you here? What's happened?'

Without hesitating, I told her that Amy had been blinded by anger and was on her way there to talk.

'She says she'll take her share of the company. She's very determined, and this could lead to disturbance in the family. I told her to calm down because I was trying to settle everything, but she won't listen to me, Lori.'

'What makes her think she should get any share?' she said.

I paused for a moment. I didn't say that Eric had told her; instead, I said that Father had made her a promise.

'It's a lie,' she said. 'No such thing ever happened. Eric must have told her. And when she got the news, she started bluffing about Father. Bitch!'

'Please, don't hold a grudge, Lori.'

While we were talking, there were noises outside, and then Amy rushed into Lori's office.

'Yes, I was sure of this. As the picture shows, you've gathered the council. V, weren't you wandering around in pain just a short while ago? What brought you here?'

The secretary appeared in the door and gestured ashamedly to show she hadn't been able to keep Amy from barging in. Lori nodded to indicate she understood and waved her away.

Amy sat on the couch across from Lori.

'Look, I won't beat around the bush,' Amy said. 'I'm gonna be very direct. We aren't enemies, so I'll ask you not to display any bizarre behaviours, Lori, okay? I have put in a lot of effort for this company, which you know very well. I just want to receive a recompense for it, if there's any. Or, let me be clearer about this: if Mr Kushner thought I should have some. This is all fair. I just want what I deserve.'

'Then here's your answer, Amy: no, there isn't any recompense,' said Lori.

'Lori, I know there is. You can't push me aside like this.'

'Look, Amy, you've earned regular salaries for your efforts every month. There isn't any other payment for the team; you know this. That's all you get, like all your other colleagues.'

'Lori, I'm not an idiot, and you know it! That's why you jumped straight on the phones to arrange lawyers as soon as Mr Kushner died. You're trying to change his will for your own benefit, but I won't let you do it. You hear me? I'll stop you and you know it, Lori. You know it very well. You chose for it to be this way!'

'What are you talking about?' Lori asked.

'You know what I'm talking about.'

'Are you blaming me for changing the will? Are you sane, Amy? You are uttering ideas that you made up in your mind. You are inculpating me. If you continue to behave this way, I'll make you regret for it for the rest of your life, girl.'

'C'mon, Lori, don't play shit with me. Both of us know what you're after. But V doesn't know it. Be careful. I won't drop this issue. I came here to tell you that you can't just do whatever you want. Don't forget that you aren't the only one who knows the lawyers you've been colluding with. It'd be better for you if you weren't defeated by your own ambitions. Control yourself, Lori, at least for once.'

'Why didn't you show this side of your personality last week at all? You're using the cheapest words. It's apparent that your jealousy doesn't have an end. My father was so right to never fully trust you.'

'Don't make me laugh, Lori. At least, don't disturb his soul by mentioning the man whose funeral you didn't even attend. Anyway, that was all I want to say. See you, V. I wish I hadn't been wrong to trust you.'

She slammed the door as she left.

'I've never understood what he saw in that woman,' Lori said. 'Sometimes just her presence in this building makes me feel uneasy. I try to think that she isn't a bad person in essence, but she often behaves treacherously.'

'You know Gary. His mind functions differently. People's treachery and ambitions don't interest him. But actually, I don't think she's treacherous either. And she might have some features that he likes.'

Lori laughed. She took out a cigarette and lit it. Its smoke filled my lungs. I sometimes liked the smoke of another person, as I did then. She raised her head, looked at the ceiling and puffed out the smoke quickly. Then, she turned back to me.

'I'm not talking about Gary,' she said.

We looked at each other and kept silent.

I changed the subject in order not to leak the words passing through my mind. I asked what she had done that morning, whether there had been any changes in her plans, and whether she could begin to think more reasonably as time passed. And whether she was still determined. I believed that I could affect Lori positively with my velvet words.

'I've already done everything I needed to do,' she said. 'You don't need to worry anymore.'

'Wait, wait, what exactly did you do?'

'I mean, the tasks relating to changing the will. I'll change it as I like. Very soon.'

Lori had just carried out her plans as if I didn't exist, and she hadn't listened to anything I'd said, and all without me even realising it until now. I was in a situation where I couldn't control anything in my life. My father was dead, and Lori was going to change his will as she liked. Looking into Lori's eyes, I was little by little becoming sure that I was desperate and ineffective. What I said and thought was meaningless to the minds of others and not worth speaking aloud.

'Why are you looking at me like that?' she asked.

I turned my face aside and tried to look at the table between us. Everything was about to become even more complicated. While I had been trying naively to prevent our problems from getting any worse, Lori had simply carried out her plans, oblivious to my attempts. I felt as if I was losing my grip on everything.

'Goodbye,' I said and stood up.

She grabbed my arm and told me she was doing it for our own good. For me, for Gary and for herself. As we deserved. As my father had desired. She told me we didn't owe anything to anyone, and that no one could take the things that belonged to us. The strong bonds that kept us together could stand up to anything, and the only reason she was behaving this way was because of the blood-bond among us, which she appreciated and was attempting to protect. Likewise, Gary and I must behave similarly and show that we were putting in some effort for the family. We might have some difficult days in the near future, but we'd get through them together. My father would have wanted it to be so. Our bonds and relationship deserved it.

I wanted to believe in what she said. But I didn't want to look in her eyes.

'I don't know whether I can be strong enough to be on your side this time, Lori,' I said.

She let go of my arm. I left her office without slamming the door.

I got into my car and suddenly felt relaxed, and relieved. What I had been afraid of had already happened. I had been trying to prevent anyone being treated unfairly, and as a result I had been blamed and complained about and called naïve by the people I was fighting for. Despite my efforts in the opposite direction, Lori was simply doing whatever she wanted to do. As a result, all that remained for me to do was to watch whatever happened from now on. I didn't need to bustle around, persuading people to act in the right way. Moreover, it was only me who believed in my own truth. Everyone was going after their own truth. There was a common purpose – money – and hence it was inevitable there would be a conflict.

I didn't care about any of them. I decided to be free of all this nonsense. I called Eric and suggested we go get a bite together. We decided to meet at a place near his office in half an hour.

It was a quiet café located at a small park between some big buildings. I was there before him and sat at a table by the window, which had a view of the pool. I started to think about my father.

He had always worked hard for us and had tried for all of his life to make us virtuous people. He never missed any chance to give us a lesson: he always associated each of our actions with something we could learn, and then shared these lessons with us immediately. And when required, he scolded us. This wasn't true only for his own children but for almost everyone who was sitting at the table that night when he'd passed away. He had directed every younger soul to become a virtuous man or woman. If he could see us today, what would he think about us? Who would have disappointed him, and who was behaving as he would have expected?

I wished he could see our shit now. I wished he was still giving me orders and even getting furious with me for the things that, according to him, I did wrong. I wished that he'd correct them. I wanted to get over this blood-bonded pain together with him. I wished he'd come back.

Then I thought about myself. I couldn't reach a positive result by behaving reasonably in this very complicated situation I had suddenly found myself in. I was desperate and ineffective, like a simple observer just watching everything. Now the best solution I had found for getting over it was for my father to come back and help me out.

I laughed at myself, just because I was too weak to feel pity.

I took out my phone and added M's number to my contacts – again. I checked the numbers coming after one another, standing next to each other as obedient as they could be. I felt ashamed, being face to face with those numbers at that moment, never having cared for them before in those happier times. They had been the most important bridge between me and her, but I'd never thanked them before, even though I had written them countless times on this screen. It seemed as if I could turn back to those happy old times with her again, if only I could press the green button.

In fact, we lived more distant and more "other" lives with every passing moment. Maybe, at the same moment in our two distant lives, we would happen to smile at our past, thinking of each other at the same time. Then, she might move her hand towards her coffee mug, while I might reach out to my pen on the table. Maybe while she was enjoying a sip of coffee, she would remember the smell of coffee on my lips. I still heard her laughter even as I wrote her name down in my notebook. All these thoughts rained over me, after being accumulated in my unconscious. Two people who miss each other might dream of one another, consoling themselves with a dream-version of their lost companion. I had consoled myself in a similar way many times, and it had been enough. Or so it seemed at the time.

I'd called M before, in my happy, passionate, passionless, angry, humorous, willing and unwilling, desperate and excited moments – thousands of times. Whenever I heard her deep and obtuse voice, I felt as if I was returning to my home from a foreign, far-away place. Now I really wanted to re-experience that feeling.

I imagined touching the green button, watching the number enter into the calling phase, and hearing the calling sound. I also imagined what she might be doing while her phone rang – what response she would have upon seeing that it was me calling. Would she feel happy or excited? Would she champ at the bit, her heart beating quickly, because she missed me so much? Or would she become upset and wonder why I was calling? Would she see that it was me and then look far away with a smile on her face, remembering how many times she'd imagined this moment – as I had done? Would she be alone, or with her colleagues, or eating out with her new boyfriend? Would she want to answer and hear my voice? Would she answer at all? I couldn't stop thinking about the possibilities.

When I started to delete the numbers one by one, a hand touched my shoulder.

'I'm dying of hunger, bro.'

A feeling of relaxation took over again, as if I was going back home.

'Hey, pal,' I said. 'How have you been?'

'Sheeeit like crazy. Work, work, work. Those people are fucking my life, bro. I should really consider whether to start from scratch, on my own. Whatever, fuck that now – how are you?'

Whatever happened in his life, one side of Eric's mind was always busy with the issues, details, possible developments and opportunities regarding his job. I was sure that he felt the pain about my father's death at least as much as I did. However, he was also able to keep planning which new steps he should take regarding his business, whereas I still couldn't even enter into my bookshop. Maybe work was his way of relaxing himself.

I was still angry with Eric because he had gossiped about our talk to Amy. After he sat down, I told him I didn't like what he'd done, and we talked it over. He tried to defend his actions, and we shouted at each other, and then fell silent. It came to an end – a cease-fire. We settled it and didn't drag it out.

We finished our meals: our friendship had won again. Whatever happened between us, our problems were never unsolvable; we'd always find a way. Though other people had come between us this time, we'd gone around them and ended up finding each other again.

It was relaxing to meet and talk to Eric, which helped me to get over my nervousness. He was the person with whom I could most easily talk about the sorrows I'd lived through for the last two days, and he seemed to shoulder some of them and offer solutions for the rest. Even though all we did was talk, I felt relieved.

But it wasn't only me who spoke.

'You know,' he said, 'I was also upset when my mother's husband died. You were there with me, at his funeral. He'd always treated me as if he was my real father. He didn't discriminate against me. He provided the same affection and fortune to me as he did to his own kids. I hope he's in heaven now, you know that.

'But, Mr Kushner is different, man. I don't know why, but we had a special bond. I loved him very much, as if he was my own father. His big belly and his gel-sculpted white hair. The scolding we got from him. Remember how he used to rebuke us when we were kids? He made a man out of us; he really civilised us. If he hadn't shaped us with his hands, we wouldn't be what we are today. We'd have hurt more hearts and destroyed the lives of more people without even realising it or knowing what went wrong.

'I learned many things from Mr Kushner and took many life lessons from his words. Not small things, but big ideas. There wasn't only one core idea in his words, but they seemed to evolve into something bigger as time passed; they meant more. I'm sure we couldn't have learned so much if he hadn't been around. He was a limitless mind. Hard, very hard. I'm also crushed, V, believe me.'

He leaned towards me, held my neck and touched our foreheads to each other. I also put my hand on his neck. We both looked at the ground. A teardrop fell from the edge of my nose and wetted the ground. Then his teardrop followed mine. One from me, one from him. The teardrops rained down in front of our feet and I stopped counting and closed my eyes. I could hear that outside it had started to rain.

We went to the toilet one by one and then ordered coffee. Both of our chairs were directed towards the window. We watched the rain. The blobs dropping into the pool.

'Do you remember the time when we swam in the sea while it was raining every day?' he said. 'That summer, when I stayed at your house for nearly a month! A month, man.... Wow!'

'Of course I do! How can I forget? We escaped from my father. He told us it would be stormy and that we weren't allowed to go out, and so, like the children in your favourite stupid book, we went to the sea, because we thought it was so crazy to swim while it was raining.'

'That was extreme, man.'

'Not obeying Mr Kushner was way extreme....'

'Then Lori came to take us back home. Then what happened, do you remember? She swam with us. With her clothes on, as she didn't have her bikini of course. She said she'd tell Mr Kushner she got soaked in the rain. He would never have guessed she'd be our partner in crime. That remained our secret for all these years, right? Plus, I must admit something else, bro...'

'Go ahead,' I said without looking at his face.

'Her dress clung to her. You were walking in front of us. I approached her and couldn't help looking at her breasts. She realised and hit my head, but with a smile on her face. She might have liked it. I think that moment is when the first spark happened. Hey, sorry bro, no hard feelings, right? Does it annoy you when I talk about this?'

'A spark? What spark are you talking about?' I stared into his eyes.

He tried to answer, but didn't seem to know what to say.

'Please shut up!' I said. 'I don't want to hear any more about what happened or is happening or will happen between you and Lori. Please, understand me. It's weird, man! I don't understand how the relationship between three of us gained this dimension.'

'It hasn't acquired any dimension. Cut the crap. You know what has happened.'

'Whatever, never mind,' I said.

I wanted to close the subject. I wondered whether Lori would be behaving in the same way towards Amy now if Amy and Eric had never been lovers. Would Amy just be an ordinary person for Lori? Maybe an ordinary person who had gained Lori's appreciation through her hard work in the company?

I told Eric what had happened that morning and the previous night, and how Amy had complained about me, and how it was all very meaningless and didn't help to do anything except complicate the whole situation. Eric told me that Amy was not an ill-minded person, but that she just wanted what she'd earned.

'I know it,' I said. 'She's told me that thousands of times: she deserves it, and she's gonna get it. But I don't understand how the situation has evolved into a battle between her and Lori. Why can't we discuss everything like reasonable people and find a way? Only James, who is not considered a member of the family by anyone except himself, remembers and mentions that we are a family. Unlike him, it seems as if everyone else has become enemies to each other in just two days.'

'Tell me, what will Lori do?' he asked.

'Are you asking on behalf of Amy?'

'Fuck you, V.'

I told him what Lori was planning to do – that she was trying to change the will.

'But I don't know the details of how she's gonna do it. She just said that no share would remain to anyone outside the family. The house would be Andrew and Nancy's. My father told Lori that he wanted to leave his library to me, and she said she'd settle that for my sake, but I don't know how she's gonna arrange all this.'

'Changing the will...'

'Changing my father's "notes" in the will draft....'

'Lori sometimes behaves in an overbold manner. She surprises me. What's the point of all of this? Why does she have so much trust in lawyers? What will happen if one of them reveals her secrets or threatens to share this information with some other people? What she's planning to do—'

'Or has already done!'

'Whatever,' he said. 'She should feel a heavy guilt about this. It's a meaningless effort, and it's a crime man.'

Crime! It was a word that scared me when used together with Lori, a person who, for all her life, had fought for discipline and compliance with the rules. It was hard to understand why she had gone off the rails and why she was acting so strangely, in a way she wouldn't do in normal conditions.

I asked Eric whether he knew about the lawyers at the company – the ones working with Lori.

'What if I did?' he said with a bitter smile accompanying his distance.

'I don't know. I just asked out of curiosity. If there are some reliable ones among them, maybe we can ask what Lori is doing.'

He became serious. 'Do you believe that any of them would admit she was committing a crime under their supervision? What's more, that makes us accomplices, because we know the shit that's happening and haven't informed the authorities. They could dismiss me from the bar for this.'

I thought he was exaggerating a bit, but I didn't argue with him. It would be best to just leave it to time. I was sure that Lori would have taken all the necessary precautions to avoid putting herself into trouble. Thinking of the issues and trying to solve them while Lori was acting so independently was like pouring water into a sieve. It was distressing me and wearing me down, and it was all in vain. The final version of the will would be shown, the displeased and pleased ones would emerge, and then, together, we'd see what would happen.

The rain stopped, and the sun showed itself among the clouds. It would be better if we left soon, before it started to rain again. I decided I would go to my bookstore and tidy up the mess waiting for me. I'd have more peace for the remainder of the day if I stayed among the books.

'You met Danielle this morning,' Eric said.

'Yes, she came to visit and we ate something together.'

'She thinks you're very down. And she feels sorry for you, too. Even she very much liked Mr Kushner, in her own limited way. She believes we will both miss him very much.'

'Yeah, she's right. I will. We will. And yes, she often asks me how I'm feeling. So nice of her. I'm grateful.'

'You're right; sometimes she asks too many questions.'

'Come on, I didn't mean like that. But if she does ask a lot of questions, you'd better get used to it, bro. You'll be her husband soon. I'm gonna be the best man, right? I know it's bullshit to ask, but I just want to make sure....'

Then, the thoughts I'd had that morning passed through my mind for a moment. I looked down.

'That depends,' he said.

'Fuck you! Depends on what, asshole?'

'It depends on whether we marry or not.'

'What do you mean? Danielle is already behaving as if you two are married...'

'She's quite ready for it. She bought it up suddenly like that during the meal because she wants to pressure me. But there's nothing certain now. I don't wanna return back to that night, but I didn't like her attitude at all.'

At that moment, I completely understood why Eric seemed nervous and sometimes became lost in his thoughts. I knew that Eric loved Danielle, but Eric loved himself more (than anything), and he didn't like being forced to accept things he didn't desire at once. Everyone may be like that, but something was a bit different for Eric: he responded to this pressure by keeping himself completely away from the person who caused it.

'Don't dive into deep waters to make your voice heard,' I said.

'Don't try to solve your problems or the matters that disturb you on your own. And don't decide on behalf of Danielle. Talk to her and try to find a solution together with her. You're not a teenager anymore, dude. Please, behave accordingly.'

'Am I hearing this right? You are saying these things to me?'

The "match" had been going well for me until that time. Though my rival seemed bulky and strong physically, I had started well enough and had thrown him for a loop with my attack. I muddled him with a couple of fists. But then I was taken unawares and, at that moment, he put a fist into my rib cage. The referee was determined to count it.

Eric was right in some ways. How had I behaved in my own recent love chaos? What did I do after that? Had I done the things expected of me, or behaved in the way I should have behaved? The questions and their answers were quite complicated and disturbing. If you asked Eric, he would say that I'd behaved in a pathetic and childish way (as he expected). If you asked me, I would admit to having behaved "as required," as a result of both sorrow and anger. At the time, I didn't and couldn't have argued about what was right or wrong.

However, when I thought of it now, it was obvious that I'd behaved improperly. I couldn't even call her, though I had felt pain deeply within and needed to hear her voice. The only thing I could do was to write her numbers on my phone screen and then, shortly after, erase them one by one.

'Forget about me. I made my mistakes, and I'm still struggling with them. They still suffocate me. But this is about you. Danielle is very hopeful about your future – both of your futures. She's happy, excited and eager. Don't break her heart. Don't leave her waiting forever.'

'Indeed, and she shouldn't break my heart either. It seems easy from your perspective. Okay, enough dealing with shit. C'mon, let's go; it's late.'

We walked to the parking lot together. Before we parted ways, I told him not to do anything silly. He swore at me with a smile on his face and then left. In that mood of his, he didn't seem trustworthy to me at all.

I got into my car and started to drive. I thought of Eric and our friendship. We'd formed a very strong relationship over the years, as happens between all intimate friends and fellows. Brick by brick, built by delicate moves. We didn't fear being defenceless before each other. We mirrored each other, and stayed face to face with all our nakedness. We tried to find solutions to our problems. I thought it was very rewarding to have a friendship like ours.

Words that I wouldn't normally pay attention to if they were uttered by any other person at a different time were shouted into my ear – as if by my inner voice – and I agreed with them: my father was dead and I was getting older.

Time was ticking away. It was flying, even if I couldn't see its wings. While I was trying to force the biggest happiness into its smallest instants, time was quickly melting away. Even while I contemplated it, and nearly became mad at it, it was still flowing out of my hand. Thankless time.

However, my inner-voice echoed in my ear for a moment, saying, "You must resist it." Life could move on; events and other things would happen. After the way Lori had just ignored me, I believed that I had to get out of the state of mind I'd entered in such a desperate way. This isn't to say I felt incapable of doing anything, or that I would just leave everything to the hands of time and see what happened. Lori would do whatever she'd planned. I couldn't change that. But I could prevent the potential outcomes of her detailed and nicely executed plans, like the disappointment, hatred and conflict.

I began to drive towards Gary and Amy's house.

Amy was the kind of person who, because of her merits, was liked by the others. I also liked her. She was a reasonable and hardworking woman. In addition, she had an extraordinarily attractive personality. She was very sociable, made friends quickly, and could easily make anyone she interacted with like her. With these traits, she could be considered a very dangerous woman – against her female opponents. However, I should also note that I'd never seen her using these womanly powers intentionally for any specific purpose. Or at least, I'd never realised she was using them. In my opinion, her degree in psychology had a positive effect on her management of human relations.

She'd dated Eric for three years, and, as far as I knew, she was the only woman who had ever left him. She'd felt uneasy about his over-dominant character and had broken away from him, almost as if to protect herself from a lethal disease. However, as I observed from outside, the importance and value they placed on each other had never diminished. She maintained quite an intimate friendship with Eric even after they'd broken up (though it was not as intimate as my friendship with Eric). Amy probably shared her problems, moments of happiness and the things that confused her mind much more with Eric than she did with Gary. A tiny detail: Eric didn't attend Amy and Gary's wedding party.

The relationship between my father and Amy had always been distant and based on respect – the faultless respect of Amy for my father. Amy had always been satisfied with what was provided to her in this relationship. Sitting at my father's table first as the lover of Eric and then as the wife of Gary had, she once admitted to me, made her feel ashamed from time to time. But on my father's side there wasn't any problem at all. On the contrary, being lovers with Eric had given her an advantage in my father's eyes. If Eric had chosen her, then she must have good qualities.

Amy thought of Lori as a successful and respected business woman. During our talks, she'd say, 'I learned a lot from her.' But then she'd add, 'Lori thinks I'm responsible for what she's experienced with Eric, and she takes revenge on me whenever she finds the opportunity.' I'd never been able to understand the details of the relationship between these two women.

Gary had never been a successful or productive artist, but what he had was enough for Amy to admire him. She appreciated his art, maybe more than anyone else in the whole world. I'd never thought she married him for his money or according to any hidden agenda such as to "continue to sit at Mr Kushner's table." But I'd never believed that she fell in love with Gary, either. In my opinion, their marriage was based on pure reason, for both of them.

Gary was Amy's husband, but Eric was the man she'd fallen in love with. Maybe the one she'd never forget.

Though she still, in my opinion, carried her love for Eric in her heart, she had never behaved improperly to Danielle. She had reacted to Eric's other affairs with the attitude of a woman who ignored her husband's flirtatiousness and was sure of him returning home – always with a smile, with a "what have you done again, brat?" attitude. But she knew that Danielle wasn't like the others.

Amy liked me. She was always frank to me and criticised me harshly when she thought it was necessary. Sometimes, when disagreed over something, we even quarrelled. However, we always recognised the point when the next step would hurt the other person, and we knew to end it there. Sometimes I wondered, however, whether the reason she got on so well with me was because her female intuition told her I was the person closest to Eric.

James was the only person I knew whom Amy didn't like at all, and she implied her dislike for him whenever possible. I didn't know whether it was a prerequisite not to like James if one wished to sit at my father's table. My father considered James a complete deceiver and therefore did not trust any words James uttered. He also thought it was obvious from James' eyes that he had the potential to do any kind of wrong to anybody, at any time. I never believed that my father could've been mistaken about this.

When I arrived at their house, Amy was surprised – in a way that made me understand she didn't like surprises. I hadn't informed her that I was on my way there – and I'd failed to do so on purpose; I didn't want her to prepare psychologically for my visit.

'Oh, V! What a surprise!' she said.

'I'm trying to find sudden solutions for my problems. This is my new method. How do you like it?'

'Well, at least you've decided to act at last, and it's good to find a solution, but the place you're searching is wrong. You should've gone to Lori. Don't you think?'

She invited me inside. How had everyone's desire to have everything they wanted – even if it meant ignoring everyone else – suddenly emerged at once. Why had I not recognised it was happening?

I kept assuming I'd discovered the source, but I was always mistaken. According to my plan and expectations, Amy should have opened the door, immediately punched me in the face, and then slammed the door again. But instead she had warmly welcomed me inside, as if nothing had happened. Because of this surprise start, it was hard to quarrel and settle everything afterwards. It was hard to refresh the mutual affection and understanding.

Without wasting any time, I told her I was visiting because I wanted to talk about what we had to do to solve this conflict before it got any worse.

'But, there's nothing we should do, or could do. I witnessed what Lori was planning to do by accident, which has unsettled her, but she's already told me she'll go on with her plans regardless of me – I wish I could say 'us' here... whatever. Now who's the one preventing us from reaching a solution? I've worked for your family – for that company – for ages, V. Mr Kushner saw this and said he'd reward me sometime in the future. After all this, should I now allow Lori or her lawyers to take what I deserve out of my hand? In the name of "providing a solution?" Get the fuck outta here, mister... I'm just trying to get what I deserve, that's all. I'm not usurping anyone else's rights or anything.'

'I have a question.'

'And, what is it?'

'Okay, I understand what you mean. Really. And I don't think you're wrong. I've already said that to Lori. But is it worth creating so much bloody drama? I mean, Gary will own one third of the company anyway, right? And you're married to him...'

'Are you crazy, V? You can't be serious. Oh, my...'

'Doesn't that mean you'll also own one third of the company?'

'V, shut the fuck up!'

'Look, don't get me wrong. I'll say it again: you are right for the things you've said and demanded. I've no problem with that. But what if Lori has been pulling our leg and has no intention of changing the will? We don't know whether if that's even a possibility right now....'

'V, wake up, for God's sake! Please! Of course we know that!'

'Anyway, whether she changes the will or not, what's the difference to you?'

'What?! Are you really asking this, V? If so, I find it very childish. It is silly. There's something wrong with this whole situation. My rights, and maybe the others' rights, are being exploited, and you say "so what?" Am I getting that right? I can't believe it. This makes me crazy! Look, V, if you're trying to do something, then do it! Cut the crap and get down to business.'

'Come on, Amy, I just want that nothing becomes any worse, and to find a middle ground for everybody. Weren't we all in a very "intimate relationship" only three days ago? And yet now we have all fallen out with each other. It's very stupid. I don't want to find out I was mistaken to put so much trust in my family. The moments we shared together – and by "we" I mean all of us together – were real. I want to believe this. That's my only concern.'

'If you are obsessed with this "reality" issue, pull yourself together and "really" do something! Don't just organise meetings with Lori and Gary without taking any real steps. Was any outcome gained at the end of these meetings, V? Any positive ones? I can answer that: *no*!'

Amy launched into another monologue about how naïve I was. While she was talking, I began thinking. Was I just knocking my head against a brick wall? Would my actions have a meaning and outcome at the end? Yes, I'd had meetings with Amy and Gary, but she was right: the things I'd said had no positive effect on the situation. Lori was simply behaving exactly as she wished, and as she had planned. I was an ineffective element. Was I the kind of person who could be so easily deceived, or rather fooled? Wasn't it clear, in light of recent events, that I was easily fooled?

'How about I call Lori right now,' I said, 'while I'm here with you, and tell her what I want her to do from now on? Would that be enough? Then would you believe in me?'

'I already believe in you, V. You don't need to show me anything. But I think your attitude won't provide a solution in the end. Really, I can see that now. First, you can't do that to Lori. She'll put you in your place in no time. Be realistic. You believe I'm being treated unfairly, right? And now you're gonna talk to the person who's doing it. What difference is that gonna make? None. You and I are just observers for the time being.

'But whatever happens or however events progress, I won't accept defeat. Either tell me "You're demanding something you don't deserve," so I'll know that I should struggle on by myself; or go and do something to solve this. Or forget everything – don't get involved and go to your bookshop and tidy up your books. You see, with this mind-set of yours, nothing's gonna change.'

We had come full circle. Amy was very talented at pressing someone's buttons while arguing. When it came to me, she got very productive results, because she could combine her talent with desire. For a moment, I leaned back and thought of this meaningless struggle I was involved in. What was it for? For company shares. Which I didn't even care about.

I was too bored to speak with her like I was a member of a negotiation team. In fact, an idea that would solve everything had come to my mind at that moment. It was obvious that Lori would reject it at the beginning, but I believed I had a chance at persuading her. Maybe it would be the most important step I'd ever take to make something right.

'Okay, I'll find a way to solve it,' I said, and left.

First I went home to have a power-nap and get rid of my heavy headache. I wanted to sleep on the idea first, and plan ahead to be sure I could execute it well: a decision-making process I'd inherited from my father. Was this habit exchangeable into company shares?

When I woke up, it was approaching nine, and my mind and stomach were empty. I ate a snack and, while drinking my coffee, reconsidered my idea. Was I satisfied with my solution? Certainly, yes!

I got into my car and went back to the house where I'd stayed the previous night. James was watching an action movie, and Lori was sitting alone in the garden.

I went out to the garden and told Lori that I had an idea that might solve all our problems.

'What's your idea?' she asked. 'Will you try to persuade Amy to give up on everything and move to the other side of the world? Don't forget, she'll certainly demand the ticket price. And I won't give a dime!'

'That's also a good idea,' I said. 'But mine is different. What's on my mind is that I'll transfer my shares to you. From what I have inferred from your previous words, the three of us should get equal shares. So I'll give up mine. That's all.

'You and Gary can take my shares, but on the condition that you give Amy's part to her, as Father planned. I don't want anything. Arrange the distribution in such a way that you take fifty percent, while Amy and Gary take the remainder. Or you take fifty-one percent and leave forty-nine percent to them. Even if they sell their shares to someone outside the family, the majority will always belong to you. Yeah, this is it. How does that sound to you?'

Lori was looking into my eyes without blinking. She seemed to have frozen as hard as stone. I could still manage to surprise her after all. She had lost that look that implied she always had the power to control everything. Surprise was dominant in her wide, bluest eyes. She remained motionless for six or seven seconds.

The silence was broken by James, who we hadn't known was eavesdropping. 'Are you crazy, V?' he asked.

I had assumed he was watching his rubbish action stuff in the living room. Lori seemed to loosen up slowly and began to move again. She detached her gaze from mine and turned her face towards the river. With slow movements, she drew on a cigarette and then exhaled it to the river.

'No, I'm all okay, James,' I said.

'No, no.... Hey look, V, have you completely lost your mind? Bro? Hey, are you high or what? Tell me....'

Lori suddenly turned her head towards me and gave me a penetrating look. 'For whom are you making this sacrifice?' she asked. 'For me and Gary? Or for Amy?'

'For all of us. All of us. This is an unnecessary battle. What I own will be enough for me for the rest of my life. I feel a big pain in me, but I can't suffer it properly because of all this bullshit. I want no more people to get hurt or cross. I wanna believe that the people together around that table before Father died have real love and respect for each other. I wanna believe that our laughter and words were real. I don't want any fights, debates or struggles. If someone has to give up their rights, it could be me, and that's okay by me.'

Lori was silent and staring at me, as if trying to make some sense out of my decision.

James broke the silence again. He was reacting as if I was scattering his money around. 'You must be mad,' he said.

Lori answered him. 'James, could you please leave us alone for a while?'

James didn't understand what was happening. He didn't want to understand it, either. From his posture, it was obvious that the problems he had with Lori were making him uneasy. He was like a bomb that was about to explode. I hoped he wouldn't explode over me – shit would be all around.

After James returned to the living room, a cool, light wind breezed through the garden. If we'd been at an outdoors cocktail party, the women would've got cold just now, and the boys would've whispered, "It's starting to get cooler; wanna go inside?" into their lovely ears, while enjoying the accompanying evening perfumes.

Lori, holding her hair behind her neck as it ruffled with the wind, turned to me. 'What's happening? Why do you feel this way?'

At that moment, I wanted to be sure of the fact that Lori and I lived the same life and breathed the same air. My mind couldn't understand how she could ask that question. I was looking at her with empty eyes in order to understand what she was really trying to ask me. My words came out easily.

'Why am I feeling this? You mean uneasy?'

'Yeah, uneasy, at least....'

'Okay. Two days ago, my father died. Then my family started to fight for the inheritance. I think that if I don't stop this fight now, everything will become more complicated, or rather, unsolvable. Lori, aren't these reasons enough for a normal person to feel uneasy?'

Without speaking, Lori turned her face towards the river. The breeze picked up again. Her hair was streaming backwards. Normally, she would feel cold in this weather. The fire in her heart might be protecting her.

I couldn't tell exactly what she was thinking, but she didn't seem to like the solution I'd found.

Her silence led me to question my own solution. I contemplated it: what I was giving up, for whom I was doing it, and what I might feel at the end. I became sure of it again. It was the most correct decision I'd made since I'd become obsessed with finding a solution.

'You're wrong,' Lori said. She was still looking at the river and did not turn her face to me. She shook her head slowly from side to side, almost indistinctly.

'You'll just give them the impression that they can take whatever they want whenever they create uneasiness. You are justifying their actions,' she said.

So she was not thinking of me but of her battle with Amy. Could Lori ever lose a battle to anyone? Of course not.

'Lori, we're not children. What are you talking about? To whom are we giving lessons? Because of your obstinacy, many people will get hurt and probably fall out with each other. Please, I'm begging you, try to understand what this means. You don't need to execute your plans. Since neither you nor Amy will take a step backward, I will do it. Why are you resisting this? In fact, how can you turn up your nose at it? Anyway, I've made my decision to do this, and it's my turn now. Mind your own business.'

Lori began to speak without pause, and quickened her pace as the minutes passed. The words tumbled out after each other as if she had quit thinking and was just saying whatever came to her mind. She told me I was not able to make head or tail of business life, or of human relations, and that while she was trying to make my life and her stupid brother's life more meaningful, we were very successful at losing what we owned. I couldn't know what it meant to live without money, she said, or understand how money could just vanish into the air, because Father had never allowed me to experience something like that. I had busied my mind with stupid ideas that I would regret later, and I not only wasted her time but made her angry with my nonsense. She would not get upset or involve herself with our problems ever again. It was the last time she would try to back up me and Gary. She wouldn't care about us – or anyone else – from then on.

I started to feel Lori's words were going to hurt me more and go too far, and leave big scars that would be hard to heal in our relationship. But I let her keep speaking.

From this moment on, she told me, I had to spend my life like a mature man, to know the value of what I owned, and realise that I couldn't start a new leaf every day. Life was not like a novel and I was not the protagonist in it. Time and conditions wouldn't always support me. If I removed all that was beautiful and promising, I couldn't just replace it all with new stuff. This behaviour, she said, was just unconsciousness and childish waywardness. It was ingratitude to life, and those who showed ingratitude to life had to face the consequences. Mr Kushner was no longer there to back me up all the time, and she would no longer support me, either. I needed to grow up, be mature and stop behaving like an adolescent. Instead of focusing on my store as I should have been over the last few days, I'd been wasting all my time running after Gary and Amy, and all in vain. My irresponsibility had no end. Isn't that why M had left me? Isn't that the reason I was still wandering around in such a silly and aimless manner? Wasn't I in a desperate situation because of the way I always lost things?

'Oh, please, Lori, enough!' I shouted, because she had already exceeded the limit of giving me a hard time.

She stood up. 'Don't you yell at me, boy! You never stopped behaving like a child because every other time you've done something stupid, I've never slammed your silliness in your face. You haven't learned your lesson, and so every day you do new silly things!'

I also stood up. I was having difficulty controlling myself. All the tension that had accumulated in me in the last few days seemed like it might explode at any moment.

'Why are you so happy, then?' I asked. 'Is it because of the "perfect life" you have, or because you can afford it for yourself? What have you done in your life, except for trying to be strong? Except for forgetting your humanity? Is that really living a good life? Lori, one day the things you consider indestructible will disappear. It'll all be gone. Then you may find yourself in an irreversible situation, because you seem to have forgotten your humanity.'

James was watching us from the door that opened into the garden. I started to breathe harder. I turned to go, but Lori grabbed my arm. She gripped me so hard that her fingernails penetrated the skin of my wrist, but I didn't feel any pain.

Her nails went deeper into my skin, and I didn't resist. She looked in my eyes, frowning, her lips tight. 'I will never forget this misbehaviour, V, never! One day, you'll throw yourself at my feet, begging me to forget this night. But I won't! Never. Never!'

'As you've never forgotten Eric,' I said.

I watched her other hand coming closer to my face, as if in slow-motion, and then I felt the slap.

With the deep burning sensation on my cheek, I re-awakened to the real time-flow again. She was still looking through me after her solid hit on my face. We gazed into each other's eyes, our breaths running fast.

James came up to us and hugged Lori. 'Come on, calm down a bit,' he said.

Lori escaped from his arms with a quick and sudden movement. She looked at me with concrete hatred, and then rushed into the house.

I watched her go, and remained watching until she passed the living room, went upstairs and disappeared. Her footsteps over the stairs were very harsh, as if she were driving a nail with every step. I knew her anger wouldn't simmer down for hours, maybe days.

My heavy breathing began to slow down. I don't know how long it took. I was still standing where I had been slapped, and James was also still just standing there, looking at me. We were eye to eye, but we didn't talk. He seemed calmer than me, but it was obvious that he also had a lot on his mind, and his explosive nature was still close to the surface. In fact, it had been ever since the beginning of the night, but Lori had stolen his role from him.

When I sat down on my chair, James sat down on Lori's.

'Stupid!' I said.

James kept silent.

'Crazy bitch!' I said.

'Hey! Watch it!'

I stood up and left as quickly as I could. James stood up too, but he didn't follow me.

As I ran towards my car, the moment Lori had slapped me ran through my mind over and over again. I didn't care to get in my car, so I passed it and walked on. I felt the slap on my face with its all intensity and bitterness. My cheek burned. I moved my hand towards my face and started to cry. Like a stupid and guilty boy. I felt guilty, like I had poked my nose into unnecessary things. The others were in some kind of conflict, and I had been trying to find a solution for them, but both Lori and Amy were just going to follow their noses and do whatever they wanted. I was only putting myself through the wringer and setting myself at odds with the others.

But I couldn't do it – I couldn't keep silent, or ignore it whenever something went wrong and disturbed me. Their money and power-play had become my concern for no reason. In fact, I was happy with my books and with what my books continuously taught me – their guidance, their light within and shining through. And I was happy with the things remaining to me from my life, from M, from my father. The family did not want me in this "holy" clash over money; if they wanted to dive into that shit on their own, why was I there bothering myself about it? For absolutely nothing. I was happy with what I had in my hand: a bunch of joyful moments and a lot to remember and even to regret.

While I cried with my hand over my face in the middle of the street, I thought of being together with M. Once more. I imagined a scene: I was looking out through the window of a train. I put M into my dream, as if we were two fugitives of a bitter life. She was happy just to be sitting next to me, while gardens in shades of green passed in front of us, as if competing, racing to give me some hope. I caught sight of a flag waving wildly among the green. It was black and flapping as if it were resisting the strongest wind in the world. I wished I could be sure, without so much thinking, that it was the flag of a pirate ship, because a pirate flag was its own master. I wanted to feel the pleasure in the moment and in its waving, though there was a conflict in having a pirate's soul and also being attached to a pole. If the wind blew harshly enough, the flag could detach from its pole, but could the wind also bring freedom?

I wished the girl sitting across from us would play some music from her mp3 player, a little flamenco, maybe some tango.... The rhythm would stir me, and a small movement from my toes would act like a spark and spread up my legs and to my heart.

I began dreaming about *being* that pirate flag, the harsh, destructive winds of life shaking me and the air from all sides mercilessly flowing through the knots and loops of my body. It made me feel cold. At that very instant, dream-M looked at me, as if I wasn't in the hardest fight of my life, and ask me whether I wanted some water. I said, "No," and she smiled at me with her beautiful lips and nice whispering eyes. She turned her face left to look outside through the window, to watch me and my struggle with life. At that moment, I didn't want to die at all. I thought, *heaven must be like this*, and I wished for it to last forever.

When I arrived back at my car, my hand was still over my face, but I wasn't crying anymore. I had been wandering the streets aimlessly, though my car was standing there outside Lori's house.

I stopped and looked at her front door, and at the path leading up to it. I hated all of them. I wasn't sure I'd ever go there again in my whole life.

I got into my car.

I hadn't chased after M following our second and biggest separation. It had been obvious that our relationship couldn't continue any longer because we'd been worn out, and we'd hurt each other without meaning to. I had grown used to her... and getting used to her was very bad. I'd grown used to her voice, words, mannerisms and behaviours. To her foolishness, silence and her looks.

If my father wasn't dead and Lori hadn't hit me, I wouldn't be feeling her absence so strongly. Time would pass more quickly. I'd focus on my work and life and forget her more easily. But at that moment... that night, at that very instant, I really wanted her to be near me. Pulling me towards her chest and saying, "Come here" and "We'll deal with it together" and stroking my hair and calming me down. If she were with me, I wouldn't have lived such a night as I just had. She would have made my mind work better and would have prevented these events from taking place from the very beginning. She always made me feel better.

I took my phone out, slid my thumb over its screen to unlock it, and began to type in her cell phone number. One by one. When it was finished, I stopped and looked at the whole number. It was as if she were in front of me. I knew that, if I dialled these numbers, I would hear her voice. It would be like I was in the past.

Just looking at the call button excited me. I wouldn't have felt excited if these numbers had been any combination other than this. At that moment, I felt as if her life was flowing like a quick river, and I was just watching it pass by in front of me, standing at its side. I could jump into it suddenly and swim in it – in her life. I could become a part of her life; I could be covered with her, surrounded by her, touched by her.

I reached her house and parked my car at the curb outside. Her bedside light was on – that tiny yellow lamp. Was she reading something? Or was she smoothing her eyebrows? Maybe she had already fallen asleep. I watched her window without blinking.

For a second, the light of the living room turned on, but then it went off again. Maybe she had forgotten her reading glasses and had gone to the living room to find them. She could be reading a book. What was she reading? Had she finished the last two books I'd given her as a present? If she was holding one of them, a book I'd touched before, did that mean we were touching each other at that moment, too?

The screen of my cell phone had gone into stand-by at some point as I watched M's home, but now it lit up again with a new message. It was from James, but unfortunately it did not answer any of my questions: "Amy the bitch is responsible for all this. But she'll pay for it. She'll see what it means to upset us and play the family."

Though I had no desire at all, I smiled at this message. I was sure that whomever we asked at that moment, they'd consider Amy more a part of the family than James. But James had undertaken the responsibility to defend the family. I was sure he had no idea what he was defending or against whom, but he just had to be anywhere there was tension, uneasiness or disturbance – either as its source or its support unit.

It was stupid of me not to answer his message. I continued to watch M's hidden soul through her bedroom window. Then, I looked at the street where she walked on her way out or as she came home. And at the door she opened every day with her keys, and at the stone column where she braced her legs to tie her shoelaces one at a time before starting to run. All of them were still there. The marks she left on them – which only I could see – were still there.

Suddenly, the light in the bedroom was turned off. Would she go to sleep? After we broke up, I believed that she no longer thought of me during her sleep. I believed that she left herself V-less in her sleep in order not to wake up with disappointment. Maybe I was wrong. I couldn't help wondering whether she saw me in her dreams – saw me approaching her with my arms opened.

But I didn't believe that at all. When she slept, we broke up again every night. That's the only reality.

I threw my cell phone onto the seat beside me, started the engine, and headed towards my home. While she was falling asleep, I advanced away, looking at the street where her shoes must leave so many marks. The marks of her legs that I liked very much.

Priday
17 SEPTEMBER

I OPENED MY eyes with peace. The day didn't start with the same process it usually did: adapting myself to the light, blinking my eyes, closing them again, and desiring to prolong my sleep.... None of that happened. I opened my eyes in an instant, suddenly, and looked at the white ceiling and at my green lamp, which I liked very much. It was a huge ball surrounded by black strings. It hung from the ceiling like a unique planet, and I was the small satellite that entered into its orbit every night, again and again.

I looked at my watch and saw that it was a little past eight. Despite the uneasiness in my head (and in my subconscious), I was surprised to wake up feeling like I'd had enough sleep. I had a clear and peaceful mind, as if I hadn't been dealing with so much trouble for the last few days. Even this was enough for me to feel happy. I smiled and rolled to the other side of the bed, burying my head under the pillow as a ray of light found its way through to my left eye – the sun was uncertain about lightening and heating the day. "Sun, please favour me today," I prayed.

Checking my phone, I saw the message James had sent. I desired to remain peaceful despite his nonsense.

After my shower, I began to prepare my breakfast. I cut the bread and took the cheese from the fridge without thinking anything and was busy toasting bread when the doorbell rang, ending the small fraction of peace I'd had.

There was an unexpected guest at the door. A person who was visiting my house for the very first time.

'Hope nothing's wrong?' I said.

'Your apartment is nice, V. I wish I'd visited you earlier. Anyway, I'll visit more often from now on....'

James stepped inside and then said, 'May I come in?'

I wished I'd said no.

I prepared some toast for him, too. With our coffee and toast, we went to the dining room. I wanted him to say whatever he had to say at once and get out of my life as soon as possible, but he talked about many other unnecessary things – everything except for explaining why he'd stopped by. When he asked what kind of books I could suggest for his daughter, I couldn't bear him anymore.

'What do you want, James? Why don't you get to the point?'

He smiled. 'You understand that I want to talk about something. How wise. Okay then, look, sour things happened last night. We both know it. I'm sure Lori's feeling very bad now. She left the house before I woke up this morning. I haven't called her, yet.'

'I don't care. What's next, James?'

'Anyway, what I want to say is that I'm going to talk to Amy and tell her she must behave, and stuff... you know. I'll tell her not to disturb the family. But there's a problem.'

'What are you talking about, James? Please, don't exacerbate anything. Let them solve it, Amy and Lori by themselves. You know that's why I didn't answer your message last night. Let's just keep ourselves out of this issue. Both of us, all of us. I've become bored with all this shit.'

'Yes, V, you've become bored with it. So has Lori. I think I need to take some action now. We must teach this woman her place, man. Otherwise she'll continue to behave in this silly way and disquiet the family more.'

Whenever James uttered the word "family," I got goose bumps. Each time I wanted to say, "No one considers you a member of the family, you silly crack!" but I didn't say anything and just listened to him. I shouldn't be the one to tell him.

According to James, "the wisdom-maker," Amy must be told what she'd done wrong, what she'd misperceived and what she should do from then on: namely, to behave and not disturb the family anymore.

'Okay, James, I'll ask you something. Isn't Amy as much a part of our family as you are?'

He smiled. 'Look, V, family is an abstract notion. Her being married to someone from the family doesn't make her a part of it. In order to become a member of the family, you need to have certain thought structures. She doesn't have them. She'll never be a member of the family in real sense... and good for her, she'll learn this today.'

He didn't realise how unreasonable his words were. While I was telling myself that one's mind couldn't have worked in such a wrong and unnecessary way, and that my sister couldn't be married to such a pinheaded man, James kept saying what was passing through his mind and explaining constantly what steps he'd take to save the family from this situation. After solving Amy's problem, he said, he'd reconcile me and Lori. Actually, Lori regretted what she'd done – slapping my face – but he considered our reconciliation his own responsibility and would do his best to ensure it was carried out.

I continued to drink my coffee and eat my toast, and after a while gave up even looking at him while he was speaking.

'Are you listening to me, V?'

I was not.

'Yes, I'm listening. But if I tell you what you're saying is very silly, will you get offended, James?'

'Silly? What the fuck does that mean? Why? What are you saying, V? I'm telling you I'll help you and Lori reconcile, and turn Amy from her current path, which is what has caused all these problems. What's silly about that? Until last night, you were also trying to solve this problem, weren't you? Didn't you come to my house last night for the same reason? I don't understand you. Why is it silly? Tell me....'

I had to keep saying the same thing over and over again... being forced to do it. 'The silly thing is that you ignore Amy, her desires and her earned rights, as she calls them. You and my sister both do. Lori's behaving in an unexpected and unreasonable way, and this is a big problem, but you trying to become involved only exacerbates the situation. If you'd said you came here to help me, I could understand it, but directly targeting Amy implies that you've accepted what Lori says as the "ultimate truth," and you are even going into combat for her. Can I make it explicit? Your actions are not directed at solving the problem.'

He stopped talking and looked at me with empty eyes. He bent his head and looked at his toast, one fourth of which was eaten. Then he turned his eyes towards me again.

'V, do I want any share from the inheritance?'

'What?'

'Do-I-want-any-share-from-the-inheritance? Have I demanded a share from Mr Kushner's company?'

'What's that got to do with our conversation?'

'Amy wants a share.'

'Holy shit! James, don't talk nonsense! Amy's been working at that company for years, and my father promised her shares in return for her efforts, even though it was not written down – or maybe it was. We don't know for sure yet. Hasn't Lori tried to change the will? That shows something was written down. So what else should we do? What's this got to do with your "demand" for some of the inheritance?'

'No, V, if Lori doesn't find the will correct, we have to accept her opinion. She's the one who worked with both your father and Amy under the same roof, and hence she is the one to make the best evaluation. And she's done it already; therefore, we should comply with it. And so should Amy.'

'Did she send you here? Tell me the truth, James.'

'Of course she didn't. I came here by myself.'

'Then, why? What did you come here for?'

'Actually, I came here for this reason: Even though Amy behaves like a very silly person, she's one of my closest friends – Gary's wife. [*One of your closest friends? How can a person live with such absence of any perception?*] I also don't want to upset or hurt Gary, but we have to solve the Amy issue. Can you support me in this by informing Gary that Lori and I are correct on this issue? You know we're both very close with him [*He must absolutely be crazy*] and often share good times with each other. I don't want any harm to come to him. If you help, Gary may agree with us and try to put pressure on Amy. Then we can solve the problem more easily. I don't want to give the impression that I'm taking action on my own. I want others from the family to support me.'

As the words from James' mouth reached me, I felt each one's weight in my ear. Listening to him was very tiring and difficult for me. I became bored with talking to such a stupid man about the future of my family. To tell the truth, it was about to drive me mad, listening to his monologue about the "Amy issue." I felt as if I was going to die due to shortage of oxygen. Every time he uttered another stupidity, I thought even less of him. I needed to end this unnecessary talk.

'James, please don't involve me in your plans. You shouldn't be involved in any of this anyway. Don't talk to Amy, Gary or anyone else. Let's just see what happens. Because if we do it your way, everything's only gonna get worse. Plus, I haven't been able to deal with the store for a long time and, well, if it's okay with you, I wanna leave now, at once. Let's close this subject.'

He wiped his mouth with a paper tissue.

'Okay, fair enough! Even though you won't support me, I'll solve this problem by talking to Amy. If it requires, I can talk to Gary and tell him what I wanna do. It's for everybody's sake.' He continued with a dozen more empty words as he went out of the door, only pausing to tell me he'd inform me if anything happened, and then he fucked off.

At last.

The peace and calmness of my quiet morning had disappeared completely. I looked out the window. The promising glaze of the sun had also worn away. There were clouds in the sky, and it looked like it might rain. I leaned my head on the window. The coolness of it erased the perplexity of my mind for a short instant. The cold killed the microorganisms that had imposed themselves on my mind with James' poisonous sentences. Trying not to think of him and what he'd said, I tidied up the table and left home.

When I got to work, it was around noon. I emptied six new boxes of books and placed the books on the shelves, some on the sales shelves in the hall and the rest on the big shelves that I used as storage in the back. Then I cleaned away the dust, checked the recent inventory, replied to some e-mails from the distribution firms, and filled out the next week's order forms. I felt real peace in my own place.

At about 2 p.m., I went to a nearby café to grab a tuna sandwich. Normally I didn't go there too often, but spending some time there that day pleased me. Visiting a new place meant my mind could concentrate on the posters on the walls, the goods and the people around me instead of on shares and allocation issues.

Nearly an hour later, I returned to the store. I dealt with some customers – I suggested books to them, wrote down the ones they ordered, and helped them to fill out customer evaluation forms.

I felt as if I'd returned to my normal life, until my cell phone started to vibrate. I had begun to feel anxious about every call I got; the phone had become a messenger of bad news. The rule didn't change for this call, either. The person calling me was Amy. She was crying. It was clear that life had decided it was enough for me to have had even that much peace.

'This man is mad. He's completely nuts! He's a pure... a pure son of a bitch! Please help me, V, please. I can't take this anymore...'

'Hey, calm down, what are you talking about? What did he say?' I didn't ask whom she was talking about, because it was obvious that "he" was James.

Her voice faltered, and then she convulsed into crying and couldn't say anything more. At first, I thought she was crying out of anger, but after a while I realised she was crying out of fear.

'Please, Amy, calm down and tell me what's happened. Hey! Where are you now?'

I couldn't understand her words clearly because she kept sobbing. With difficulty, I finally understood that she was in the car park of the company. When she said she was very afraid, I told her to wait for me there. I left the store at once and went to meet her.

Her car was not in the car park outside the building. I called her, and she told me she'd gone to another car park because she didn't want to be around the company anymore.

When I found her, her eyes were swollen and red. She was looking around with empty eyes, her hands covering her shoulders as if she felt cold.

I sat next to her.

'Are you okay, Amy?'

She hugged me and, with her arms around my neck, started to cry again.

'Everything will be okay,' I said. However, I didn't know whether it was true.

'V, that son of a bitch was waiting for me at the car park.... Then he came up to me. "Let's talk," he said. And then he started to talk like, "Give up this battle. You won't gain anything from now on." When I said I wouldn't, he told me he'd keep his eye on me and if I didn't listen to his "orders" I'd regret it! Fucking orders. V! ORDERS! Then, he said, like, "Go deal with your own business. Take care of your husband..."

Her crying became more intense. I tried to console her, but her tears and boogers were dripping onto my shoulder. She was very afraid.

I had become extensively involved in this struggle, whether it was necessary, true, or a long-term battle. And there was no point in keeping myself away from it, unless that would solve it completely. Even though I'd tried to push myself away from it, it constantly pulled me back inside, like a whirlpool. Actually, by that point, I no longer wanted to abstain from taking part. Lori's behaviours of the previous night, James' rude attitudes of that day (though I hadn't been aware of the details until this morning) had brought me to the end of my rope. If it was a war they wanted, I would fight. No one had the right to make someone's life miserable for no reason.

I remembered the last night we'd all been altogether – the night my father had passed away. We had still been a very happy, sincere and intimate family, all sitting around that table three days ago. I gave up believing in the honesty, beauty and sincerity of that moment; I left all my naïve beliefs behind. I felt enlightened about the realities about that moment and, in accordance with what I had experienced afterwards, I decided to take concrete action. While Amy cried deeply on my shoulder, I swore not to die until I solved this absurdity.

'He told me, "Take care of your husband,"' she continued. '"Why are you interested in shares of the business? Go behave like a normal woman and protect your husband.... If you don't care for Gary, he'll find someone to do it on your behalf." That fucking idiot. What was he talking about, V? What?'

I never ceased to be surprised at how far James' nonsense could go. I couldn't understand how he dared to say those words.

'Gary might have found someone,' she said.

After saying this last sentence, she began to sob as if she'd been exposed to all the bitter things in the world. I hugged her tighter but gave up saying calming and soothing words. I just tried to make her feel that I was there, even though I knew it wouldn't help much. After a while, I released her from my embrace and let her cry and discharge her pain. I waited.

Six or seven minutes later, she raised her face and looked at me. Her eyes were even more swollen and red than before, and her face was pitiful.

'V, I don't want the shares,' she said. 'I don't wanna fight for them. How merciless these people are.... Why do they consider me an enemy? Who the fuck is James to say those words to me? How has he become a part of my life?'

I couldn't find the words to answer her. There was no point trying to anyway. While I was aware of the inappropriateness and improperness of James' behaviour, one side of my mind was thinking about what he'd said to Amy. Gary and James often spent time together, especially over the last two years. If Gary was involved in an affair, James might have guessed it, or even know about it.

I didn't think James and Gary were confidants who shared their secrets with each other. Perhaps James would tell his secrets to Gary, because Gary was a member of the "family," but it was obvious that Gary wouldn't trust James with any secrets. Then again, James didn't need to be a confidant in order to know about an affair; he could have witnessed a phone conversation, seen Gary with someone, or overheard gossip. He could also have just guessed – or just made it up. I shouldn't forget to expect anything from James.

While trying to console Amy, I planned how to take action. What should I do first? Should I search for evidence of James' claims, or make James account for what he had said, or should I talk to Lori about the latest news and ask her to be more prudent, make her see the indirect results of her actions. Make her see how far things could go. Thinking about so many things at once meant I couldn't decide on any of them.

'Is it true, V? Do you know anything about it?'

Even if I knew, would I have said so at that time?

'To tell you the truth, I'm very angry and surprised right now. I hadn't heard anything about this. You know Gary best; he's your husband. If such a thing was going on, you'd probably sense it.... I don't think he'd do anything like this....'

'No, I haven't seen anything or been suspicious of him. But, V, what if it's true? What if what James implied was real?'

'I think James just wanted to confuse your mind, so he chose to hit below the belt. His only concern is to make you do what he wants, by whatever means. Please, stop crying and calm down. Everything will be okay, do you hear me? We'll take strong steps; nothing's gonna be the same from now on, don't worry.'

We sat on the bench for a while. Though Amy seemed a bit calmer, her energy went down to almost zero. The last few days had worn her out, as far as I could see it. She was hurting, not only from the things she'd heard but also from what she'd experienced in recent days, after everything had exploded. Maybe she was also tired from everything that had happened in the last few months or even years. Perhaps she had recognised at that very moment how many memories and scars she had accumulated in her heart. Someone had tripped her up, tilted the basket and made its contents visible to her. James had done a favour to Amy, although of course unawares and without desiring to. I wished very much to say this to his face.

Every now and then, she wiped her nose and gently touched the inner corner of her eyes. However, sitting there in such a way and pretending to be waiting for something made me bored. It must have bored her, too.

'Come on, Amy, let's leave. There's no point in sitting here in complete sorrow, or in some kind of desperateness.'

'You can go; I'll stay some more.'

'Come on, what will you do by staying here? Rethinking everything, over-thinking everything.... Let's go to another place so you can let go a bit....'

'I can't bear any more distractions, V. You go. I'm fine. I'll stay a little longer and then go home.'

I left Amy there and returned to the car park, wondering where to begin. The most reasonable plan would be to talk to Gary first; I needed to go to the atelier as soon as possible.

I didn't inform him I would be stopping by, because I wanted to catch him off-guard. I didn't even turn on the radio while driving so I could concentrate on my mission.

I was barely able to contain my anger, but I didn't know where to unleash it. It wasn't against Gary. If he was having an affair, that was between him and Amy in the end. The thing I was most angry at was James and his defiant and violent attitudes. Even if what he'd said about Gary was true, it wasn't his concern, and it wasn't related to the problem we were trying to solve. Whenever I witnessed the way he activated his rude attitudes and mafia-like problem-solving mechanisms, I was revolted by him, and felt shame mixed with some embarrassment whenever I talked to him or did him a favour. I felt like a traitor to the good people whom he tried to put his shit on.

After parking my car in front of Gary's atelier, I greeted the stair rails and went upstairs quickly. I knocked on the door and waited patiently for five seconds. Just as I was ready to knock on it harshly for the second time, Gary opened the door. He was wearing his apron and looking at me with a paint brush in his dyed hands.

I went inside without waiting for an invitation.

'Easy, young gun,' he said. 'Hope nothing's wrong. What has happened?'

'I have bad news, brother. We need to talk. Get your stuff together. We have to leave.'

'Leave? Why? Why don't we talk here? What's happened? Tell me. Don't keep me in suspense. Has something bad happened to someone?'

'It isn't related to health, don't worry! I'll tell you all about it, but first let's leave here. Come on, hurry up, and then I'll tell you....'

Suspicious, and without understanding what was happening, Gary washed his hands and then took off his apron. He put on his coat, and we left together and went to a pub two streets away. I didn't say anything on the way.

I took a sip of vodka before explaining, but he couldn't wait any more.

'I really can't understand why we didn't talk in the atelier. Come on, I'm gonna go mad. Tell me!'

'James has finally become involved in this inheritance shit – or, inheritance fight, whatever you may call it.'

'No surprise for me. What else?'

'He met Amy today at the company and talked to her.'

'Talked about what? What did he say?'

'What would you expect him to say?'

'What would I expect? What does that mean? I wouldn't expect him to say anything. I just asked what he'd said.'

'Maybe it won't surprise you.'

He stopped.

'V, stop talking nonsense and tell it straight. What's happening?'

'James warned Amy not to talk so much about the shares, the will, or the company any more. He told her she shouldn't be so demanding and should be content with what she has.'

'Immoral bastard!'

'He told her that if she goes chasing new shares, she might lose what she already has, and that she should wake up and open her eyes —'

'Idiot! Idiot, son of a bitch.... What crap. What does Amy have to lose?'

'You.'

'Me? What?'

'He warned Amy that she might lose you. Or maybe had already lost you.'

'What the fuck are you talking about!? What are you saying...? Are you sane, V?'

'Of course. And I'm serious! What's going on, Gary? Are you into any shit?'

He started to punch his own hand.

'I'll kill him!' he said, and suddenly went to leave the table.

I grabbed his forearm and made him sit back down.

'First we need to talk, Gary. Then we can do whatever is needed. But I have to know what's going on, okay? Look, it's your life. Your relationship with Amy, or with anyone, doesn't matter to me. I don't care. My only concern is that neither you nor Amy is harmed in these stupid circumstances. We were all already struggling with a nonsense problem, and now we also have to deal with James – just to make things worse. But I don't wanna drown in his shit. Now, are you gonna tell me what's going on?'

He gritted his teeth and tightened the muscles in his chin. He looked at the people around him and kept silent.

Then he started to speak.

'He's right,' he said.

I felt myself sink a little more into the sofa where I was sitting. My shoulders were about to be crushed by the weight hanging over me. I was loaded more and more by life each passing day. What kind of a test were these things I was experiencing? A force was trying my patience. How long would I endure? How would I behave? But still, I had told myself that I wouldn't lose this game.

'I'm seeing a student of my friend. She's a painter. Everything started in a very sudden way. Four or five months ago. Like a river that swept me off my feet...'

'I don't wanna know the details, man! How on earth does a schmuck like James know about it?!'

'I had no other choice. I had to trust him.'

'Trust James! Are you fucking out of your mind, man! How can somebody trust James! What shit are you into that you feel obliged to trust James?'

'The girl got pregnant. I didn't know what to do. When I found out, I was at his place having a drink. One thing led to another, and I told him after becoming drunk. It was not something I did intentionally.'

Had my brother remained an adolescent, even though he was twenty years older than me? Was I older than him in the more real sense?

'I can't believe you,' I said.

'Slip of the tongue, man. I was drunk... I didn't mean to....'

'Gary, hey... shut the fuck up! This is shit. Deep shit. I mean, James, for God's sake! How can all these things happen at the same time?'

A terrible headache struck me suddenly. I couldn't speak without holding my head. 'You had to know that you MUST NOT talk about such things with someone like James!' I said. 'Why were you getting drunk at his restaurant? I don't understand, man. No!'

'Okay, stop it, V. Stop it! Don't bear down on me like this. I didn't do it intentionally, I said!'

'Intentional or not, you told him, and this is all.... Then what happened? Gary, hey, is it... still continuing?'

'Yes, it is. It is...'

'Fuck! What are you gonna do now?'

'I don't know. How is Amy? What did she tell you, huh?'

'This... is the reason we couldn't stay at the atelier. Do you see? I met her at a car park near the company and told her to wait for a while, but she might go there to hunt you down and talk to you. She doesn't know, of course, that I'm talking to you right now. I wanted to reach you first, you know, to be sure about everything.... Now I am.'

'We were planning to marry...'

The torture wasn't coming to an end for me.

'Say what?! Marry? Do you mean marry the girl??'

'Yes. She's three months pregnant.'

My vodka glass was already empty by then. I grasped Gary's glass and drank his whisky in one gulp.

'Hold on...,' I said. 'Let's hold on a second. Please. Just do it one by one. Haven't you solved that issue yet? I mean, oh God, she's going to keep the... baby?'

'Yes,' he said.

I remember looking outside through the windows at the front of the pub and questioning whether I deserved all of this. What could I have done to deserve all this mess?

But actually, none of it was related to me. I could easily go aside and continue on with my life, and just watch.

But I couldn't do it. All these people were my family. I felt responsible. I couldn't be someone who said, "Life is good; it's perfect that we're together," while everything was okay, and then decide everyone should go their own way when the rot set in. Only James could behave like that, and I had nothing in common with him, in this life or the other.

I didn't want to observe how they were making life miserable for each other in such stupid ways. On the other hand, it was sad to see the situation Gary had made for himself – and all by himself, without any help from the others.

I had totally quit thinking the idea of becoming an uncle because of Lori and Gary and their way of life. I wasn't sure how to react to this unexpected surprise. We renewed our glasses of vodka and whisky.

Gary sometimes looked up at the people around us, and other times looked down at the table without speaking. Whenever he raised his head, we caught each other's eye. After we finished our second round of spirits without talking, I felt we needed a break from that "peace."

'Gary, we have to do something.'

'I know, V, I know....'

'To put it another way, Lori's whole argument on this inheritance issue has been that Amy is your wife, and so your shares also belong to her. Therefore, Lori claims, she doesn't need to give extra shares to Amy. But the situation is... different now, as Amy won't be your wife from now on, or she might think she's not going to be.... Just a sec, Gary, she's not gonna be your wife from now on, is she?'

He would not look at my face.

'It seems not... I don't think so. I don't know...,' he said.

As expected from Gary: an answer that did not much ease the problems at hand.

'Will you pull yourself together? Hey! You said the girl's gonna give birth to this baby. You said you were thinking of marrying her. So? You have to think about all this, man. Amy, the girl, divorce, marriage, a baby. What is all this? I don't understand it... I should be excited I'm going to be an uncle... but this is so strange. I mean, look at how I learned about it, in a great chaos. Can't you see?'

I ordered another glass of vodka. As I didn't know what else to do, I was resorting to alcohol, as if it contained some magical formula that would help me solve my problems.

As time passed, I moved from light-headedness to the first stages of drunkenness. Maybe it was the right thing. We had to become as drunk as we could. Weren't we celebrating something anyway? I would be an uncle, and Gary would be a father.

'This is complex, bro,' I said. 'This is deep shit, in a sense...'

'I know it, V, I knooow.'

'What're we gonna do now?'

'Nuff. I don't know.'

'Gary..., here's a plan.... Or, something as close as a plan I can think of.... I'll first go and settle accounts with the bastard James. Then I'm gonna go talk to Lori and learn what she's being doing till now, and ask that she, as his wife, takes care of her son-of-a-bitch husband.... By the way, you don't know, of course...'

'I don't know shit...'

'Yeah, you don't know shit.'

'Is Lori pregnant too?'

I smiled. 'No.... Respect, bro, as even in such deep shit you can still joke. But, I'll make you laugh soon. Lori... Boom! She slapped me last night.'

'What? Lori?'

'Yeah... Boom! Here.'

'Fuck that... No way.'

'No, really....'

Gary paused for a second, looking at me, and then burst into laughter. He laughed like crazy, and as he continued to laugh, the germ also contaminated me, and I started to laugh too. I think the spirits had begun to show their effects. We laughed uncontrollably. From time to time, he started to slap me for fun, mimicking Lori, and then his laugh would gain intensity. We were officially drunk. Our laughter continued for roughly seven or eight minutes, without stopping.

Eventually, we became calmer and quieter, and then I saw a woman's legs on my left side. My forehead was resting on the table and I was looking down at my legs. (I said we were drunk.) She approached the table with small steps and stopped about thirty centimetres away. I was sure I'd seen those shoes before, but I couldn't remember where and when. I was unable to access my memory, as if it was hidden behind a glass wall. When the owner of the shoes started to speak, the glass was broken.

'Well, boys, what's the celebration for?'

I didn't want to raise my head from the table at all. We must have seemed extremely happy; it would be the hardest job in the world to convince this person that we were exactly the opposite. I had no choice but to keep silent.

As I didn't have the courage to raise my head, I tried to understand what was happening around me by following the shoes and listening to the voices. I was watching with my mind what Gary was doing, and wondering whether Amy would kill him or not.

'Oh, God.... It's a very hard situation now, V. It's like something from a dark comedy film, you know, back-to-back misunderstandings, right? We aren't celebrating anything, darling, hey honey...'

Though his answer seemed reasonable, my inner-voice whispered into my ear that we were in deep shit. I still was not ready to raise my head.

'I need to talk to you, Gary,' Amy said.

'Of course, baby, come. Sit here.... Come, yes... Let's get something to drink for you – hey, Susan, can we get—'

'Please, Gary. Of course I'm not gonna talk in here. Let's go home. Come on. V can stay here. Look, he's about to go sleep....'

When my name was said, my game was over; I could raise my head. More precisely, I had to.

Amy was looking at me in an exhausted way, like a collapsed body whose spirit was gone. We might say "dead," in short. She'd completely cleaned off her make-up. Her eyes were swollen and her nose was red.

'Hey, Amy! How've you been?' I said.

She didn't answer me, only turned back and walked towards the door.

'I'm going to wait in the car. Please, hurry up.'

Gary was looking at me with a stupid smile on his face.

'How did she know we were here?' I asked.

'She must've guessed it. I usually either come here or go to that son of a bitch's place. She's smart enough to eliminate one of the alternatives under these circumstances....'

'Then, what now?'

'I dunno. Nothing, of course. Maybe.'

'Nothing? Gary, wake up! She's gonna ask about what James told her... What will you do? You're drunk, for God's sake....'

'No, no..., I'm fine, don't worry. You're drunk. Drunker.'

He laughed.

'Okay, fuck it. But tell me what're you gonna say?'

'I-don't-know! I'll think of something before I get there....'

'There? Where, to the door? Are you crazy? Hey, look at me. I'm gonna say something very important to you. Listen to me. Hey!'

'Stop yelling at me, will you?' He stood up. 'See you soon V, I'm leaving now, but don't worry, not forevah! And you, boy, don't do stupid things okay? Don't get slapped or whatevah.... Do you like me talking this way, huh? Don't make me deal with that James, that fuck-face, okay? I'll kill him if he does any harm to you. I-will-kill-him. Okay, you got me?'

'Gary, you just take care of your ass, okay. Don't worry about me. Never mind James. What are you gonna say to Amy?'

'We can discuss these issues tomorrow, V. Relax, you can go home now.'

Then he walked towards the door. I watched him helplessly from where I sat. Right before stepping outside, he turned back and looked at me. My eyes were still on him. He winked at me, waved goodbye, and left.

I laid my head on the edge of the table again, looking down at my legs. I didn't feel drunk any longer; in fact, what I had been feeling before wasn't only because of the alcohol. It had also resulted from the joyful fact that I was going to be an uncle. When Amy turned up, my joy had been suddenly eliminated, as if I'd just had a cup of strong espresso and instantly woken up.

I wondered what they'd talk about. Would Gary tell the truth? What would Amy feel? Under these bitter circumstances, the share she'd get from the inheritance would become very important for her, if she still had the mind to think about it. I predicted she would become very aggressive toward Lori. If Amy attacked, Lori would maintain her dignity and keep herself away, but her dog, James, could get wilder.

Until now, we'd had trouble because of personal ambitions and conflicts, and getting these mixed up. From now on, another phase could begin, with events resembling those in a bullfight arena where one person would die and the other would kill. Things might get physical, and the slap I'd received might become pale by comparison.

I looked at my shoes through my legs, with my forehead still on the edge of the table. I was wearing the same shoes I had been wearing the night my father died, when we had our last meal together as a family.

I remembered wearing these same shoes on another night, when we had something to eat at Lori's house, M and me. She used to like these shoes very much. We were together and happy then. No one was thinking of any shares, or inheritance or pregnant lovers. We were together, and that was all. The joy of being together, the tinkle of plates, the laughter of women and men, my father's rebukes in his deep voice.... And the dreams we had, nice dreams about the future. The ones we dreamed together, the ones we all dreamed individually in our own hearts, and that hope belonged to all of us. We always make the mistake of believing that time will keep the promises of our dreams.

I'd often dreamed that M and I travelled far away, somewhere where only she and I lived with no chaotic, grumbling, crowded existence. We had dreamed about taking small vacations while we hugged each other. We imagined staying together and leaving the business and other problems behind, only packing irresponsibility and selfishness. Each of our voyages would be a bit further away and to quieter places than the previous ones. Each would bring us closer to each other. However far we went, our spirits would become closer.

I wondered whether she too, from time to time, remembered the things we dreamed. Did she find herself, like me, dreaming about these moments over and over again in her daily life? Or had all our dreams been left behind with me? Did she demolish this spirit by creating contrary dreams in her mind? Could she bear the dreams of which I was also a part?

A hand touched my shoulder, and I returned to the world.

'Are you okay?' white ballerina flats said.

I raised my head. The edge of the table had left a mark on my forehead – I could feel it. I looked at the waitress and told her I was fine, and smiled at her. When required, I could tell little lies relatively easily. I don't know from whom I gained this feature. It might have been passed on to me bit by bit from James, with one tiny difference: he was a wild liar, whereas I could only lie about feeling good.

I decided not to lose any more time there and to take action.

Walking in the fresh air would help me get my head together. I got out.

The cold air felt good on my hot cheeks, which were burning after drinking so much alcohol in the warm bar. That cool consoled me and led me to laugh meaninglessly at the people passing by me for a moment, enabling me to forget my problems in the most childish way possible.

I didn't know in which direction I should walk. It was about half past four. Where should I start? Even the hours were important from then on. My problems were snowballing. I had to hinder them somehow – had to take action quickly and not lose time or pass the no-return point.

I tried to walk properly, looking at the paving stones. I started to put in order what I had in my hand: James had to pay for his arrogance, and for putting his nose into everything. Lori should be made aware of what was happening so she could re-evaluate the ideas she used to support her behaviours. Would she need Gary's help? How would Amy behave after finding out about Gary's secret, and how this would change her psyche?

I stopped and tried to listen to my inner voice. It said I needed to go to Nico and talk to James. Having two doses of James in one day would be too much for me. But I had to do it. Then I could talk to Lori. Meanwhile, I would wait for the news from Gary's side.

James wasn't at Nico. The place had just opened and been prepared for the evening. There was a rush of activity among the staff. James was usually at the restaurant during the opening hours. Why he wasn't there on this day might be related to some secret events. I sat at a table, ordered a glass of mineral water with some ice cubes, and waited for the big boy.

I watched the people of Nico hurrying around. It was obvious that they carried out their duties meticulously and with pleasure. It was hard for me to understand how a person with such a boss could still work with peace of mind.

While the younger ones rushed to arrange the table cloths and accessories, the experienced waitresses directed them and checked the arrangement of tables and chairs. James didn't employ waiters as a principle; all of the staff were waitresses. This was such a signature move for James. I was sure he'd done it just to entice himself into work every day.

I drank two glasses of iced mineral water in half an hour and continued to watch the femmes working feverishly. One of the waitresses was standing just a short distance from my table, her back facing me. She wore her hair in a bun. Just as M used to do, from time to time. M would sometimes tie her hair up for me and then turn towards me and ask, "How does it look?" Actually, she knew that I liked it, but she still asked every time. Her asking this question with wonder would make her hair look better to me. The hair coming out of this bun during the day would fall over her face. It would hover and swing a little while she was writing something with her head leaned forward. While watching her, I would dream of falling down to a distant part of the world after first clinging to, and then letting go of, this swinging hair.

The sound of a glass smashing into pieces on the floor threw me back into the restaurant. I needed to get my mind together and escape from the romantic and somehow melancholic atmosphere. I had to talk to James, and hence had to be as serious and dedicated as I could be.

I turned my head towards the right, taking in the view of the restaurant garden. Though I didn't visit there so often, the bulky oak tree in the back garden was the thing I liked most about this restaurant. The oak looked like a strong and wise man. He had a reliable side. James didn't deserve to have him there.

When I was alone, waiting for the devil to come, the tree became my close friend. I took a trip down memory lane while watching it. From time to time, its leaves swung to the sweet tune of the wind. I found myself murmuring a song that M loved. I liked the song too, but she liked it more than me. She used to say that she listened to it whenever she remembered me and thought of her love for me. Whenever she crossed my mind, I became sad. Even when we were together. But I was very happy that she harboured such strong emotions within such a delicate nature, and loved me with her vigorous love.

After a while, my drifting with the dancing leaves caused some dark sadness to whirl in my heart: the thought of my death, without her. Then I thought about the days after our break-up, the days I'd thought I couldn't survive. Time had flown, minutes had flown, hours had passed me like fast trains, and I could do nothing to stop it. It felt like I was just watching life passing by, like I was a sympathetic stranger, and my soul was mending itself at the same time without my knowledge. If only it could stand on its feet, without its eternal support – the other half, some might call it.

'Don't worry about it so much. Not good for your health, boy,' James said.

He had come up to me like a silent snake. He was the one who wanted to spoil that sweet time, when someone is dreaming by himself. I really wonder whether there was any person whom he hadn't bothered at some time with any of his behaviours.

'I'll come back soon, after checking on these chicks.' He pointed at the waitresses. 'And I'll order some men's spirit for you to drink, as mineral water is always forbidden at my table.'

Whatever I said wasn't important to him; he just produced a strange and meaningless 'Ha-ha-haaa' sound right after I uttered my part. As if he'd tried to laugh but couldn't do it humanly.

If it was up to me, I might have sacrificed whatever I owned in order not to meet him again. Especially after what he'd recently done. I didn't have any sympathy for him left in me. Then again, depending on the way our conversation went, I might not have to meet him ever again; I had a bit of hope.

He wandered around, asked the waitresses some unnecessary questions, gave someone some orders and signed a few papers – possibly the most unnecessary tasks being performed in the whole restaurant. In between, he signalled me with his hand as if to imply, "Wait a second, I'm coming soon," like he was in a hurry.

In my mind, I was quietly begging, "Please, do not come any time soon." However, our meeting was inevitable; I needed to face him.

After a while, he went to his private room at the back of the restaurant. I hadn't been in there before, but Gary had once told me that it was a dull and gloomy room where goods were stockpiled over each other: an unaesthetic way of doing things, which was something very well expected from James. In addition, his private room was very close to the ladies' room. I thought this was a strategic decision on his part in order to create chances for himself. I wished that tipsy women would mistake his room for the toilet and (at least) pee on his rugs.

One of the blonde waitresses brought a glass of vodka to the table without asking me. If I was going to be forced to drink something other than mineral water, I wanted to continue drinking whisky, so I sent it back and asked for a glass of Scotch. But, right away, I regretted it: I couldn't understand why I'd given up drinking mineral water just because that Neanderthal wanted it to be so, and got angry with myself.

James came back at that instant with an empty vodka glass in his hand. While taking a seat, he showed his empty glass to the blonde waitress, ordering a new one without a word spoken. His order was processed in a flash, and he had a new glass of vodka in his ugly right hand. He took a sip and grimaced. Disgust served at the speed of light. Good job, Nico.

'Same shit every day...,' he said.

'Okay, I came here to talk to you, James. I won't beat around the bush—'

'Oh boy, you know about the bushes?' He took another sip as if he wanted to eat the glass.

Could he be for real?

'How can you be such an.... Whatever. Look, the thing you did today wasn't good, okay? At all....'

He didn't respond quickly; instead, he moved his hand over his chin. 'You heard what happened, right?' he said. 'I would be surprised if you hadn't.'

'What? You made a big deal out of nothing. You exaggerated something, okay? I mean, you can't be that merciless, right? You don't have any right to poke your nose into other people's lives....'

'I haven't poked my nose into anyone's life. I just wanted to warn her about some issues – real issues, boy. I also informed you about my plan, didn't I? I didn't decide to do it all by myself.'

I could no longer understand how this guy's mind worked. I mean, I couldn't be sure it'd ever worked in his whole lifetime.

'What!? Decision? What decision are you talking about? Are you fucking nuts—'

'Watch it!'

'Of course you did it all by yourself. Whatever shit you did, you went there alone and did it by yourself. Why are you talking as if we planned something together? Stop talking shit.'

'I told you what I was gonna do this morning. I visited you in your apartment and told you about it.'

'James, you.... Oh, God, does telling me you were planning something mean we decided on it together? Are you mad, James? Moreover, you didn't tell me what you'd do.... You didn't say you were going to give Amy a hard time by irritating her and threatening her! Wake up to yourself for once! You can't solve anything with these stupid attitudes.... Put the threat shit aside. What you said about Gary is very fucking rude, man.'

'I didn't say anything bad about Gary. I just said she should take care of her husband. That's all. I did a favour to her, boy.'

He ate his glass one more time.

'Enough, James! I'm not a kid. I've become very bored of your Mafiosi behaviours. Look, please start behaving like a proper adult, okay? Just try. What is there to gain by hitting below the belt? You always emphasise the importance of being a family, remember? Does what you did fit the concept of being a family?'

'I don't do anything to anyone who belongs to the family...,' he said.

James was like a cartoon character, specifically created to drive the people around him mad. He was overwhelming me. His ignorance and rudeness made his eyes blind and his ears deaf. It was impossible to have a reasonable conversation with him, but I was determined not to leave there without reaching a solution. Upon seeing that the waitress was bringing some vodka to him, I knocked my whisky back and asked for a new one with a gesture she was used to from her boss, just the swinging of the empty glass.

'V. Hey, V, listen to me. Calm down. Look, I love you, though I don't spend so much time with you as I do with Gary. We aren't that intimate yet.'

'Do you think you're intimate with Gary?'

'What does that mean?'

'What does that mean? I asked a very clear question, man. Do you think you're intimate with Gary? Just a simple question.'

'That's nonsense. Of course I am. We're close. Why would you ask something like that?'

'Because, he thinks you're a stupid person. When he heard that you consider him a close friend, he burst into laughter,' I said.

Now the flames were getting higher. The fire had been fed. When I uttered that last sentence, I knew at that very instant that nothing would stay as it was before.

James was looking at me woozily, as if he'd been slapped. But he contented himself with just opening his eyes and warping his mouth, because showing surprise like a normal human didn't fit his stern and macho nature. It seemed to me as if he was mimicking a behaviour he'd seen in a movie. He drank his vodka in one gulp, looked at his glass, and asked the waitress to bring the bottle to the table this time.

'When did he say that?' he asked. 'That... that I'm a stupid person.'

'James, please don't behave like a child. You're not seeing the point! We need to be serious. It isn't important *when* he said it. You don't know what people think about you. Seriously. People don't like you because of your rude manners – your poor behaviour. Pardon me, but it's true. You still resist telling me what happened, as if there's nothing to say. You still believe you'll solve all the trouble we're in with your rudeness and, you know, macho moves. How can this be, man? How do you have this meaningless courage? Why bother? Do you have the right to behave this way?'

While I was speaking, he had filled his glass with vodka and drank it. I knew that he drank quite a lot, but I'd never witnessed him drinking so fast.

'V, I don't care about what people think of me. But, what I think about myself is important, okay? And for me, I'm not a stupid person.'

He was "not" stupid, but he argued like a kindergarten baby.

'What my wife thinks of me is important. Do you see it? Her happiness, our marriage. By the way, my daughter is also important. I shouldn't forget to mention her. Apart from those two, I don't give a damn shit about the rest of the world. Do you understand me, boy—'

'Stop calling me boy, James.'

'I don't care any bit for your brother the drunk painter, or for his bitchy wife, or for you. Do you hear me, boy? No shit! Now, get the fuck out of here, V!'

'What!? Are you sane?'

'None of you is worth a dime. None of you. Except Lori. How can she be your sister? She's something else, very different, and proper? I can't understand it. Also there's your father. I loved him. But he didn't love me back. Grumpy bastard. Hah! I knew him well... so well. He was a devil. Yes! But I still loved him....'

His uncontrolled words, defining my father as a "grumpy bastard" and "devil" were enough to drive me crazy. I started to feel a little dizzy due to both the alcohol and my growing anger. I didn't look at James' face again but instead watched the restaurant and the rush of people moving through it.

James had been busy filling up his glass and knocking it down, one drink after the other. He was about to knock down the glass he'd just filled when I held his arm. Some vodka spilt over my hand and onto his wrist. He didn't let the glass go, though.

'Enough. Look, if we continue like this, we'll all fall out. I'm going to leave after one last thing, but promise that you'll listen to me and do whatever I say, okay? Please, from now on, just try to behave and don't threaten anybody else. Leave them all alone, James-less, okay? Amy, Gary, Lori, everybody. Let them solve it by themselves, okay? Do you understand?'

He pulled his arm away sharply, spilling more vodka over the table from the overfilled glass. He drank the remaining amount in one gulp, looking directly into my eyes.

'What will happen if I don't, huh?' he said. 'Will we get bitter?

Come on..., let's talk the shit out of that, then.'

'James, look, you don't understand me.... First, calm down. Whoever starts out in anger will end up with a loss. I haven't threatened you, or anything. I'm not making a power play. I'm just saying how it should be. There's no point in creating such a stressful mess around yourself, as you are now. None of us needs it. Do you see my point? Let's talk in a human way and solve our problems without losing our control. We were like that three days ago....'

'That was then... three days ago,' he said, and stood up. 'Get the fuck outta here!' he shouted.

It was like a bomb had exploded in my hands. I think before then I had never been forcefully shown the door from anywhere – or, if I had, at least not with the word "fuck," I was sure of that. Worse, this was James, a man of straw with whom I hadn't spent even one sincere second, sending me off from his restaurant with swearing. In front of so many people.

I was in a situation that was difficult to digest. It was humiliating, even though James was a man I hated and from whom I expected every stupid thing. Still, I'd never imagined that he could be so low. I couldn't understand for a second whether the moment was real or a nightmare. If real, it would serve to keep me away from him forever, but I felt deeply humiliated and didn't wanna leave without reaching a conclusion.

'Stand up! Now! C'mon, now. Fuck off! Go away!' He showed me the door with his vodka-wet right hand.

I stood up, but I had to do something. I wanted to squeeze his neck till his face went violet-black, but I didn't dare.

I threw the glass of whisky I was holding to the floor. When it smashed, a silence fell over everyone in Nico. They had all stopped what they were doing to watch our show. Three bodyguard-like doormen were walking towards us with quick steps. I needed to leave the place fast. I stared at James as I headed to the main door. The customers, waitresses and the doormen all watched as I left.

I felt lucky to have escaped the situation with only that – the stares. If I'd grasped James by his throat as I had wished, his door-dogs might have pulled me into pieces.

Both of us had drunk too much in too short of a time. I had difficulty walking. I felt dizzy, but I came-to a bit with the cold weather touching my face. His swearing still echoed in my ears. I put my hands into my pockets and started to walk, my eyes on the ground. I didn't know where I was walking to and didn't care either.

I started to laugh as the echo-loop came back to "Fuck off" again. The moment I'd smashed the whisky glass onto the floor was still before my eyes. The glass pieces flying away from their boss, the little drops of whisky wetting the sober floor.

The echo repeated: I heard "fuck off" and the smashing of the glass again and again.

I was sure that he had enjoyed that moment to the fullest, his showing me the door, the swearing, me breaking the glass. All of these were the small doses of unrest a sick mind like James' sought after. Actually, he had remained more passive than I expected. But, if I'd punched him in the face or clung to his throat, it would definitely have ended up worse for me. James could have beaten me easily even by himself, but there were also his paid-dogs. Attacking him would have been my foolishness. Maybe that's what he had wanted from the beginning, and why he had provoked me. I didn't know at what point I had decided to smash the glass, but I was certainly feeling better.

In just two days, I had been both slapped by Lori and "fucked off" by her husband from his restaurant. Humiliation at its best.

I was drunk, and it was getting colder. I desperately needed M beside me. The smile I had borrowed from the broken glass of whisky was starting to diminish slowly. I raised my head and continued to walk. Though the pavement stood flat and motionless, the walls around me, the trash bin and the road next to me were all moving with waves. I felt a bit afraid of their coming my way, but I continued to walk without hesitation. I was very lonely and started to feel colder.

I didn't have the enough courage to call her – no, maybe it wasn't a lack of courage; I just knew that it wasn't right to call her.

I thought of sending her a letter. A real one. It wasn't a big thing, but it would be better than nothing. How about the mood I was in? Would it be a wise move to write her while experiencing these bitter flows of thought? At least I could scribble something on a small piece of paper and just send it to her. It would be enough for her to learn that I was thinking of her at the moment. And at some other moments. Also, it wasn't obtrusive like a phone call. An action carried out from a distance, one that wouldn't disturb the usual flow of her life. Like, for instance, if we were sitting face to face at a table and I wanted her to look at me, instead of calling her name or touching her, I just leaned slowly left to right to catch her eyes in the space. Hook them to mine, and then her soul to mine, in the most innocent way.

As I couldn't stop the walls coming towards me, I quickly entered a stationery store on my left. The floors were stable (still), but the walls were moving (again). I walked towards the middle of the store where I found a small plain white card, nearly the size of two business cards or maybe slightly bigger, and took out my needle-tip pen. I was determined to write down what I felt or thought at that moment, and then send it to her without too much thinking.

I sat on a chair located at the far corner of the store, near the shelves stocked with notebooks. I paused for a second, raised my head from the white card, and looked outside through the display window. At the sky. The weather was indecisive, as if it'd bring some rain but was also somehow clear enough not to leave people hopeless about living. Though it was only a slightly bright sky, it might be enough for those who wanted to breed hope inside.

I wondered how she'd reply if I wrote many pages to her instead of just a lonely card. I remembered some of those little instants we had left behind, those short hours, the sincere laughter, the cosy feeling of mutual understanding, the moments that were impossible not to wish to live again and again; and the love transferred itself from my heart to my brain, and then to my hand. I wrote it down:

"Getting to know you was the most beautiful journey I've taken in all my life."

And I put the card in an envelope.

Keeping myself away from the walls, I went to the cashier and paid for the card, envelope and stamp. There wasn't a post box in the store, but the cashier said I could find one just outside, on the street. I left and walked in the direction she told me.

The turning of objects in the environment, everything except the pavement, continued, but their speed had decreased. I was feeling a strange excitement. It was stronger than what I had felt when dialling and then watching the numbers on my cell phone screen, but similar to what I'd felt while holding my finger over the call button.

A littler further on, I saw the yellow post box. At that moment, a feeling of hesitation found its way to my heart. I couldn't be sure of whether to send it. I began to feel afraid. Twenty seconds later, I was in front of the box and needed to make a decision. I took a deep breath, and looked at the name and address on the envelope. Then I raised my head and looked at the sky. It surprised me how quickly it had become dark.

There were things I needed to do. I have to take action before it gets too dark, I thought. And I threw the card into the post box.

I felt both relaxation and regret. I held the box with my two hands. If I could've managed to open it, I'd take the card out. I tried a bit, but I couldn't open it. I punched the post box a couple of times. But nothing changed.

In fact, I felt happy I could not open the box; deep within, I didn't want to take the card back. I gave up and continued my walk. Relaxation stayed; regret flew away.

I couldn't decide what exactly to do after being kicked out of Nico. I was motivated to meet Lori, but, on the other hand, I also thought that I should follow a policy of wait and see. As if contradiction was the only thing I needed then.

Even though the regret about the card issue had gone, I still thought myself a little cowardly and inconsistent as I had done something I'd never normally do if I weren't drunk. I felt as if I had quit holding the bicycle handle-bars while still riding. I might fall off, or not, but it was something I wouldn't do normally. I'd never felt so reckless before.

I was in desperate need of talking to someone close to me. I took out my cell phone and called him.

'What are you doing?' I said.

'I'm just leaving the office. I got bored, fella! I got bored – with capital letters. I felt extremely suffocated today. What's today's problem, man? It should go and get a life. What are you up to?'

'I'm wandering around in a semi-drunk and nicely done manner. Or, am I fully drunk? James has just kicked me out of his restaurant.'

'What? Look at that fuck-face...'

'And he did that shit by telling me to fuck off! How do you like that? Dude, I lead a very fast and exciting life. Come and join me. I'm sure you'll enjoy it....'

'Are you serious, bro? That son of a bitch!'

'Of course I'm serious. We were drunk. We were trying to talk, but he ruined our conversation. After he told me to fuck off, I got angry and couldn't restrain myself—'

'Man! Then what? Did you fight? Oh, punch him, ma' boy!'

'Listen, I bought a card from a stationery store and sent it to M— I mean, I wrote something on it and then I sent it. I wrote a note, did you hear me...? Ha-ha! Plain perfect!'

'That idiotic son of a bitch! I'm so angry now, V, and frustrated, very frustrated.... Hey, let's crash his place, huh? What do you say? Let's settle his hash. Let's go to his damn restaurant and do this shit together. Okay? Hey bro, are you in?'

'Do what together?'

'Whatever's needed, man. I don't know. Crash his place!'

'Are you crazy, Eric? Calm down.... He has a dozen dogs inside. They'll break our necks in no time. In-no-time! Even if he's alone, I mean, he can beat both of us.... Can't he?'

'Fuck him, c'mon!'

'Don't you know he's like a polar bear?'

'We can also be bears, man. It's all in the mind—'

'Fuck that Buddha shit!'

'We're used to fighting, man. C'mon, I gotta relieve this shitty frustration and anger. Let's break his neck, cut him loose....'

'Bullshit.'

'No, it's not! Where are you? Let's go and do it. Let's meet in front of Nico.'

'Enough. Don't be mad, Eric. Would you behave? I'm the one who's drunk. Are we kiddos, bro?'

'Fuck you. Hard.'

'I already have enough trouble and don't want to add any new problems to my existing ones. Stop it.'

'I'm leaving now to go to Nico. Are you gonna come?'

'Eric, sometimes you get really sick-minded. You know that, right?'

'Are you gonna come, V? Are you with me? Say it!'

'I'm already walking near Nico. Oh man! You're really an asshole sometimes. Come and pick me up. We'll go after a quick bite somewhere, okay?'

'How could I know where you're walking? Let's meet in front of Nico. Then well go straight in. Rush in!'

'Enough, Eric! Okay? I need to talk. Please cut the crap. I'm walking towards the park across from Nico. Go there, and call me.' I hung up.

Though Eric's momentarily excitements sometimes led to positive results, it was rare. Most of them were meaningless – as going back into Nico would be.

It could take him up to thirty minutes to get from his office to the park, so I decided to wander around a bit more. If I stopped walking, I would either think of M or James, both of which would lead to unreasonable results. I'd either end up calling M before my card reached her, or I'd think about attacking James at Nico, now that I had been infected with the idea. I had to keep my mind busy with something else.

Despite my best efforts not to think about M, questions started rising in my mind: How long did it take my ex-girlfriends to completely erase me from their thoughts? Had they all forgotten me so easily? How long did it take for them to completely forget me? Could I learn whether M had forgotten me by asking others about their experiences with me? Would it work if I called one of my other ex-girlfriends instead of M and asked whether she had forgotten me? And, if so, how long it'd taken her? Was the forgetting complete, or was it a still continuing process?

While dancing and boxing with these questions in my mind, I stopped in a store and bought some whisky in a small metal flask, like I'd seen in movies: something portable to keep in the inner pocket of a jacket. I started to enjoy it. I'd missed whisky in just a couple of hours since I'd been kicked out of Nico.

I started to look at the contacts list in my cell phone. I'd erased M's number, but it was carved into my brain. The number of one or two other women with whom I'd had short-term relationships caught my attention, but I couldn't call them. And I didn't want to. We'd never been "lovers" and they wouldn't answer my questions – and even if they would, their answers would probably be meaningless to me. I needed to ask someone I'd been in love with, or something close to it.

After I scrolled up and down for about thirty seconds, I found what I'd been searching for. She was someone with whom I'd been together before I got to know M – for seven months.

Chelsea was then working for a magazine. Not as an editor or content creator but someone responsible for sales channels. We'd met for business and, after realising we were having a good time together, started to date. Our chemistries danced, and we were having crazy sex. (Oh, those animals.) For a long time after our break up, I missed making love to her. But she was a very determined and proud soul. And also stubborn. After our break-up talk, she didn't contact me at all.

While we were together, I'd made no plans regarding our future, and this had made her bored with my love, and depressed about it too. I hadn't wished to make any such plans back then, and I wasn't good at planning anything either. Nor did I know how it could be done – not in those times. She'd meant a lot to me. She was different from the rest, and while dating her I'd come to understand what the previous women had been lacking, but – if I might be a bit frank – I'd never thought she was the one I should be doing any "planning" with.

It was a win-win situation for us to end our relationship – I guess.

She could fulfil her dreams with someone who wished to "plan a future with her," and I could chase my own dreams for an even greater love. God, I was lucky to find the love of my life, and unlucky to lose her right away – now my love existed only on a small postcard.

On that evening, I didn't care too much about how Chelsea would react to my sudden call after more than three years. If I hadn't been drunk, I wouldn't even have thought of such an act let alone done it. Of course, she wouldn't know that my courage came from alcohol.

I drank a little more. The whisky wasn't of high quality, but I liked drinking from the can. I pressed the green icon on my phone, took a sip of whisky, and listened to the ring tone. While peeking at the legs of a woman walking in front of me, I realised it had become dark.

The phone was ringing, and I felt as if I was waiting in front of a door I hadn't knocked on for a long time.

'Hello?'

'Aw... hello.... Hi..., umm, I just called to check how you are...'

Silence.

'V? Is that you?' Chelsea said.

'Yeah, yeah, this is me.... Hey, that's good. You haven't forgotten me.... I mean, my voice.... Okay, whatever.... How's life going?'

'I'm very good? And you?'

I couldn't speak for a moment. I was thinking how stupid I was.

'Are you okay, V? Is there a problem? You sound a bit... strange?'

'Yes, yes.... No, I'm fine. There's no problem. Anyway, am I bothering you?'

'Well, no. It's okay,' she said and fell silent again.

I moved the phone away from my mouth, took a full-mouth sip, and then tried to continue. 'Well, Chelsea..., I... I wanted to see how you're doing.... And one more thing, I wanted to ask... uh...'

'Yes, what else?'

'What else?' I laughed. I was laughing at myself, my miserable condition. 'Look, actually, I called to ask you something....'

'And yes, I'm listening?'

'Okay, as I trust you and value your opinions, please don't misunderstand me.... I wanna be sure of that before asking.'

'V, to tell you the truth, I don't have much time right now. Martin, my husband, is waiting, and we were about to leave. I'd be happy if you could hurry up a little....'

'Oh, Martin! Yes.... Okay, yes. Congratulations. You got married. What then.... Sorry... I mean, I didn't know it. If I knew, I wouldn't have called....'

'Please V, what do you want?'

'I wanted to ask you something, but it isn't important. I can ask it later. It isn't urgent. See you soon,' I said and hung up.

I already felt ashamed at calling her, but after I'd hung up on her I felt even more ashamed. I had become very unbalanced recently. The behaviours I had displayed within the last hour were things I'd never do under normal circumstances. As time passed, I was losing more and more control.

I drank the remaining whisky, turned back and started to walk towards the park to meet Eric. Passing by the liquor store, I wondered if canned whisky was the new trend. I bought five more cans – three for me, two for Eric.

When I reached the corner where the newspaper kiosk stood, Eric was still absent, but I could see Nico and the big green sunshade in front of the restaurant – the restaurant from where I'd been kicked out. Would that sunshade be reluctant to open if it knew it was in the service of a man with such filthy attitudes and behaviours?

'Hey, what are you looking at?'

'At the sunshade of Nico....'

Eric turned towards Nico. 'Let's go there and break it. Let's break the shade, and then go into the place and punch that bastard in the face! Break that big nose. Come on!'

He grabbed my arm and pulled me towards Nico. But, I resisted.

'Oh, don't start again. Don't act stupid,' I said. 'C'mon, I've bought whisky for you, too. Knock them down.... But, I must say, you're behaving as if you don't need these, if you know what I mean, boy.'

'Perfect, let's drink these first. Then we can take action. Boozed up! Give them to me—' He looked at the cans. 'What the fuck?'

'It's wonderful, isn't it? I've just discovered it. I took one to carry in my pocket, but I sucked it up so quickly I had to get some new ones. Perfect idea.'

'What's the point of carrying these in your pocket? Oh, V, why didn't you get something proper? Are we getting drunk? We'll drink it just to kick up a fuss.'

'Let's go to the other side of the park,' I said. 'We'll knock these down and chat a bit. There's another thing I need to talk to you about. I've done something stupid....'

We went to the other side of the park, behind Nico's summer garden. Eric was wearing his suit and looked relatively "dignified." He took a sip of his whisky.

'It isn't as bad as I thought...,' he said. 'Drinkable....'

'I just called Chelsea.'

He wrinkled his face as if I had said something impossible. 'Chelsea? "The" Chelsea? The blond chick?'

'Don't call her a chick.'

'Why did you call her? After so many years, oh boy! Did you get that horny?'

'No. I called her to ask whether she'd forgotten me or not.'

'What?!'

He looked at me and started to laugh. Shook his head, drank some more whisky, and turned back to me again. Laughed – again.

'From the shitty look on your face, I can see that she must have forgotten you....'

'No, she recognised my voice. She hadn't forgotten my voice. But she's married.'

He laughed so hard he looked as if he'd die of laughter.

'Then, she didn't forget you,' he said, and his laughter made his voice come out as if he were shouting. He got up and took a few steps forward.

'Stop laughing like an idiot. Anyway, fuck that. Let's talk about James. He dropped by this morning and gave me the impression he was going to do something wrong, but I didn't know what. Then, after he went out and caused shit by talking to Amy, he told me I'd approved his plan. I rejected that idea, so we quarrelled. We were on the verge of fists, bro. That bastard tried to involve me in his shit.'

'Wo-wait, James talked to Amy? About what?'

'Oh, you know nothing.... Okay..., James came to me this morning and said he'd talk to Amy and force her to stop demanding any shares from the company. I told him he shouldn't get involved and to leave them alone; they can solve it however they want.'

'I'll beat him hard.'

'Then he asked me "why" he shouldn't get involved. Idiot considers himself a member of the family. He always speaks of "family." He can drive me crazy even early in the morning.'

'Sucker! And then what? Fuck! I just remembered Amy called me today, but I was in a meeting. I completely forgot to call her back afterwards.'

'He made her cry – hey, wait, don't call her now.'

'Cry? How dare he?!'

'They're talking now.'

Eric put his phone back into his pocket.

'What the fuck are you talking about, man? Who's talking to who?'

'Gary and Amy.'

'So what? She sometimes talks to me, too... still.'

'Forget her, just for now. What should I do about James, huh? I quarrelled first with Lori, and then with her stupid husband. I don't know what she's gonna do about this shares issue. Everything got muddled.'

'If she changes anything in the will, then she's guilty. It's a crime.'

'I know, I know, but it isn't even certain a will exists. We're talking about notes, this and that.... We can't prove anything. She must have taken all precautions.'

'I remember that Chelsea was a very beautiful girl. Will you meet her again? I mean, hidden agenda-wise, you know. Are you gonna try your chance to get... you know...?'

'Why are you bringing up that now? Of course I don't intend to do that. She won't wanna see me again anyway, I'm sure. I hung up on her.'

'Hung up on her? Why?'

'She said her husband was waiting. I said sorry and hung up. That's it.'

He started to laugh again. He emptied the second can.

'Is there any more?' he asked.

We decided to share my third can. We were getting drunker.

'Before coming here, I also drank a bit at the office,' he said.

'Why?'

'I didn't wanna fight sober. We might find ourselves in a situation... but, thanks anyway. These cans were like a remedy. Polishers.'

'Enough! What fight are you talking about? There's not gonna be a fight.'

'If no fight takes place, then we can break that shade. C'mon, let's do something to him!'

'Oh Eric, are you a kid? What's the use of breaking the sunshade of a restaurant?'

'Nothing very practical. It'll just freak him out. He'll know that you had a hand in it, for sure, but he won't be able to do anything. But if you say, "Breaking the shade isn't worth shit; we must fight," then I'm all for that, too. Let's go and break his nose.'

'C'mon..., how are we gonna break the shade without getting caught? This is bullshit.'

'We'll break it and then escape at once.'

'Are you serious? What kind of a lawyer are you? Is this the best plan you can come up with? Give up your profession; you ain't worth your hourly charge. Don't you know there are guards and valets waiting at the entrance?'

'Isn't there a shade at the back, towards the garden? Maybe we can see it from the park. We can break that instead.'

I was starting to get used to Eric's idea to freak out James. He wasn't insisting too hard, but his idea had poisoned me little by little. I felt trapped. He had shaped the plan step by step in a way he knew I'd like it and couldn't resist. The whisky in tin cans had also worked for him.

Since James had kicked me out, I'd done two very stupid things; I decided another one would change nothing for the worse. We started to think about how we could cause some trouble in James' life. It was clear that we wouldn't break the shades – that wasn't wise. They were very high, and we didn't know which parts we could break or how to break them. (I refused to talk about "why.")

We thought of waiting until midnight and breaking the huge lamps that lit the restaurant entrance, but we concluded that it wouldn't drive James crazy enough. Another idea was to write swear words on the front window with spray-paint. This idea lasted only a couple of seconds because not only was it "not bad enough," it was also very childish – as if our other plans weren't childish at all.

'Let's break the big windows overlooking the back garden,' Eric said. 'We can wait here until late. They don't accept any more people to the back part after a certain time, so there won't be anybody there, and we won't harm anyone when we smash the windows—'

'Is our plan bad enough now?'

'Yeah, doing something while there're still people inside will hurt him. It's a great idea, isn't it? It's also a distant operation; no one will see us in the dark. We can hide behind these trees and throw big stones. After the *boom!* we'll run towards the road, cross it... and disappear into the night, bro. That easy. Look man, giant windows... big crash, big noise!'

'Yes, big windows. Can you hit them?'

'It's a perfect plan in all respects. What do you think? Is it okay?'

While Eric was enthusiastically telling me the final details of his great plan, I was thinking of Chelsea. I wanted to have sex with her again. But it was too late. I drank some more whisky.

'Okay, it's a perfect idea...'

'Is it? Really? YES!'

'We'll break the two back windows completely. Throwing apple-sized stones will be enough for that. We'll shoot from over there.'

'That tree over there? Behind that one?'

'Yeah.'

'Yes,' said Eric and stood up. He drank the remaining whisky in one gulp, swallowed it with difficulty, and threw the can at the trash bin – but it didn't hit the target. He stumbled a bit.

'You won't be able to hit the window in this state,' I said. I stood up and drank the rest of my whisky. Then I threw the can into the trash bin, but I couldn't hit the target either.

To wait for the proper time to execute our plan, we found a modest and small café. First we ordered some whisky and then some food.

'Where is Danielle?' I asked.

'Probably at home.'

'"Probably?" Why probably?'

'I don't know.'

'What's the problem, man? Tell me. There's something.'

'Please, V, don't suffocate me. Shut up. I'm making a plan now,' he said.

I felt dizzy and didn't want to ask any more questions or hear his answers.

When our dishes arrived, I remembered Gary and Amy. I checked my cell phone, but there were no messages or calls. I wondered what was happening at their side. I sent an SMS to Gary: "How are you?"

'Does the upper floor belong to Nico? Should we also break those windows there?'

I started to laugh at how Eric was trying to develop our primitive and childish plan in detail.

'I don't know. It might, or not. Let's forget it all. How proper and interesting is it for you to break windows? At this age and with this anger, don't we need to take more serious action? In a more chevalier spirit. Like—'

'The best idea is to go and break his neck, or nose at least. I say that's the most suitable action for a chevalier spirit. But you hesitate, pussy!'

'Yes, because it's certain we'll become the "chevaliers" who got beaten in no time!' I was being realistic.

There was nothing left on our plates, but the whisky was constantly renewed. Actually, I hadn't drunk so much for a long time. The ambiance and the talk with Eric had done me some good.

We drank and talked until 11 p.m., killing time. We came up with other stupid ideas and said them out loud – like having Eric express his "love" for Lori and then getting her to change the will as he wished. We entered into an adolescent thinking spree. With both our words, our laughter and the actions we planned, we were behaving like high school kids; and we were probably gonna be kicked out of school the next day as a disciplinary act.

Eric asked for the bill. We left a heavily loaded tip for the waitress so she would know we were not "really" stupid. I wasn't quite sure whether that tip worked for or against us on that matter.

It was a little colder outside, but there was no rain. We passed by Nico, walking along the pavement on the opposite side of the street. After walking about two hundred and fifty meters, we entered the park from where we would carry out our glamorous plan. Though we were very distracted, we began to walk towards the back of the park, be careful not to unsettle the people in the park. After a while, we could see dim yellow light of our prey reflected over the green.

Eric gripped my arm. 'I'm excited.... That son of a bitch is going to be furious,' he said. He was shivering out of fear and cold.

I was still not very sure about carrying out our perfect plan. In spite of our drinking, the time we had spent together and our motivating talks, if someone had approached me and said, "Think about it for a moment; what you're planning is petty. Are you stupid or a child?" then I would easily have given up on James' big surprise. I think Eric was aware of this because he kept forcing me to contemplate the plan in such a detailed way.

We stopped near the back of the restaurant, facing the big windows that looked out into the back garden. The ambient yellowish light inside the restaurant seemed very beautiful from the park. Nico seemed bigger and more gorgeous from that angle. There were chic women and handsome men inside, some standing and others sitting and dining. The waitresses were in a rush; the place was full of luxuries and seemed alive. One could dream of the scent the women inside must be radiating: a mixture of reckless wealth with a hint of diamonds.

As far as I knew, this dynamic nature of the restaurant usually lasted until 2 a.m., but they didn't allow anyone into the back after 11 p.m., when they slowly began closing the service to that side.

We needed to wait for the remaining four tables to become vacant in order to carry out our plan. We were going to behave like shit, but we weren't so low as to throw rocks right in front of people.

'Fuck you, guys. Haven't you had enough?' Eric said. 'Go home! Now.'

I pulled him under one of the big trees. First we waited, standing, and then after half an hour or so we sat on a bench near the tree. From time to time, I checked my cell phone, but there was no news from Gary.

We had lost some motivation and were fighting off sleep when, roughly fifty minutes later, two more tables of people left at the same time. We recovered our hope again with this tiny forward motion towards the big time. We straightened up on the bench, tried to flex our eyelids.

'Hey, enough with the sitting. Let's collect some stones,' Eric said. 'The time is coming.'

'Right. Maybe we should practice a bit, right? On the opposite side. There, for example?'

'Why the fuck?'

'To test ourselves, see whether we can hit it or not.'

'There's nothing to target on that side. What if someone is sleeping there, or making out and we hit 'em?'

'But we don't know—'

'What difference will it make? Are we gonna quit? So stupid. Also, there's nothing to target.'

'We'll find something white ahead. I dunno, a bag, for instance. A shoe, maybe. Then we'll try to hit the target?'

'A shoe?'

'I don't know, Eric! What the fuck is with you? Something to aim for? That's it. Jeez!'

'We don't need to. We should just find enough stones for the plan. If we practice first, we might not have the strength to do the real job later. I'm about to fall asleep right now.'

Victorious General Eric felt sleepy. The army had weakened.

We started to wander around without going too far away, trying to find "proper" stones for our mission, our eyes on the ground. We had to search for the stones that were willing to be on our side, on our death-squad – loyal stones. All because James had become indirectly involved in this issue and hadn't hesitated to help us feel disgust for him.

'Look what I've found! A grapeshot!' Eric said. 'Perfect. I'm gonna throw this into the eye of the window, and boom! Crash! A very aerodynamic thing this is.'

'Oh, God, why do we have to do this? Stones, crashes, booms...'

Eric seemed very excited and happy.

'Do you remember when we lost your key to the house, huh?' he said. 'Instead of searching for the key itself, we tried to find a four-leafed clover so we could get some luck... to help us find the key....'

'I still can't help but feel surprised at our foolishness whenever I recall it.... Eric, this is the same stupid urge, isn't it? Years later, a whole lifetime later for God's sake, we are doing the same stupid shit again!'

'Why is it stupid? It was a very good indicator of our determinacy and belief in ourselves.... If, now, we can still do such things, I mean if we've got the balls, man, it's grounded on those stupid acts. We owe it to our stupid days and—'

'Eric...'

'What?'

'I feel sick. My stomach... I'm feeling dizzy after searching for some shitty stones to throw... and now I'm gonna throw up. Oh, no..., just stop for a while, please....'

I sank to my knees. It wasn't a trick or a lie; I really was feeling seriously nauseated. Apart from the exact point where I was looking, everything else around me was circling.

Eric appeared beside me just as sour saliva came up in my mouth. Unfortunately, he put his hand on my shoulder to ask whether I was fine. At the very moment, I raised my head and saw that he was also circling with the rest of the world. It was too late then.

While I was throwing up, I couldn't care less about Eric's trousers.

Shouting and swearing, Eric leapt back. He stopped a short distance away and looked down at his legs. He seemed about to cry. I leaned back and laid on the grass for about twenty minutes, I suppose. I came to with Eric's shaking me.

'C'mon, dirty drunk fuck. The rest are gone, too. We're done. We need to take action. Get up!'

I felt as if it was already morning; wake-up time had come.

'Hey, I'm talking to you. Where are your stones?'

I was just about to suggest we give up the plan when he grabbed me under my armpits and lifted me up. He handed me a couple of stones, which had been next to me while I was sleeping. They were *my* stones.

'C'mon, asshole,' he said and propped me up on a tree trunk.

While I was trying to say, "Do we need to do this...?" he ran behind the big tree and hid himself. Then, he threw the first stone. The stone (without sin) hit the concrete space between the windows of the upper floor, and produced a strong sound. It was the time I'd been his partner in crime – on top of everything else we'd been.

'Throw it with all of your strength, pussy,' I said. 'But be careful: don't aim too high. If we break the upper window first, we won't have enough time to hit the bottom one.'

'Shut your mouth and get your ass up here!'

I approached and looked at him. He paused and stared back at me.

'What? Why are you looking at me?' he said.

'This will cause trouble for us later – like, some deep shit.'

He took the stones from my hand and compared the biggest one with his grapeshot. Then he made a decision and threw the grapeshot at the window. This time, he hit the target.

The window broke into pieces with a high-pitched smashing sound – and the pieces fell down on the ground like a new form of rain. A violent and out-of-this-world rain. The exact moment the glass yielded was impossible to see, but exhilarating to imagine: grapeshot's clinging to the window, the window's little flexibility, its effort to resist the dash, its insufficiency.... The window on the right sight had been knocked down. Eric completed half of our task.

Anyone observing us from inside the restaurant at that moment would have seen that we were gawking at the damage as much as everyone at the tables was. The customers sitting at the back of Nico looked shocked and fearful. Perhaps they thought it was a terrorist attack.

While some diners ran away to the front of the restaurant, the security guards who had been at the entrance were walking quickly but cautiously towards the broken window. In other words, James' hunter dogs were on their way, with hunger saliva on their mouths.

The whole restaurant seemed to be experiencing a shock and panic wave, with everyone trying to both keep away from the windows and also see what was happening.

Without losing time, Eric threw another stone at the left window – but the stone hit very low on the pane and didn't break it.

This time, I reacted more quickly: I took a stone from Eric's palm and threw it at the left pane.

On target! There was a crash and all heads turned towards the imploding window. The people then gave up their wonder and, perhaps believing something serious was happening, started to make their escape through the front door with shouts and little pushes. Among them, I saw James walking with slow steps in the opposite direction.

I was about to say "Let's go!" to Eric, when he touched my arm and said, "C'mon!"

As we had planned, we ran through the dark side of the park towards the road.

I still felt both dizzy and sick. It had been ages since I had run that fast. After a while, I started to think that my legs were touching the ground properly only out of pure luck, or by the grace of God. The security coefficient was zero in the commands given by my mind and the behaviours reflected by my body. I couldn't believe how fearlessly I was running, or how I had put myself into so much potential trouble. We had crossed the park and reached the road. We were only looking forward. At least, I was doing so. I didn't see any car lights coming down the road. If I'd been mistaken or if someone had forgotten to turn their headlights on, I'd probably be dead by now.

We reached the opposite side. I could see the street lights reflected on the small puddles. The chances of one of us slipping and landing on our backs in a puddle was very high. Turning left from the left side of the road, we continued to run. We didn't look behind or talk; all I could hear was our heavy breathing. Eric was one and half meters in front of me, and running as fast as he could. He was opening his legs extensively and his heels were touching his butt. With moccasins on his feet, he had it more difficult than me, but we hadn't had time to think about the pros and cons of particular footwear.

Saying "Here!" he turned right from the end of the road. At that time, my fear came true. My left foot slid and, like a talentless ice dancer, I continued to slide on my palms and knees and then, when "out-of-gas," fell over.

My heart was beating very fast and I felt dizzy. My nausea suddenly reappeared, as fast as a bright idea, and I couldn't control myself and threw up.

Eric saw me, turned back and approached. He grabbed my shoulder.

'Get up, hurry!'

'Enough, I can't run any more...'

'C'mon, there isn't much left. We'll take a cab soon. Get your ass up. Come on.'

He pushed his head under my armpit and we ran, him half-carrying and half-dragging me, till we saw a vacant cab waiting under the street light.

He opened the back door and threw me inside. I lay on the seat. Eric kicked my legs inside, got in and closed the door. He uttered his address.

The taxi driver asked whether he had kidnapped me. Eric said that I was a diabetic and he needed to give me an injection to me at his place, so we had to hurry.

The driver took him seriously enough to start the engine and begin driving, but he was still suspicious and frequently checked on us from the mirror.

'As far as I know,' the driver said, 'diabetics don't drink this much....

He seems to have drunken too much tonight, right?'

'His case is a different one,' Eric said, looking outside. I could see the sweat droplets running down his neck.

'Everybody knows what diabetic is. How is his different? What type is his?'

'A type you don't know, okay?'

Eric stared at the man. The driver understood that he must not ask any more questions, and he didn't open his mouth from then on.

When we reached Eric's, we realised that the door wasn't locked. He made me sit on the stairs.

'Wait here.'

He entered the apartment as silently as he could. I heard him talking to someone inside, but I couldn't understand what they were saying. Continuing to talk, he returned to me.

'Danielle. It's okay,' he said.

'Were we already afraid?' I said.

But he didn't reply. He picked me up by my arms and pushed me inside. Danielle came up to us.

'V, what happened? You're a mess! What did you do? Are you okay, V? Gosh, did you fall down?'

When I felt the panic in her voice, the shitty reality of our situation echoed in my mind.

'Nothing happened. There's no problem. Let's bring him to the bathroom,' Eric said. 'Or, you bring him some clean stuff to wear, and I'll take him to the bathroom.'

Eric pushed me under the shower and turned on the tap. I was startled by the cold water and quickly recalled what had happened over the last couple of hours (yes, like a film strip). I was still feeling dizzy and sick. The cold-shower operation enabled me to better understand how I'd been drinking like a teenager.

Danielle said that she had brought some clean clothes. Eric took them in and left them on the sink.

'Come and put these on.'

There were grazes on my hands and knees, but neither of us cared about them.

As I approached the sitting room, I heard Danielle and Eric talking passionately.

Eric said, "I am such a person. Accept it, or—"

When I entered, they quit talking. Danielle stood up and hugged me.

'Are you alright V? What happened, tell me....'

'I said, nothing happened!' Eric said.

He was looking at me from the sofa where he was lying. He'd changed his clothes. When he caught my eye, he started to laugh.

'When was the last time you vomited from too much alcohol, you cocky drunk,' he said.

'I still feel dizzy. But not because of the alcohol. Your "perfect" plan also made me drunk.'

'What plan?!' Danielle said. 'You two are hiding something. What did you do? Tell me! Now!' She sat on a chair next to me.

'Oh, enough, Dani. We didn't do anything,' Eric said. 'Stop asking over and over again. James asked for a bit of trouble, and we answered his call, that's all. What's wrong with that?' He was still laughing.

'What?!'

'What? He annoyed V, so I got annoyed too. As a counter-move, we did something to bother him. That's all.'

'Don't, Eric! What did you do? I mean, really, are you guys in trouble?'

'Fuck that! What trouble?'

'You know... James.... You said...'

Eric didn't like Danielle's insistent questions and comments. He had been laughing when he spoke to me, but his face fell when he talked to Danielle. I felt that, any moment now, he'd utter some words that would hurt Danielle. I wanted to prevent it.

'It's nothing important, Dani, relax,' I said. 'We became flies in his delicious food, that's all—'

'Flies?' Eric said. He laughed. 'That's good, man, really good....'

'And? Please, V, tell me. What happened?'

'Nothing, calm down. Really nothing. We broke the windows at the back of Nico, the ones facing the back garden.'

'What?! You... broke windows?! Quit talking shit, please.'

'Yes, we broke them. See, nothing important.'

We looked at each other, and Eric started to laugh again.

Danielle looked at both of us with a serious face – of course, not laughing.

'What does that mean? Are you aware of what you're saying? Please say that you're just making fun of me. I'm begging you, guys...'

She was looking at us desperately.

'No, we did it. Really. No big deal,' I said.

'No big deal, Dani,' Eric said.

She stood up angrily and turned to Eric. 'You are one stupid son of a bitch, Eric! You're doing your best to make V a person like you! You're not kids, for God's sake. This.... How stupid.... Crazy.... It's childish nonsense! What does it mean? I can't believe you...'

'This is none of your business,' Eric said. 'NONE of your business! We can do WHATEVER we like!' He straightened up on the sofa.

Danielle was breathing fast, and no longer speaking. She looked at Eric carefully for some seconds. He looked back at her. Then she turned, took her bag from the table and left the apartment, slamming the door after her.

If Eric had really been about to marry Danielle, would he have become as angry as he just did, under the same circumstances?

He tilted his head back, leaned back on the sofa and groaned.

'Stupid!' he said.

'Why are you so wound up? Why is she so nervous? Calm down. Your stress affects her in a bad way...'

'I'm gonna sleep. Wait, I'll bring a blanket for you,' he said and then went to his room. He came back with a blanket moments later.

'Won't we talk about how we did it?' I said. 'The most enjoyable part should be the conversation we have after all we've done. Am I wrong?' My aim was to calm him down.

'We can do that later,' he said. He went back to his room but, before closing his door, he turned back. 'Dream sexy dreams tonight. We've earned it.'

I didn't reply. I lay down on the sofa and turned off the standing lamp next to me. I hugged the blanket and closed my eyes. My ears were whistling, and I still felt dizzy. Everything around me was shaking and drawing circles in the dark. I felt something sour in my stomach. Sometimes I felt as if I was relaxing, but it was deceiving, because the next moment I would be reminded of my vomiting, drunken condition, and I'd remember doing silly things like a young boy. I wanted to forget all of it. I would sacrifice all I had in order to fall asleep at that moment.

However, while I was struggling to go to sleep, lying on my friend's sofa in his sitting room and wearing his T-shirt and shorts, I suddenly recalled M – that I wanted to be next to her. She wouldn't get angry about what we'd done; she'd try to understand me. She'd understand me completely.

I reached out for my cell phone. There was a message. I was excited and straightened up at once. Was this M, surprising me? Could the world and all the energies on it have prepared this magic for me?

No. The world was a spherical bastard, as it had always been.

It was from Gary.

"I didn't say anything."

I couldn't decide whether that was a good or a bad message. What would happen to the girl? Or to the baby? Or to Amy? It was clear that the following day wouldn't be calm, either.

As these thoughts crossed my mind over and over, I turned to my left and right, watching the ceiling spin over me. Then my cell phone rang. I was excited again, and hopeful about the world and the energy, till I saw the caller.

Surprise: James was calling. I straightened up. The phone and I looked at each other. He didn't quit; he rang again and again.

Eric opened his door. 'Either answer that damn thing or turn it off!'

'James is calling...'

'What? James? Why is that son of a bitch calling now? Answer it and swear at him!'

'Fuck that. Don't talk nonsense.... What would I say?'

He started walking towards me.

'What would you say, V? You could say, "Fuck off, motherfucker! Don't you know the time?" And blah-blah.... Fucks, shits, etcetera.'

I couldn't do it.

Eric was next to me. 'Give it to me...,' he said, looking at me and extending his hand. If he answered it, he could push James back, because he had a gift for gab – he was a lawyer. But it would be impossible to explain to James why Eric had answered my phone. Therefore, I did it.

'Hello?'

'If you're in this shit, V, it's gonna be so bad, boy... so bad. I won't show mercy.'

'What? What are you talking about? Are you insane, James? Do you know the time?'

'Shut up! I don't have any evidence right now, but I feel it, V, from my gut. I smell bad things.... If you're involved in this, I'll fight you, too. Believe me, boy.'

He hung up.

'What did the bastard say? Why didn't you shout at him!'

'He says he feels it—'

'He feels what?'

'Tonight.... He smells bad things, he says. And if I have anything to do with what happened, he'll fight me, too...'

'Fight my ass! We should have beaten him! Broken his neck. His ugly nose at least. If we'd broken his mouth and nose, he couldn't have called you.'

Then Eric turned his back and walked towards his room, swearing.

I lay back down on the sofa and closed my eyes. In order to wake up from this nightmare, I had to fall asleep.

Wrathday
18 SEPTEMBER

WHEN I OPENED my eyes, Eric was standing by the sofa.

'Wassup yo!' he said.

'Get out!'

'Rappin' deepa, ho! Dani is on her way here. For breakfast, you'd better get up.... Now!'

I straightened on the sofa. I felt as if my head had become a big globe and its northern hemisphere was moving more slowly than the southern one.

We woke up into a sunny autumn day. Eric had opened the window shades so we could gain some of the hope we needed from the sun. I stood up and went to the bathroom, attempting to find my balance.

I looked into the mirror. Strangely, I didn't feel any regret regarding the previous night's business. I didn't feel tired, either. I felt a bit dizzy because of the adverse effects of the alcohol, but I believed that would disappear after I had some coffee and breakfast.

At that moment, it was impossible to reverse what we'd done. There would be a big fight, but it wasn't clear who was gonna win. Maybe someone would help me, or maybe I'd be fighting all by myself. I didn't know for sure what would happen. The only thing I knew was that I wouldn't give up dealing with this knot (whose reason for occurring I still didn't understand). I wouldn't allow any injustice to happen to anyone, or close my eyes to anyone's attempts to gain possession of something through brute force.

The new day came with this determination tattooed on my heart. It stuck to my mind like an inspiration (or command) that I'd been bestowed in my dream.

After taking a shower, I went to the sitting room wearing the clean trousers and shirt Eric had given me. He was staring at me from the sofa.

'Did the bastard call you again last night?' he asked.

'Nope.... To tell you the truth, I should have called him back and said, "What the fuck is going on? Why are you calling me at the dead of night?" But I was in a terrible condition and didn't have enough strength at the time—'

'You should've...'

'But he might have become suspicious if I had...'

'You should say it, though. We should also tell him what we've done, and drill it into his head that if he causes any more trouble, we won't fucking take it.'

'Oh Eric, don't start, again. How can we tell him we broke his windows.'

'Nothing's gonna happen. They've committed more serious crimes —'

'They?'

'That son of a bitch and Lori. Every day. He's too afraid to make a move against us.'

'He isn't afraid of anything. He can't think properly, but surely he won't let us get away with this.'

'What will he do?'

'Dunno.'

'Then we'll defend ourselves...'

'Okay, can we please quit this nonsense, just for now? Have you and Dani made up?'

Eric turned his head to the side and looked outside. He grunted and didn't give an answer.

I couldn't understand why he was behaving so depressed and uninterested in the matter.

'What's the problem? You get mad when the girl speaks, and even more when her name is mentioned. You lose your temper...'

'I don't feel that Danielle is the one I want to share my whole life with.'

I hadn't expected such a definite and clear answer. They had been dating for about eight months, and I'd never seen them unhappy or depressed. They always seemed to love each other and take pleasure from spending time together; it could easily be seen in their eyes. If I were to use typical magazine language, I'd define them as "a match made in heaven." They looked so harmonious, as if they had sex every day and didn't spend even their shortest free time alone. They were a clean-cut match, like they'd been taken out of a film frame.

At least, I saw them like this. I couldn't understand what disturbed Eric's feelings, or which behaviour of Danielle had so strongly affected his point of view on their relationship.

I didn't ask any more questions. It wasn't the time. Danielle would arrive soon, and our talk would be left half-finished, and this could spark a depressive mood in Eric again. I could see how badly his mood reflected onto Danielle and charged her with negative energy. I kept silent.

He turned his head and looked at me. We didn't talk for a while. He felt that I understood him – as usual.

'I don't know what's lacking between us. When I think of it or deal with each part independently, I can't see what's wrong. But... but I'm sure. If I continue in this relationship, I won't be happy. I'm sure...'

'But you're making marriage plans, for God's sake. What's the point? Why, man?'

'That's the problem; I don't make any of our fucking plans! She does.'

'Then why don't you tell her? If she knows anything about your reluctance, she won't breed so much hope in herself, or behave so hastily.... She's about to print the invitation cards, Eric. Why are you waiting?'

He turned his head to look outside again. The sun fell upon his cheeks.

The door rang. Reacting more quickly than Eric, I went to open it. I didn't want Danielle to see him in such despair.

'Oh, you've woken up the glass-breaking kiddo?' she said. She was wearing her poisonous perfume – again.

'Yes, I have,' Eric shouted, 'and I'm very hungry. What you got?'

'Yes, he has...,' I said.

Danielle went inside. Eric hugged her as if nothing had happened the previous night. Both of them were calm. I went to the kitchen with the bags so as to leave them alone.

While dealing with the breakfast, I recalled Eric's words. Did he too miss the past? That is to say, had he begun to think about Amy again? I knew they had decided to remain friends after their relationship and that they still met each other often, but my inner voice had always suggested that friendship was not the only thing that remained after their love. If Eric compared Danielle with Amy, and searched in Danielle for things similar to what Amy had, it was natural for him to be disappointed. That's not to say I thought Amy superior to Danielle, but they were two very different women. If Eric dived into such thoughts, it was inevitable that he would find himself in a tight corner.

On the other hand, I started to wonder how Amy would respond to this mind-set, if indeed it existed, and whether she knew about the "trouble" Gary was having. He hadn't informed her about his affair or the baby, but he would have to someday. On that day, the person to whom Amy would first resort to for friendship would certainly be Eric. If Eric had such a psychology, synchronously, their love would revive out of its ashes.

I felt as if I were being surrounded by more and more dynamite day by day. Like, each stick was connected to another so that, when one exploded, all the others would explode too, one by one – and I was right in the middle of them. The funny part was that I had no direct connection to any of these things happening around me. Had I been unconsciously looking for trouble, to have so quickly found myself a bunch of quality stuff? I had tried to behave like a responsible person and solve inter-family problems, and I had taken precautions in order to prevent conflicts among our "loving" family members. But what I'd come to learn was that everything only ever became more and more complex. How talented I was to accomplish this!

The three of us had an enjoyable breakfast – there was no sign of a post-war struggle. Eric started to smile, and so did Danielle. It was obvious that the peace and calmness they had was temporary, but it was still perfect to see them happy for that moment. The sun was shining over our table. On these days of autumn, sunshine was like a birthday present given late, but which still made one happy for not being forgotten.

After breakfast, I left them alone and went home. In order to remove the evidence of the previous night – vomit and mud – I put my clothes into the washing machine, and then watched the water pouring into the chamber and mixing with the detergent. The absolute sureness that the clothes would end up clean created an elusive relaxation in me. I wished all seven of us could be cleaned in that machine, like those dirty clothes.

I stepped back from the machine and walked away in order not to drive myself crazy; that was the last thing I needed at that time.

I put on a shirt and jeans, and then prepared a strong black coffee for myself. On a sunny Saturday like this one, the best thing to do would be to spend time with M – just an ordinary getaway, without big detailed plans. Everything I'd done felt good and right with her. I came to realise that I missed her so much. Even a terrible love poem written by a professional urologist/amateur poet could make me cry at that moment.

I spent time at home until the afternoon. I read a few pages of a book and then had a nap. When lazy clouds began to appear, I had to turn on my table lamp. It was interesting that I had not yet been disturbed by James' threats or Amy's reproaches. Actually, I wanted to talk to Gary, but instead I waited for him to call me. I had no idea about how things were with him and Amy, so I wanted to avoid making the first step.

About half an hour later, I admitted defeat and decided to call him. I figured that if I could at least hear his voice, I could guess about the rest and act accordingly.

They were at the atelier, together. That sounded like good news, at least for now.

'So, what are you doin'?' I asked. 'Will you be working all day?'

'Yeah, but if you like, drop by, and, you know, we can have a chat or something....'

I accepted his offer and went to the atelier. Amy was still there. She seemed calmer and more relaxed compared to the previous day. This was a good thing.

'Do you have any good news for us, V? Surprise me,' Amy said and smiled.

'Actually, I don't know what's been happening recently. No, really.... What's the procedure for revealing a will? I want to get this problem over with somehow... and as fast as we can.'

'As James is also involved in this,' she said, 'we can expect the problem to be resolved one way or another soon. Did he try to warn you or threaten you too? You know, tell you to tread carefully and mind your "own" business and stuff...?'

'Oh, please don't do this,' Gary said. 'I can't even bear hearing his name. Let's change the subject. Let's keep ourselves away from that bastard.'

'What do you mean?' Amy said. 'Would you prefer to leave everything in his hands? Why are you talking that way, Gary? We can't avoid him; on the contrary, we must confront him!'

(The sleeping giant had woken up?)

'Come on,' Gary said, 'I don't want to deal with all this.... Can't we just leave it behind, Amy? You should just drop it. I don't care about what they're doing, and I won't care in the future, either—'

'NO! No, Gary! I want what I deserve, and I'll get back what's already mine,' Amy said. She was still determined. She didn't intend to give up at all.

'Calm down, darling,' Gary said. 'You can't gain anything by fighting with them. Not with Lori or James, for God's sake. I.... Look, Amy, I don't wanna—'

'Shut up, Gary!' she said. 'Your sister might be able to tyrannise you, but she can't do that to me. She's gonna learn this, and you're gonna learn it as well.'

We were all silent for a moment. I didn't want to get involved in their quarrel because I felt there were dimensions in their tension that I had no idea of. It wouldn't be proper to take a side, or explain my own opinion.

'Would you like a coffee, V?' Gary said.

'Well..., yes... I'd like one....'

'I'm gonna go get some fresh air. I need to unwind,' Amy said and left.

'Wow..., you drove her mad,' I said. 'Congrats.'

'Yes, I saw.'

'What happened yesterday? Is this overtime or what?'

'Nothing. We talked, and she told me what James said.'

'And you? What did you say?'

'I said he was lying.'

'Did she believe you?'

'Yes. I mean, I think so.'

'What about now? What's gonna happen?'

'I-don't-know, V, okay? Stop firing back-to-back questions at me, please.... I feel too tired to think about anyone, or anything. I'm very tired.... Please.'

Gary always seemed to let everything slide. It seemed impossible for him to make any decision and apply it. But the situation in which he was involved required exactly the opposite. He had to talk to the pregnant woman, and to Amy, and try to solve the problem. He didn't have the right to be tired when time was flying. He was talking as if his spirit had become numb.

'Gary, look. Listen to me. If you continue to behave like this, you'll eventually lose control of your life, and it might turn into something you can't put back into order any more. You have to do something.... Now.'

'I can't, V. I can't do anything. I don't feel like it. I don't have any power to take action now. Please understand. You at least... you must understand me, V. Don't do this to me....'

That was classical Gary, this attitude towards life. He didn't have the time or strength to deal with any crucial matter. He never had – not even to deal with problems that resulted from his own behaviours, like the pregnant secret lover.

Gary had always had the same character and it hadn't changed throughout the years at all; he postponed everything, especially when he was required to think about a subject he didn't like, act during hard times, form plans, solve problems, or make decisions. If he lived alone, his life would be destined to end with a heart-attack, after he'd become buried under increasing troubles and their corresponding stress. He was a lucky man to have had our father, Amy and even me around him. He'd always been supported by us, in every way.

Years ago, before I was there, my father had called Gary in and told him he would give him a try at working at the company. He'd hoped Gary would get used to working with him and that he'd like business life. As a result of my father's hopes and pressures, Gary spent seventeen (seventeen!) days in total at the company. But he couldn't bear any more than that, and nor could my father. The final day had been a complete disaster, a very foreseeable one.

During those seventeen days Gary had worked at the company, he hadn't been able to carry out any task – big or small – in the proper way. He'd accepted every task my father gave him without objection, and yet he was unable to accomplish any one of them. My father realised his incompetence and warned him once or twice, but that didn't change anything for the better.

Finally, he talked to Gary face to face and told him he was giving him a last chance: he asked whether Gary could help him with a very, *very* important meeting. Gary said he would take advantage of this last chance and promised to do his best.

When Gary told me about this conversation some time later, he said he hadn't wanted to destroy my father's last piece of trust in him, and so he'd answered in the way he thought my father wished him to. Gary promised to help him, but only reluctantly, without a true desire to provide any help at all.

What my father had asked for wasn't actually a complicated thing. He was attending a meeting with a new potential customer and wanted Gary to carry out the icebreaker presentation about the company. This kind of meeting was something my father had done thousands of times before and was very good at. Therefore, it was impossible for Gary to cause the meeting to be unsuccessful. He couldn't spoil anything, because my father could jump in if something went wrong and solve the problem in a flash.

As far as I can remember, Gary had been excited about the task, but his excitement didn't emerge into reasonable preparation, and he didn't pay his role the attention it required. My father had asked him about his preparations every night, and Gary would always say something like, "It's not one hundred percent ready yet..., but it's going good. It will be awesome; don't worry, Dad...."

Even though my father hadn't fully trusted that Gary would be successful, he never quit motivating Gary or acting as if he had complete faith in him.

Gary's involvement in the "real" business left everyone in the family feeling unsettled for the five to six days leading up to the meeting. On the last night before the big day, during dinner, my father claimed that he'd won Gary's heart in the end, and that Gary wouldn't even think of leaving the company after he had experienced his first meeting and "the joy – no! the *pleasure* – of ruling the room." My father was happy and proud. Gary was dull and distant, as always. He'd shared in only a little of passion in the air that night.

My father had some other stuff to deal with before the meeting, so he and Gary decided to meet at the boardroom where the meeting would be held. Gary dressed in his black pinstripe suit, and left home in the morning. Everyone waited to hear some news, curious to know how he was going to do and whether he would want to be a part of the company as my father expected (or wished).

In the end, we didn't get the chance to evaluate the result of the meeting, because Gary never showed up there. He disappeared without informing anyone, and my father managed the thing all by himself.

When my father returned to his office, frustrated, he found a short note on his desk. Gary had gone to the office instead of to the meeting and had left a note, which read, "Dad, I want to become a painter. I don't want to work here. I don't wanna work with you, either. I'm begging you, please, understand me."

That same night, all hell broke loose at home. My father said whatever he could to kill Gary with his words. In reaction, Gary lost his temper and began trying to knock down the shelves in my father's study. He managed to tip one over and was almost crushed when it fell. We all tried to break up the fight and calm them both down.

After that day, the relationship between my father and Gary was never the same. Both of them experienced that night again and again whenever they looked into each other's eyes, and hence none of us could get over it. I don't think their love as father and son died, but the heartbreak caused that night was never mended.

My father wouldn't talk to Gary for weeks afterwards, and even up until his death he never asked Gary about his art or told Gary about his own work. But he didn't ask for his shares back either. He'd never believed Gary would earn enough money to sustain his lifestyle, and so, in a sense, he'd always intended to guarantee Gary's future.

I think Gary had known this from the very beginning: that he could manage his life without having to work at any time. He'd known my father that well.

I'm sure that whenever my father thought something positive about Gary, his heart was probably penetrated with a gloomy feeling. A dagger strike coming from a person he'd never expected it from.

Something that wouldn't kill, but would always hurt.

Those hectic days had also created a negative effect on Gary's relationship with other members of the family. Not so with me, because I could understand him, even though I found his style of quitting wrong. If I'd had the chance, I would have done anything to prevent Gary from failing to turn up at that meeting.

Gary might regret having behaved like that now, but unfortunately the past is the past. It would always remain broken and would always hurt when the sorrow rained on him, in his mind and in his heart.

Things were different according to Lori's perspective, however. She thought of that day as a betrayal rather than just disrespectful to my father. She wasn't a person who could just forgive a betrayal, especially not when it took place among family members. Not only could she not forget, she'd always wanted to punish Gary for doing it. If it had been possible, she would've punished him forever.

Gary had always respected Lori because she was always there when my father needed her and had taken her job seriously, but Gary and Lori never showed their love for each other at all. I saw them hugging for the first time in many years on the morning after my father died.

Gary used to like me, before. Maybe still. He knew that I didn't judge him for his perception of life or reality, and that I tried to understand his conflict with my father. We both valued intellectual assets more than physical ones, and we both tried to earn our living via our passion for art – something Lori could not accept. But it was conceptually true that we couldn't have sustained our life without our share dividends. Maybe I could have managed, but Gary definitely couldn't. How noble, graceful and consistent Gary and I had been; we hadn't wanted to work at the company but had surely benefited from its income.

As Eric was very close to me, he also became unavoidably close to Gary. They never became very intimate, but always knew of each other – about each other's faults, attitudes, happy times and sad times.

Also, more than this, they shared another emotion, reluctantly and apart from the others: Love.

Gary had met Amy because of Eric. Gary had been there at the same table, in the same room, at the same garden when Eric and Amy loved each other very much (the beginning), got used to each other (the middle) and thought that they were no good anymore (the end). I hadn't felt that Gary was interested in Amy at all then. Nor Amy in Gary. They hadn't shown any clues that they "loved" each other. Moreover, I didn't think they knew each other well enough to be in love. From my point of view, they had no chance together.

But, against all odds, they had started to date surprisingly quickly. When Amy and Eric split up, Gary also split up with his then-girlfriend, whom we all thought he would have married in the near-future. Then, something happened – as if, in a flash, Amy and Gary were spellbound with each other and realised that they got along well.

After a very short while, they got married. All of this rush was difficult for us to comprehend, which resulted in a wave of gossip in the family. Everyone asked each other about the details of this new "burning-love."

Though the details had never captured my interest, I'd often wondered how Eric would deal with the issue and whether our family dinners would still include the same people. I also wondered what Lori thought about all that had happened: Amy, who Eric had once preferred over Lori, had become a member of the family and gained my father's trust, and she would soon start working for the company. Maybe the break-up had made Lori a bit happy – in a womanish way. Then again, it was a mixed-up situation.

Acquiring Gary could be counted as a victory for Amy in the keeping-her-enemy-closer sense ("enemy" may not be the correct word, but Amy and Lori had always tried to keep control of each other; they watched each other's every step, shared smiles over hidden agendas, watched each other warily and everything). Amy was even closer to Lori than she'd been at other times when Eric was in her life. And now she was Lori's relative, on paper, signed with ink.

Amy had managed to move closer to Lori without making any change in her social position at the table where family meetings were held. If we assumed there was a cold war between these two, it was 2-0 to Amy. But nothing was over yet – not till Lori made her move.

Eric had accepted this "love" between Amy and Gary, and the marriage that followed, in a very mature way. Whenever we were alone to talk about this matter, he said that it had been his and Amy's mutual decision to split up; they had burned their bridges, but they would always remain invaluable to each other and hence wanted each other to be happy. He also thought that Amy would be happy with Gary and therefore didn't display any negative attitudes or behaviour towards them.

However, he hadn't attended Lori's marriage ceremony, nor had he attended Amy and Gary's. I'm not sure whether this was intentional or just "how things appeared," as he said. The real thing about those two weddings was that neither woman had the man of their heart standing next to her – not as a guest or as a groom.

Amy had first fallen in love with Eric and spent some happy years with him, and then she married the man before me now, to help her forget her lost love. My interpretation of Gary and Amy's relationship is hidden in the previous sentence. I have never thought that Gary and Amy were really in love – they didn't act or sound like they were. In my opinion, their relationship was based mainly on reason. I don't say it to scorn (or judge) them or their marriage. Even looking at them through an evil lens, a spirit would be unable to find anything sinful about their relationship.

Though they didn't love each other, it was obvious that they were good to each other and had been happy. After they were married, Gary worked more effectively at his office and entered into a more productive period, and Amy began to manage much more at the company than was expected from her. They took a step as two reasonable people who, having already left their younger years behind, did not want to lose any more time in life.

But both had sacrificed passion for the sake of "peace of mind." It was probably the only thing missing in their marriage.

'Is everyone like this?' said Gary. 'I mean, all families? Does everyone just try to tolerate others instead of love them?'

He had uttered the concept that for days I hadn't been able to describe to myself. The answer depended on who I defined as my family. "Tolerate." We used to sit around the same table, eating the same thing, enjoying fun and peace together. All of that was an illusion? Perhaps we had never gathered around a table as a group of people who loved each other. While some were experiencing communication and social relations based on affection, the remaining pairs were practicing only tolerance. In fact, when I turn my mind back and think about those times, I realise that sometimes we couldn't even tolerate each other.

While we all separately created our "real" families by choosing our friends in a conscious way, we could only tolerate those we couldn't choose: those who were family by birth, and of course their tails: whomever they chose as their partners.

'I don't know, maybe it's the same for everyone. This chaos can't be something that has only happened to us. I mean, we can't be such a special family...,' I said.

We laughed.

At that moment, someone knocked on the door of the atelier. Gary stared as if he hadn't been expecting anybody.

He answered the door, and I saw it was the problem who always appeared at the most unexpected times.

'V!' James said. 'So, you're here. How nice to see you, kid. You know what, I've come to complain to your brother about you and that son-of-a-gun friend of yours. Huh! Young ones, Gary. Anyway, how lucky, V, because now you'll hear what I was gonna say about you. Then it won't be a secret, and I'll get the results faster. How nice.'

James walked inside, nearly stepping on Gary, and walked towards me without waiting for any invitation, trying to hide his nerves that were about to burst. Gary, without having a clue what was happening, seemed frozen with shock.

James came eye to eye with me, put his hands on his waist and stared at me, his mouth half open – like he was about to utter the most angry profanity he had in mind.

Gary closed the door, walked over to us, and gazed at James, but with a more nervous attitude than his counterpart. Maybe I should've stared at Gary to complete the "Staring Triangle Installation" show at the painter's atelier.

'Hey, James, what's happened, huh? Why are you in such a hurry? Relax a bit,' Gary said.

James silenced Gary with a hand gesture, still looking at me.

'Don't worry, Gary, I'm here to tell you everything. But you know..., V being here now is like a gift. It's good. So good. Anyway, let's start with you. Let's sit down.'

He hurried over to the table to find a place to sit.

I couldn't keep my temper low when I saw his arrogant, bossy attitude. I stood up and took a few steps towards him.

'James, you're talking too much these days,' I said. 'You're talking to everyone around. Why so talkative lately?'

James couldn't care less about the concept of "family" that he'd created in his own mind. He started to walk towards me again. Seeing that the atmosphere was getting tense, Gary interfered – maybe he didn't want to watch a cock fight.

'Come on, V, calm down,' Gary said. 'Let's talk. Let the man talk, V.'

James turned his back by swinging his head like he was warming it up for a head-butt, and then sat down on a stool in the corner. Gary told me to calm down with his eyes. I sat in my chair.

'Yes, James, we're listening to you,' Gary said.

'I'm a little nervous, Gary,' James said. 'You know, I don't want to do anything bad. I'm actually more angry than nervous. Indeed, angry and disappointed.'

'In whom?'

'Amy, in the first place. Then in him, and then in you. Look, Gary, we've spent a lot of time together. There shouldn't be unease in the family, you know that. We must prevent it. We must do our best—'

'Whenever this guy says "family," I lose my temper,' I said. 'Sorry.' I couldn't tolerate James any longer.

'Shut the fuck up!' he said. He held his index finger out in the direction of my face. I stood up. James also stood up, kicking his stool. I pushed him twice in his chest, and he did the same to me.

As I stumbled backward, Gary got in the way and shouted,

'Enough, James! Hey, enough! V! Go outside, now! I'll handle this, okay? I'll listen to what he has to say. Please, go away, now. Otherwise this could get worse. Come on.' He tried to move me towards the door.

James smoothed his collar, grinning wolfishly, and again showed me his finger.

'You have something to do with what happened last night, V,' James said. 'I feel it. I sense it from your foolish and childish behaviour. If you had the balls, you would tease me like a man. But you can't. Never mind. You'll be made to account for it!'

'Fuck off!' I said. I tried to escape Gary's hands and lunge at James, but Gary held me with all his strength. He dragged me over to the door.

'Please, calm down,' Gary said. 'Please. I'll listen to him first, and then we'll act accordingly, okay? Please leave us alone for the time being.' Touching my back, he directed me towards the stairs.

I went down, but I don't remember how I moved my legs – my anger erased time. I couldn't console myself.

I saw James' car parked in front of the building and wanted to kick it, break all of its windows and puncture his wheels. But I couldn't afford to behave in such a childish manner, not for the second time. The next step should be taken "like a man," as he'd said.

I decided to wait for him outside and settle the score with him in a manly way. If I harmed his car, it would make clear that what happened previous night was my shit – it would be the exact same style of the silly-doing: a high-schooler kind of attack.

I waited there for a while, leaning back on the trunk of his car. I hoped that when he saw me, he'd see this as an invitation to fight.

About forty-five minutes passed, but James didn't appear. As time passed, my anger lost its soul. I grew calmer every second. I knew very well what I'd do when he showed up. I would run towards him and throw a hard and well-directed punch right at the scar on his ugly face. My fading anger and lack of desire to fight would probably save my bones though.

But also, I didn't want to back down. James' attitudes were getting worse from day to day, and in his own vulgar way he was now trying to impose his stupid ideas on everyone else too. I wanted him to understand that I wouldn't allow his nonsense behaviour.

I was looking around with empty eyes, holding these thoughts in my mind, when I heard an anguished voice.

'What are you doing here, V?' Amy said.

'Oh, you.... Hey.... I'm fine. What are you doing here?'

'Don't mirror my question back to me. I didn't ask whether you were fine. I asked what you're doing here – sitting on that son of a bitch's car?'

'This car? Oh, yes.... This.... It's James' car.'

'What the hell is he doing here? Is Gary with him?'

'Well, yes.... Yes, he is. After you left..., he arrived. We quarrelled a bit, you know. I mean, James and me. Gary kicked me out. They're talking now, and I'm waiting for him to come out. I was waiting here in order to give him a punch in his face, but as time has passed I've been thinking it might be unreasonable to fight with him. I've been waiting here for forty-five minutes, now.'

'Forty-five? What has that moron been talking about for forty-five minutes? Why is Gary even allowing him to talk? Why does he listen to him?'

'I don't know. Gary said, "Let's listen to him first and understand what he's saying." Or, something like that. And now he's in the listening phase. The bastard has talked too much, though. He's very talkative these days, you know.'

'I don't believe it, V. What Gary should do is say, "How can you threaten my wife? How can you make up lies about me, you son of a bitch!" and punch James right in his big nose! Why the chatting? There isn't anything to listen to. How can that piece of shit have anything worth saying? He knows Gary will hear him out. But I won't – I'll let him have it!' She started to run towards the building.

I went after her and took hold of her arm.

'Wait, wait, Amy..., listen for a moment. Gary's right. He's spent so long talking to James. Let's first learn what James said. They might make up. I don't know, just wait for a while.... Let's talk to Gary first.'

'Cut the crap, V! Are you losing your mind? They can't "make up," not after his threats against me and his dirty lies. Neither you nor Gary does anything to that fuck-nut, which is what shocks me the most. You don't even punch him! Like... like pussies! You just wait, wait, wait and wait without doing anything.'

I thought a little about whether I should let Amy know of what we'd done the day before, or keep the childish secret to myself. When she saw that I was keeping silent, she freed her arm from mine and started to storm towards the building again. In order to distract her mind and hinder her from going to the atelier, I decided to prove that I wasn't a pussy – at least, not that much.

I caught her hand and pulled her towards the next street.

'What the— Hey, let go of me, V. Hey! HEY!'

While pulling her away, I told her about what we'd done, and suggested it would be best if neither of us were near the car when James came back to it.

'Oh my God, are you silly? What you're telling me is one of the stupidest things I've ever heard! Are you aware of what you've done?'

'Yeah, sort of...'

'It's not less stupid when we consider what that fucking idiot has done to me, or what he's trying to do up in that atelier now, or will do in the future as long as you continue to behave like that. What does it mean, for Christ's sake, breaking the windows?'

'It's a move. Against him.'

'Who benefits from that? How stupid you two are. Oh, boys... and what's even MORE stupid is— You know what? You're just telling me that shit as a justification. "We don't just wait without doing anything. We DID something." I really can't believe you, V.'

She didn't appreciate our efforts.

Then again, I didn't have any reasonable explanation for what we'd done, even though she asked me over and over again. Yes, I accepted that it was silly and childish, but "childish" was better than nothing. It was obvious that we had disturbed him somehow. If there was a battle of nerves, we had contributed to it. Like Eric had suggested, going directly into Nico and attacking James would have been an alternative strategy, but I believed that breaking the windows was more reasonable than having our skulls broken.

'Okay, I can see your point. These days are hard for you. Your father has recently died. I can see it. I'm not a heartless woman. You can talk nonsense if you want – I can understand that. But why didn't Eric prevent this insanity of yours? Why does he follow along with the things you do? I can't understand it at all. He's usually sane.'

'Actually, if it were up to him, we would have gone into the restaurant and attacked James. We'd certainly have had a harsh fight and got beaten up. When I suggested we find an alternative to this, he made the window-breaking plan. It's a small thing but, you know... enough to irritate James. We were like small flies in his delicious food. I must admit I found it far more reasonable than being beaten up—'

'But why did Eric want to attack James out of the blue? What's his problem with James?'

'Out of blue? Why do you say that? He knows what happened – I mean, what James did to you.'

'What?!'

'He also knows how stupid James is. I told him I'd talked to you, and about how that idiot had unsettled us, and hence we had to do something. We were very angry and determined to teach James his place.'

'And for this reason you broke his windows, is that it? Well done. He must have been vee-ry surprised. I'm sure that he learned his lesson. Yeah. He'll be a better person from now on.' She started to laugh.

Actually, her laughter resulted from another thing: she liked that Eric was acting as a chevalier for her. After all those years, after so many days and nights spent separated, Eric was there for her again.

She kept silent for a moment. I was sure that questions – and the answers that favoured her heart – were passing through her mind.

As my aim was to keep Amy away from the atelier until James was gone, I left her free in her daydreams. I imagined that in her mind, she met Eric, and they fulfilled each other's longing. She went back to him. I watched them without saying a word, hardly breathing. Their unspoken words for each other, accumulated over the years, were revealed in a language known only to them. Amy was not with me anymore. Amy was not in the moment anymore.

We walked side by side a little more. No talk, no words. Only the sound of our steps, a gentle wind passing between us from time to time. We left the tension and battle of the previous minutes to the wind of love. The big mass of emotions made us believe that life was worth living, despite people like James, and the concept of money – discovered by men like him.

Our silence was shot dead with my cell phone's ringing.

'What are you doing? Where are you?' said Gary.

'We're out.'

'We? Who's with you?'

'I met Amy after you kicked me out. We're walking around the block now. How about you? Is he gone?'

'Yes, yes, he left. Wait for me there, I'm coming.... Where are you now exactly?'

Gary joined us, and we walked to a park nearby. Amy was still wistful and also very frustrated. It wasn't so clear with whom or over what she was that angry. Her inner world was reflected to the outside in such a mixed way.

Gary told us about his talk with James. James had explained how he'd met with Amy and warned her to keep calm so that nothing would get any more complicated. He also told Gary about the tension he had with me, and about the previous night's window incident. He was sure that I'd been involved, and warned Gary that if he was right, they were now at odds with me. I would be punished for embarrassing him.

'So, what did you say?' I said.

'I said, "V wouldn't become involved in such matters." Of course. I wanted him to stop thinking such nonsense, that you would do such things. What more could I say?'

'So what, you didn't reject the punishing part? That he's gonna "punish" me for embarrassing him, huh? My ass...'

'That isn't important, V. I just pretended not to hear those words, because I was sure of you. I know you wouldn't do those things....'

'Oh, Gary, I can't understand you sometimes – not a bit, man! He's plainly threatening me in front you, and you don't say anything! I don't understand why you're so passive towards him.'

'Passive?'

'Yeah, passive! Any problem with that?'

'What's the point of dragging it out and making everything tenser? That incident doesn't have anything to do with you. So why are you making it an issue? Please, don't become obsessed with details.'

'This... is a very important detail. That man can't just talk however he wants. We all have to put it into that stupid head of his that he can't just utter threats like, "If you do that, this will happen, or I'll do this, do that, blah, blah." He has to KNOW his place. You also need to KNOW that I broke those goddamn windows. YES!'

'What? You broke them? Are you mad, V? What were you hoping to achieve by breaking some windows—'

'Oh God, will you please stop,' I said.

'I mean, what are you? A primary school student or what? Oh, my...'

Same things, again. Why didn't anyone think of the efficiency of being a "fly"?

'At least he's done something, right?' Amy said. 'I mean... they've done something.'

'They? With whom did you do it? Oh... yes, how silly I am. With whom else could you do it anyway...'

'But Gary, they *did something*, see? Something! They didn't idle around but instead tried to unsettle that bastard. They might do a bit more in the next step. They wouldn't just listen to him in a kind and understanding manner, like you did. They would stand up against him.'

'I'll tell you why we did it,' I said. 'That bastard threatened your wife and then wandered around like he was the boss. Indeed, you should be the one to stand up to him and make him hear what you have to say. Instead, he comes to your place, makes you sit down—'

'Nobody made me sit down!'

'And makes you listen what he has to say! And you keep silent and listen to him!'

'I didn't listen to him in silence,' said Gary. 'I said my own things....

You don't know!'

It was obvious that he felt under pressure at that moment. Our expectations of him conflicted with his worldview and his own expectations. We wished for him to behave against his nature, and that could destroy his own perception of life. Or, destroy him. He didn't want to do anything for anyone under these circumstances, even though the people demanding action from him were his wife and brother. Whatever James had done, Gary saw his visit to the atelier as "a kind of effort towards explanation," and it was somehow enough for him. But I knew that James was really in the last phase of showing us, one by one, where we "must" stop. Gary couldn't see this easy truth standing clearly before him.

I tried to tell Gary that Lori might have used James as a hit-man while dealing with the technical details of her master plan, and hence James might be just trying to keep us busy. It was only a guess, but it was much more realistic than anything Gary had come up with.

Actually, it wasn't realistic to think that Lori had appointed James and asked him to behave "shit." It was clear that Lori had directed events how she'd wanted without even considering James. Behaving officiously, James had eagerly created some missions for himself. If Lori somehow learned that James was bossing everyone around, it wouldn't be any good for him, because the word "family" meant different things for Lori, despite how often James mentioned the word as if he were one of us.

The three of us talked about the same issues and same details once again. We became depressed, bored and angry. We shouted at each other and then tried to understand each other. We tried to find a common ground. We produced new ideas about how to behave. Amy and I thought we had to react against James, and also talk to Lori at once to learn what she was doing regarding inheritance issue and what she would do about how rude her husband had become. But Gary believed that any step taken against James would only complicate everything more, and that possibly Lori had already got what she wanted, and so it would mean nothing to talk to her once more. He thought that the best – and actually the only – thing to do was to keep silent and wait for Lori to explain what happened and what would be. After that, we could go to the court and defend our rights legally, if necessary, without any more fighting or heartbreak.

'Money isn't worth any more struggle,' he said. 'It isn't worth dealing with someone like James. Understand that. Let him alone with his rudeness and shallowness. We should just remain aware of what kind of person he is and keep him out of our lives. That would be enough for him, enough punishment.'

'Gary, would you please come back to the real world from wherever the hell you are,' Amy said. 'For God's sake! What you're saying is bullshit! Total bullshit! Please say that you're joking – I'm begging you. Please say that isn't what you're really thinking...'

'No, what I'm saying is not bullshit. It's the truth. It's what I think.'

'Gary, you talk like you're living in a fantasy world,' I said. 'I can't make sense of what you're trying to say. Really. You're saying – as far as I can comprehend it – that we need to keep silent for the sake of "peace and wisdom," and protect our honour and pride, but that while we do so James can display dishonour and vulgarity in whichever way he wants. How can you ask us to keep silent against this? How can we live without bringing him and Lori to account for what they've done? How can we disregard this injustice?'

'Because it's unsolvable, V. They are the powerful ones, not us. All the cards are in their hands; we're just their tools. We have no choice but to abide by what they say. This is not an issue of honour. We simply haven't chosen their path, that's all. This aggressiveness is their gun, and we don't have one. We can't go into combat with them under these circumstances. We'll be defeated at the very beginning. So the best thing would be to stop—'

'Gary, shut up!' Amy said. 'Shut-the-fuck-up! NOW! Enough! I don't wanna listen to you and your stupid ideas. How can you be so submissive and display such an abiding attitude? Which planet are you on? What kind of a person are you? Stop being lazy and take some action! Open your ears, eyes and mind, and wake up! For yourself... if not, for me. I'm begging you... before it's too late, please wake up!'

Before Gary could answer, Amy left us there, as if escaping for the second time that day. I was alone with Gary again.

He seemed very tired. The stress of recent days had caused him to lose his way. Before, he had been trying to avoid facing his problems, but now he had to deal with them all at once, and in detail. Pressure made him see his problems as bigger than they really were. He took a deep breath, looked trapped. I put my hand on his shoulder.

'Don't worry, Gary. We'll get rid of all this. Together. Don't worry.'

'How? Everything has come to a deadlock. It seems impossible to knock all these problems down. I mean, our problems aren't going to go away until someone – or more than one person – gets hurt. I know it. That's the only thing I can think about now.'

'Things can't get worse than they already are, right? We'll find some balance somewhere. Pull yourself together. Sometime later, our situations will be reversed, and we'll have the advantage. You'll see. Believe it.... We must have some hope, bro.'

He smiled. 'Your words remind me of the movies, V, a character talking in such a hopeful way when the tragedy is at zenith.... It's difficult though. Life isn't like the movies – it's more difficult.'

'If it's difficult, we can act accordingly. We'll KO our problems, trust me. Hey, how about taking a few steps?'

'Like, walking, you mean?'

'Yeah, walking, man. C'mon, get your booty up. Let's walk some. I'm bored. We shouldn't just spend the whole day here. Let's go somewhere else...'

I don't know why I didn't suggest that we visit Lori, me and him together. Everything would've been easier if the three of us had come together and talked. We might have put everything in order in just a flash. We might now understand each other better and be able to put our egos aside. But, our meeting hadn't happened. If we were sly foxes for once, we'd talk. But neither Gary nor Lori had thought of getting together to solve our issues.

Not even my walking-talking idea with Gary worked, as he refused to join me for the following part of the day and returned to his atelier, mentioning a "need" to be alone.

I didn't know what to do. While walking towards my car, I decided that talking to Lori (again) was the most reasonable plan. James' involvement in matters, and his insistence on driving us mad, were not good signs for how the following days would play out. The cat wouldn't be able to pass through the vases without touching any of them – some would get broken.

I would have called Lori and suggested we meet some place where James was unlikely to drop by, but I didn't want to avoid him. If he was going to be there, let him be. I was determined to say whatever I wanted, even if it clashed with that monster's plans. Maybe he'd perform some irrational nastiness in front of Lori, which would work in my favour. Indeed, I was already sure that Lori was aware of his clear-cut stupidity, ill-manners and poor behaviour. My inner voice told me that James' days at that house would end in a short time.

When I got to Lori's home, I found she was alone.

'I'm sorry. I mean, for last night,' she said.

'If I should, I can also apologise to you. Cool with me. I must say, I'm very sorry for how things got so out of hand.'

'I know. Come here...,' she said and hugged me. It made me feel good, and more than that, comforted. I had experienced so many complicated and intense emotions recently, and felt so tired. Lori's sincerity brought me all the peace that I needed, even though it was only temporary.

She looked me in the eyes and tidied my hair. Then she kissed my right eyelid, like I was a small kid, like she'd done more than thirty years ago. She hugged me again. I felt her head shaking, and heard her snuffling. I didn't say a word and left her alone with her tears. She was like a victorious but wounded warrior. Still beautiful, and there was not any bit of difference in her usual grace and posture. I was proud of her.

'You won't do wrong, Lori. You don't make mistakes... I know you....'

She touched my face with the edge of her ring finger. She was both smiling and crying.

'I don't, do I?' she said and smiled. 'But I'm your older sister; I can either love or slap, whichever I want.'

'Yeah, absolutely. You're right. I'm sorry,' I said and smiled.

She stood up and walked towards the garden. I followed her.

Outside, we stood side by side and stared at the river. The sky was dark-grey again, as if it was going to snow. Human beings, who were the protagonists of their lives while we just considered them walk-ons, were out on their boats, enjoying what the day brought them.

'Cold, fresh air. I don't want anything else these days,' she said. 'Just coming here and breathing this cold, fresh air all by myself. That's all I need.'

'I can't even think of what should I be doing to relax,' I said. 'Can you imagine that? I've become so depressed and driven away from one side to another that I can't think of what will do me good. I feel as if I have been eternally poisoned.'

'It seems that we've all been poisoned, doesn't it? All together. We seem to be waiting for someone to come and clean our poisoned blood. Who will come, hmm? Mr Kushner?'

We kept silent and continued to watch the river flow. The waves hooked my mind. We listened to the deep peaceful hum of the silence, even though it only lasted a moment.

'How are you coping with missing him?' she said.

'Missing who? Dad? Well, I miss him, of course. Very much.... If he was alive, he wouldn't allow all this chaos. He would rebuke everyone and settle it in just two minutes.'

She looked at me, into my eyes. She bowed her head a little and leaned towards the cold steel barrier between her and the river.

'You miss her. You miss her very much. It's in your voice. In your eyes. But have you called her and told her about... you know, Father's death?'

At that time, a thrill started to conquer my being. A load of chilly cold waters started to flow from my feet towards my torso. They made a pit stop at my neck. I looked at her. Then I took solace in watching the river again. My heart was beating very quickly. Did she really understand it from my eyes, or my voice, or had my card reached M? Had M somehow talked to Lori? No, that was against all odds.

'Why haven't you called her?' she said.

Lori was torturing me gently.

'I wanted to... but I couldn't.... I dialled her number, but I couldn't press the green button. I drove to her house, but I just parked outside and watched the light from her window. I looked at the streets where her feet have walked. But I couldn't call her.'

'She loved you very much. Very much.'

She looked at me again. 'I wish it hadn't ended the way it did. You should have stopped her...'

'Okay, but why don't you wish that she didn't go away at all? Is it only my fault?'

She smiled and then took a deep breath. Silence again. Then, she hugged her cardigan, which was a sign that she was about to talk about something serious. It had always been her sign.

'Don't do this,' she said. 'Don't... please, don't do it anymore. Please, appreciate each moment you live, each step and each word in your life, V. Don't you see that you're a grown man right now...? Your adolescent days have come to an end. Say goodbye, wave goodbye. You've become a nice mature man—'

'Wow... look at what Lori says...'

'Don't behave like you're still a high school kid. When you have trouble, face the realities. Accept your faults bravely. Try to correct and repair them, or at least the ones you can handle. Don't repeat them over and over again—'

'Oh, c'mon, Lori.... Are you really one to tell me this?'

'Yes, I am. Accept it: say, "I lost her. She slipped from my hands. I didn't want this, but she did. I lost her." Accept it, and try to correct it if you want. Search and find the power in yourself to correct it. If you can't, then try to live with your losses. This is also a wisdom: to accept, to welcome bitter situations... when required....'

I felt as if my mind was being washed with her voice.

'I sent her a card,' I said.

She started to laugh without looking at me. She was staring at the current. Her hair streamed from time to time because of the wind. The sound of her laughter increased.

'You sent her a card?' she said and continued to laugh.

I didn't reply. The strength of her laughter decreased, and when she turned to me there remained only a sweet smile on her face.

'V, you were a very clever boy in the past. What has happened to you?'

It was my turn to laugh. She smiled.

'I don't know, Lori. Maybe it's because of love...'

She hugged me. She leaned her head over mine.

'Look,' she said, 'do you see how beautiful the flowing water is there...? Very dark, but promising. Its essence and flow include hope and life in itself. It's obvious. If it didn't exist, didn't flow in front of me every day, I'd probably die.'

'Don't talk shit, please. It's not you.'

She hugged me harder.

Then we heard the grating and impatient sound coming from behind: 'You, V, oh boy.... You aren't fed up with getting beaten,' James said.

We turned, and he grinned wolfishly. 'Don't worry, it'll all be taken care of....' He approached Lori. 'Honey,' he said, and kissed her.

Lori was standing motionless like a sculpture.

'So, what are you up to?' he said. 'Is there a chance that V has been telling you what improper things he's been doing, hmm?'

It was clear that it would be a long night. We would settle accounts; I felt it. I turned my back to him and let my mind dive back into the current, without caring about what he said.

'Calm down, James. What's this? Why aren't you at the restaurant?' Lori said.

'Can't I come to my house whenever I want? I had something to do and hence dropped by. What's wrong with that?'

Lori also turned her back to him and looked back at the river. The dark colour we'd been enjoying moments before had become even darker.

'Guys, were you chatting about these problems the family has been dealing with?' he said. 'I wonder whether V has told you *everything*, Lori? There shouldn't be any secrets kept, boy.'

We were still within the cold war process. I turned to him. 'No, "boy," I haven't yet told Lori that you threatened Amy....'

Lori turned and looked between him and me, trying to understand what was going on. Before she could ask, James started talking.

'I was soft on her – softer than I needed to be.'

'What?!' Lori said. 'Amy? What's going on? James, what are you talking about?'

'Nothing, dear..., nothing. I just warned the silly Amy to leave things alone, but she didn't like it and only got worse. You know her kind. She started to create some new lies, but I'd rather talk about them with you alone, later. After V has gone. Let's first talk about V's adventures.'

'Watch your mouth!' I said.

He took two steps towards me. 'Achtung, boy, I'm warning you. Don't forget where you are right now. You have no chance any more. You'll tell Lori what the fuck you did yesterday, every little bit....'

He was so wound up that the veins in his neck were visible. We were like two mad street dogs, on the alert and ready to attack each other at the slightest provocation. Realising this, Lori attempted to take control.

'No, V should not forget where he is,' she said. 'He's at his sister's home. James, would you behave? Get over this aggressive posturing. Go and drink something. You know better than me how you can relax yourself. Go, and don't spoil the moment.'

James continued with his implications. 'Yes, I know, Lori. I know lots of other things too... lots of things. Don't you worry.'

At that moment, I understood that he had more problems than just me.

He took one or two steps back and sat down in the middle of wicker bench. He opened his arms to each side. 'How should we proceed, V? Should I send you the bill for the windows? In addition, what are we gonna do about the loss of prestige of Nico? All those customers saw what you did.... That should also have a financial equivalent. What do you think?'

Lori walked back, sat in her chair and turned to me.

'What's he talking about, V?'

I wasn't sure whether to admit everything or hide it all. Not only had I been childish, but Lori might become angry with me for behaving so stupidly and messing with James. Moreover, James looked as if he'd got some new information, although I wasn't sure how. He seemed very certain about blaming me for the windows. His gaze was unwavering.

'Wait, wait-wait.... It's clear that you are a bit confused, huh,' he said. 'No worries; I'm gonna help you.'

It was an injustice that bad people are always ready to fight and that they are bestowed with such a power by nature.

'I'm not confused—'

'You're not?' he said. 'Then tell us why you and your brother-like friend broke Nico's windows like two stupid kiddos? Why have you disturbed people – my customers? Why, boy?'

He was speaking in a disgusting tone and rhythm. I tried my best not to punch his dirty mouth.

'James, can you stop for a moment?' Lori said. 'V, please tell me what's going on?' She seemed both curious and a little angry – with both me and James. She was probably nervous about me putting her into a difficult situation with James.

I sat on the patio sofa near Lori's chair. Maybe it was high time to talk about everything. It seemed meaningless to deny what had happened any longer.

James was waiting curiously to see what I'd say in front of Lori.

'I need to start from the beginning, Lori,' I said.

'That's nice!' said James. He started to laugh as if drunk on victory. Though he hadn't yet heard the confession he desired, he took his cigar out of his pocket with the pleasure of knowing he would get it in the end, and lit it. An angry man enjoying a victory. Too disturbing to bear.

First I told Lori about what James had said to Amy, how he'd upset her and worn her out, and how he'd flung dirt on Gary (I tried to hide my knowledge that he was right.) When I said that James was backbiting Gary, James didn't say anything but laughed loudly, leaning his head back. I explained how James had also threatened Amy and warned her against demanding any share of the inheritance, and more precisely insisted she give up chasing anything.

James couldn't stay still. 'Oh boy, but I told you that same morning everything I was gonna say to that woman. I visited your apartment and told you what I would do. You didn't try to stop me then.'

'Don't be such a prick, please. You've tried to put the blame on me before, but this time you won't manage it. No, "boy," you didn't tell me about any of the shit you would do. You didn't mention you were going to threaten Amy, or tell her theories you made up about Gary. You said you were going to talk to Amy, and I told you not to put your nose into others' business. But you didn't listen to me!'

'What I said about Gary is true. It isn't a theory. Actually, I didn't even say it; I just gave that woman some clues so she could find out for herself and enjoy....' He started to grin wolfishly.

That night, he was being even ruder and more annoying than he normally was. It was very clear to me that the rest of the talk wouldn't be peaceful. James was sitting next to us like a bomb that was about to explode.

'Wait.... What did she find out?' Lori said.

'V might know. Let's ask him. What do you say, V? Were the clues enough? Have you reached the right conclusion?'

'Lori, please shut that man's mouth. Let's talk alone. I'm begging you.'

'NO!' James said and straightened. 'No, I am staying here. You will talk to me, too. We will all talk together. Everything will be clarified. Tonight. Now!'

'James, calm down!' Lori said. 'Lower your voice!'

'I'm fine. Don't worry, baby. I know what I'm saying. And you'll see that I know what I'm saying.'

'What does that mean?' she asked.

'Nothing,' he said. 'It means I know something, and I'll talk to you after I've settled accounts with this boy.'

I had been attempting to ignore his bad attitude with self-control and lip-biting, but I couldn't bear his disrespectful behaviour to Lori, and once he called me "boy" again, I couldn't control myself any longer – I attacked him.

When I jumped on him, the bench tipped over backwards and we both rolled off behind it. We pushed our hands into each other's faces and tried to punch each other. Lori tried her best to split us up, but couldn't. I was about to hit James on his chin when he caught my arm and held on so strongly that I couldn't move it. Steven, the butler, came running and tried to break up the fight. James swore and told him not to intervene, and then said he'd kill me.

'Steven, do something.... Please!'

'I'm trying ma'am...'

'Garcia, hey! GARCIA! Where are you.... Oh, sweet Lord!' Lori was crying.

Garcia, the gardener, also ran towards us, and he and Steven managed to split us apart.

During the chaos that followed, while Steven and Garcia were still holding James, I managed to punch his chin. Enraged, James attacked me again. He started to beat my stomach and kick me with his knees too. Finally someone managed to pull him away from me.

I felt as if my stomach had been wrenched after all those hits; the pain was intense. In grand total, he had scored punches and kicks to my stomach, caressed my face with a couple of fists, and then retired.

'Take him away!' Lori was crying. 'Go away! Go!'

But James had lost his temper and couldn't help swearing at everybody around him, including Lori.

'This is just the beginning, boy! The first party. You still haven't paid for the damage YOU caused! You'll see, V, you'll see....' He freed himself from the hands holding him.

'I'll also have a talk with you!' he said to Lori and went inside.

I let my head drop onto the grass and closed my eyes, praying that none of my internal organs had been ruptured.

'It will be over soon; don't worry,' Lori said. 'Are you okay, baby? Are you alright? Let's go see a doctor. C'mon, help him.... HELP! No, Steven, you go get the car.... We'll leave immediately.'

Lori was saying something to the people around, hurrying them, sometimes leaning towards me and asking whether I was okay.

'Relax.... Hey, I'm fine, Lori. Agh..., I don't have nothing.... Okay....

Fuck the doctor. Did he touch you? Tell me that.... Say that he didn't or...!'

'Ssshh! Don't talk,' she said. 'We'll see a doctor for sure.... C'mon, try to get up.'

It was difficult to persuade Lori that I was fine and didn't need to go to the hospital, but I succeeded in the end. We moved to the sitting room, where she and Steven laid me on the sofa. Lori forced me to drink various beverages, like water, tea and fruit juice, but I couldn't drink any of them. The filthy owner of Nico had put my stomach out of order. Later, I even vomited up blood in the toilet, but I didn't let Lori know about that. Besides, it might have been related to the last punch he landed on my chin.

Lori's hands were on her cheeks. 'I can't believe what has happened.... What's going on V?' she said.

'Lori, that's why I came here tonight... to talk to you. Talk to you about everything, including your douchebag husband who gives himself the authority to do any stupid thing he feels like. Like threatening Amy—'

'What's the thing he made up about Gary?'

'He implied that Gary had a girlfriend. Fucker!'

'I can't believe... why would he? James is not... he's not like that. I mean...'

'Yeah, tell me about it. He also kicked me out of Nico yesterday.... He shouted, "Fuck off! Fuck off!" Moron!'

'What?! Is that.... Oh God.... Why didn't you tell me before? But why did he do that? Did you have a fight? About what?'

'I didn't tell you because the previous night, you'd slapped me. I was cross with you.'

She started to cry and hugged me.

'Don't worry, V. It will end soon,' she said.

'No.... No, Lori. What's gonna end? Please, Lori, don't be silly. It's just between me and that bastard. Okay, and Amy, but you don't need to end anything because of this. C'mon..., I'll take care of him by myself....'

'Have you talked to Gary? How is Amy now?'

'Yes, I have. Actually, I was with them today. James even came to the atelier – overdose James. We also had a small thing there.... Gary pushed me out and tried to settle the fight. But Lori, James provokes me a lot...'

'That window thing... James kept saying it over and over. What's that about?'

I had nowhere to escape; I had to tell her. Lori listened to our window-breaking adventure from beginning to end. I told it in a shame, feeling surprised and angry at the naive stupidity of our actions again (yes, again).

She didn't like what she'd heard. She didn't find any bit of it funny, either.

'Why do you mess with that man, V? Don't you know how he loses his temper when he's obsessed with something? Look what happened tonight... God knows what else he wants to do to you,' she said.

'Yes, you're right, unfortunately.... It was childish, okay. But it's his fault too. He just wants to fight or find someone to tease. He's continuously saying "family, family." Believe me, no one in the family likes him except you. He thinks Gary is his dude. Bullshit! Actually, Gary hates him. Even more after his last move.... By the way, if it were up to Gary, we'd all just keep silent. He says that no matter what James does, we shouldn't mess with him. Amy naturally got very upset and angry with that. Lori, I wanna show James that he's wrong! All wrong!'

'How? By breaking the windows of his restaurant, V? That's like throwing a stone at an angry dog. You triggered him... to attack us.'

Us.

It was sad to learn that both Lori and Gary were having problems in their marriages, and that their homes were not peaceful. I was also unhappy to know details of their private lives that should belong only to them. Seeing them upset brought me down. Not being aware of their problems certainly didn't eliminate them, but I still preferred to be unaware of them.

'So Eric... was also with you when you broke the windows.... Gosh,' she said and took a deep breath. Then, she leaned back on the sofa and looked out into the garden.

'Yeah, we did it together,' I said. 'Hey, don't worry; I'll take care of everything.' I really believed that. Everything would be okay.

She turned to me.

'We'll suffer some losses, V,' she said. 'Unfortunately, we'll need to part ways with some people. We have to pay for those we wore out, because of our ambitions, desires, faults, laziness and timidity. We must all prune our souls in order to grow again.'

For a long time, we had believed that everything was going well; we had each been obsessed with our own lives. The dinners we'd had together from time to time hadn't been aimed at reviving our affection for each other; they were just a play. We'd all acted our parts and then left the scene. It had not been important for us to know about each other's deeper offstage lives. I understood better now, after all these problems we had experienced. We might have chosen the wrong people for our lives. We might also have chosen the wrong jobs and reduced our efficiency, and blocked our own paths by becoming obsessed with wrong-minded fears. What we needed was to shake ourselves up to recover. This was what I inferred again and again from all these things.

But I couldn't stop myself wondering whether it had to be so difficult. We'd had to face not only my father's death but also inter-family conflicts and lies. All of them had been great burdens that had mauled both me and all the others.

I imagined myself as a big and beautiful tree. It was as if I'd needed to drop my leaves, but had been holding them against my branches by force. Then a powerful blow had come out of nowhere and shaken me, causing me to drop all of my dead leaves, right before my eyes. The decayed and faded ones, my zombies.... Then the pruning period came.

After the fight with James, I felt that I was moving into the second phase of these tense moments, one that would be even tenser and more painful. We had to be pruned in order to become strong again. Lori had uttered a word of wisdom and opened the blocked ways of my mind. And my heart.

She was lying on the sofa, apparently engrossed in thinking about what she'd win in return for those she would lose in the near future.

She appeared to be reflecting on her ambitions, perhaps regretting the mistakes she'd made, wanting to clean them all away with an imaginary eraser – if only she could.

I too was thinking of my latest mistakes: how I'd lost M, how I could've said "Stop, don't go!" when she'd released my hand. I thought of my cowardice, of my irresponsibility, and of the feeling of peace I'd had, as if I owned everything, when she had been beside me and in my life.

I thought of how simple, worthless and easy it had seemed then to "have it all." I'd considered myself an ordinary person, and thought that my life was composed of simple and accessible components. In fact, the peace and love that I had defined as simple to achieve could be gained only with the most difficulty.... The simpler it looked, the more difficult it was to get.

When my life turned upside down, I understood better that the world doesn't keep its balance on its own. It depends on the unified effort of all of us, all the pain we stand. We keep life in balance through our sufferings. When we suffer, the world keeps turning.

The desperate feelings I'd had after losing M passed through my mind, and couldn't even find a place for themselves. They hit the walls of my brain, turning over and over themselves again and again. These feelings I'd never wanted to re-experience had combined their powers in the depths of my mind in order to hurt me even more. Maybe for the last time they waved goodbye.

I would recover. The darkness I'd created would clear up. I believed that with my heart. We would have more beautiful, clear and peaceful days than we'd had before. Us, the people around us, and even the ones we didn't know. It was our turn. It is, I thought, high time that we shake ourselves awake, become aware of our humane deficiencies, and see how they get us into trouble – and then learn how to deal with them, control them, and even escape from them. Time to relax and renew ourselves, and then go on.

Recovering from the hard days and "waking up again" to life afresh was like a humane duty. It was this duty and renewal that our ancestors had built our civilisation upon, and it was passed on around the world as if it were a wave of energy. Today it was our turn to fulfil our duty; tomorrow it would be someone else's. I felt this with all my being. One day, everybody would be shaken up and see his humanity for himself. He would feel pain. He would wear out. He would experience the pain of having skin taken off. He would cry his eyes out. After this "pruning," his next step would be very clean, and his wisdom, belief and power would become true again. The volume of his inner-voice would turn up and guide him. He would enjoy the pleasure of small things, the value of moments, and the happiness of giving someone something without wanting anything in return. He would realise that knowing more things about someone would make him feel less "important," because the simple life brings so many wisdoms within itself. So many wisdoms that he couldn't consume them all, no matter how long he lived.

Everyone would experience the same things. Those who became green again warm our hearts by smiling. Those who had almost decayed would go deeper into the earth with their dark and unsmiling faces.

With these thoughts in my mind, I stared at the river. Lori was beside me. She was standing in silence. Without uttering a word, both of us moved into deep conversation with the flowing water.

Slothday
19 SEPTEMBER

WE WOKE UP into a sunny Sunday morning. Lori was curled up on the big armchair with a blanket over her, and I was lying on the sofa, hugging my coat. I couldn't remember when we had fallen asleep – only that we had been talking about our lives, hopes and disappointments.

Lori had asked Steven and the others to leave us alone, so I didn't know who had put the blanket over her – not until I saw James sitting on the wicker bench. The reason I'd been left to make do with only my coat for a blanket was now clear.

I woke Lori. She left the dream world for the real one, and seemed surprised.

'Oh, how are you...?' she said. Then she saw James sitting outside in the garden, and her expression changed: she looked flustered.

'I'm gonna leave now,' I said. 'I'm fine, relax.'

'No, no, no... don't leave. You don't need to go anywhere. Stay. We'll have breakfast together. You can go after that.'

'No, thank you. I should go and, you know, have a shower and get some rest. If that fella's at the breakfast table, we may end up stabbing each other. It's best for me to go.'

We hugged, as if we were being forced to be separated this way.

'Don't worry, okay?' she said. 'Everything will be alright. Take care of yourself. We'll drop by Gary's for a moment later and talk to him.'

I was both happy and curious to see Lori more relaxed and getting over her very ambitious nature. She was not used to being a tender person – at that moment she seemed susceptible to getting hurt, offended and torn. They weren't the best vulnerabilities for someone married to James. I prayed that she would return to her "iron lady" state in the shortest time possible, even though I had been longing and waiting for this relaxed version of hers for ages.

I left there quickly to avoid meeting James and made my way home. The only thing I could think of while driving was to get in the shower and stay there for a while, without doing anything else. I felt a little stomach ache, and my chin still ached when I moved it. I took a quick look at it in the rear-view mirror, I was lucky to find it hadn't turned black.

I parked my car outside my building. As I approached the entrance, I heard Eric's voice calling after me. When I turned back, I saw him walking towards me.

'Hey,' I said. 'What are you doing here? I didn't see you. Were you hiding...?'

'I parked a little further down the street. How are you? Where have you just come from?'

'I have some news for you, man. Shock! Come on, let's go upstairs, grab a bite while I tell you.'

I put Eric onto preparing some coffee and making toast for us while I went to have a shower. Though I couldn't turn the shower into the relaxation session I'd wished for, it still felt so good. When I was done with the bathroom, the table was ready. (Last meal.)

'I am starving,' I said.

'Where were you last night?'

'Oh, God... terrible things happened again.... I got in a fight with James the idiot. A real one. Look, he punched me on the chin, hard.'

'A fight? Are you serious?'

'Yep.'

'Let me look— No, there isn't a bruise or anything... but where did it happen? Why didn't you call me?'

'At their house. He was mad, like crazy. He was speaking his bullshit again, and I couldn't bear it anymore and jumped on him—'

'What couldn't you bear?'

'I went there to talk to Lori about James, after he went to the atelier to see Gary yesterday. Anyway, I'll tell you that part soon. First the action part. So James turned up to Lori's and started ranting. He turned to Lori and said something like, "I'll settle accounts with you, but V is first to go." I don't remember it exactly, but something like that. I couldn't just stand there and listen to his shit, so I jumped on him. He was sitting across me on the wicker bench. In the garden.'

'And then what!? Go on...'

'I tried to punch him, I guess, but he's as strong as a bear. I couldn't manage it; he was holding my arms. Then the butler came and tried to split us up. I freed up one of my arms at that moment, and boom! Punched the motherfucker on the mouth... slightly. Steven and the Garcia were holding both of his arms, so I just reached out and punched!'

'YES! Perfect! Great man! But, just a slight knock?'

'Sort of. Never mind—'

'Who are Steven and Garcia?'

'The butler and the gardener. Anyway, he went crazy after that. He escaped from their hands and attacked me. He punched me twice in my stomach and a harder one caught my chin.... It might not be bruised, but it aches like hell, man. I still can't get how it's not got black. But, anyways...'

'What was Lori doing all this time? She must have been very

afraid...?'

'Of course she was. She sent James away somehow and tried to take me to a hospital. She was afraid I might have internal bleeding and stuff. I talked her out of it and so we just stayed at home, and I put some ice on my chin. We talked a little and fell asleep in the sitting room. After I woke up this morning, I ran away so I wouldn't have to see his fuck-face. James must have found us there during night because he'd laid a blanket over Lori but nothing on me—'

'Maybe he pissed on you, man!'

'Maybe. Do I stink? When we woke up, we saw him in the garden, sitting alone.'

'Sucker! I wish you had super powers and had broken all the bones in his body.'

'Impossible. It was the best decision for us not to attack him at the restaurant that night. He and his dawgs would have ruined us, Eric. We'd have been scattered in pieces. That punch was vicious. What does that guy feed on to hit like that? What a grudge!'

'It was a double dose. I guess you received a little something for me, too. He gave my share of punches to you.'

'And why's that?'

'Because you were there, I was not.'

'But why would he want to punch you? He was one hundred percent sure that you and I did that shit. He had no doubt at all. How could he be so sure, for God's sake? Does he have some cameras in the park?'

'He didn't need any cameras. Amy told him everything.'

'WHAT?! Fuck! But why?! Oh GOD! When did she tell him?'

'She's got really angry after seeing Gary behaving so nicely to him and decided to fight back on her own terms. Alone—'

'Bullshit!'

'Then, after realising she couldn't deal with him alone, she asked for my help.'

'For what? For the battle with James?'

'Yes.'

'And what did you say?'

'What could I say, V? You know how precious Amy is to me... "Of course, I'll help you," I said.'

'Fuck! And? On how many fronts are we fighting with James now? And more importantly, what THE FUCK are we gonna do now!'

'I don't know what "the fuck" we can do. But I'll do whatever Amy asks of me. That shit-head can't just behave however he wants to Amy as long as I'm around. And, there is one more thing...'

'What else can there be? Oh, God...'

'Actually, I got angry with Amy for this, but it was too late. She told to me after it had all already happened...'

'Would you just spit it out please.'

'You know James implied Gary would cheat on her. Well, Amy took her revenge by saying that Lori had been in love with me once, and added something like, "Be careful. You can't understand, but I can. I'm a woman. I think your wife's still in love with Eric." 'Nuff said.'

'Jesus Christ! We're fucked!'

'Why's that?'

'Don't you hear what you're saying, man? This is deep shit that we're in now... de-eeeep shit.'

The thought of how Lori would react crossed my mind. This was going to be too much for her.

'That must be why James was so anxious and so certain. He knew it was us who sabotaged Nico, and about the issue regarding you and Lori. God... he knew it all.... He won't behave himself from now on...'

'That's why Amy asked me, and I will ask you: are you with us?'

I became stuck with the question. I stopped. I had to take side in a battle. It was not a simple battle, though. It was combat against someone like James, who would no doubt do anything for his ambition and pride. Though I always thought "nothing can get any worse," whenever we had some kind of tension in the family, it always got worse – and more complicated – with every step.

'Well... of course I'm with you, Eric. You know it. But, are you talking about declaring a war against James the son-of-a-bitch? How wise would that be?'

'Of course, we aren't mafia. Starting a war doesn't mean attacking and killing that jerk-head. But Amy will defend her rights and not steer clear of James. And I will help her on this. That's all. Actually, it wouldn't be so bad if we attacked him, but...' He smiled.

My neck was straining. I wanted to surrender myself to a masseuse and spend my whole day in her hands.

'Look, Eric... there's nothing to discuss. If you say, "I need you," then I'll certainly stand by you. As you know, I've been standing against Lori in this since the very beginning. For what? Myself? No, only for Amy. Actually, Amy defines it as a new war, but I've been carrying out this shit on her behalf for about a week—'

'Just a second—'

'No, listen, Eric. I'll say it again: James is not like us. Do you understand what I'm saying? And though I know we have to stand against him, Lori is also involved in this. I'm worried about James' violence-prone nature. I'd better inform Lori of what Amy told him. She should know...'

I took out my phone and typed her a message: "Amy told James everything. That Eric and I made that mess, and something more: the thing between you and Eric."

It seemed strange for me to write "you and Eric," even in an SMS, because I couldn't imagine them together. But I was sure the only thing concerning James was that his wife might love Eric, with whom he'd always been in conflict. He merely looked down on me and Gary, but he considered Eric his rival in the family. James would also question why he'd never heard anything about this "thing" before. More and more provocation for a mad dog.

I was suddenly engrossed with the fear that James might still be angry, lose his temper, and do something bad to Lori. My worries for her took over my mind. I started to wander the apartment, trying to figure out what I could do. If I went back to their place again, it would make everything more complicated. I waited for her to reply to my message.

While I walked up and down aimlessly, a message was delivered to my phone. I checked the screen.

'Chelsea...,' I said.

'What? Why the fuck is Chelsea sending you a message? What does she say?'

'She wants to know what I wanted to ask her the other day...'

'Never mind. Don't reply her,' Eric said.

I didn't reply, not because Eric told me not to but because I was too busy worrying about Lori. I wanted to be sure she was okay. That was the prerequisite for my peace of mind at that moment.

'Hey, V, I need to talk to Lori...,' Eric said.

'So talk to her. Why are you telling me?'

'I wanna talk to her about Amy. About what Lori's gonna do about the will, whether she changed it or not. I want to talk about everything.'

'After what James just heard, is it reasonable for you to meet Lori and talk to her? She hasn't replied yet, by the way.... Should I call her? I can't wait any longer.'

'I don't know. You could... or just wait a bit more. What do you think of my plan to talk to her? Forget about James for a minute. You and Gary can be there too. We can all talk together.'

'How will Gary react to you defending Amy? Won't he say, "I'm here, for God's sake, so why on earth do you wanna represent MY wife?" They've both been hurt. I can't believe everything that's happened. Our family has been knocked down like houses made out of playing cards...'

'Is it true, V?'

'Is what true?'

'Gary and another woman. You know. What James talked about.'

Eric had asked me a difficult question. Why he was so interested in this, I couldn't understand. Actually, it was neither his business nor mine. It wasn't right to just talk about it. But Amy asking for help from Eric and giving up expecting anything from Gary was not normal either. I couldn't make sense out of it. Or, I didn't dare to.

'Why?' I asked.

'Don't mumbo-jumbo with me. Just say it.'

'What do you think?'

'What I think isn't important. But Amy thinks it's true.'

'Did she say so? Really? That's strange...'

'Why? In fact, it isn't so strange; Gary and Amy did not marry for love. We both know it. Everyone knows it. Amy was still under the influence of what she'd lived with me, and Gary was still thinking of the girl he'd just broken up with. It started from a vacancy – indeed, two vacancies. Remember, everyone thought it was strange at the beginning. Gary might have discovered that "marriage for reason" is actually an "unreasonable" act. What do you think?'

'It's better not to talk about this, Eric. It's their relationship and their marriage; it's none of our business. I haven't talked to Gary about it. Whether he's having an affair or not, it's their problem, and they should decide what to do about it.'

'I know her, V, the girl,' Eric said.

I had been trying to escape, but I fallen into a new line of fire. I was surprised to hear that Eric knew her. It was a small world.

'Huh... what? Who do you know?'

'Don't fuck with me, V. I know the girl. The one he's having an affair with. She's the sister of one of Danielle's friends. The girl is pregnant now—'

'Wait-wait—'

'She panicked and told her sister everything, and then her sister told Danielle, and—'

'Okay! I got it! Okay.'

The situation was even more complicated than Gary had assumed.

'So you haven't told Amy? From what I can tell, it's now your turn to tell someone.'

He looked at me. 'No. I haven't.'

'So, will you?'

'You're right. They should solve it on their own. We shouldn't intervene.'

'When did you learn about it?'

'About a week ago.'

Eric had again behaved as I would expect from him. His attitude was an example of nobility. If he'd told Amy, everything would have become even more complicated for Gary. Eric and I both needed to keep calm as long as we could, and hide what we knew. As Eric had done till then.

Eric suddenly changed the subject, enabling us to destroy the disturbing silence between us. 'Danielle asked me yesterday... whether we would marry or not.'

'Wow... and? What did you say?'

He sighed and leaned back. 'I said... that I don't know.'

His answer was the worst possible. It was not only unsatisfying, it was the kind of answer that would make any woman go crazy – it was even worse than a "no" because it wasn't the truth, but it shouted the reality.

'What we have is something like a scar that can't heal,' he said. 'It hurts when it's touched. I don't know when we got the scar anyway. We've lost the living core of our love. Maybe we haven't even bred it yet. I don't know. What I feel is... this is not love.'

'Maybe you're right,' I said. 'But don't be so quick to be sure. Once, I gave a short piece of writing to M – one of hundreds – after one of our fights—'

'As a make-up "sext"!'

I smiled. 'Yes, sort of. It went something like this, though I may not remember it exactly word by word... "When I look back, I wish we hadn't upset or hurt each other so much. All the hurt we caused each other could mean we never really loved each other – but I don't believe this. And even if I lived thousands of times, I would do it all over again. Loving you is a scar that I never want to heal..." It was exactly how I felt. I loved M so much, I desired her so much, that I wasn't interested any bit of the rest of the world. Nothing else was important for me. Shouting, swearing... conflict. I thought a lot about why we harmed each other so often even while we'd loved each other so much. Why did we get stuck in the love-passion-agony triangle? Addiction, it might be.'

'If you hadn't been in that triangle, you'd know it wasn't true love, and you wouldn't still be thinking of her after so much time. Love is something like that: it puts you in a triangle. You run around in that triangle like a mad dog. It exists with its conflicts, fights and unsolvable problems. Chaos. You stand by with folded arms. You can't move. You both hate and desire her. You want to die and burn while having sex. Wearing away. Pain, love, affection and hatred. All of them. It's like being addicted to a drug. THAT is the real love. It isn't the girl you give some flowers and kiss to on her birthday; it's the woman with whom you disagree, you fight, you surrender, you clash. The one who doesn't give in to you. The one you hate and love, desiring to fuck her while you hate her for an instant, at the same time. And unfortunately, Danielle isn't this woman for me...'

It became clear that the reason Eric had been so depressed and thoughtful in those recent days was only to construct this sentence and say it out loud. Eric knew that simply being a partner was not the same as loving someone in the real sense. He might have felt this before too, and just ignored it; but now he had begun to accept it. I could see that this dead-end "love" and the mixed feelings of hesitation and regret held him back from living his life.

'Who is it then?'

He looked at me. He didn't say anything out loud, but just mentioned something with his eyes, and I listened to him with my heart.

'But it's difficult... very difficult, Eric. After all those things, after the different paths you've walked...'

'I know. I'm not chasing anything. But, it is the truth. I won't deny it any longer. I will recognize and accept it. And for this reason, I wanna be fair to Danielle. She deserves this at least....'

'How long have you been feeling like this? Was it always like this? I mean, have you always felt it, but suppressed it? Why didn't you mention it to me before?'

'No, it wasn't always in my mind. That is, I've had issues with Danielle for some time. We just didn't quite fit.... It... it just wasn't for me. Not that it's not good or, I don't know, enjoyable, and... I loved Danielle. Only, being in love is something different, V. I mean, it must be different, otherwise why on earth do we call that more intense experience being "in love"? You also know this.

'Maybe I started to understand what was disturbing my mind or maybe I heard my inner voice.... A strange feeling I couldn't control anymore got hold of me and... made me feel this way. I feel so depressed and bored, as if I were alone in the middle of a fire, feeling the flames getting closer, but unable to get away. I have no hope of escape, and... and then this other woman came up to me and said, "I just want to stay with you. Let's not talk at all.... Let's sit side by side and just breathe in life. You, next to me."

'While she was sleeping, I thought of our quarrels, debates, ego combats... and of our harmony. I could have never felt the same with Danielle.'

I understood what Eric meant very well. He was talking with all his sincerity and in a defenceless manner – no walls, no shield around his heart.

He was hurt because he couldn't be with the woman he wanted most, and didn't know how to explain what he felt to the woman who was dreaming of marrying him. He was as desperate as a wheat kernel about to be crushed in a grinding stone.

We were putting our hearts on the table. We had some questions for which we couldn't find the answers. We had ambitions whose ways were blocked.

Silence came back again, as, without talking, we tried to understand each other.

The sound of an SMS being delivered to my phone called us back to life.

'It's Lori,' I said, and then read out her message: "'I'm going to visit Father. Wanna come with me?" Why would she go there now? What for? Eric, I gotta go, now...'

'Okay, then. Go.'

We both left my apartment, and I ran to my car. After "that" day, I hadn't had the opportunity to visit my father. I'm not sure whether that was because there had been no opportunity or because I simply couldn't bring myself to go. I think I hadn't dared to do it. But this time I had no other choice. I had to see Lori.

I drove as quickly as possible. I swore to myself that I would tear James' flesh with my nails if he had hurt Lori one bit.

When I arrived at the cemetery, there were people around – people who were making use of the Sunday calmness to remember their loved ones at their eternal beds... their fathers, mothers, siblings, grandfathers, aunts, friends, sons and daughters. Each person was now leading a different life without their lost one's shining smiles, to-the-point jokes, wise guidance, relaxing presence, or strong arms to hold them when there was a need. Maybe these families had been turned upside-down like ours.

Everyone had similar expressions on their faces and were looking at other passers-by as if they understood each other. It was the kind of look you never forget: an understanding one gains only upon experiencing a loved one's death. The only truth that beats all humanly sins.

I ran past the people remembering and those being remembered, and then saw Lori, satisfying her longing to be with our father again. She was standing at his gravestone. I approached her.

'Tell me the truth: has that son-of-a-bitch James done anything bad to you?' I said.

She was crying. Despite that, she tried to smile. She held my head and kissed my forehead. We hugged each other, and she let her tears fall freely.

I looked down at my father. I hadn't seen him so silent before.

'He has missed us, V. He used to miss our mother too, but they are happy now, don't worry...' She started to sob.

'Lori, don't cry. Tell me, are you okay? Did James do anything to you? Why are you here...? Tell me.'

She shook her head swung slowly, and then laid it on my shoulder again, still hugging me loosely but determinately.

We stood this way for a while. People passed us by from time to time. We were all silent and, even though we didn't know each other, we were the strangers who understood each other the best in the whole world, on that Sunday afternoon.

Then, Lori quit hugging me and started to walk around my father's gravestone.

'So, what are you doing? Are you okay?' she asked, sniffing.

'Yeah, I'm fine. I've done nothing special. When I went home, Eric was there waiting for me. We ate something and talked for a while. I was waiting to hear from you. When you told me to come, I raced here immediately. That's it...'

'How is he? Is he okay, too?'

Like Eric, my sister had also dropped all her shields and was standing in front of me with all her naked soul bared. She had asked about Eric with tears in her eyes and in her heart, like in a post-rain calmness, but her eyes also shouted her love. She was a woman who had loved someone very much, but he hadn't been able to love her back. And her love wouldn't accept being buried deep inside; instead it flowed out with her tears.

'Good...,' was the only word I could utter. I didn't say, "The woman he's with now wants to marry him, but he's in love with another soul, and hence he's very wistful or maybe depressed."

'I'm happy to hear he's okay. I always want him to be fine...,' she said. She was looking at my father.

'Lori, I want you to be okay, too. Where's James now?'

'I don't know. We talked, and then he left home. And I came here.'

'What did you talk about?'

'He said he didn't rip you to pieces because he loved me.' She turned to me and tried to smile.

We sat near our father. She told me that James had been calmer that morning compared to the previous night. He told her the reason he'd behaved so badly was because he cared about Lori, and that he'd only talked to Amy in order to take some of Lori's burden. Everything was for her.

'But that doesn't explain why he'd behaved like an asshole? Why, for example, did he dish on Gary?'

I didn't know why I still couldn't accept or admit the truth about Gary even to Lori. Maybe because of James: maybe if it had been someone else who revealed this secret, I wouldn't reject it so easily.

'I didn't ask him,' she said. 'He was behaving as if he knew something or had learned something recently, but I don't know what. I only wondered what he wanted to talk to me about. His explanations didn't actually interest me at all.'

'What did he ask?'

She smiled and turned to me. 'He asked whether I love Eric,' she said.

We looked at each other and tried to smile. This time, together.

'So... what did you say, then?'

She stopped for a moment and thought. 'I said, "I love him."'

I couldn't believe she'd said that to James. It was respectable in terms of honesty, but the person with whom she was dealing wasn't normal, and therefore I was afraid of Lori's fearless behaviour.

On the other hand, it was interesting that she'd told me in such a comfortable and relaxed way. She might not have behaved so openly before. She wasn't hiding herself or any of her feelings from me.

'Do you mean love him like a lover?'

She stopped again and looked at the ground. She was swinging slightly – as if her inner voice was shouting, "Come on, tell him!" She obeyed it.

'I love him... like a lover,' she said.

It was the first time I'd heard my sister say she loved someone. I didn't know what to do; I was surprised and wanted to support her openness.

'Well... I... I understand,' I said.

She smiled. 'Won't you tell me I'm talking nonsense?'

'Noo.... Why would I? And, why should it be nonsense? It's... it's love. It doesn't require any defence, or justification.'

'James said that I'm foolish.'

'Do you expect me to agree with him? C'mon.... Bravo!'

She punched my shoulder and smiled. 'Isn't it foolish?' she said. 'Loving someone without any hope that he'll love you back. Not touching him, or crossing his mind, but still carrying on loving him. Isn't it foolish?'

'No, it's not... but... but, I admit that I don't understand something... I mean—'

'What?'

'If you love him so much, why didn't you do anything about it? You just left it like that.... Maybe he's in love with you too..., or with another person... but not doing anything.... This is kind of strange.'

She smiled. 'Did you ask me that to make me laugh, or are you really wondering about it?'

'No, I'm really wondering about it.'

'Because he's not in love with me, V. I can see it. He has a complicated mind that even he can't find his own way through. He isn't in love with Danielle either, but with another woman; I can see that, too. And if you ask me, the other person loves him back. They just don't wanna recognize it – as far as I know, of course. I don't have a place there. I don't want it, either. I'm tired, very tired. I don't want to struggle any longer, not for love or for any other thing...'

Despite the accuracy of Lori's remarks, their timing was also interesting. I had just been together with the subject of her comments only a couple of hours ago, and he'd openly told me what Lori was decoding about his life through her intuition. I thought she had surprised both of us – herself and me. While what Eric had said was now coming through in front of me, I felt very naïve for not having recognised it before. That Lori, despite having kept herself away from Eric's life, had made such accurate discoveries about him, forced my mind. Was there, somehow, an invisible red telephone between the lovers, over which they could understand, hear and see inside of each other.... Was there one between M and me? Could she also see my inner self or hear my inner voice?

After M crossed my mind, I thought of the message Chelsea had sent me that morning, which I hadn't answered yet. I didn't want to be rude to her again, so while Lori was busy watching our father in silence, I sent Chelsea a reply:

'I wanted to ask whether you had forgotten me or not. Forget it. It was nonsense. See you soon. And I'm sorry.'

We stood up and began to wander around the cemetery. We didn't talk any more. We had nothing left to do there, but neither of us wanted to leave.

We had a long walk around, saw people who met our eyes. I tried to understand them too. Most of the time, I thought I succeeded. It seemed to me that they all felt alike. We all had gaps in our hearts, the places we had failed to fill, and it was obvious in our eyes. But the ambiance around dictated to us that life goes on and we should go on living. Taking another step forward in our own lives didn't mean "forgetting." Living didn't require self-guilt. We were all feeling the persuasion in our hearts, and trying to understand and surrender to it. But, it was difficult.

My phone beeped. I was sure that my apology would not have been accepted. But why did she need to say so?

My prediction regarding the sender was correct, but not the content.

"No need to apologise. I emailed you something. Check it out when you have time. Take care."

Chelsea was the same for me as Danielle was for Eric. I loved her and she loved me, and we were good friends and got along well, but something was missing. Even though I couldn't explain what that thing was, it had successfully obstructed my "falling in love" with Chelsea. Maybe we'd done the best thing; everyone continued on with their own lives when the time came. But still, our memories were with us. These memories sometimes made us feel a little bitter inside, but they were beautiful enough to care about, even though they don't include the "dream love" of our lives.

The cemetery was quite a huge place. Though it did not seem to be a proper place to search for inner peace at the beginning, the calmness around provided us both with a sweet serenity.

As we approached my father's grave again for a last goodbye, I saw from far away a surprise waiting there for us. Eric was sitting at the edge of the stone in silence. Motionless.

Lori also saw him and took her arm back from my shoulder.

'Isn't that Eric?' she said. 'What's he doing here? Why is he here?'

'I don't know. He knew I was coming here to meet you, but that was this morning. He wanted to visit my father, too, but...'

When we reached the grave, Eric also looked surprised. He stood up.

'Wow, are you still here...?' he said. 'It's been hours, man.'

'Yeah, such a nice surprise, bro.'

'Yes, well, I hadn't visited yet, you know. I never had the opportunity. When you mentioned coming here this morning, I realized I had some time and, you know, wanted to come. So, why are you still here? It's been hours....'

'We're a little mad, don't you know?' Lori said. 'We just wanted to really "feel" our emotions...'

Eric laughed, and Lori smiled.

'I know that "mad woman,"' Eric said, and they hugged each other.

It was a scene I would never forget. They were probably the two people that I loved the most – out of what was left of our family. I could not deny their value to me. I would do anything for them, without even thinking about it for a second: no matter what they asked or what the consequences might be. They were together now in front of my father, as if he'd wished to see this scene unfolding. Lori's eyes were closed. She might not have the chance to hug Eric close like that again – maybe not for the rest of her life. Her hands were on his back. She held him as if she wanted to get possession of his personality, body and soul – maybe imagining in her mind, behind her closed eyes, that she had all of him.

Without saying a word, Eric seemed to understand what she'd told me before about her love for him. He didn't question her tight embrace and let himself be taken into her arms, at least for a moment. Rather than struggle against a woman's passion, he waited. He let Lori enjoy her hopeless love.

They split after some seconds. Lori's eyes brimmed with tears. Neither I nor Eric asked why. This was one of those moments when none of us needed to say a word, because everything was already being said clearly. We were not misunderstanding each other.

Eric had brought some flowers for my father. We mixed them with Lori's flowers and put some over my father's stone and the others over my mother's.

I stood next to my mother's stone while Lori and Eric sat at the corner of my father's.

'It hasn't been a week yet,' Eric said.

'He would be planning another night together and busying himself with the preparations,' I said. 'He would be impatient to laugh again....'

'I wish he'd never planned those evenings at all,' Lori said.

I couldn't respond.

'How crowded it is here today. I wonder if it's always so busy,' Eric said.

'How are you Eric?' she asked.

Eric paused and looked at her. Then, he smiled. 'I'm fine. Not so bad. Normal, I mean....' He looked at my father for a moment, and then turned to Lori again.

'And you?' he said.

Lori smiled. 'Fine-not-so-bad-normal.'

The atmosphere was getting depressive and heavy. A father recently dead, a woman with hopeless love, an intricate heart inside the man she loves, and me, with a very complicated mind and a broken heart.

'Let's go,' I said. 'Otherwise, I'm gonna die here.'

It was a meaningless joke. It failed to sound like a joke.

'You go, guys. I'll stay a bit longer,' Lori said.

She and Eric hugged each other again. This time it was a shorter and more "formal" hug. They seemed as if they'd woken up from a dream.

Lori turned to me. 'I apologise on behalf of my stupid husband. Everything will be okay, V, alright? Don't get sad. We'll be okay....' She kissed me on my cheek. Then, she hugged me, too.

While walking back towards the main entrance, I didn't talk to Eric at all. Sometimes we caught each other's eyes and that was enough. Then, Eric destroyed our silence.

'The three of us, together. What a coincidence.'

I smiled. 'You're right. It's strange. But maybe it's also good. The three of us, without the others. I don't know what you think... I mean, it was good for Lori. She very much wanted to see you.'

He didn't answer me. He understood it all and continued to walk, his eyes on the ground.

We walked among the people entering or leaving the cemetery. It was quite a huge place that included a small forest of woodland. I thought of where I would want to be buried after I died. I couldn't find a specific answer.

When we were near the entrance, we saw the only person who could have destroyed our peace.

'I'm not surprised at all,' James said with a laugh. 'You, your accomplice, and the woman in love with him. A family visit all together. How graceful you are...'

Eric grabbed the collar of James' jacket with a quick move. 'Look,' he said. 'I know what an asshole you are. Your words have no limit. But don't do it here. Please, be respectful for once!'

'Take your stinking hands off of me or I'll make you regret it for the rest of your life, you son of a bitch!'

James stood still and looked directly into Eric's eyes as if he would kill him. Then, suddenly, he hit Eric's arms off his collar, freeing himself.

'Listen to me, Eric-the-fuckface,' he said, pointing his finger towards Eric's face, 'you, your coward friend and his null brother and his slutty wife—'

Eric jumped on James and they both fell down, wrestling and trying to hit each other. Everyone nearby stopped to look at us. I thought of Lori and hoped she wouldn't see this mess.

I wanted to stop it before it got worse. James had only lost control because Lori had openly revealed her love for Eric. I wanted to prevent that bastard from behaving badly to Lori too. The most reasonable thing was to split them up and get Eric away from there.

I tried to intervene. They were struggling on the ground, so I dropped to my knees and tried to pull Eric away while holding James' strong arm. They seemed to be knotted together. When James felt my hand on him, he must have thought I was trying to attack him too, and he landed a punch on my chin and shouted, 'So now you have the guts, you bastard?'

'Shut up, you stupid fuck! You... you ruin everything, asshole!' I said.

I stood up and shouted at Eric, 'Let him be. Let's go!'

Eric didn't listen, so I grabbed his shoulders and pulled him backwards. As Eric rose, James, who was still on the ground, kicked Eric in his stomach.

'Enough, you pathetic motherfucker!' I said and kicked him in his kidneys. He didn't seem to care about the pain.

'ENOUGH!' I said. 'Get away from us!'

'Away?!' he said, getting up. 'ASSHOLES! I will ruin you. I'll make you cry, girlies!' He moved closer to Eric. 'I will ruin you, first,' he said, and then looked at me. 'And you next, baby boy. You'll both shit your pants! You'll shiver like pussies! I'll pull your tongues out! Just be patient, cocksuckers... Your time is near – so near.'

'FUCK OFF!' Eric said. 'You won't do anything to either of us, or to Amy, or anyone. Do you hear me, asshole? Do you HEAR ME! I'm the only one who will stand against you. On behalf of all of them, all of us, I'll deal with you! You'll pay for all the shit you've done. Got me? I won't lose to you, asshole! You'll see... I won't lose. I never lose.'

James put all his hatred onto Eric. 'I'll pull your intestines out and tear you to pieces. You'll beg me not to hurt you anymore, you pussy. You don't know who you're dealing with. Huh, you're just two kids to me. But I won't show you mercy! I won't—'

'Fuck YOU!' Eric said.

'My payback is so close now, boys. Just be patient... only a little longer.'

Both of their outfits were dusty. Reddened faces, untidy clothes. People were casting scornful and angry looks at us. Three men fighting and swearing at the entrance of a cemetery, as if there was no other place left to do it on Earth, as if we had no respect for the peacefulness of this place, and no decency.

Eric and I began to walk towards the car park, feeling both anger and shame at the same time. We checked behind us, not forgetting that we had "fucked" with James and could expect anything from him.

James had started walking towards my father's gravesite but

suddenly seemed to give up on this idea and changed direction. He was heading back to his car.

'Let's get out of here before that son of a bitch gets to his car!' I said.

'Isn't there any police or security around here?'

'Why? Why on earth would there be police at a cemetery?'

'I mean, these are all dead people, right? What if there was a crime and... I don't know, maybe.... Oh God, how can that fuck-face so easily insult us?'

'Eric, c'mon.'

We just needed to walk past a group of trees to where our car was parked, jump into the car, and drive away.

'We've had enough, okay? Move!' I said.

'What the fuck am I doing, V? I'm walking, you see...'

With all that anger, I wouldn't be surprised if James tried to drive his car into us.

'What kind of a man is he?' Eric said. 'I mean... he's on the limit of being the biggest asshole on Earth, man. What a bastard! I've never met such a shabby person in my whole life, V! Never! Lori's married to some son of a bitch. I don't understand how she can bear him....'

You had some indirect effect on that, was the sentence I wanted to say. But I kept silent.

Just as we reached my car, James began shouting, 'Yo, bastards! Mummy's bo-ooys! Papa is here...'

'What da—' Eric said.

'Don't turn around. Get in and we'll get the fuck outta here.'

Eric didn't listen to me and turned to James. 'What up, you crack?'

James was walking towards us with quick steps. His manner was strange, but everything was developing in a flash. I didn't know what to do; thinking quickly was impossible. The fight, cemetery, sorrow, all that swearing – I felt as if I'd been narcotised with some opium and was no longer in control of myself, like I was just watching everything from a distance, out of the scene.

James approached and then stopped a few feet away. We were isolated from the public eye by the trees.

Eric turned to me. 'This guy's really itching for trouble, V. Is he nuts?'

'Look at me, four eyes!' James said.

Eric began pacing side to side, not looking up at James. He put his hands over his face like a man experiencing the final intrinsic quarrel one has with himself before getting involved in the final deadly round of a big fight.

'I said, look-at-me-fucking-four-eyes!' James repeated.

Eric put his hands on his hips, threw his head back, and started to talk to himself: 'Oh, sweet Lord, help me. Help me so that I won't kill this motherfucker—'

'LOOK AT ME,' James roared with such force that all the veins in his neck were visible, as if his capillary vessels were so filled with blood and hatred they might burst. His face was as red as a dying bull's spilled blood.

Eric turned and moved so close to James that the tips of their noses touched. He took hold of James' collar with his both hands.

'What's up, asshole! What's UP? What'ya want! WHAT!'

James pulled his hand out from behind his back and stabbed a hunting knife so deeply into Eric's right hip that the handle pressed up against Eric's body, leaving none of the blade visible – it was all inside Eric.

The first instant after Eric got hit, I was in deep shock, which prevented me from comprehending what was really happening. The world as I knew it disappeared; the absurd violence I was witnessing disconnected my mind from reality. My perception of the world narrowed to almost nothing. I felt as if encapsulated in a vacuum, just seeing images of Eric, blood, the knife, James, his hatred.

Eric let go of a vague "Ah!" after a couple of seconds, as they continued looking into each other's eyes. Eric's hands were still on his collar. James had a very adamant and furious expression.

Then, time started to move again, and I returned to life. But I didn't know what to do. It was like a supernatural moment for me, more than just a nightmare. James' daring at doing this, and my inability to prevent it. A deep carving feeling of pain was showing on Eric's face.

Eric started to shout as if in enormous pain. James pulled the knife out of Eric's hip and directed it towards Eric's face. The knife was red, very red.

'Now, son of a bitch, listen,' he said. 'This is the first move, just the beginning. Enjoy it... okay? The next one will be much more painful. You'll beg me to stop.... Understand? Beg-me-to-stop... and I won't.'

Then, he roughly knocked Eric's hands off his collar, freeing himself from Eric's grip. Eric sat down. James looked at me and didn't say anything. He looked back at Eric lying on the ground.

'This is just the beginning, boy!' he said, and turned and walked away.

As soon as James started walking, I ran towards Eric. His hip was bleeding. I helped him to his feet and started to pull him towards the car. He was still in shock. Words, mixed with utterances of surprise and pain, were coming out of his mouth, seemingly without him knowing exactly what he was saying.

'What did that son of a bitch do, V? He stabbed a knife into my ass...! He stabbed me, man! Is it bleeding too much? Hey, is it bleeding too much...? Tell me!'

Yes, it was.

'No, no!' I said. 'Get in the car now.... Don't think about the bleeding, okay. Don't worry.'

Half-running, half-wrestling, we reached my car and got in. James was walking back to his car. At that moment, I agreed with him: we were pussies – mummy's boys – and he was the street dog, grown up out in the streets. We had broken his restaurant's windows, and he had taken his revenge with a knife. He had shown us very clearly and quickly that it was not wise to challenge him. He was very different than us. While he was a real outcast, we were tabbies that pretended to gad about but couldn't succeed even at that.

I'd lived in a dream where everyone behaved properly and no one hit below the belt, not even when they quarrelled or lost control. But now I had woken up. No one could have reminded me better than James that there were no rules in a war. The bleeding wound on Eric's hip had taught us that.

We were in the car. I glanced at Eric. He was sitting on his hand, and the wound had not stopped bleeding. I didn't know what to do. He kept asking whether it was still bleeding or not, even though he could obviously see that it was. He would take his hand out, look at his hand, and ask whether his wound was bleeding. Then he would sit on his hand again.

As if I was using the car for the first time, I carefully started the engine, pushed down the handbrake, and stepped on the accelerator, slowly and step by step, being sure that I was doing nothing wrong.

'V, that motherfucker stabbed me... you see? He stabbed ME, V!'

'ENOUGH! Enough, okay.... He stabbed you. Now, shut the fuck up!'

He stopped talking for a moment and looked at me in surprise.

'Just shut up, Eric, okay! Behave! I'll take you to a hospital and they'll deal with it. But right now, I'm begging you to shut up! Calm down!'

Shouting like that seemed to make us both return to reality. I felt that Eric was coming out of his state of shock.

There was a background noise in my ear. I felt as though I were in a vacuum – everything sounded muffled. My mind seemed frozen, unable to process any stimulation. It was as if there were only three people in the world at that moment: me, Eric, and James – and we would meet James again soon.

I looked at Eric from time to time. He looked back at me as if he wanted to say something but couldn't open his mouth. He had a strange expression on his face, as if I was to blame for all that had happened, and very blank eyes that I couldn't read at all. I tried to focus on the road and look for a hospital nearby.

The game had changed. James had shown us his hand, and I was sure that he wouldn't give up before he'd dealt me my round. Either James would kill us or we would kill him. However it played out, someone's death seemed inevitable. But I was not ready to act yet – not to die or to kill.

Eric punched the front console and started to swear again,

repeating the same words over and over. He looked at his hand, seemed surprised about the blood again, and again shouted, cried, and swore. He couldn't keep silent and still.

'We need to call Lori!' he said. 'She must know about this. She must know....'

The possibility that James might harm Lori as well was almost too much to bear.

Eric was looking outside through the window and producing sounds like something between crying and groaning. Suddenly, he turned to me.

'I had sex with Amy!' he said.

I couldn't make any sense of what he'd said, and yet it seemed very crucial at the same time. When I thought about it more, in a blink of an eye, I couldn't denominate the feeling that came over me: I experienced a mixture of shock, anger and violence simultaneously. 'Fuck off!' I said.

I was now looking at Eric's face, giving up the road.

'After you... today,' he said. 'I went to her house... we had sex....'

That he had done such a thing, and then admitted it to me, was unacceptable; so terrible was his timing. Suddenly, my whole body filled with anger. All my cells were composed of just anger. I had once shaken with a similar rage against James.

Actually, what he'd said was something I had foreseen. But his timing was completely inappropriate. I was furious.

'Fuck off, Eric! Just fuck off! Or wake up! What are you saying! That son of a bitch just stabbed you! He stuck a knife into your ass! Are you aware of what you're saying on top of all that now?!'

I was yelling so loud my throat hurt. I felt the veins in my neck swelling up. The edges of my vision became a little dark.

'Don't give me a hard time now, please!' he shouted. 'Don't push me! It's bleeding, V! It's-fucking-bleeding!'

'You are such an asshole! A bastard. They are still married! MARRIED! He's my brother, for God's sake! My-brother! How could you? Couldn't you wait? How could you do it?'

I felt both furious and desperate. Gary's passivity and obliviousness to everything going on, and my inability to stop anything, gnawed at me. On the other hand, Eric was writhing because he had been stabbed. I wanted to cry.

'We love each other, V! Please understand that. Everyone should understand it! That bastard should also understand it! That son of a bitch! Oh God, motherfucker stabbed me!'

'Is it all you have to say right now? Is what you did right? When everything is so complicated, is it right? Shut up! Asshole! You are an ASSHOLE!'

'No one stands by her, V, no one...,' he said.

As he spoke, he kept checking the blood on his hand under his hip, groaning, pausing, and then resuming talking again.

'Neither Gary nor you... I can't bear leaving her alone. I won't allow people to humiliate her.... I won't allow anyone to do that, V. No one, and especially not that motherfucker who stabbed me! Never!'

'Don't talk to me like that, Eric! Stop it!'

He stopped talking and started to cry, looking outside.

The road was flowing in front of us, but we still couldn't find a hospital. I kept driving, lost in the moment. Eric's voice pierced through me.

'HEY! Here, it's on the right, V! On the right! There it is... on the right!'

I looked, saw a red emergency services sign, and turned the steering wheel.

I parked the car carelessly, got out, and ran around to Eric's door. I placed my head under his arm and we started to jump-walk towards the entrance. He was still saying, 'The bastard stabbed me! Motherfucker did it!' He seemed to have recovered from the initial shock enough to realise what had happened.

After seeing us at the entrance, the nurses pushed me aside and took care of Eric, taking one arm each and helping him inside. Two bulky health officers assisted them in taking Eric into one of the rooms in the back. I ran after them.

As Eric was helped onto a stretcher, I caught his eye one last time, and then a nurse pulled a curtain closed around him.

One of the nurses instructed me to go to the entrance hall to answer some questions at the patient registration desk. When they asked me how it had happened, I thought for a while.

'An accident! An accident occurred. We're very old friends and... we were playing with a knife – stupid, I know... but, we were playing-acting and... I was showing the knife to him... I mean, I had bought a knife. We were just making up nonsense, but... I know it sounds strange and childish. We were joking, just fooling around, and he just fell onto the knife... and I couldn't... pull my hand back. I know, it isn't... I mean, it seems strange, but... it was just a stupid mistake. That's how it happened. Write down what I say, please....'

I couldn't believe what I was saying. Why was I attempting to protect James? I wasn't completely sure of whether I was protecting him, or Lori, or the dignity of our family. Obviously, I wouldn't want to protect James.

'Sir, you need to know that I'm going to check Mr Stanza in just a moment and ask him the same things, if his doctor allows me to—'

'Yes! Of course you will... You can ask him. I mean, yes...'

'So, this isn't finishing with your signature, am I clear? First, I need to talk to Mr Stanza about this, and then of course we'll need to report it to the police. We can write down in the report that it was an accident, but as there was a weapon involved the police will want to question you either way.'

'All okay, man,' I said. 'They can ask. Whatever.'

In fact, I was afraid because a professional would easily see that I was lying. The nurse filling out the report could probably see it too, but he didn't ask me any more questions; he was leaving it to the police to embarrass the liar (and press him for information).

After he was done with me, he went to check Eric.

From time to time, I asked how Eric was doing, but they wouldn't tell me anything. Eventually they told me to go park my car properly so it wasn't blocking the entrance.

While doing that, I wondered whether I should inform Danielle about what had happened. I had no idea about when Eric had met Amy, or what he'd said to Danielle, or whether Danielle knew he was meeting me. In other words, I knew nothing about what Eric had done during the second half of the day, and if I said the wrong thing I could leave Eric in a very complex situation. Furthermore, I didn't know how to tell her about the incident. "Eric has been stabbed!" or "James has stabbed Eric!" or "Eric has been attacked!" What could I say?

I sat on one of the empty benches located at the edge of the waiting room. I saw many people in pain around me, looking for hope and support from the eyes of the others. I spoke to them with my eyes as much as I could: "I stand by you. I understand your pain." And tried to believe what I said.

The air smelled of hospital disinfectant. I felt ashamed of myself for everything I had ambitiously looked for all my life. For not appreciating what I already had. I couldn't stay inside any longer and went out to take a deep breath. Don't we all forget how valuable it is to have one deep breath in peace and calm?

I thought of how Eric had quickly told me about him and Amy before we reached the hospital. It was as if he'd thought he would die and wanted to make sure that someone knew it beforehand. I grew angry with him again. Then I thought about how love was something unplanned and uncontrollable, like theirs. But then I became angry with myself, because I didn't respect their love. This anger rotation didn't come to an easy end. It was Eric's turn, then my turn again – and that went on.

I decided that the first person I should tell about what had happened was Lori. I called her.

She had gone to her house and I'd caught her sleeping. I asked whether James was with her. He was not. I told her to get up from bed as I had some bad news.

'What? What bad news? What happened?' she said, panicking after hearing my stupid introduction.

'Calm down a bit. Yes, there's a problem, but it isn't "that" terrible. You shouldn't panic, I mean. I'm at the hospital right now...'

'Hospital?! Why? What happened, V? Did you have an accident or what? Which hospital? Where?'

'Please, Lori, calm-down. This isn't an emergency. But it's very important to be calm. Please—'

'V, cut the crap! Tell me, where are you? What happened?!'

'Eric had a small accident. We're at the hospital right now...'

'Eric? What accident? Is he OK? How about you? Are you okay?'

'Yeah. Yes, I'm fine. So is he. He just had an accident, but not an accident in the real sense...'

'Oh V, don't make it a puzzle! Where are you? Tell me at once...'

'Lori, calm down. This is important. While we were leaving the cemetery, we came across James—'

'What!'

Before I told her anything, she understood that something bitter had taken place – and that her husband was involved.

'Yes. We had a row, and... James followed us to our car... and stabbed Eric... in his hip.'

'WHAT?!'

'Yeah. He had a knife.'

'A knife?! Oh my God! That son of a bitch—'

'Yes. You're right. But Eric is fine now. It isn't serious..., I guess. The doctors are with him. But, there's a problem, uh... when they were registering him, I said something strange like, "It was an accident. I had a knife in my hand and he fell on it by mistake." That sort of stuff. I don't know... they didn't buy it, I suppose. The police are going to question me again. No one has come yet, but if you'd bring one of your lawyers for me, that would be good....'

'Okay, okay, of course. But, why did you— Anyways, where are you now?'

I gave her the address.

I went outside and sat on the short wall by the emergency exit. I was feeling more shaken day by day. I imagined being broken like a porcelain vase, not being able to endure anymore impacts; my pieces wouldn't hold together anymore.

How was it possible that everything I'd considered proper and stable in my life had been turned upside-down? That question had come into my mind often during that week. I'd given up contemplating the answer. I had to focus on how I could recover from these catastrophes and save the people in my vicinity from this mess. I needed to help them get through this without suffering any more losses of any kind – not of money, dignity, trust, or lives. There was no point in feeling sad or pitiful about what I had experienced. I had to regain my balance after being shaken. Then I would be more durable and ready to take more strong blows.

Why did I need to be shaken to wake up to reality? Maybe it was like doing the laundry. Why do we wet our clothes if afterwards we need to dry them again? In order to make them clean. We wash and dry our dirty clothes to bring them back to their previous condition: relative purity. Maybe we too need to be "washed" from time to time in order to become clean again. Life insisted on making me wet, so I had to learn how to dry myself again.

One of the nurses came outside and waved to me. I hurried over to her. She told me that Eric was fine and that the knife hadn't harmed any vital muscle organs or nerve tissue. He was in surgery and would probably be released in the next few hours.

That was good news. I had been terrified after seeing that much blood. Was it James' relative kindness and street-boy experiences that had resulted in a harmless hit, or was it Eric's lifetime luck that had saved him? I didn't know, but the outcome was calming. With the relaxing news, I felt that I must call Danielle, though I might need to tell a few quick lies.

'Hey, beautiful. It's me... um, V.'

'Of course, I know who's calling; your name is on the screen. Are you drunk or what?'

'No, no....'

'Are you okay, honey?' she said.

'What? I'm fine. Where are you now?'

'At home, reading. It's a boring Sunday today. You? Where are you?'

'Sundays... yes, fuck Sundays. Look, Danielle, um, I need to say something to you, but it isn't something good.'

'What? What's it?'

'Okay, it's no big thing; you can relax. It isn't... such an important thing..., but there was a small accident. But it isn't serious—'

'V, what the fuck! Say it!'

'Eric had a small accident. I wanted to, you know, let you know—'

'What?! An accident?! What kind of accident? Oh, God, is he okay? Where's he? Let me talk to him! Is he okay, V? Where are you?!'

'Hey, calm down, he's okay. He's fine. Don't worry. There's nothing to worry about. He's in the emergency room—'

'God! Where?!'

'Doctors are, you know, treating... I think they'll let him go in, I dunno, two or three hours.'

'What happened? Where are you? I'm coming there... please, tell me what happened?'

'Nothing big, really. We'll talk later. Don't worry; it's nothing serious. He's fine, now.'

I gave Danielle the address and then went back into the reception. I asked the nurse how long Eric's surgery would take. She told me it would take about an hour, and then they would keep him under observation for one more hour. If everything went as expected and he was fine, he could leave after that. I could do nothing but wait, and gaze at people, implying that I understood them.

I went out and sat on the wall again, playing with my phone. I re-read the messages from Chelsea. I tried to read what was between the lines, but I couldn't find anything. While I was keeping myself busy with the messages, Lori arrived, along with Mr Elkins, the lawyer.

She got out of the car and ran towards me. We hugged, and she started to cry. She was crying more often these days.

'Did you see James?' I asked. 'Did he come home?'

'No... no, don't worry. Oh, that bastard.... He was supposed to pick me up from the cemetery, but he didn't show up. I found my own way home. Since I didn't care where he was, I didn't bother trying to call him. V, keep away from him, do you hear me? I implore you. Keep away from him, please. He may do the same, or worse, to you...'

'Okay, Lori, don't worry,' I said. 'Everything will be okay. Don't get upset at him. Maybe we deserved this.'

'Mr Kushner, we should talk about what happened,' Mr Elkins

said. 'We don't have much time.'

'Okay...'

First, we revised what I'd already said in my report about the accident, and then decided to add one or two more details at his suggestion. Even though I didn't feel quite ready, when we returned to the waiting room we found two police officers there, looking for me.

'Mr Kushner?'

'Yes? Yes, I am...'

'We need to talk to you about the incident which involves Mr Eric Stanza. Would you please follow us to a more private room?'

'Well, yes, of course...'

Mr Elkins stepped forward. 'I'm Mr Kushner's lawyer—'

'Yes, sir, this way please.'

'V,' Lori said, 'I... let me go check on Eric's status, okay?'

'Okay, I won't be long... I guess...,' I said.

The police officers questioned me and checked some of the inconsistencies in my statement, but with Mr Elkins by my side, everything seemed easier. Actually, the story I told was very clear and simple: I bought a knife, and Eric fell on it while we were joking around. The only problem was that we didn't have the knife with us, and this had captured the attention of the police officers.

'After he got stabbed, we panicked. I was afraid the knife might, you know, harm him more if it remained in his hip, so I pulled it out. Then we rushed here. I don't remember anything else, honestly. I don't even remember driving here. We must have left the knife there, on the ground in the cemetery car park... towards the back of the car park behind the trees.'

'If everything was just an accident, and there's nothing to worry about, then why did you think that you need a lawyer, Mr Kushner?' one of the officers asked.

This was a part that we haven't reviewed with Mr Elkins.

'Mr Officer, if I may?' Mr Elkins said. 'As a general practise with The Kushner family, I try to be present in every bitter situation, regardless of whether the incident is serious or not. It has nothing to do with a "need" but is more of a custom, we might say.'

If I had given this statement on my own, maybe they wouldn't have believed me at all. I thanked God for Mr Elkins' convincing presence. The police said a team would examine the scene of "accident" and would question me again if required. Eric was still in surgery, but the police wanted to talk to him once he could take visitors. I hoped the nurse had mentioned the accident before his surgery and that Eric would understand and not ruin my story: our statements had to match up.

When we returned to the entrance hall, I saw Danielle was there, talking to Lori. As soon as she saw me, she ran over and began hugging me and crying.

'James did it! James stabbed Eric... why did he do it V? What does he want?!'

I took her arm and pulled her outside where we wouldn't attract attention.

'Hey, Dani, look... calm down. Calm down! Okay? Please, lower your voice! And don't mention James, either—'

'Why?! After what that asshole has done?!'

'I just told the police it was an accident.'

'WHY! Are you kidding me!'

'It was my knife, and Eric fell on it while we were joking around. That's it. Okay? Do you understand me! That's it. No James involved, and no one else either.'

'Fuck you! Bullshit!'

She was crying and let herself fall into my arms. While I was trying to calm her down, I saw the doctor who was treating Eric enter the waiting room. Lori got up right away to talk to him.

'Look, that's Eric's doctor. Come... and don't forget what I said, okay?'

I ran towards a nurse and asked when we could see Eric. She told me they were going to bring him in just a couple of minutes.

'Please wait there in the corridor,' the nurse said. 'They are bringing Mr Stanza to room 143.'

Lori, Danielle and I waited at the door of room 143. Then we saw Eric being wheeled towards us on a gurney. He was awake. I wanted to make him aware of my testimony, but the police officers were following him and the nurses, so I had no chance to contact him. I caught his eye for a moment, and that was all. Danielle was crying.

'I'm fine, Dani, calm down,' Eric said as he passed us by. 'It was a simple incident... nothing to worry about.' He was looking at me.

'Is it...?' Danielle said.

The police officers followed the gurney into room 143, and one of the nurses closed the door behind them, leaving us out in the corridor.

After about five minutes, the police left the room, and Danielle and Lori rushed in. The officer who took my statement approached me.

'Our guys are looking in the car park for the knife you described. If we don't find it, we may ask you more questions, Mr Kushner.'

'Sure, whenever you want officer,' I said.

I went into Eric's room. Lori was standing near the door, while Danielle was leaning over the bed, trying to hug Eric.

'I'm glad you're OK,' Lori said. 'You're lucky. I mean, we're all lucky.'

'I don't understand it at all,' Eric said. 'Really. You and he... I just don't understand....'

'How could that man dare to do such a thing?' Danielle asked. 'What happened, Eric? Tell me. Did you have a fight with him? Tell me, please.'

She was looking at all of us with curious eyes, trying to understand what was happening.

'Later, honey,' Eric said. 'Let's quit talking about it. I'm tired and... don't want to think of him now. Or later.'

Lori headed towards the door. 'I'm going outside to have a cigarette,' she said.

I closed the door after her.

'I can't believe it, V; that son of a bitch stabbed me with a knife and what?! He earns "family protection!" What the fuck is going on!"

'I didn't do it for him! I did it for Lori, suddenly and without thinking. If the police learned what really happened, they might investigate further, and then the inheritance, the will, the money. If that asshole James told them he did this for Lori – and I'm sure he would – they would ask him why. Then everything would get more complicated —'

'Fuck! Bullshit!'

'C'mon, Eric, you see it. I behaved instinctively, to protect her. But don't worry; we can deal with this somehow, on our own…'

'What?! How will we deal with this, V? Are you out of your mind? That man gads about like a Mafioso. Before you said we couldn't deal with him. What has changed since then? I'm gonna go crazy, agh! I could go and kill him now… and I mean it…'

'Stop it!' Danielle said. 'Please, Eric, stop…. Don't talk like that. Please, that's enough. Let's not talk about him any longer. You're hurt because of this man, but he isn't worth anything like that. You know he's a vulgar man; how could you deal with him anyway? But… Lori will punish him for this, won't she, V?'

She wanted me to answer a very difficult question. Everything had become so complicated that I was afraid that James might even try to hurt Lori. Daring to stab Eric showed he was already losing it.

Though I didn't believe my own words, I said, 'Certainly. Don't worry about that!'

'Certainly, my ass,' Eric said.

'Eric, that's enough,' I said. 'Please, try to pull yourself together and stop quarrelling with me!'

'I'm not quarrelling with you. I'm just angry that we ever gave him any credit. He stabbed me today and may shoot you tomorrow. He also said, if you recall, that you're next. He'll fuck both of us if we don't press charges against him! Now! Oh, the bastard! He's outdone himself…'

Eric was in fact right, but now that he was okay and we were getting over the first shock and fear, I was starting to focus on different issues – like him and Amy. Therefore, I couldn't feel empathy for him, only anger.

Eric considered my father as his father too, and loved him with all his respect. Eric had always been like a brother to me, and Lori had been "our" sister, until she fell in love with him. Even though he hadn't returned her love, Eric had always stayed respectful to her. But, not giving Lori what she wanted had always been a problem, for everybody.

Eric had not treated Gary any differently from Lori in terms of respect. They had never been very close, but they had always behaved quite well to each other. Neither Lori nor Gary had ever considered Eric as someone outside our family; he was the second little brother to them.

What "Eric and Amy" had done to Gary was not much different to stabbing him with a knife, right in his back. I was sure he'd never imagined such a thing happening to him – not from those two. Gary trusted Eric so much he would consign his life to him. In Gary's mind, Eric could be anything but a traitor.

'Everything gets worse, every day,' Danielle said. 'What's happening? Why don't you do something to correct all this, V?'

I started to laugh – I couldn't stop myself. 'Me? Am I not doing anything? How can you be sure of that?'

'I don't know. If you were, something would be going better, right? But, huh, what's happening, that asshole comes and stabs Eric...'

'C'mon, Dani, stop it,' Eric said. 'What has V got to do with all this? What could he do? He's the only one trying to fix things. Things that, in fact, aren't even our business.... This should all be their problem.'

'If it should all be "their" problem, why are you the one who gets stabbed?!'

'Enough, Danielle!' Eric said. 'Enough... please, stop! I don't wanna listen to your never-ending nonsense questioning! Can't you just pause for a moment? Even now?'

'DAMN IT!' Danielle said.

She snatched up her purse in fury and headed for the door, high heels pounding the floor. When she opened the door, she came face to face with Amy, who was just about to enter the room.

Amy! Amy, who'd had sex with Eric only a couple of hours before he was stabbed. The two women looked at each other in a surprise. Amy stepped aside to let Danielle pass. Danielle left without saying a word to her.

Amy stood at the door, looking at us. I sensed her thinking, *Does he know? How should I behave? What will he do?* as a weird tension rose between the three of us.

'How are you?' she said to Eric, walking towards his bed-side.

'Hi, V,' she said without looking at me.

I didn't reply.

Amy asked what had happened, and Eric told her about his confrontation with James. Amy, listening to Eric with worried and fearful eyes, turned to me.

'You haven't pressed charges?! Why not?!' she said.

'No, we haven't. But not for James' sake – in order to protect my family.'

'Your *family*,' she said.

I didn't want to open my mouth and say even one word to her, though I had more to say. They were both obsessed with their "love" for each other, which they had only recently discovered, or revitalised. I thought they had lost their ability to make healthy evaluations and remarks about what we were going through. If I'd told Amy any of my thoughts while they were in this state, it would only cause a rift between us and add another burden to all of our tired shoulders.

After a while, I guessed that they wanted to be alone.

'I'm gonna go talk with Lori... outside,' I said.

They didn't protest.

Lori was sitting on the wall I'd discovered earlier. She was alone – and appeared lonely.

'Where's Danielle?' I asked. 'And Mr Elkins? Has he gone? Why aren't you sitting inside, by the way?'

'I'm smoking. Mr Elkins was done, so he left. Danielle is in the toilet. She'll be back soon, I guess.'

I sat next to her.

'Amy's inside,' I said. 'Did you see her? I wonder how she got the news—'

'I called her,' Lori said.

'You called her? Why?'

She took a deep drag on her cigarette. 'I thought she might wanna see him.'

So Lori knew. And she had shown her respect for love by calling the woman who had the very love she herself desired. Bowing one's head and standing in homage before love – like a real lover: decent and honourable. All the things related to Lori showed themselves (again) as a sign of courage and virtue. Except one pain in the ass.

'Has James called yet? I mean, have you talked—'

'No. He hasn't. I haven't talked to him.'

'Um... then, what now? What are we gonna do?'

'Don't worry; everything will take its course. Everything's gonna be okay. Don't lose your hope.'

'I won't, Lori. But c'mon, I'm still worried. I fear that James may upset or harm you. What can I do to prevent that? Tell me what to do....'

She smiled. Her cigarette finished, she threw the butt into the trash holder and stood up. She took my head with both of her hands. 'I said don't worry. He can't do anything to me. Don't you know me, V?'

'I do, but... but he's an asshole. If he hurts you, I swear I'll kill him, Lori.'

'Shut the fuck up! Don't talk nonsense, boy. He won't do anything else. To any of us. Now, stop worrying, okay? Don't become obsessed with these things. Go to your bookshop. Don't you have things to do?'

'I'm very rarely going there these days. Unfortunately. I wish these fucking issues would come to an end.... After that, I swear I won't leave there even for an instant.'

'Good. Books are your life. Don't neglect your life. Think of them instead of getting caught up with worthless things – like that asshole.'

'Watch your mouth.'

'Go fuck yourself.'

'I'm thinking of you, Lori. Seriously,' I said.

She smiled and squeezed my nose.

'Come on,' she said. 'I'll go say goodbye to the wounded bird and then leave. It's very crowded here... no place for me....'

'I have a question: how did Amy behave towards you? I mean, she should be hating you right now.'

'I don't know. She might hate me. We didn't talk too much. I just said, "Eric is in the hospital. I thought you might wanna know." I told her it was nothing to worry about, just a minor issue, and blah, blah. She thanked me, and that was all. Nothing more. Then she showed up.'

'Who told her about James... stabbing him?'

'I did. When she arrived she asked me what happened, and so I told her.'

I stood up, and together we walked back inside. Danielle was at the coffee machine. She joined us as we walked towards Eric's room, and I began to pray to God that when we opened the door, we wouldn't see anything that would end this all in a complete disaster.

When we entered the room, Amy was sitting on the same chair I had been sitting on earlier. They were only talking. Danielle, apparently forgetting that she had left the room so suddenly before, approached Eric and kissed him.

'How are you, honey?' she said.

Lori stopped to wait at the foot of the bed. "The women of Eric" were around him, like guardian angels, at full strength. The one he wanted to remove from his life was closest to him, while the one he had fallen in love with was farthest away. A picture worth remembering for all my life.

'I have to go now, Eric,' Lori said. 'I hope you'll get over the physical and psychological effects of this unpleasant event as soon as possible. I mean..., I hope we'll all get over it.'

She approached and hugged Eric. He controlled himself very well and didn't mention anything about James. Instead, he thanked Lori and smiled.

'Later, girls,' Lori said, nodding to Amy and Danielle. Then, calling me outside with only her eyes, she left the room.

I went after her and followed her to her car. She turned to me.

'Be careful. I'll deal with my stupid husband, don't worry, but pay attention to what I say: don't mess with him. Please, don't. I don't care about anyone except you. Do you understand me? There's you on one side and the rest of the family on the other side, understand? It's not all the same to me: there's you, and then there's the others.... Don't forget that.'

We hugged. Then, she got into her car and sailed away.

I was alone in the garden of the hospital. The stars in the sky started to appear one by one. There were three people inside, attending a complicated, knotted relationship ball. I returned to the room in order to help Eric with the checkout.

'So, what now? When are they gonna let you go?' I said.

'In around fifteen minutes. The nurse said so.'

'Let's go to my place tonight...,' I said.

'Your place? Why?' Danielle asked. 'You can come to our place, and stay if you like. I need to take care of my little boy.'

I looked at Amy out of the corner of my eye. She was counting the floor tiles.

'Yes, thank you, V. I will certainly need a friend by my side tonight,' Eric said. 'But you can come to us.'

While we were debating about who would stay where, Amy stood up.

'I also need to be leaving,' Amy said. 'Eric, get well soon. I hope your wound gets better quickly and you return to your old days...'

"Old days." Then, she left the room, acknowledging me and Danielle with just a distant look.

'Sometimes Amy behaves like a very strange person,' Danielle said. 'I mean, I know she isn't happy these days, but that's not our fault; it's because of James. That idiot! He's to blame for everything....'

'Again and again, you must always remind me of that son of a bitch, right?' Eric said.

Though her concern was something way different, it was again Danielle who was rejected, who was silenced and from whose heart a small piece fragmented – again.

Eric had been given two crutches, but when he got up he used only one and began "walking." I carried the other one.

When we reached the car, Danielle yelled, 'Oh my God!' The passenger seat was covered in blood; it was not an easy sight to look at. Eric took a glance and then they both got into the backseat.

As I drove, I met Eric's gaze in the rear-view mirror from time to time. Danielle was resting her head on his shoulder, looking out at the road. Although he kept silent, I could read his mind. The pain resulting from the unspoken words to Danielle was much greater than the pain from his knife-wound. He couldn't feel anything about Danielle's emotional closeness to him at that moment. His mind was wandering in a very different place. Meanwhile, unaware of the reality, Danielle was just trying to be happy.

We reached their home. Eric wanted to walk inside on his own, wounded and noble. It was forbidden for him to take a bath, so he simply changed his clothes and lay down over the sofa in the sitting room.

The apartment was very silent, as if a new-born baby was sleeping there. We couldn't utter any meaningful words, and the time was passing over us like a road roller. Suddenly, I remembered that Chelsea had sent me an email.

'Dani, can I use your laptop? I want to check my email....'

'Of course. Help yourself. It's there, on the console.'

I moved to the farthest corner of the room with the laptop. I logged in to my account and saw the email. I couldn't say that I didn't feel excited. I hadn't seen her name in the "From" section for ages. I felt a kind of longing. I was happy that we had once been together, but also happy for her that she was not with me at this time.

I started to read her email.

Hello,

First of all, I want to mention that I didn't write the email you will find attached with the hope that you would see it one day. I wrote down my feelings to cure my soul, believing that they would belong only to me throughout my life.

What you will read does not require a response, and I expect nothing from you. Just read it. That is all. Don't even reply, please.
For the sake of all the nice days we had, sending you this was the best answer I had to your question. You deserve to read these.

I'm very happy now. Very happy.

I hope you'll also be happy one day.

C.

I opened the attached file. It was a photo of a white page on a dark-brown table. I remembered her handwriting.

Today, it's your birthday, again. To celebrate, again without you, I sat at my desk and opened a bottle of Riesling 2008. 'The Way We Were' is playing in the background. As you can see, I have made a change: from this time on, I will listen to this woman instead of the other. I don't know how long it will last. It took me three years to move from the heart-melting lyricist to this diva. We will see.

It is about 11 p.m. right now, but earlier there, where you are. You might be at a romantic dinner, or maybe you're out dancing with all your friends. You might be spending the night listening to a lot of small-talk. I really, really want you to be happy on your birthdays. I want your eyes to smile and your laughter to echo around you. I don't want your heart to feel any bitterness, nor to remember your regrets or losses. You should think only of the things you have gained. Don't even think of me.... I loved you so much, you see? And I still do.

I've let my hair free today, as you'd liked it. I let it be as free as it wants to be. I let the air dry it, and it has gone wavy now. Like the wavy state I remained in after you left. I'm smiling; I don't get upset that easily... I'm not complaining. Those days have already passed. They are now way behind me, and behind us. Now, I just have your beautiful words in my mind.... They are almost always with me during my happy moments. When I am unhappy or sad, your shoulders are with me to lean on. Your beautiful supportive words. Your ambitious looks. Your touches on my arm as you ask, "Are you okay, now?"

Okay, I admit that I'm crying a little, but don't worry! My tears are going to dry; they always did and always do. I'll get over it. Just a sec, I'll have a sip from my cool German mate here...

Today, I told the rainbow-haired woman that I would write the sixth letter to you (as her anger towards you has not died yet, she doesn't look at me when I call her with that name). By the way, she dyed her hair a reddish yellow this time. But, it doesn't look nice, oh God! I told her she doesn't look like "herself" at all, but a stranger. It is a colour that hinders me from showing tolerance for her untimely perversity.

She has been perverse today. Actually, she wasn't just perverse – she became angry with me. She rebuked me. She said I must wake up to reality and that you were a selfish snob who always thought only of yourself and would still be thinking only of yourself. She said I should pity my husband, if not myself, since my mind is still on you. And that I should have more respect for myself, because everything in the past remains there, and now it's absolutely over... and that I need to look ahead, and enjoy the day and my life. Without you. Without your memory. Without your eyes, smile and words, the stupid words. (I'm smiling now.) And of course without your clumsiness, your missing glasses. Maybe I can just enjoy your pens secretly, which you left at my place in your hurry to leave me.

You can't imagine how angry I was with her today. She's behaving like one of those people I don't like: those people who are always realists, behaving as if they do not need dreams or empty hopes to endure all of life's difficulties, and never interested in the past but always looking ahead. None of them are as realistic as they think; they don't gain anything, but deceive themselves. Moreover, they leave their beautiful memories as orphans and their vivid dreams unfulfilled. They are vulgar, but I'm not.

And she has that hair, my God.... I was furious at her, but then I realised that I was just wounded by her attitude. Why does she leave me alone? She knows how much you mean to me, that I've evolved with you, that you helped me become the person I am now.... She says I am a child, apparently for my own good. But I'm not looking for parenting... I've passed those ages. They have ended. "We" have ended, you and me. What I want is for her to try to understand me and say, "Come, let's read your letters. Let's cry together and then laugh together, remembering him. Yes, let's remember him!"

You. I remember you, my love.

No, no... I'm not crying. These fallen tears don't count – they are not mine anymore, but my desk's. I'm smiling even. Where are you now, honey? Are you happy? I swear that I want you to be happy. As happy as you can be. I want anyone who's sharing your life now to make you happy. You are a good soul. Even though you're not mine right now, you are still a beautiful soul, darling.

When I write to you, I always drink the whole bottle so quickly, and now I have finished it. But you know, I don't have more than one bottle for you. A bottle once a year. And it's empty now. I had better go out on the balcony and breathe in some fresh air. The night is charming here. The stars are shining brightest in the sky. It's a bit chilly, a little windy. If you were next to me now, your hair would wave in a rebellious way as if it was standing against the strongest wind. I'd first watch it, and then look into your eyes and kiss you. I'd say, "This is your present, this year." I know it would satisfy me. I know it would satisfy you. Is there any wind caressing your beautiful hair, my love, in whatever faraway place you are... a place that is as faraway as possible... from me?"

Tears had accumulated in my eyes, waiting for me to blink so they could fall freely. I couldn't breathe, my heart was beating fast. I was dumbfounded, scared to blink. I didn't want to shed my tears for this letter, the author of it, her lovely voice, her sincere attitude, her passionate love. I didn't want to be in another war within myself.

I closed my eyes. Two drops fell, leaving two lines down my cheeks like slight cuts from a knife, causing me to suffer as much as possible.

I closed down the laptop, stood up and yelled goodbye to Danielle and Eric, heading for the door without looking at their faces.

Eric shouted after me.

'Hey, what happened? What's the matter? Is it James again or what?!'

I was trying to leave as fast as I could, but then Danielle, who I had assumed was in the sitting room with Eric, walked out of the kitchen and into my path. We came eye to eye in the narrow hall for an instant. She saw me crying. She stood before me and looked at me. I looked back at her. She then touched the wetness on my left cheek with her index finger, frowned slightly and tilted her head.

I reached past her side and opened the door. Danielle didn't ask anything or suggest that I stay. She didn't speak a word.

When I got into the car, I was sobbing like a child. Hearing such sincere words after all those years and after the last week had destroyed my balance completely. I wasn't crying because I missed Chelsea or wanted to run back into her arms. I didn't even have such a right anyway, and she had told me she was happy. I was crying for all the memories I had accumulated, for the beautiful scars remaining in my soul, for the love and longing in my heart, for my father, mother, sister, brother; for my despair, hope, and existence; and for M, for her absence.

I knew that I had to take shelter at my home in order to come through this blitzkrieg I'd pulled myself into.

I drove.

Lustday
20 SEPTEMBER

I SPENT THE night without quite sleeping; I kept turning in the bed, trying to free my mind (but failing), re-running the James incident over and over, and thinking of what Chelsea had written to me, of her sincerity, the strength and hope she had given me. I fell asleep for one or two hours towards morning. Then woke up like a miserable drunk.

It was another Monday, and the gloom and complexity in my head were at full strength. Even though I had slept, it didn't seem to have helped – and lying on the bed in the darkness wasn't giving me any relief either.

I got up, checked the news online, and then prepared myself a green tea. After refreshing myself, I found the courage to read Chelsea's letter once more. Then again, and again. I didn't cry this time;

I kept calm. But I felt a pang of sorrow in my heart whenever I read it. Again and again.

She'd said she wasn't expecting an answer, and I did not intend to reply. Even if she had expected it, I would have had no idea of what to say. Should I thank her because she hadn't forgotten me, or because she'd made me believe there was no possibility of her forgetting me? Or, should I apologise? I had no idea.

I was considering all these things, feeling empty inside, when Eric called. He asked how I was.

'In fact, I should be asking you,' I said. 'How is your ass?'

'Still gorgeous. I'm fine. It aches a bit, but it's okay. I can even go to work today. I won't stay there the whole day, but it feels good that I *can* go there. What about you? Last night, you suddenly got the blues.'

'I'm fine. It's all okay. I got a bit, you know, when I read the email...'

'From who?'

'Chelsea.'

'What? She sent you an email?'

'Yes.'

'And? What did she say?'

'That she hadn't forgotten me. I mean, to get straight to the point.'

'Really... and what now?'

'Nothing.'

My answer pleased him.

'Why did she need to mention that all of a sudden?'

'Remember, I asked her...'

'You've really become strange,' he said.

Perhaps, since he'd recently become involved in a complicated triangle between a lover, husband and his miserable self, he just didn't want me to experience the same thing.

After hanging up, I read the letter once more and then decided a shower might be a good idea. "Crying in the Rain" was playing on the radio.

After my dance with a towel, T-shirt and jeans, I was ready for a beloved friend of mine.

My bookshop was always there, safe and sound. And I wished that it would always be. I tried not to think of anything else except for being there. Despite everything that had happened, I needed to spend time in the shop. I had to do it in order to breathe in the fresh air of reveries, words, imaginary friends, even if only briefly. It was like some kind of a sanatorium for my wounded soul.

As I hadn't dropped by for days, everything in my shop – the little office at the back, my desk, the unpacked new arrivals, the stay-home books on the shelves, and unanswered emails – were all looking at me biliously. They had missed my presence, but they wouldn't forgive easily or bow to me just because I was there at last.

I began to tidy up with huge enthusiasm, as if I were starting everything from scratch, like this was my first day at the shop. I saw and felt my stuff and fellow books anew. Unlike in recent days, I forced myself not to rerun in my mind's theatre the disasters I had experienced. I focused on my errands and pretended nothing had happened the previous week, as if everything related to that time frame had been erased completely from my memory – as if those sorrows, surprises, tears and fights had never taken place.

The silent morning brought no customers. My cell phone didn't ring. No one intervened in the mutual flow of emotion between me and my books. I dusted the shelves and watered the flowers. I looked over the ordering lists and paid the due and almost-due bills.

Then I wandered around, touching the book jackets. I imagined that thousands of other lives were re-lived on every read, in every other mind, in every other heart. Different on each day. Stories that were both known and not yet experienced, stories that would be read in the future, and the mistakes that people make in them – those that would be repeated again and again. The books stood docile on their shelves. Stories about loves, betrayals, wars, indecencies, families, brothers, mistresses, kids – all side by side. Who, I wondered, was the first owner of the story I had been experiencing for the last week? Had it been lived before? Why on earth was I living it again? Who would live it again, and when, and where? What could I suggest to the "lucky" guy or lady?

The peaceful hours I'd spent alone didn't make any contribution to our conflicts and fights, though. Why had we gone through such a disaster? The whole story was about how an old man's money would be shared after his death. It had set people against each other, busied their minds constantly, and changed the whole flow of their normal lives. It was all because of that meaningless money, which was unable to buy one millionth of a view of a fair blue sea on a breezy day.

As of that morning, I decided to let things slide from now on. I didn't feel the need to follow the truth or show it to anyone, to correct their mistakes or hold their insolence against them.

There was a feeling in my heart (for no particular reason) that everything could just "get better." Though we couldn't remember it at every moment, self-improvement was the core essence of life. I'd woken up with the magic of that feeling in the morning.

While hope continued to breed in my whole being, the first client of the day arrived.

'How nice it is to see you at your work again,' she said.

'How nice it is to see you here again,' I said.

'Yes, you're right. I've been a stranger to this place for so long. If I hadn't been able to find you here, I'd have fulfilled my longing by just looking inside through the window. How about you? Have you been missing anything?'

'Missing you?' I smiled. 'Yeah, I could say that I've been missing you, though I saw you just ten hours ago.'

Danielle smiled back.

'You must have been missing me, of course... I don't even need to ask that. But did you also miss the books, the smell...?'

'Of course. Terribly. For me, this is the most beautiful place in the world – these four walls and the shelves inside.'

'How nice,' she said and smiled again.

We smiled together.

I prepared coffee, and we each took a chair next to my desk in my small office at the back of the store. Danielle told me Eric was feeling better and had gone to work again. She seemed more relaxed than the previous night. She didn't seem so worried.

'What happened to you last night? You vanished so suddenly....'

'Nothing. I mean, I read an email – a letter trapped in an email to be precise. From an old friend. It was... a bit touching. But I'm fine now. It wasn't that she wrote horrible things to make me feel that way.'

'I know. I mean, I felt it. You had tears in your eyes, not for bitter things but out of longing, I saw. Not because something'd ended, but because of a voice and breath coming from past days. It seemed so... I don't know. But when I saw you like that, I sensed what you were going through.'

I smiled.

'Yes, you guessed right. I felt pain, but it was not simply because an old love had slogged my heart. It was a different feeling, of happiness from having experienced love and sharing the same memories together, knowing that someone you'd loved is living somewhere, thinking of you from time to time. I was thankful, and sort of lost myself in that joy, I suppose. It's not easy to describe.'

'I understand you,' she said. 'The cons of being emotional; not everyone feels so deeply. Life is difficult for you and others like you.'

She was smiling, and she was very beautiful.

'Most people can feel, but they probably prefer not to,' I said.

'Maybe. I've also felt similar things... and perhaps will again soon.'

'What do you mean?'

'I don't know. Gut feelings. Opinions – never mind. What shall we do?'

'Sorry?'

'What will you do today? Will you stay here the whole day?'

'Well, I guess I'm planning to stay for the moment, yeah. I don't wanna get involved at anything or deal with anyone like James, or Amy... I wanna stay alone in my cave, here....'

'Alone? Am I disturbing you?'

'No, no..., you're excluded from "anyone." Nobody else but you.'

'Nice. Then, can I stay with you? Here?'

'If you like, of course you can....'

'Yippee!' she said, and jumped out of her chair in joy to give me a hug.

In doing so, she tripped slightly, unbalanced, and fell into my arms.

We came eye to eye and found ourselves looking at each other, very close, feeling each other's breaths on our lips for an instant. I had never noticed the tiny yellow lines in her eyes, like meticulous ribbons placed within the brown. It looked as if a wind was blowing in her mind and the ribbons were turning with it. *The woman in whose eyes the ribbons turn.* Though my heart had started to beat more rapidly, I felt I had to wake up at once. I took her arms and stood up, helping her regain her balance. The "sinful fall" had come to an end, but then the "dangerous-thoughts ball" blew up.

'Okay, if you're gonna stay with me, let's tidy up the shelves at the front...,' I said, and ran away into the store.

She spent some time with me, but it was obvious she was growing more bored with every passing minute. Then she didn't want to stay any longer.

'I had better leave, V. This much cultural activity is enough for today. I need some more feminine things to do, like trying on some new shoes and clothes. A peaceful mind is not for me right now. I wanna get lost choosing the right colours and designs.'

She smiled and went to the back office again, took her bag, and walked to the front door. She paused to wave.

'Goodbye!' she said, and then left without waiting for my reply.

I watched her leaving. I watched her legs moving her towards her sins, her feet beautifying the world every time they hit the ground.

I made myself wake up from this dream that could soon turn into a nightmare and surrendered myself to my office.

I started to tidy up my drawers, and there I encountered my notebook, in which I sometimes wrote down my thoughts. The last entry was dated more than two months ago. I had written to M, to whom that notebook was mostly dedicated.

I read some of the pieces. There was one that sparked a memory of exactly when and where I'd written it. I had been at a movie theatre alone, and I'd seen a woman there who resembled M. After realising it was not her, I'd taken up my pen and found comfort in filling a blank page.

I see you from a distance. You meet your friends and shoot the breeze. Even in this very short instant, your joy for life gushes from your eyes. I'm walking towards you; we are approximately seventy-meters apart. It seems that I can reach you within about eighty-five steps. You are laughing while you speak. Not because you want to show off your happiness to the people around you, but just because you feel like it.

I like you very much when you behave like this – sincere. When your smile comes from your heart, your lips turn into a different shape; the inner side of your upper lip turns a little outward. A very tiny part, more wet than the normal, represents your inner side, like your deeper flesh.

Now, I've taken forty-five steps – you are moving your hand towards your hair and playing with your curls. You do this whenever you get bored. I don't know why you are doing it right now though; you don't seem bored. Maybe the person you're talking to has said some vain words to monkey around, and you want to run away but you're stuck because of the burden of friendship. You are moving your hands over your hair to keep yourself busy. Instead of my hand, your hand. Your left hand. Your thin fingers and red-polished nails have taken over the smell of your strands.

When I have twenty-two steps to-go, I want to take your left hand and smell it. Some people are passing me by. I had to stop for a while, but I haven't given up. You turn your back to me and reply to the silly questions coming from the people sitting at the table. What will happen to my questions? Do you also have answers for me? Or will you answer my questions with your own questions?

When I have thirteen steps more to-go, questions flow in my mind; who is right, me or you? Now I'm able to hear your voice. You'd grown bored and left the office without finishing the report you were asked to do. As you've still not gone home on this fresh spring evening, you must want to stay in the afternoon sun, the light of which is confirming all your beauty.

Now, the distance has decreased even more. We have just seven steps between us. You pause for an instant and feel my presence in your vicinity, turn around, look for me. First, your gaze meets my new shoes, and then you raise your head and see me. We are now eye to eye. For the first time in twenty-two days.

Your breathing got quicker. I saw it, even though you are trying your best not to reveal it. You tilt your head a little left. The others follow your gaze, start looking at me. I still have not given up looking at you. After touching your hand slightly, your friends move back to the table and you turn to me.

After that last step I took, only six more steps remain. Six small steps for the sun to rise in my life again.

Then, on another page, I encountered a piece of writing that made me very sad. We had just broken up, and I had been driving around the city, thinking of her. I'd heard a piece of music on the radio, a song we'd chosen for a future journey, and had taken up my pen again to write something down on the back page of my car's service booklet:

Tonight, while I'm listening to "I Drove All Night," I can come to you without any bit of hesitation. While the night is standing over me, darkest blue, and the black clouds are carrying the night towards the morning, I can still hold the steering wheel and think of you without getting tired. While the wind is sneaking through the window, your darkest hair is still on my mind. While your looks are still burning every eye that they come along, or any flower or tree, I may come to you to get burned voluntarily. I can still be on my way to you, anywhere you go.

There was no limit to the memories these writings evoked. If I had continued to read them, my fragile and temporary peace would have broken up completely. Having difficulty in breathing and feeling very depressed, I squeezed all the notebooks into the drawer and decided to chase some errands to reset my mind.

While my head was trying to end the journey it had been on, I was startled by a phone call. It was Gary. I answered it, scared that my peaceful day might come to an end.

'What's up, V? Where are you?' he said.

'I'm at the store, doing some regular work, a bit of this and that. How about you?'

I asked that question under the shade of the betrayal I knew of, but he was not aware of that, of course.

'I'm fine, too. I'm going to the atelier soon. Amy isn't here; she left early in the morning. Anyway, this morning when I was having breakfast, Lori called me... V, do you have some spare time?'

'Yes, of course. Why?'

'First, a question... though it's a bit strange. Anyway, I heard that James stabbed Eric. Lori said he was okay, but... is it true?'

'Yes, it happened yesterday.'

'How is Eric?'

'He's doing fine, don't worry.'

'Good. I'm glad to hear it. What's James' problem? Has he just completely lost control?'

'I don't know. Eric and I leaving the cemetery after visiting Father, and we stumbled upon James at the exit. He got mad and attacked Eric. I had to take him to the hospital, but fortunately he got off cheap. He's fine.'

'Good. Anyway... I talked to Lori a bit—'

'Hey, Gary, she's okay, right?! Tell me that motherfucker James hasn't done anything to her?!'

'No, no, no... not at all. She's fine. She apologised to me.'

'Apologised? For what ?'

'On behalf of James, for his "stupid" behaviour towards Amy. "Stupid" is Lori's word, by the way.'

'Didn't you say, "Don't apologise to me – apologise to Amy!" Or, "You should not apologise, but your asshole husband—"'

'No, no, I didn't. That was kind of her, though. What do you think? Is everything going to get better from now on?'

'Oh, Gary... that bastard stabbed Eric yesterday. Before that, he quarrelled with me and punched me in my face and stomach. I really wonder how you can conclude that everything is going to get better?!'

'Not for James. Never mind him—'

'How can I not mind him? He's the one buggering everything up!'

'Lori will handle him. Don't worry. I hope Lori will begin to behave reasonably. How is she doing?'

Gary's attitude was disturbing. He was unaware of reality, and his perceptions were closed. Moreover, becoming involved whenever he wanted and then keeping himself away whenever he didn't seemed so selfish. I couldn't understand how he could stay so indifferent. Gary's unnecessary calmness on top of my mixed feelings felt like torture.

'How could I know, Gary? I hope she'll make reasonable decisions at last. Look, I need to hang up now. People are waiting for me here. Talk later, okay?'

'Oh, okay... and... oh my! James has just arrived.... He's parking his car... why is he here, V? Anyway, we'll see.'

'James?! What the fuck is he there for? Gary, don't mess with him. If he does something odd, let me know quickly. Or should I come over now—'

'No, no, you don't need to be here.... He seems calm. Don't worry, I'll let you know if he tries to kill me...'

He laughed at this joke and hung up.

I felt sorry for Gary, but I couldn't help feeling angry with him too. He seemed to live in a bell glass. How could he misperceive and misinterpret all the realities? I was aware that subjectivity dominated my view too, and I didn't expect him to find everything I said right, but he had various roles to fulfil: he was a husband, a brother, a relative and an enemy. I couldn't understand how he maintained an attitude of indifference to his responsibilities. I didn't want to accept that he was considered an ineffective person by most of his acquaintances. There was a common link between Amy's inability to stay indifferent towards Eric, and James' expectation that he could use Gary – and the common link was Gary's weak stance. He acted as if no matter who punched him, he would never punch back.

But no matter how Gary behaved, he didn't deserve to be treated like shit. And his younger brother didn't deserve to see, hear and feel it.

James jumped into my mind, pushing Gary aside. Why was he at Gary's? I wanted to go there and wait outside as a precaution – that way I could help Gary quickly if required.

A young man who had been browsing through the shelves suddenly found what he'd been looking for: he took Stephen King's

Misery from the shelf, approached the counter, and paid for it. As he left, I decided it was a good time for me to leave the store too – it was a time to take action, or at least to go and think.

I got out, locked the main door, but then paused, unable to decide whether to go or not. Counting the pavement tiles, I began to walk. I didn't want to see or hear anyone, but the neighbourhood was packed with people. I pretended not to overhear the words of the people passing me by.

Absolute indecision. On one hand, I wanted to stand by Gary; I felt that I should. On the other hand, I wanted to leave him alone to deal with this problem on his own. He had to learn that if he didn't stand up and defend his honour and life, nobody else would do it on his behalf. It seemed too late for him to gain such a perspective.

My desire to isolate myself from the world by staring at the ground as I walked was not accepted by the flow of life. It had been just two or three minutes since I'd left the store when I heard Danielle calling after me.

I turned back, and waited. She walked towards me one tiny step at a time. I watched each step of her legs, despite knowing that I shouldn't. I regretted each step and promised not to stare at the next one, but couldn't keep my promise.

'This time I'm fed up with shopping,' she said. 'What's up with you?'

'Not much. I was just thinking of heading home,' I lied.

'Come then, I'll drive you home.'

'No, thank you. I have my car with me, over there.'

'Please, come on, V. I need to talk to you.... I'm not feeling so good.' She hugged me suddenly and started to cry.

I didn't know what to do and chose the wrong move: I hugged her back.

'Hey, calm down. What's the matter? What happened?'

'I'm not feeling good, not at all...'

'Hey, don't cry. We'll find a solution, whatever it is. Don't worry now...'

We turned and headed back to the store. I didn't want her walking around the streets in such a sad mood. "Angel" me.

She walked through the door in my arms where, previously, she hadn't waited for me to say goodbye. We walked down the corridor, to my office at the back. She seemed a little calmer and wiped her nose and eyes.

The stress made me break out the emergency bottle of whisky, which I kept in my drawer for urgent situations.

'We need to drink from the bottle...,' I said.

She smiled. I took a big sip and then passed it to her. She smiled again.

'Thank you, but I don't want any,' she said.

'Well, that's good. One of us had better stay sober,' I said.

She was looking at me without speaking, leaning her head on the wall behind her.

'So, what's the problem? Go on..., tell me,' I said. I took one more sip.

'Can't you see the problem?'

'What do you mean?'

'You should be able to guess.'

'I mean, I have some idea about why you may feel depressed, but I'm not totally sure...'

'What might be my problem?'

'What might be...? I think you're at odds with Eric.'

I immediately felt a deep regret. By saying it out loud, I had confirmed that the reason for her sorrow was real and obvious. That was not proper in my situation. Not proper at all.

I decided I had to stay politically correct from then on. My very tiny mistake could cause irreversible trouble between Eric and Danielle, and I didn't want to become involved in an issue between them. The problem was all theirs – at least for the time being.

'You think we have problems, don't you?' she said.

'Well—'

'No, a correction: you don't *think* so, you *see it*! You SEE that we have problems...'

'I don't know... You might have problems like every couple has....

Probably.'

'Come on! He must have told you. Don't lie to me, V.'

After that comment, I became nervous. Maybe she'd come back to my store to ask me to spy for her.

'Lie? C'mon, Dani, I won't lie to you. What must he have told me?'

'About us. About me. You can't convince me that you two don't talk about us. But relax. I'm not planning to use you as an insider. I don't need your information. I can *see* everything by myself. It is... very obvious. Everything's oh-so obvious.'

I needed to get help from the whisky.

'I have a confession...,' she said.

'Say it.'

Whisky.

'Once upon a time, I told one of my close friends that... if I had approached you instead of Eric, my life would be much happier...'

(That confession really deserved a church and a real father.)

The whisky bottle remained at my mouth. The blood in my body seemed to drain away, and my heart started to beat as fast as it could.

She was looking at me. She appeared very relaxed, her legs crossed, her head resting against the wall behind her and tilted a little to the left. She had a slight smile; she was playing with me, dangling a string-toy for a bewildered cat.

I swallowed the giant sip of whisky and put the bottle down on my desk. It was as if someone had erased all my vocabulary from my brain. I couldn't find anything to say to her, nor to myself. I forgot all the words I knew, including "mistake," "behave," "trap," "regret," "betrayal," "stop," "don't!"

She smiled at my situation.

'What? Are you surprised to hear that?' she said.

The word "surprise" wasn't enough to express my feelings at all. I felt a cocktail of emotions, but shame was on top. It didn't result from the fact that she liked me or had desired me some time ago, but from not being able to reject her words or the idea at once. I'd allowed myself a few seconds to dream of it, and worse, was feeling pleased with it.

I smiled.

'I thought Eric had stolen your heart...'

'C'mon, V, you are old enough not to believe in such bullshit. That a man choosing a woman..."

I took a deep breath and then a big sip.

'Yes, you are correct,' I said. 'I mean, I think so... yes.'

She was smiling.

'What?' I said.

I was glad the whisky bottle was in my hands.

'I could seduce you, if I wanted,' she said. 'Whenever I want. I could have done it yesterday, last week or last year. I can do it still... tomorrow, next month, next year. I could even do it now...' She raised her left eyebrow.

I knew I would be punished in the hell of friendship and brotherhood for staring at her, spellbound, and for letting my bond with Eric weaken.

I kept silent. I took another sip from the whisky, and a deep breath from the hellish atmosphere around us.

'Yes,' I said, admitting my defeat.

'Yes what? You agree that I could seduce you anytime I want?'

I couldn't deny it. She was all-magical. 'Yes, you could,' I said.

She smiled.

'But what would we – you and me – do then?' she said. 'Wouldn't it be degrading... sinful?'

"You and me:" this combination was the most exciting thing I'd recently heard, side-lining both "Lori and Eric" and "Eric and Amy." This combination froze my mind and stirred my blood. This combination stopped the reason in the world I lived in.

Whisky. Deep breath.

'It would be an incredible betrayal,' I said. 'Beyond belief. A sin that would wound more deeply than any other in humankind...'

She smiled. But it was not a modest smile. She was really playing with me. I had no control over my body, or my mind, at all. I was totally captivated by her spell. Without even touching me, she had managed to get hold of me. A pure magician, and I was the puppet of her broken soul.

'*Beyond belief,*' she said. 'I think so too, V, but... let me ask you this: where would we belong – you and me? To heaven or... to hell?'

She then pulled her head away from the wall and stood erect. She looked through me, not moving her eyes.

Whisky.

'In which one you want it to be? In heaven or hell?' she repeated. Then she leaned forward.

Whisky, deep breath. Whisky.

'In hell...,' I mumbled. A definite surrender to my lust.

She smiled.

I knew that her lips were bold, but I hadn't noticed how beautiful they were before. Her lips were as red as a fresh apple waiting to be bitten.

'Why do we people all prefer hell, V?' she said.

She stood up, her body before my eyes. Fit and curvy. Her clothes seemed to have been produced in a special way to reveal and enhance her beauty and features. They fit her in the sexiest way possible.

I left all my values behind and started to take greater sips that filled my whole mouth. Before the burning taste of the last sip vanished, and while my throat was still hurting with the fire of the hell, I answered:

'Because truth and benevolence belongs to heaven. If I had to make a decision right now, I'd choose to get burnt in the fire. The fire that one deserves, in the depths of hell...'

I was regretting my attitude even as I heard the words coming from my mouth.

'Will we create a hell here, if your fire is burned in mine, V?' she said.

Then she put her hands on my desk and leaned towards me. Her fingers were long and thin, polished in claret red.

'Will our lust give birth to a hell of our own?'

I was already feeling the hellish fire all over my body. I leaned my head forward, towards her.

The dice were already cast. We had to pull ourselves apart. If this was a game, it had to end at this point. The next step could mean our lives would be destroyed in an irremediable way. All my values (if I had any left) and wisdom might vaporise. My mind had been confused for days, my heart was full of longing, and my body yearned for affection; then again, I should not be defeated by a sweet and dark surprise of life, under the influence of a few sips of whisky.

She looked at me with shiny eyes, her eyebrows resembling daggers, waiting in the wings to take my heart from its place.

I said, 'Probably,' and without hesitation she touched her lips on mine, giving me their plump softness like a savoury dessert. Her heart-carving spicy perfume was winding from her smooth skin towards my face.

I don't know how long that moment lasted, or whether I also kissed her back or behaved like a robot – because of both her spell and the clouds of (too much) whisky.

I felt as if I were gliding in space, within some kind of beauty, within a happiness and excitement that I didn't want to surrender myself wholly to. It might have lasted three seconds, or three thousand years; I couldn't comprehend.

I was a fool to have wished for hell without having any idea about the flames there. I had felt desperate, and had forgotten that every moment we live might be a test. But life is a smart-ass bitch and catches us at moments like those, when we are most unprepared and most-selfish.

A voice I heard, while I was still enjoying her spicy perfume, soft flesh and slippery red lipstick, showed me that the whole of hell and all its demons could fit in my small office.

'Tell me this is not happening for real...,' Eric said.

I came to know, at that very moment, that I was indeed cheating myself; I wasn't weak, and my perception wasn't so much influenced by the whisky, or by Danielle's magic.

I felt that I was actually a dead person then, lying forty floors below the ground, and couldn't breathe at all.

Eric, wearing a suit, his formal law-firm attire, was standing in the doorway holding a crutch in his right hand. His left hand was still on the door jamb, and his eyes were cauterising me.

'Everything else I could believe,' he said. 'Everything... but not this. I'm begging you...'

A rebellious teardrop slid down from his left eye across his cheek. He didn't have the stereotypical "crying man" expression; on the contrary, his face was emotionless, like an impassive statue, despite the tears cutting through his face and through our hearts.

Both Danielle and I stared at him, frozen. He shook his head and then, suddenly, threw his crutch behind him into the store and made two leaps forward. He reached the desk, leaned over it, and punched me over my left eye with all of his strength.

Till then, I might have fooled myself that all I'd experienced was a dream, or a nightmare, depending on the viewpoint. But when he punched me, the bright stars shining in my eyes proved that the moment was in fact pure reality. A very bright reality.

I was now in hell, as I'd decisively said I preferred only a couple of minutes ago. Eric's punch was the first flame of fire burning me.

Danielle jumped on Eric, shouting 'Stop! It's not what it looks like.'

Eric pushed her back and said, "Go away!" Then, he stood directly in front of me and looked me in the eye. I looked back at him with my left hand over my left eye, unable to move or speak.

'WHY!' he shouted with a volume that felt like it could make my ears bleed.

He then turned and, awkwardly, with a movement that resembled something between walking and jumping, left my office. I watched through the open door as he walked down the corridor that led to the store. He pushed over the first shelf he came across, and then walked over the fallen books, kicking a few across the store, and steered himself towards the front door.

Danielle remained motionless, looking at me. I was still watching Eric with one hand over my face. He was crying as he exited. I, on the other hand, couldn't cry at all.

Even though it had passed, that hellish moment when I heard his voice was still burning me. Thousands of times before, Danielle and I had been alone in this room – always in total recognition that I was a man and she was a woman. But we had never lost ourselves in this way, and we had always done the best we could not to hurt the soul of the one we both loved most.

Eric knew about our friendship and about me spending a lot of time with Danielle. He had never complained or been suspicious about it – I was the one he trusted most in his life. And that feeling was mutual: he was the one I trusted most. I'd been carried away with the joy of the moment and broken the bond of trust, to which I owed a lot. I'd lost Eric's trust for no good reason at all.

I believed that I had to shoulder all the blame for the situation with Danielle: my behaviours, the thoughts I had accumulated in my sub-conscious, my continuing to drink despite knowing that it would cause me to lose my self-control. All these faults were mine, and I had no excuses. Also, Danielle's path had been ruined. Even though it was a mutual act, I should have taken control and not let that kiss happen. Anyone can make mistakes, but not me, not at that moment – and not against Eric. Our friendship required better. Our friendship deserved better.

We all were born to make mistakes – but Danielle and I should not have made this one. We should have denied ourselves in that moment, no matter how strongly we felt. One of the main aims of my life was to eliminate obstacles from Eric's life and brighten his path, and he felt the same towards me. We tried to never disappoint each other. One day, it would all come back to us, whether good or bad.

Danielle might have been conditioned – because of the problems she had with Eric, and maybe with the motivation of revenge – to take a wrong step towards me, despite knowing the suffering it could cause. I should have been the one to stop it. It was my responsibility. I should have had the wisdom to stop her move.

After Eric left, a hidden whisper continuously said in my ear that nothing would ever be the same as it was before. There wouldn't be a common path for the three of us any longer.

I turned to Danielle. 'You can still catch him...,' I said.

I couldn't say any other word.

As if Danielle had read what was passing through my mind, had seen my vision of the disaster we'd experience if Eric left for good, as if my words had magically transmitted this secret message to her, she suddenly stood up and ran towards the front door, flying over the fallen books and shelves.

I walked to the window and watched them outside: Danielle caught up with Eric and hugged him from behind. Eric stopped but didn't turn back at first. Then suddenly he looked over his left shoulder, and met my eyes.

He was crying, but his expression was still emotionless. There was no hatred direct at me. It was as if he'd never seen me before, as if he didn't know me and we hadn't shared so many years together. He had the right to feel numb. I had turned all those hours, days, months and years into a disaster. We were caught in a complete darkness.

Danielle stepped in front of him to look him in the eye. Whatever she said, she might as well have been talking to a wall. Eric didn't say anything; instead, he turned and began limping away. Danielle stood still, following him only with her gaze. Even after he went out of sight, she remained there, watching after him.

After a short while, she came back inside and sat on a chair.

We looked at each other, neither of us speaking. We couldn't. She was not crying; she simply sat as still as a statue.

I reached for the bottle of whisky, but fumbled and knocked it over. The remaining whisky spilled out over my table and then onto the floor. Danielle didn't react or make a movement – not even a tiny reflex. Neither did I.

While the smell of whisky conquered the whole room, the knocked-over shelves caught my attention. Then the open door. It would be a shame if, at a moment like this, someone came in to buy a book. In that instant, I came back to life – waking from the horrible nightmare to run to the front of the shop, avoiding stepping on the books on my way. I locked the door, sighed, and looked around. A whisper ordered me to kneel and start collecting the books. I obeyed.

I heard Danielle's high heels. If I looked up I could have seen her legs, but I didn't. She stopped.

'I'm pregnant...,' she said.

Could the world really turn upside down in space, in just half an hour of time?

I felt a very deep pain and sting, as if someone had heated a sharp silver dagger and had unhesitatingly thrust it into the back of my head. The cold, dense and dark wave of pain was in my brain. Beyond the pain, I felt a strong wave of shame.

Having chosen hell was the biggest regret of my life. It was surprising how quickly that wish had come true. On the bright side, maybe it meant I was the kind of person who deserved to have his wishes turned into reality, a.s.a.p.

We looked at each other. I was too tired to talk and shout and drown in shame. Then, some power gave rise in me.

I threw all the books I'd collected onto the shelf on my left, and then began to collect the others off the floor and throw them on the shelf too – two or three at a time.

I kept on with that until only three books remained on the floor. I didn't care about them and wanted to make a bolder move; I knocked down the big shelf on the left side. Then, the other one standing next to it. The scene I was creating and being a part of was making me feel terribly sick. I had only one wish on my mind then: to die. I wanted to move away from this life, to avoid seeing anyone, to get burnt and be reduced to ash, to be pulled to pieces and not come together again. I wanted to become nothing.

Danielle was still standing right in the front of my office door, unresponsive towards my actions. Then she started to talk.

'He doesn't love me anymore.'

I wanted to cry, but I felt as if my eyes had become blocked. None of the fluid in my body wanted to be my tears. My being wouldn't allow me to cry for the situation I had put myself in. Crying would not alleviate my pain. I sat at the edge of the first shelf I had knocked down.

'Did he know?' I said.

She didn't reply. I looked at her, caught her looking at me. She turned back to the office, took her bag, and then moved to the front door without saying a word.

I kept silent.

'Can you unlock it?' she said. She was not facing me.

'Did he know?!' I repeated.

'I just told him... after he saw us.'

My brother from another mother had discovered me kissing his fiancée, and then a mere two minutes later had discovered she would be the mother of his baby.

I bowed my head and thought of the troubles I'd been battling over the last week, and saw the reality: it wasn't coming to an end. Whatever my sin was, I must have engraved it deep, layer by layer, because I was paying for it in the same way – deeper and deeper.

What did all this mean? Where had I gone wrong?

When I looked at what had happened, the problem couldn't (or shouldn't) be the "others." I must take on all the responsibility.

I – my hands, legs, eyes, arms, ears, veins, blood, lungs, the air inside me, the taste on my tongue, my memories, thoughts, loves, sorrows, joys... all of me – must be wrong. So wrong that my life, which I had once loved and admired, could be turned upside down so quickly, and so tragically. If the universe had some balance, my being, and all its faults and all the other things surrounding me, should come to an end at this moment. The "end," whatever that was, must be close. It couldn't be anywhere else.

I stood up. I wanted to hug Danielle, but I quit the idea in an instant – it sparked in my heart but couldn't make it to my mind; rather, it would stay in my heart forever.

I unlocked the front door and went outside. When I looked to the left, I saw Eric sitting on the ground. My heart began to beat as if I had received the happiest news in the world – my sun had risen again.

'He's here!' I said.

Danielle ran past me and looked outside. Then, she ran towards Eric. I'd never seen her move so fast.

In front of him, she stopped. She sank to her knees and put her hands on his thighs. They looked at each other, without talking.

I walked back inside and locked the front door again. I took shelter in my small office – locked the door, turned off the lights, and sat on the sofa where Danielle usually sat. I started to cry, and soon I was crying so intensely that the sounds and movements I was making were all very unfamiliar to me.

The room smelled terrible. I groped around in the dark, found the whisky bottle, and shook it. There was still a little juice in it. I drank it all, and then threw the empty bottle at the wall. It smashed, and if I hadn't closed my eyes reflexively, they might have been filled with the tiny pieces of broken glass I felt spray into my face. I didn't give up crying and leaned on the wall behind me. The wall felt cool, but it was no help for the fire in my head and lungs. The coolness existed only to give me a false hope.

While I was dreaming about the coolness carving its way into my skull and demolishing my brain, I fell asleep. But it felt less like falling asleep and more like leaving a place for good, or dying.

After a while, though I didn't know how long, I heard my cell phone ringing and opened my eyes. It stopped, and by the time I had woken up in the real sense, I was not sure whether it had really been ringing or not. There was a disconnection in my timeline.

I took my cell phone out of my pocket and saw the time – 7:44 p.m. There had been several calls, but I hadn't heard any of them. The last call was the sixth one I'd missed. The first five I couldn't give a shit about: Gary had called three times and Lori twice. The last call was only a number.

Whatever I had experienced and however drunk I was, I recognised the number as soon as I saw it, because it was carved into my heart. That I had lost my mind and all the information in it didn't change anything. My heart was declaring war on my skin, wanted to tear it apart and set itself free. I got scared, ashamed and excited. I got terribly excited. She had called me two minutes ago, at 7.42 p.m. Was it for real?

While I was thinking of what to do, whether I should call her back or go out to take some fresh air first, my cell phone made the new-message sound in my hand. At that moment, my cell phone was more valuable than a million gold blocks.

"Hey! I received your card today. I wanted to hear your voice and say thank

you, but I got no answer. So, I'm boarding a plane now. Gotta go. Take care."

I thought I was dying. But I didn't want to die at all. Never. That was the moment I came back from hell, after my time wandering there. Surely, this was the sign of my return. Just as my experiences were becoming too bitter to be real, this message was too good to be real too. It was as if I was waking up from my nightmares, one by one.

My hand searched for the switch on the wall in the dark, and turned on the light. My poor office: the floor was covered with whisky and broken pieces of glass. Worse, it carried all the invisible marks of the wisdom I'd lost. It had none of the blame though; all the mistakes had been mine...

I opened the door and stared at my store. It was dark, but the war that had taken place could easily be seen. Not even that view could take away my joy. My phone in my hand, I re-read the message over and over again, ten times, fifteen times. I checked the number. I realised how much I'd missed seeing that number on my cell phone's screen.

I needed to answer her. It was not really a requirement, but I was dying to do it. Should I call her or just write a message? If I called, how would my voice sound? Tired, exhausted, sad, worn out, off-putting... I wasn't sure. Writing a message was easier. But it was such an opportunity; I had to use it well. Calling her would be much better. Voice beats text.

While I was thinking of what to do, my cell phone cried out with another beep: a second message from her. But I didn't dare read it. I worried that she might have regretted sending the first message, or that she'd written something to kill all the hope in my heart. She might have written, "Don't get me wrong, you know, my sending you a message."

Though I didn't want it at all, my hand opened the message without waiting for my approval. My racing heart beat in my head, hands, lungs and legs – everywhere at the same time.

"When I look back, I usually regret how we upset and antagonised each other. Maybe we shouldn't have loved each other so much; that would've eased everything. But, I think, I'd never prefer that."

I kneeled down. My legs could no longer carry me. I couldn't re-read her message. I started to cry. All the fluid in my body was being turned into tears and beginning to flow down my cheeks. As I cried, I felt I was being cleansed, as if some invisible poison was vanishing.

I'd missed M very much. Her voice, attitude, her love. Her way of talking to me. I quit thinking and acted.

'Hi,' I said and sniffed.

'Heeey, are you okay?'

'Well, no... I'm not... I'm not okay... but I will be.... I will be.'

I was crying.

'V, are you drunk? Is it because of what I just said? Look, I—'

'No! Don't say anything, please don't say anything. I miss you. Very much. There's so much to say now... so much....'

'What's the matter, V? What happened? Where are you? Are you alone?'

'I'm at my store.... My father died... then... everything got worse... one thing at a time... and—'

'Mr Kushner died?! How? When?!'

'Last week. On Tuesday. Suddenly. We were not expecting it... I mean, who would expect it but... he died, suddenly...'

'V, why didn't you let me know?! Why?!'

'We'd broken up. We weren't talking at all. I didn't call you, but I came by your apartment one night. I watched you from outside. Your sitting room and bedroom. You were probably reading a book...'

'V, why! Why are you like this...?'

'Like this? What have I done? I just didn't call you. I couldn't. I set you free. Didn't you say so...? You wanted it that way. So I didn't call you. And now you're asking me why not?!'

'V...'

'Please, I'm begging you.... Okay. Let's talk calmly, okay? Like you and me, like us. I'm begging you.... I need that so much. So much! I need you terribly... please.'

'V, calm down. Get out of there and go to Lori's. C'mon, please do that for me....'

'Okay, I will. I can do whatever you want.... Please talk to me like you did before.... Please...?'

'Look, V, first relax a bit, do you understand? If you calm down, we'll talk. Okay? But right now I'm at the airport and... I need to hang up. Okay? V? Do you hear me?'

'Yeah, I'm... okay... I'm fine, don't worry about me.'

'Okay, perfect! Please, leave now and go to Lori's. I'll now call her and let her know about you, all right?'

'No, don't say anything to her. I won't go there; I'll go to my place. I can't go to Lori's...'

'What do you mean you can't go?! Why not?'

'I had a fight with James when I went there last time – we punched each other. Then James stabbed Eric yesterday, on his ass—'

'WHAT THE!? He stabbed Eric?! What the hell are you talking about? What's going on with you all, V?'

'A lot, M. Lots of things happened... lots of things. Let's talk about them later, okay? Later... You should go now. I'm fine....'

'Get out of there. Go somewhere else. Go to Eric. I don't want you to stay alone.... Meet Eric, okay? Gotta go now!'

'No. I can't meet him, either... but I'm fine. Go....'

'Why can't you meet Eric?! Oh God, be quick, I gotta go!'

'Go. Later, I'll tell you everything.'

'Shit! Okay. I have to go now.'

'Bon voyage!' I said, and she hung up.

For a while, I just sat on my knees, without moving. I was calm. I checked my cell phone once more – looked up the call time, and the number to which the call was made. It was real. It was too beautiful to believe. I was very happy.

I re-read the messages, again and again. I read the second message slightly more often than the first.

I stood up. There was a strange feeling on my left eye, like it was swollen. I checked it with my hand and took a selfie with my phone. Both of my eyes were dark red, and one of them was almost closed, as if I was a beaten boxer, hesitating to leave the locker room. I was surprised that I hadn't felt the swelling as soon as I'd woken up. There was also a cut on my cheekbone; a piece of broken whisky bottle must have done it. The blood had flowed down my cheek and slowly dried there. I tried to clean the blood with a mouth-wetted finger, but the pain stopped me.

I was like a war veteran, both psychologically and physically. The day had passed in such a bitter way, and then suddenly it had changed to give me a surprise I'd only dreamed about. But questions rose in my mind: Had she called because she was interested? Did she miss me as well? Or had this all been because of the condition I was in?

Chelsea had played a big role in my decision to call M back. The intimate letter with its indefinable beauty had given me a subconscious power and motivation. She had made me believe that M might not have forgotten me so easily. If I hadn't read Chelsea's letter, I would have replied to M with only a dull message. Then I wouldn't have heard her voice, and she wouldn't have heard mine, either. And she wouldn't have learned that my father had died.

I walked towards the front door of my store. Before I stepped outside, I turned back to look at the wreckage. I loved it there, despite everything that had happened to me. It had first become my hell, and then my paradise, all within a couple of hours. It gave me peace again – a real peace... like the relaxing affection of someone I longed for. Her voice had seemed to come from my dreams. I smiled and whispered to my books that everything would be okay, and then I went out and locked the door behind me.

With every step, I left Danielle, Eric and our battle farther behind, as if they were all just parts of a tale. I couldn't tell whether what we had experienced was for real or just a nightmare, not till I felt my swollen eye again.

I paused for a moment, remembering how Gary had said that James had just turned up at his house. Had James done something disastrous again?

I called Gary.

'Oh boy, where have you been?' he said. 'Why haven't you been answering your phone? I've called you a thousand times.'

'Oh, thank God, you're alive...'

'What?'

'Look, I fell asleep at the store, okay? Never mind me – are you okay?'

'You fell asleep at the store? Wow, I've never heard such a thing from you before. Why did you do something like that?'

'Gary, I don't know, okay. I don't know. What about that horseshit James? Why did you call so often? What happened? Answer me, has James caused a problem?'

'No, no... he hasn't. Unfortunately, this time, he's the victim....'

'Victim?! Oh no!!'

'Where are you now?' Gary asked.

'Fuck where I am, Gary. Why don't you tell me what happened?!'

'Okay, okay... I'm with Lori. At Father's house. I think you should come here....'

'Lori? Is she okay?! She's been calling me too. Tell me she's all right!'

'No, there isn't anything wrong, relax...'

'Damn! Hey, Gary, I should warn you... oh, never mind. I'll see you.'

I didn't know how I was going to explain my swollen eye or the cut on my cheek, and would have preferred they not see me like that, but Lori and Gary together and at my father's house: this was not a normal situation.

When I arrived at my father's place, I felt myself going back to the day of his death. I had been wrong to think that a sorrow as deep as that would go away so soon, or that it would be easy, or that I might have gotten used to it already.

I was very wrong. There hadn't been even a tiny decrease; it had all stayed there and still hurt me deeply.

While I was trying to walk up the seven stairs on my shivering legs, I came to know that death was the biggest truth I'd experienced during the last week.

I reached the door and rang the bell. Before Gary opened it, I heard him yelling, "I got it...!" in pure joy.

He greeted me with his peaceful face and a wide smile, but, after seeing me, his smile turned into a worried frown in an instant.

He took two steps towards me.

'What is this, V?'

He was fussy and excited, and his hands were shaking.

'Nothing, Gary. I'm okay. I'll tell all,' I said, and went inside.

Lori was sitting on one of the sofas, looking out into the garden with her back facing me. I wanted to act immediately to diffuse the tension that would last until she saw my face.

'Hey, Lori, I'm here, and my eye is swollen, and black and blue! But nothing to worry about,' I said as quickly and sincerely as possible.

Lori suddenly turned towards me. It didn't take too long to remove the smile from her face either. She stood up and ran to me, and grabbed my shoulders.

'Who did this to you?! Don't say James...'

'Relax, Lori, please calm down. It's nothing to worry about; I'm fine. C'mon, sit down. Gary, you too, please.'

Gary was watching us with excited and fussy eyes. Nancy closed the door we had left open behind us.

'V, tell me quickly! What happened!' Lori said.

'Lori, I-will-tell... I'm here, you see? But, please, let me have a breather. It was a hectic day today...'

'I can see that! Whatever! I won't beg you for the story. Fuck! Are you okay, V?'

'Yes, I am.'

They were a little calmer after our initial encounter. They sat down, and I leaned back on the sofa, half-sitting and half-lying. Lori brought me some ice and ordered me to hold it over my eye, and I obeyed. They were drinking coffee, and Nancy brought me some wine. I was gonna drink for M, *the love of my life.*

'Why are you here?' I asked. 'Why are you two here together, I mean...? As strange as that question may sound.'

My question broke the ice a bit and moved the attention away from my eye. But it was obvious that Lori would dig for information as soon as she found the right time.

Gary told me that James had visited him neither to cause any more disturbances nor to give any more "general warnings" about the inheritance. James had had a big quarrel with Lori the night before, after Lori had arrived home from the hospital.

At this point, Lori interrupted Gary's story to correct him: she and James had not actually quarrelled, she said, but had verbalised some problems they'd recognised. No one had raised his or her voice, or said any bad words.

I could imagine the situation – Lori would have been in control and said what she wanted. She would have struck James with a sour note and left him answerless. It was almost impossible to argue with Lori, or to move the quarrel (or conversation) in any direction apart from wherever she desired.

As a result of this "conversation," James hadn't known what to do and had resorted to Gary for help, as he considered Gary "his closest friend."

'Until then, I would never have imagined James crying, or even coming to the edge of it,' Gary said. 'Really. In my opinion, he had a very strong nature. You know, tough as a stone...'

'Strong nature my ass!' I said. 'All the stone he has is in his heart, man!'

That Gary still insisted on misunderstanding James so much upset me again. I couldn't believe how weak his comprehension about that idiot's character was.

James had cried and told Gary he was terribly hurt by what Lori had done, and that her attitude had revealed the differences between them and their expectations from their marriage. I was pretty sure that these were Lori's words – James could never have come up with them by himself.

James had told Gary he had no desire to upset or depress Lori – in fact, he'd done everything for her. There was nothing he wouldn't do for the "family," for me and Gary. He suggested I'd only been acting with Eric, the bastard, when I'd done all those things to his restaurant. He hadn't gone after me because I was a member of the "family," and family meant everything to him.

In order for James not to lose this sense of family, he needed

Gary's help. Gary, James had said, should help Lori see how all James' intentions were right.

'Gary, wait...,' I said. 'I have a question: did you ask him whether he's aware he's not really a part of our family?'

As I predicted, Gary hadn't asked.

Apparently, James had also apologised about how he'd treated Amy (without her being present for the apology, of course) and had made out that she'd simply misunderstood him. According to him, he hadn't done anything with the intent to hurt or upset her; he was just trying to solve the problems as soon as possible. He'd even informed me of what he intended to do, and I'd allegedly approved and not discouraged or tried to stop him. We (me and James) had no bad intentions; we were just trying to find a way out.

'FUCK OFF! Son of a bitch!' I said. 'He didn't tell me what he was going to do, and I didn't approve any of his shit! He only told me he was planning to talk to Amy and asked me not to intervene. Does that mean I didn't stop him? Why the fuck would I stop him doing that? How could I read his bullshit mind?!'

James had interpreted everything as he'd wished, and behaved accordingly. Actually, he was in desperate need of help, and knew he had to give something to Gary (an apology, for instance) to get what he wanted. According to James' mind-set, everything in life came down to exchanges – he was that simple and shallow.

I asked Gary whether James intended on apologising to Amy, but Lori answered instead:

'No, he isn't. But... I apologised. On behalf of my family,' she said. 'I called her today.'

I straightened up. I just wanted to be sure I was understanding it properly: James had gone to Gary, crying and asking for help; and Lori had apologised to Amy on behalf of James and herself. Everything seemed to gain a surrealistic dimension. The climax, however, still belonged to me and Eric.

'How did she react to your apology?' I said.

'How else? She was happy, of course.'

'Wow. I honestly wasn't sure what would make her happy... That's why I asked.'

'Amy and I worked in the same office for years. We've shared much more than you might assume,' she said.

I saw that Lori was relaxed. Her calm and peaceful demeanour was in sharp contrast to the things she'd been doing for the last couple of days. It was nice to witness it. I felt that she wanted to ask questions regarding my eyes and cheek but had given up, maybe deciding it was not the right time yet.

I changed the subject.

'Then what Gary? Have you been able to persuade Lori about... you know, James?'

Gary looked at Lori, and she looked back at him. They smiled.

Lori said, 'I can say that he did his best...'

I didn't ask anything more. Everything was clear. Lori had endured her marriage for a long time. She and James were completely different people in terms of their world views and intellectual backgrounds. As far as the notions like having a child and fatherhood were concerned, their parting of ways was inevitable. James would never make the kind of father Lori or any other decent woman would wish for.

While we tried to warm up the evening and talk about other issues, the love triangle between Gary, Amy and Eric was still sitting right in front of us. On top of it was Gary's affair, too. And not to forget Danielle's pregnancy. And me and her. And me and Eric. And Eric and Danielle. And hell.

Had they talked about these things? Gary and his affair. I wanted to get Gary alone, even if just for a moment, to learn how much Lori knew. But I couldn't create an opportunity.

Lori created hers before mine.

'Okay, that's enough,' she said. 'Tell me about your face. Now. I'm asking explicitly and waiting for your answer!'

I thought for a while. If I could have made up something credible, I would certainly have said it. But my mind emptied as soon as I recalled the moment when I was punched. I couldn't think of any other story. I had to tell the truth.

'Eric did it; he punched me.'

It was impossible to define the effort I saw in their eyes as they tried to make sense of what I'd just said. If they had been asked to guess who was to blame for my face, they would never have said Eric, not if he was the only person left alive in the world.

Lori stood up, approached me, and took my wine from my hand. She drank the whole glass, which had been newly filled, and then sat down.

'V, we need to talk as openly as we can. Please, I can't take it anymore. What's going on!'

She was yelling, and her eyes too seemed to shout at me, telling me this was enough. It was too much for her, for me and for all of us.

The worst thing was my inability to ask "why?" What was the reason for all this? Why did the owner of a small bookstore, who had been alone after breaking up with love of his life, have to witness the death of his father while he was going to the toilet, and then experience a week of hell... as if he was the most sinful person in the world?

'What's going on? We can all see what's going on.... Our father died... the fight about the money started... and while we were battling over that, we revealed our wounds – the cracks and problems we used to just smooth over.... Everyone has come to the end of their tether. While we were trying to find solutions, we dived deep into the shit... and now here we are. We are still here in this house, as we were before, but with a lot of loss. We are the ones to blame. Our lives. The things we have done or not done till now. I don't see any other reason. I can't find any... my new solution is simple; we must try to correct our mistakes.'

I looked at Gary, as if he was the only one who could correct any mistakes – underlining, it couldn't be me.

'V, stop saying "we," please,' Lori said, 'and please cut it short... I don't have any more strength. What happened today? I just want to know. Be brief.'

'Eric got angry at me, very angry, and couldn't control himself. I didn't have enough time to explain what he'd seen. Besides, he'd already punched me by then. That's it. That's what happened.'

I took a sip from my refilled wine glass.

Naturally, Lori didn't let go until she had learned every detail. She punched me with questions of "why, how, when" and so on. After doing my best to endure, I stumbled and, in the end, threw in the towel and told her everything. Everything.

'V, wait... is this you? I mean, is this really you telling me all these things? My God! Why couldn't you stop yourself before it got so complicated? How... how could you behave in such a... V, how—'

'I know, Lori, okay. I was drinking. And I was very sad... I was so lonely. I was missing M so much... I don't know. It just happened, somehow, and I couldn't stop it, or I didn't want to at that moment, I'm not—'

'I can't believe this!' she said. 'I just can't believe it. How could you be so stupid? If your defence is to say you were "drinking" and put the blame on that – hah! – why on earth are you drinking now then?'

'Lori, please... I was about to say "no." Despite the state I was in, I was thinking it. I was about to... but suddenly she kissed me, and at that exact moment, we saw Eric at the door. Everything happened in a flash, in one second. Maybe shorter. There was nothing I could do. And even—'

'Enough! I don't wanna hear any more. Just stop.'

'I didn't have enough time to explain, Lori. Eric came in at the worst possible moment. He wouldn't listen to me. Everything just happened. I couldn't do anything except watch what was happening in front of me...'

'I'm not asking "Why didn't you try to explain it to Eric?" I want to know why you didn't prevent it from the very beginning! You are all the same, you dickheads! None of you is any different, none! You're all the same shit. I wonder who should punch Eric in the face. That's another issue...'

I felt as if all the blood in my body had been drained. I was frozen, looking at Lori. She noticed my strange countenance. It was impossible for her to know about Eric and Amy – the recent development – but she had made such a correct assumption that time stopped for me.

She was right: Eric had also done wrong – so he had behaved

unfairly by punching me. He hadn't given me the chance to defend myself, even though he was in a similar situation to me. He could have shown some empathy.

Lori was looking outside, standing in front of the door that opened to the garden. We were all silent. I continued to drink my wine. Gary just stared, sometimes at me, sometimes at the floor.

'If even something like this can happen, whom should one trust?' said Lori. Then, she turned to me.

'Trust, V, a virtue you once believed in. What happened? Why on earth did you lose it?! All through his life, the owner of this house tried to show me, you and Gary how to trust. "Believing in someone, trusting someone." Isn't that meaningful to you anymore?'

'Look, Lori, this is not trust or—'

'Eric must now think that he was wrong to believe in you for all these years! To trust you! And he has a point. He must think you have been deceiving him and doing things behind his back throughout all his life, all those moments you spent together. Yes, he's now thinking about all those moments, how "empty" they are now, how he was fooled! Is it worth it? Is it worth all those years you spent together? V, do you think life is a game in which we can do whatever we want at any given time? Self-denial, responsibility and sacrifice.... Do these words mean anything to you? I know they did – once. But what has happened to you? If you haven't become mature enough to realise how important these things are, then what on earth have you been doing all these years? I can't... I can't put my disappointment into words. I can't even imagine how Eric feels...'

Before arriving there to meet them, I'd hoped to get healing for my physical and mental wounds of the day. Instead, Lori was torturing me Middle Ages style – without any mercy. Trying to take revenge for all the immoral things I'd done, and all the things she'd observed everybody else doing. She had held it all in her heart.

She didn't stop.

'We three didn't meet here tonight because James desired it; we met here because we – all three of us – have concluded that it's enough! Enough of everything! I'm fed up, Gary's fed up... and we thought it would be a good idea to talk to you, as well. We were not like this, V. We've never been through anything like this before...'

'Maybe we are like this, Lori, but we just didn't realise it before?'

'No, V, we are not. We never were and won't be in the future either. We'll get over these times. We have made mistakes. Maybe more than a few. But, we'll correct them all. Together. We must.'

'Maybe *this* is the problem?' I said. 'You and Dad have always believed that all moments spent, all works done, all words said, must be faultless... as if our lives could be faultless. But life is not like that! First Father and then you forced us – Gary, me, Amy and everybody who joined our family – to be flawless, to always act "correctly!" Maybe this is what's wrong, Lori. One can't live like that. Can't you see how stressful and depressing it is? It's not human! It destroys everything in an instant.

'And our father... maybe he is the source of our problems..., because he didn't prepare his "perfect" and proper will or complete this task "perfectly" as he "should have." Maybe Father is to blame for all we have experienced since his death! Because life isn't perfect, and nor was he. He died all of a sudden, despite all his imaginary perfect—'

'Enough!'

It was the first time I had heard Gary shout in maybe decades. It was unexpected. He was sitting and looking not at me or Lori but at his legs. He didn't move at all. He brought silence. We let ourselves flow into his silence.

After a couple of seconds, he started to talk: 'Don't disrespect him, V. Please, don't do it. It's not you; you aren't like this. I know you've had some very hard days, and you've tried to shoulder all these problems and – maybe more than anybody else – tried to solve them. You wanted to do some good for the others by involving yourself in matters that don't involve you. It's very noble of you, I can see that, and so can Lori. But I can also see that all this has worn you out. It's more than you can take. You can see it too.'

'Hell yeah! What should have I done, then? Watch you all get tangled up from a distance?'

'Please... don't say things about Father that he doesn't deserve. Yes, he tried to be a "perfect" man. Yes, he tried to make us perfect too. He forced us! Oh God, that old prick forced me a lot! But he also gave me – *us* – opportunities, and helped remove the obstacles. What more could he have done? He did everything. And what did we do in return? I've had an affair with a girl and she's pregnant.'

When Gary mentioned this, Lori slid down and sat on the sofa next to the door that opened onto the garden. Her right hand found her mouth, and then her cheek, and remained there.

Gary didn't stop: 'You... you kissed a woman in front of the man she loves, a man who is maybe your closest friend on this planet. Oh man, what happened to the concept of virtue? Is there anything left to ruin? Have we reached our lowest point? Is that when you would blame Dad?'

Lori appeared to be in complete shock. I couldn't count how many times she looked between Gary and me, like she was watching a tennis match – Wimbledon, tie-break, last set, championship point.

'Look, V,' Gary said, 'I know it's not something he could control, but maybe Dad leaving us unprepared was on purpose. Maybe he wanted to smash our faults and defects in our faces. Maybe he wanted us to regain our balance after wobbling side to side, so we would find our real and true selves, and become cleansed. It's gonna get better, V, for all of us, but we need to see it: we need to face it all and understand. Maybe we need to embrace these sorrows. Only in this way, by not rejecting them, can we be happier and more powerful in our future. Reacting against all this will bring no benefit to us.'

I had never heard Gary speak so provocatively before, but he'd spoken so deeply at that moment, and illuminated so much about us, that his words would bond us together. All of his remarks found their places first in my head, and then in my heart, as if they were coming from a holy source.

We were all in the same boat, going in the same direction – towards the iceberg. We had realised this finally and wanted to steer away. Together. We would first become shattered and then rebuild ourselves again. We wholeheartedly and quietly believed it.

After the short speech, I was calm, as if I'd just been meditating. I might even have fallen into the optimism trap if Gary hadn't said the "pregnant girlfriend" part. It was still echoing in my ears.

Lori, trying to appear calm or at least as a more "controlled" version of herself, stood up, took a couple of slow steps, and then sat next to me. She picked up the wine bottle and drank what remained in one gulp.

'Is it true, Gary?' Lori said.

Now it was her turn to take the stage. This could be fun, I thought. We both looked at Gary.

'Is what true?' he said.

'The affair, for God's sake! What else could it be?'

'Oh.... Yes.'

'"Yes"? It's all true?'

'You mean—'

'I mean, the girl and the baby. Is it all true?'

'Yes... yes, all of it, one hundred percent. Yes!'

Lori leaned back.

'Then, tell me everything, from the very beginning,' she said.

Gary started to tell his story. He explained how he and the girl had met, what they had shared together, and how it had made him feel alive. Happy. Peaceful. New.

I listened, and so did Lori. She didn't talk about what was right, what was wrong; she put aside her "correct-self" and respected the love that had happened somewhere away from her.

Then Gary talked about Amy, about his love for her and for what they had shared, and how precious all those years were to him. He spoke with admiration about her ambitions, business approach and worldview. It was probably the first time I'd ever heard Gary fawning over someone. He said nothing bitter about her. It was obvious that he'd loved her very much. But it was also obvious that now he was under the influence of another fire of love.

When Gary finished speaking, silence wrapped us again. We didn't say anything more; no one commented.

Then, Lori started to open up.

'I want to have a baby,' she said. 'But I won't give birth. I mean, I can't. So, I'll adopt one. I'm determined to do this.'

That Lori had suppressed her "righteous" comments on what Gary had told us, and had instead embraced the ambiance and broken down her own walls to share something, gave me hope about the near future. Then again, maybe instead of being a sign that everything was going to be good, it was just Lori's maternal instinct kicking in early, making her more empathetic even before she'd actually become a mother. She told us why she had made such a decision, what she was expecting from life, and how she hoped it was not too late for her to do it.

But thinking of adding a child to the family could make one look at their chosen life partner in a whole new way. Lori needed to decide on James, if she hadn't done it yet.

'So, what does James think about having a child?' I asked. 'I mean, he has a daughter, so I know he's experienced. Maybe that's an advantage for you two.'

'He doesn't know anything about this. No one does. This is the first time I've talked about it with anyone...'

'He doesn't know?!' Gary said. 'But shouldn't you tell him soon? He needs to... I mean, he should be involved in such a... decision!'

'I'm gonna do it alone.'

It was Lori's turn. Hers was the third shock wave to spread that night. She told us that although she hadn't said anything to James, he seemed to have sensed her pulling away from him, and when he realised it was only getting worse he'd gone to ask for help from Gary. He might have seen it coming a long time ago. That's why he was so interested in the notion of "family" and had declared himself as the man in charge of it – just to mend his relations with Lori. It was too late for him; Lori had already made her decision. It was obvious that, as a woman who knew herself and was also sure of herself, she would not change her mind.

Gary stood up and went to the other room without saying anything. I hugged Lori, and she kissed my forehead.

Gary came back holding two bottles of wine and two glasses. He gave one of the glasses to Lori and filled it. Then he poured my share into my glass and handed it to me, along with the half-filled bottle.

Taking his own glass and bottle, he moved towards the sofa and filled his own glass. It was going to be a wild wine night.

Sharing a night like this had been a long time coming. The disappointments, sorrows, expectations and problems didn't leave us alone, but it was still good to be together. It was as nice as listening to the sound of a calm sea in a beautiful evening, lying on fine sand, feeling the wind on your face and breathing in the salty smell it brings. It was like being grateful for no one thing in particular, just for life as a whole, for being alive, for that regular breath.

'Not everything went badly today...,' I said.

'Something nice at last? Oh, no way...,' Gary said.

'Tell me something good, V, I'm begging you,' Lori said. 'Please..., tell me.'

'After being punched and drinking the rest of my whisky, I fell asleep at the store. You know – when you were unable to reach me. Anyway, I woke up because my cell phone was ringing. Well, I guess it woke me up—'

'Cut the crap, boy,' Lori said. 'What happened?'

'Don't expect anything big, Lori. I don't see anything good on the shore,' Gary said.

'Hey, wait... listen... I missed the call, but I couldn't believe my eyes when I saw the number. M had called me!'

'M? Are you sure?' Lori said.

'Yes, of course I am!'

'That's wonderful news, then,' Lori said. 'Thank God, at last. Although don't deserve such a good thing after the shit you've done.... So?'

'I didn't know what to do because I was so excited. Then messages —'

'What did she write?' Gary said.

I read out loud the two messages she'd sent. Lori was moved to tears, and Gary smiled.

Lori's cheeks were red and wet. Tears went very well with her at that moment under the dim light. Sitting on the sofa, leaning back, she seemed to me in her twenties.

She turned her head to the right, as if looking outside through the window. A yellow light glittered over her tears. She was watching the cruel world through wet eyelashes. Lori was still very beautiful.

'Well done for her. She wrote some touching things. Good stuff,' she said and sniffed. Then, she turned to me. 'So why are you here then and not with her *somehow*?'

'Because she was at the airport. We'll meet up when she's back – I mean, I hope so. I don't know. If she still wants...'

Lori smiled.

'Figure it out. Now! You *must* be with her, idiot!'

'*If she wants...*' Gary said.

'Yeah, if she wants....' I said.

Lori straightened up. 'V, you're still surprising me. You can't be this naïve? Listen to me: this is an insider tip: she-still-loves-you, silly!'

This time, I was the one on the spot.

They carried on talking about my successes, my job, M, my "great expectations" in life, my endless daydreams – till all the wine bottles were emptied. Then Lori brought out two new bottles, and Nancy and Andrew joined us with their delicious sandwiches. We talked and talked... and laughed. About our memories, Mom, Dad, and the days we'd happily spent. And the days we couldn't. 'Of course, there's no rewind button in life; those days will never come back—' Andrew said, speaking of the beautiful past days we wanted to re-live over and over again.

'Really, Andrew? Oh, don't do this to me, please...' I said.

'Shut up, kiddo.... Let the wise man talk.'

'Thank you, Lori,' said Andrew. 'Yes, even if the good old days are gone, we can still enjoy other days, maybe even better ones. We should just believe this, and imagine that everything will be good. Think of a picture of a beautiful view. Draw your dreams and the people you like into it, the people who you want to be with you – all together in this picture. And enjoy this view in your free times, when you get bored, stressed out, when you feel the weakest. One day, you will suddenly find yourselves an indispensable part of that view. And if you wished and drew the sky sunny and clear, you would look at the actual blue sky that day, and then remember tonight....

'Myself, I always imagine the sky as partly cloudy – a very clear blue with cream-like white clouds that don't block out the sun. They symbolise *hope* for me. I always have some hope, no matter what. There in the sky. Like cream, very sweet cream. The clouds are signs of hope for those who seek it – and they offer them a delicious taste too.'

'Taste? Water vapour taste?'

'No, V, the sweet taste of hope. I always dream of cream clouds, delicious hopes for both me and my loved ones. V, you should have some cream clouds too, boy. It isn't bad, or harmful. It's always a good idea to have some cream in your skies – it may change your life.'

Andrew had raised the sun in our minds for a hopeful tomorrow. After taking the last sip from their wines, Andrew and Nancy left us alone. Their family had been long-standing friends of ours in this long journey of life, but since my father died, we'd begun inevitably separating our lives. It was painful, but reality. Andrew had summarised all those years and moments we had spent together with his words, and I would never forget them for the rest of my life.

That night, the curtain was closed on a life spent together by our two families.

We left the house in a happy, sad, longing, loving, drunk and hopeful mood. Two hours had passed since midnight. James didn't call Lori. Amy didn't call Gary.

'How can we end tonight in the best possible way?' Lori said.

When I said, 'Let's visit Mom and Dad,' we all seemed to agree without speaking.

We took a cab and went to the cemetery with our saddest smiles on our faces.

It was not the kind of visit where we carried with us some uneasiness mixed with pain or longing. It was obvious that we missed our parents and had pain in our hearts, but, mostly we just wanted to thank them for what we had: our characters and our chances in life. For the echo of the essence of life and love even after they'd passed away.

Lori sat next to my mother's grave, and Gary sat next to my father's. And I was in between, kneeling. We were silent as our joy vaporised and our faces fell. When I heard Lori sniffing, I moved closer and hugged her. She started to cry more deeply. Gary came over and put his hand on Lori's back, and Lori twisted around to hold his elbow. I couldn't control myself and started to cry too. Lori sobbed in my arms, as if every tear she shed was coming from the deepest parts of her body, and with pain. I hugged her tightly, and Gary secretly wiped his eyes.

After a couple of minutes, Lori became calm and cleaned her nose with some tissue paper. Then, she smiled and apologised for having cried.

'This is a funeral, isn't it?' she said. 'This many tears is a must.... Sorry....'

I came to realise that I couldn't stand seeing Lori crying. I promised myself to avoid anything that would make her cry again. For a moment, I believed this could be achievable.

'Now, guys,' Lori said, 'we must each deliver a speech—'

'What?!' I said.

'Yes, V, this is the real funeral ceremony for Mom and Dad. We'll say goodbye to them as they deserved: in a happy mood, with our thanks, especially for the way they gave us eternal hope. Come on, Gary, you start. Then you, V, and me last....'

'Me?' Gary said. 'You know I can't do such things, Lori.... Normally —'

'Nothing is normal tonight, as you can see,' Lori said.

'Yes, yes, I know. Thanks to wine. But don't expect anything *good* from me then. I'll just... say things, okay?'

'Say things, bro!' I said.

'Begin!'

'Okay, okay,' Gary said. 'I... well, this might sound strange, but... I'm very happy now. I mean... this is one of the happiest moments in my life. Because I... I haven't spent enough time with my family, with all of you, though I've always wished to. I mean, I wanted to, but... but life, things... I don't know, maybe—'

'Wow-wow-wow. Go, Gary, go!'

'Shut up, V, or grow up,' Lori said.

'Okay, wait guys, wait.... Now, I'm talking only to Mum and Dad. Don't interrupt me, V, okay? Anyway, I was saying I haven't managed to spend enough time with my family, not in the way I've wanted to. But now I've just spent a perfect night with V and Lori, together. I shared myself, my feelings, with them. I felt dependent on them, which is not bad—'

'Not at all!' Lori said.

'Thanks, Lori. Yes... umm... Mum, Dad, we talked about you a lot. Maybe you don't have your ears right now, but—'

'Gary, c'mon man!'

'Okay, okay, that was bad.... Anyway, I'm just happy to be standing here with them, and with you.... Thank you for all the good feelings, sacrifices and beautiful memories you left behind. I don't know. I think that's all... that's all that I can say....'

'Bravo!' I shouted.

'Hey, V, calm down,' said Lori. 'This is absurd enough already; don't shout like that.'

'Who will come if I shout, Lori? Ghosts? Wooo—'

'Shut up and make your speech.'

'Okay, but this is our ceremony and I think saying "bravo!" to my brother should be legal?'

'V, enough. It's your turn. Instead of talking nonsense, start! Please.'

'Alright. Okay. Now, I'm really the one who loves the others more than they love me... I mean, I love Lori more than she loves me and I love Gary—'

'V, don't do that, please!' Lori said. 'Talk like Gary: talk about your feelings.'

'Hey, don't interrupt me. It's my speech, isn't it? Anyway, I love Lori more than she loves me, and I love Gary much more than he loves me—'

'Bullshit,' Lori said. 'Why are you raising a subject like this? It's nonsense!'

'It's the truth. You should see and admit the fact. Anyway, I also love you very much, Mom, Dad... and I've always missed Mom, like all of us: we've all missed her. Dad is a newcomer there... here? Whatever.... Sorry, Mom, Dad, I must put the blame on wine tonight. Well, it's good that you aren't lonely there anymore, Mom, but on this side, we are a little lonely. We're bewildered and shaken. Maybe we haven't still realised what's happened for real... we're only now starting to feel reality, slowly. But this isn't bad... no... yes, it is bad; our father died. But then again, we'll all die one day, won't we? At least Dad died by leaving us as virtuous as we could be. It was hard to deal with it though... I admit that I've felt angry with you from time to time, Dad. But after tonight, something I already knew dawned on me. That's a bit strange, isn't it? Anyway, I'm nearly done with this... speech— Is it raining?'

'Yes, it's raining,' Lori said. 'Please conclude.'

'Okay, okay, I'm nearly done. One last thing. Hey, Mom, Dad, I've always loved you very much. I still do. And I will always love you – as long as I can. The feeling of missing you will never go away. Okay... done.'

'Quite a rain,' Gary said.

'Yes, but it ain't a problem,' Lori said. 'It will clean our souls, if we need that. Purification. Anyway, it's my turn.

'Mom, Dad, we've all lived through hard times. I don't mean that our lives have always been hard, but you know, first you left us, Mom, and then Dad. You wanted your boys to help you, work with you, but it never happened. They chose their own ways, as they desired—'

'Wait, wait,' I said. 'What the fuck does that mean?!'

'V, please respect my turn and listen. I didn't interrupt you.'

'But I didn't say anything bullshit like that to need interrupting, right?'

'Ssshhh! Keep quiet and listen. Anyway, the boys preferred to do their own businesses instead of working with you, but I chose to stay and work with you. I did it in order to please you, to make you happier, and also I wanted it! I don't regret anything about that. I never have and never will. These guys don't need to get upset because of what I just said, either. I don't blame them for doing their own thing. It's their lives, and they've lived them as they wished. I respected their decision, and, Dad, you did too. They must be grateful to you, Dad, even if for only that—'

'Yeah, we are,' said Gary.

'I know, Gary,' she said. 'Dad, don't feel guilty at all, you know, if you still think I sacrificed my life to work with you. I don't see it that way. I wanted to work with you, and I did my best because I wanted to, not because I felt obligated. I learnt everything from you, and it was all invaluable. I thank you for everything: for your all your effort, time and patience. I've always tried... to deserve all this, in a sense. It all means so much. All three of us know how much you gave to us. I hope we can make use of it all...

'Also, Mom, oh, how I miss you. You... you taught us how to love when you were... with us. And now you've taught us how bad it feels to miss you, how limitless this feeling is, and how desperate and alone and small one feels against it. I miss you much more these days because... I'm going to have a baby soon. I'm going to be a mother, too. I wish so much that you were here with me.

'Okay, no tears... Anyway, during this last week since we lost you, Dad, we've made some mistakes and been defeated by our own ambitions and laziness – and by our own natures. But in being defeated, we've learnt to become aware of ourselves, to observe our lives from a distance. Each pain enabled us to be more cautious, more prepared for life's blows. We've come to know that love will save us... under your light.

'We wish you to sleep in peace. We promise to be stronger and more hopeful from now on. Despite our faults and the pain of our losses, we'll do our best to walk towards happiness and goodness. And to appreciate what we already have....

'Oh, how I love you two, and these two guys here.... I love them much more than they love me... if that's okay with you, V?'

'Wow... is this your speech?' I said.

'Yes. I think I'm done as well,' Lori said.

'Wait,' I said. 'Was that a prepared text you had memorised or what?'

'Why, of course not, V?'

'I mean, that couldn't have just come out of the blue, you know, improvised. It was, oh God, amazing, Lori.... I mean, my speech was a primary school essay, and yours, I dunno... wow! Say something, Gary?'

'V, calm down and give your promise to them,' said Lori.

'What promise?'

'Didn't you listen to me? Promise that you'll be stronger and more hopeful from tonight on!'

'Yes, yes, okay... I promise. Mom and Dad, I promise to be stronger and more hopeful.'

'There will always be cream clouds in our picture, I promise,' Gary said.

'A painter's promise. How could I expect anything different from you?' Lori said.

'Guys, I don't wanna ruin this emotional speech session,' I said, 'but are you aware it's really raining now?'

'Yes, and it's raining perfectly, V,' Lori said. 'How about... shutting up and feeling it.'

The rain clouds moved over us, rolling towards the morning sun. We farewelled our Mom and Dad in a special way. We embraced each other once more, and revitalized our love for each other – which had not died, but maybe had been forgotten. I felt that it was going to be a totally new life for each of us.

At the main gate of the cemetery, the darkness started to vanish, and we were quite wet.

'Are you guys taking the same cab?' Lori said. 'I'll take mine separately.'

'Why don't you come with us?'

'I wanna go alone, V, thank you. Also, after all these hours, I'm fed up with you. It's starting to feel like an overdose.'

'Ha-ha.'

'But there's one more thing....'

Lori took out two envelopes from her coat pocket. She handed one to me and the other to Gary.

'There was one for me too,' she said. 'And... I must admit, I've already read both of yours. Sorry for that. But after reading mine, I couldn't stop myself—'

'What are these?' Gary said.

'If you like, you can read mine as well,' Lori said. 'Anyway. Talk to you soon. Till then.' She flagged down a passing cab.

'Hey, Lori, wait,' I said. 'Don't play with us. What are these?'

'Letters from Dad. He gave these to the lawyers as part of his will before he died. While I was struggling with his notes, or I should say, "decoding" what I assumed to be his will, one of his lawyers gave these letters to me. Dad had requested, not in writing but verbally, that they be given to us one week after his death. Long story short, I got them and read them earlier than he desired. This was my only fault, and I want you to excuse me. I thought here, tonight, would be a good time to give you yours. And, I'm leaving now.... Later.'

As she got into the cab, she blew us a kiss. That was so not like Lori.

The cab pulled away, leaving Gary and I just staring at each other with the letters in our hands.

'We can't read them here. It's raining,' Gary said.

'No,' I said, and we both stuffed the envelopes into our pockets to protect them from the falling rain.

'Well, I don't know what to say,' I said. 'These letters are quite a surprise for me. Did you know about them?'

'Of course not.'

'Strange, man. Dad has surprised us again.'

'Lori has too, hasn't she? Like father like daughter.... So, what now?'

'Let's go read our letters, in private. I don't know what we should do afterwards. We'll talk...'

Gary agreed, seeming as stupefied as me. As he ran towards a cab, I turned and flagged down another one.

On my way home, I kept thinking of the letter in my pocket. I felt as if Dad was going to guide us – again – from wherever he had gone.

For a second, I thought about reading it right at that moment, in the cab. I buried my hand in my pocket and touched the folded-over envelope, and immediately felt a huge weight on my shoulders.

I didn't dare to face my father.

Tuesday
21 SEPTEMBER

I ARRIVED HOME and took off my coat, trousers and T-shirt. They were all very wet. I sat on a chair in the sitting room, wearing only my boxers, put the envelope on the coffee table and smoothed it flat. Parts of it had gotten a little wet and then dried in my pocket on the way home. These patches were obvious to the eye; the paper was a little worn off. As the envelope was so fine-textured, it was a bit transparent: I could see the vague outlines of the writing inside.

I cut the envelope lengthwise and opened it. The tiny torn parts looked like the edges of a saw blade. The letter seemed to have the intention of breaking me to pieces, even before I read it.

I could identify my father's handwriting. He'd written in blue ink, and with his beloved pen. The part I could see, upside down, said,

"Dear V, my dear son..."

When tears started to flow down my cheeks, I knew it was going to be a hard reading – I wondered if I could manage till the end. Then, I heard my father's voice. *"Don't cry like a baby, you blackguard... Can't we just talk decently for a couple minutes? Just behave, for God's sake. Be a man!"*

I became a man. I stood up and wiped my eyes. I opened the window and breathed in a bit of fresh air. Then, I turned back, picked up the envelope, and took out the letter.

Dear V, my dear son,

I am aware that you will find what I'm doing quite strange. Lori may not find it so strange. She has witnessed all of my fluctuating moods and behaviours throughout the many years we've worked together. Therefore, she might have expected such a thing from me... maybe. As for Gary, he lives a debauched life with a shit bohemian mind-set, and he will hardly be surprised at anything I do. But you... you will be surprised. Am I right, son?

'Yes, you are, Dad...'

Firstly, I will say that if you are reading this letter it means that I am not with you anymore. I am calling you from the other side. At the time of writing, I don't know yet whether it's heaven or hell for me. I wish I could give you some insider news though, about the other side – maybe a bit about the sin issue. Would it be good news to know about sins, such as they really exist or not?

'Nope...'

It shouldn't be. I'm sure you don't expect to live sinfully; I know you. You're a good man, V, a really good man. You have all become virtuous individuals without thinking of what rewards you will get in return. Your mother and I always tried to teach you what is right and decent. And, to be fair, you all received these lessons well; you haven't straggled at all. You are good children.

Son, even if I were to send you a message and say there was no hell and everyone was in heaven, and that you could do whatever you want, I am sure you still wouldn't lose yourself. Nor would the others – not even Gary. I know you all too well. This is fatherhood, V: you know your children very well; you feel them close in your heart, in your bones. I can even read your minds, though most of the time you don't realise it. I can even read Gary's mind – can you imagine that?

'Hardly, but yes, Dad.... Yes.'

There's only one thing that remains unfulfilled for me, V. I've experienced all other happiness with you. You've made me feel honoured. I'm grateful to all three of you. Yes, at times you've also made me angry, or disappointed, but I've forgotten all the bitter moments, son. Believe me, there isn't any bit of sorrow here – I haven't brought the hard days with me in my bag. There's only good times here with me.

But, still, one thing is missing... It might be something trivial, and I have thought so more lately, especially as I got older, but I want to say it now – this could be my last chance, as you know.

I've always wanted a grandchild, son. That's the only thing missing in my life, as of today. But I accept that one can't always get whatever he wants, right? At least I have my children. You are here, and I am happy about that.

Nevertheless, this is my will: the first request is that you should marry a good girl and have a child. You'll be a good father, V. I know you will. Gary could also be a good father, but it's too late for him, I guess. He wouldn't want it any longer, anyway. But you, son... become a father and enjoy the happiness I've enjoyed for all my life. Enjoy the serenity that I'm feeling right now.... Feel it while you're still living. Do you understand? I can assure you that it's a perfect state of being – including even the fights, the arguments, the clashes and rebellions; they are all worth it.

Now, I want to say something about this girlfriend you've been bringing to our family dinners. She is beautiful, by the way. I love her curly hair, and I like her. I have concluded that she's not an ordinary lady. Here's my advice, short and brief: Don't lose her. You seem to get along well. She's a little unruly, it seems, but such a woman is good because she'll keep you alive; she'll keep you fit for struggles in life. A woman should fight in a real sense and show her teeth whenever required. But she should also love properly, and I think I can sense that ability in this girl. I wish that everything goes well, and that, in the end, you marry her. Then, I will have a grandchild.

Son, become a father. Have a daughter or son who resembles you, and transfer your merits to them. Love them and tell them about me and your mother. We'd be very, very happy if they'd love us in their dreams. Remember us. I hope they won't grow up without knowing us. Hey, and don't say that I was an asshole, okay?

'No, Dad, I won't....'

Because there's only one asshole in this family. Okay, I shouldn't be steering off subject; this is my will. My will! My lawyers forced me to make this. They said I should think of this as a precaution, in case of sudden death. Anyway, I agreed to write down one or two things that I had in my mind, but only in the form of letters to my children, not for the law or any of that bureaucratic shit. I'm sure you three will do whatever is required whenever it is required. Meaning, after I die.

Anyways, here is the last advice I will pass on to you, and my last requests.

More than one commander is not a good idea, neither in war nor in companies. One person should talk and the others should obey. Yeah, I sound like an old prick. Because that's what I am! But I feel there should only be one commander in dealing with my will too. If I just wrote you three letters explaining the details, you would discuss it among yourselves, but of course there's a chance you would not find "the" most proper solution. Maybe you'd have arguments. I want to prevent that. Don't hurt each other at all, son. I know you won't, but I am still warning you, as I am the father.

With all this in mind, this letter is my will, V – the other letters are more like farewell letters of a sort. "Thanks and never forget me" bullshit. I must admit, I even cried while writing Gary's, the bastard. Being a father is like this. I fought with him, quarrelled hard, but I've never resented him.

You are all my dear children, my everything. Love and protect yourselves, and each other. And respect each other. Always be together. Watch each other's backs. Do you promise me, son?

'Yeah, Dad, I promise...'

Listen to what I say, and then tell the others my thoughts. I mean, I'd appreciate it if you do this, but if you say to yourself that I am dead anyway and hence should not intervene in your decisions, then that's up to you. Do whatever you want. But, if you go bankrupt, then you will one day pay for it. On the other side – to me.

'We'll do whatever you want, Dad... whatever.... Oh, God...'

This may get a little detailed from now on, but we have to do this. Now, as you know, I own 70% of the company and you three own the rest – 10% each. When I go six feet under, I want my dough to be distributed as follows: 20 percent to Lori, 17.5 percent each to you and Gary, 10 percent to Amy, and 5 percent to Andrew and Nancy.

This is my plan, wish, will – whatever you want to call it.
I also want to tell you my rationale behind this decision, so that you won't have any doubts in your mind.

I need to start with Lori. As you know, she has put up with me for years and worked hard, really hell of a lot. If the company has survived until this day, she has had much more to do with that than me. So, I can comfortably say she already deserves it – to have a little more than you guys. This is fair. Because of her hard work, she couldn't find the right guy for herself, nor have a kid. From time to time, I can see the regret in her eyes over this. She must also be unlucky, to have never met a proper man. Look at James, for God's sake! What kind of an asshole! In order not to be alone, she's married that prick. And what could I say about it? Should I have said "no"? Do I have any right to? She knows what to do with her life – she must know.

And Amy – she has always respected me as if I were her real father, and she has also worked very, very hard over the last couple of years. Doesn't she also deserve a reward? Yes, she does. In fact, we talked about this once, and I told her I'd give her a part of the company – shares, I mean. I don't want to be unfair to anybody. It's her right to have something.

Andrew and Nancy: oh boy, you know what they mean to us. Maybe more than I do. They must have a rest and live their own lives at some point, right? Clark is now a young man, and he's going to make his own living, separated from them. We should – no, we MUST – make a contribution to their lives.

As for ownership of the company, what I'm planning to do is as follows. It's up to you guys whether you implement this or not.
The management should of course belong to Lori. She knows best how the business runs. And Amy should be a vice-something – they'll figure that out. Two of you will sit on your asses at your homes while the other two earn dough for you! Now I'm getting pissed off just thinking about this!

Anyway. You are struggling to do something nice – I see that... but Gary... oh God. Whatever. This isn't the right time for his shit. I need to shut up.

'No, don't stop, Dad... Talk forever.'

Now what? The house. I think Andrew and Nancy should take the house. You can take some of the furniture, though – you know, as a memento – but the rest should be theirs; they should enjoy the house.

I know that now you are wondering about the books, right? Hey, boy, I know you. The library is completely yours. Take it and get lost in it, like in the old days. Check my underlines. And then show them to your brother – maybe he'll learn something. Read and read and read, V, and never become fed up with reading. Keep in mind that no matter how much you've read, it's never enough. You can never read enough. So don't stop. Drop those phones, or laptops, or whatever else you're killing time with and go read, boy.

Look, I need to mention something about that prick James... God knows, I hate him... whatever. If by any chance he gets mad about these new share partitions – if he, I don't know, expects some dough or questions why Amy gets some and he doesn't – please find a way to shut his mouth. Who is he to me? What good has he done to me or my company?

And never, never let him abuse Lori. She wouldn't allow something like that anyway, but then again, be on her side, and stay close to her. Protect her and consider her word as law. Is that clear, son?

'Yes, Dad. Don't worry... I'm on her side, always...'

Yes, I guess that's "the will" thing. Easier than I thought.... If I've forgotten anything, get together with the others and deal with it. My lawyers will help you if there's any need. You know how much I hate monetary issues.

What I want to say now is much more important, son. I want your full attention, please.

First listen to me, and then share the nutritious stuff with the others. They are... well, one is busy with her job and the other is... you know. I can only trust in you. I'm sure you will listen to me and do what I want.

'I'm all ears, Dad...'

First, you. As I said before, I hope you hold on to that girl, and marry her, and then have a child. Become a father. Always follow your virtues. Always aim to see the glass as half-full. Be always happy. And hold on to life. Nothing is impossible in life. If you try, you can shape it as you want it.

Don't try to take everything under your control: learn to let go sometimes. Pay attention to your energy, and use it sparingly. Sometimes one does his best, and sees that it's not enough — so drop it there and focus on other things; you can learn and evolve. Let matters condense, and then attack again. Believe me, nothing will get worse if you struggle for the best. Everything will always get better. You have to be hopeful. Be always hopeful, son.

Don't hesitate to show your affection towards your friends, the people you love, and your family. Become a bridge between Lori and Gary. Don't let them stay distant — make them get closer to each other.

You know that I like Eric very much. My relationship with him is almost no different than that one I have with you; after so many years spent together, he is like my own son. He never disrespects me — only loves me back. Keep getting along well with him; don't be at odds with him, ever. I know you won't, but I wanted to stress this once more. You two have a bond that has been getting stronger every day. Don't let anything ruin that. If you two keep this strong bond you have together, no one can stand in your way. Friendship requires self-confidence, effort and sacrifice. And it's worth it.
I know, I know, you don't need to hear this, but I am a father, so I'm saying it just in case.

'Dad, don't do this to me, please... I've made mistakes. Oh GOD! But... I'll compensate for them, don't worry — I'll keep the bond alive, Dad.'

Son, Lori... she's tired, very tired. She has worked very intensely for a long time, and not even formed a decent family because of her job. Talk to her, and tell her that if she'd like... she can quit. I mean, I won't feel bad or blame her for leaving. If she quits, I think Amy would be an appropriate successor to take over the management of the company. We should let Lori rest and live her life from now on. She should quit. She should do whatever she wants. She deserves more than this, but, you know, what more could I offer her? I can't change the past.

I know I don't sound very fond of Gary, but of course I love him, too. Help him as much as you can. His mind is busy with painting, with artistic thoughts and stuff. I guess. I mean, I've never understood what he's doing, but I hope he can put in some real effort and have success in his art, if this is "the" thing he wants to do. He should have an aim – a dream to fulfil.

I told him things like this in his letter, too, but I need your help, V. You'd better impress these ideas on him as well. He should not carry out this profession for vanity. Now that he has chosen to do it, he must produce successful and worthy results. Then I can be happy – and maybe even understand him, wherever I am... maybe I won't hear about it, but I'll definitely feel it. Anyway, fuck it.

And don't use the F-word so often, not like your father.

'Fuck! FUCK-FUCK-FUCK!'
I let myself go. I couldn't hold in my tears any longer.

You must also do your job better. You should try to get better every day. You are on the right track, as far as I can see, which makes me happy. Though you have a humble job, you pay attention to doing it well. I like this. Keep that bookshop always nice and cosy. And tidy – this is important. If you can't deal with everything that needs doing, employ some people to help you, part-time students maybe. Selling books is a respectable thing, and so you should show the greatest respect to your shop. Look after your books well. Don't let them suffer dust and humidity.

'Dad, please, please, forgive me... forgive me... Oh my books... They have suffered a lot... because of me. Forgive me, Dad...'

I just re-read what I've written so far. I've made a lot of repetitions – sorry for that. But I let myself write freely, however I liked. I'd be glad if you read it carefully even though it is repetitious. I mean, if everything goes as planned, you'll be reading this when I'm dead, for God's sake. Which means this is going to be our farewell talk. Fuck the repetitions then! Repetitions... If one day you become a father, then you'll understand that repetitions are your best friend. Have you counted them yet, in this last paragraph? If not, I'll tell you: there's five. Whatever. I know that you are a "right" soul; you need no repetitive warnings about anything. You'll do good, V, I feel it.

'Oh God... don't do this to me...'

I had only one request for Mr Elkins. He will give you these letters one week after I pass away. This one-week period is important. You see, I'm concerned about that son-of-a-gun James... I'm wondering how he'll behave, and if his true self will come out. If he does any wrong – any wrong! – then it must be revealed so you can all get to know him well. Maybe I can do this one last favour to Lori, before I go. I mean, after I go, but you get what I mean.

The delay is also because I want Amy to wait a little, you know. She lacks a bit of patience. No... that's bullshit. I think I am wrong about her and she does know how to be patient. I have promised her some shares in any case; she should wait a little and enjoy anticipation. Afterwards, she can celebrate as much as she wants.... She's a good girl, son. She will wait and behave patiently, I'm sure. She's ambitious but knows where to stop.

Look, V, if you notice that anyone – I said, ANYONE – has done wrong in the one-week period before you read these letters, behave accordingly. You'll decide the best option, I'm sure of it. You can change my words, or my will, or whatever these are, however you like. I trust you forever, son. Forever.

'Don't do this to me, Dad, please. Enough... the pain... this is...'

Well, boy, I hope you won't have to read this letter, and that you'll have to bear with me at least twenty more years. I will see 100! I will play with your kids in the garden. I won't pass my company on to anyone. Maybe we'll read these letters together one day, who knows?

That's all for now, I guess. There isn't anything more to discuss. If there are any problems, you'll be able to solve them on your own. You don't need any written guidance to do what's right. Our love and our bond is much stronger than any monetary issues.

Okay, V, time to say goodbye. I mean, tonight I'll see you and Lori, but of course I won't say a word about these letters. One day – with or without me – you'll read my last words to you. Till that day, enjoy my laughter and anger, son! And always remember, our hope will keep us alive, our hope will turn our ordinary days into life – real life!

Goodbye son. With all my love.
BK.

I was sobbing. I left the farewell letter on the coffee table, and then buried my face into the sofa and cried like a child, as loudly as I could. I felt a great burden on my shoulders. I had disappointed my father. He had put unending trust in me, and I had made mistakes in return.

It was a moment of regret as well, for all the times I could have showed my love to him but had not. That cloud of regret, which perhaps I'd feel for all my life, emerged for the first time as I cried after reading the letter. I swore to myself that I would do whatever it took to pay his trust back. I had left him alone at the company once; I wouldn't leave him alone twice.

I grew calmer after a couple of minutes and read the letter once more. Then I thought of Lori, and of how she had read my letter and Gary's too. I should have been furious about that; how on earth could she have done such a thing? But I couldn't get mad. And I now understood the dramatic and sudden changes in her attitudes, her fluctuating moods. She must have woken up after reading the letters – especially mine.

I had a shower and prepared a French omelette for myself. I felt a deep cut bleeding heavily inside my heart, but I was trying to mask it with living joy. It was somehow relaxing to know that all this trouble, turmoil and uncertainty could (would?) disappear at last. We might reach a conclusion. An end to an episode of conflict in our lives. My father had taken the burden off our shoulders, as he'd always done.

I thought of everything he'd mentioned in his letter: it was like a cloud over my head, his words raining on me continuously. He'd made no point that I disagreed with, nor any claim I thought wrong. He'd created a blueprint for the future that I wanted to apply completely.

I had to inform or consult Lori and Gary beforehand, but then again, my route was destined. Lori already knew what was written in my letter, and Gary would never reject it. It dawned on me suddenly that Lori might have made new decisions in accordance with my letter and even begun to take steps in order to execute them. Her discretion was worthy of appreciation. She had given us our letters at the requested time and hadn't given us any clues about their content prior to that.

I needed to find a way to let everybody know of the new situation. Should we all get together, or should I talk to them individually? Gathering at the company with a relatively small group could be a better idea.

I called my father's secretary and asked her to arrange a meeting at 2 p.m. with Amy, Gary and Lori, but decided to visit my father's house before the meeting and talk to Andrew and Nancy about their share of my father's will.

When I arrived, Nancy was busy gathering up their stuff in order to leave.

'Hey, are you guys taking time off? What's this?'

'Well, it's time, V,' Nancy said. 'You know, after Mr Kushner— I mean, we're done here, I guess. You'll have your plans for the place and we... we don't want to interfere with anything, so we thought we'd get going as soon as possible.'

'You don't interfere with anything, Nancy.'

'We would have evacuated the place sooner, but you know, everything happened so fast and... there was stuff we needed to take care of. It ended up taking a whole week. Sorry for that, for the delay....'

'Hey, would you relax a bit, for God's sake? Why are you saying these things? And where is Andrew? I must talk to you both.'

'You know the small village house we bought last year? We're moving there. Andrew's there taking care of the arrangements, but he should be back soon. Wait for me in the living room; I'll get us coffee.'

'Okay, but I'll be in the garden. I don't have much time. Let's give Andrew fifteen minutes and see if he can make it.'

'Hurrying never ends here in this city. Never...'

In the garden, the tree was swinging with the wind. A million things had happened that week, but the tree didn't care about any of them; it just kept dancing. It was always there, always would be. Exactly one week ago, it had witnessed my father passing away, but it hadn't collapsed. I couldn't help watching its solemnity. The light breeze rustled its leaves, and the branches moved from side to side calmly, confidently. As if the tree was talking to me with gestures, and motivating me.

I didn't dare to leave before talking to Andrew, and half an hour later he arrived. He and Nancy came out to the garden.

'New plans, huh?' I asked.

'Yes, V,' Andrew said. 'We need to take action; we've got nothing left to do here.'

'Well... I need to talk to you about... let's... um, look, I read my father's will this morning—'

'Oh, Mr Kushner,' Nancy said, and started to cry.

'Well... I know this is hard. You know. But anyways... he wanted us to wait for one week before reading his will, and so Lori— Look, let's just skip the details and get to the points in his will that will interest you. Actually, I have some good news.'

'Mr Kushner's death can't bring any good, V,' said Nancy.

'Before you start to talk,' Andrew said, 'I want to say that we don't expect anything. Anything.'

'Okay, look... my father wanted me to do something, and I'm gonna do it no matter what. I don't care about anything beyond that, okay? Here it is in a nutshell: right now you are my hosts, and you have served me this delicious cup of coffee at your beautiful new house. Enjoy!'

Their lips trembled. I couldn't tell if it was longing, or gratitude, or both. Nancy was already crying, but now Andrew too?

Andrew took Nancy's hands into his.

'This kind of happiness is difficult to define, V,' he said. 'This house has a special place in our memories and in our hearts. Almost all of our lives have been spent here. We've loved it like it was our own, and taken care of it accordingly. What Mr Kushner is trying to do for us is... an unusual gesture. But as I said, don't feel obliged to do this, because we don't expect anything from you. We were preparing ourselves to leave, for good.'

'Enough, Andrew. Please, stop it. I must do this. This is the old man's will, for God's sake. Please. He wanted you to be happy and have this house. Okay?'

'Well, this is more than good, ain't it, Nancy? But...'

'There are some minor details. Mr Kushner would like to allow Gary and Lori to come and see, you know, whether they want to take any items or furniture from the house – as mementos. And to me, he gave the library. Can you imagine? Isn't this amazing? All those books... Oh God!'

'Yes, V, very, very good for you. I'm happy for you. We're both happy for you and—'

'And one final thing,' I said. 'You together – I mean, not each – will also own five percent of the company's shares.'

Nancy started to sob out loud. These were tears of gratitude. The indefinable happiness of not having been forgotten, and of being appreciated for all those shared years.

We sat in the garden a little longer, the wind carrying away our feelings of happiness, sorrow and gratitude. The tree was still swinging slowly, greeting its new owners and saying goodbye to me.

'By the way,' Andrew said, 'I would have asked yesterday, V, but I couldn't find the chance. What happened to your eye? Is everything okay?'

He knew that everything was not okay.

I smiled. 'I will say that... I hit my head on a door while running around the store. And you should believe me... and ask no-further-questions....'

He smiled back. We all fell silent. And I realised that it was time to go.

After carrying out the first step of my plan, it was time to deal with the second one. Just before noon, I parked my car in front of Eric's office-building. I didn't know whether he had gone to work, but if he had, he'd likely go out for lunch around this time. I decided to wait for a bit, and then, if he didn't come out, I would try to visit him upstairs.

Seven or eight minutes later, he exited with a couple of other fellas, all dressed in suits with sharp haircuts and black shades on. He was without his crutch, wobbling and walking slowly. He didn't seem happy; rather, he seemed dull and listless.

I got out of the car, locked the doors and started to walk in parallel with them on the pavement across the road. I planned to cross the street at the first traffic lights. In order not to attract attention, I avoided looking directly at them but instead checked with the corner of my eye every now and then.

In my last vague attempt, I realised that Eric had dropped back from the group and was standing still, looking at me. There was a hectic flow of traffic flowing through the avenue between us, but we gazed at each other as if we were the only two alive in a deserted world: sound vanished, people disappeared, life evaporated.

I waited a moment for the traffic to loosen up, and then ran across the street. Eric turned and started to walk back towards his office as fast as he could.

I caught up and snatched at his arm. 'Wait, wait for a moment...'

He stopped and looked at me.

'Your eye... nice job,' he said. 'But less than you deserved. I should've done worse.'

'Please..., just listen to me. Please, just for three minutes, and then kick me out of your life—'

'I've already kicked you the fuck out of my life, asshole!'

'Look, give me three minutes—'

'Get out of my way.'

'No, I won't! Listen to me, and then I'll go the fuck away! Okay?!'

'Fuck you!'

He pushed me and tried to pass by, but I grabbed his shoulder. He hit my arm hard and released himself. I grabbed him again, and he hit me once more and released himself. I grabbed him again.

'Look, motherfucker, I'll ruin your other eye, too, and then you won't be able to see shit! Get the fuck out of my way!'

'Do whatever you want, but first listen to me. Hear what I have to say! And then go.'

He was muttering and looking at me. There were people around us, acquaintances of his from the firm and elsewhere. I knew he wouldn't want this thing to get any wilder and nastier there. He was in a situation where he had to act calm – which was to my advantage.

'What?! What do you want?' he said. 'Are you looking for trouble again? Isn't it enough, all that you've done?'

'Listen. Okay, I was wrong. And Danielle was also wrong—'

'SHUT—' He cut himself off and changed his voice to a hiss. 'Shut the fuck up!'

'We were stupid for a moment. We misbehaved, okay—'

'Look, really, I'll break your chin if you continue talking this shit. You have no time left, asshole.'

'She came to the store, as always—'

'As always!' he said and gave a harsh laugh.

'And we talked. I was drunk. And she was sad. She was sad because of you—'

'Which is none of your business.'

'We lost our control. And that's *all*. A stupid mistake in the moment. That's all. And, neither of us approve of what we did, of course...'

'Are you serious? I mean, you're here, telling me THIS shit? "Neither of us approve..." Who the— Get lost man, get the fuck away from me, now!'

'This is not shit—'

He pushed me. 'Fuck off! NOW! Shut up and get the FUCK away. Go! GO! Get lost motherfucker!'

'CALM down! Listen, it wasn't right, us losing control. But you must know that... you KNOW! Nothing like that has ever happened between us before, nothing... nothing! Not even a very small thing. We were standing face to face, and on the verge of saying, "Enough, this is ridiculous," and then we found ourselves... just kissing each other—'

He hit my chest with both his hands and pushed me away.

'Enough! Fuck off, V. I don't wanna see your face, hear your voice or anything. Just fuck off. Have you lost all your dignity? Huh?'

'I'm not blaming Dani for anything—'

He hit me again. 'I said fuck off, asshole.'

'I am much more to blame. I am much more guilty.... We lost our control suddenly, and that's the exact moment you saw us... but we would have stopped there. Right there. With shame. But you saw us, and it was too late to explain—'

'Betrayal, you prick, can't be explained! Just CAN'T!'

'You wouldn't listen—'

'And I'm NOT listening now, either!'

'We were involved in such a stupid and complex situation that I got in a tizzy... and my mind... just stopped functioning. I... I couldn't say anything or defend myself.'

'Defend yourself?! Are you out of your fucking mind?! Defend?! DE-FEND?!'

'Look I don't mean that I'd try to make it right—'

'How could you defend yourself, you motherfucker?! We were brothers... WE WERE BROTHERS! How... how could you even think of defending what you did?'

'I DIDN'T think of anything! We didn't plan anything. You just saw us at a very stupid moment... in an absurd situation that is difficult to explain. Yes, I accept that it's our fault it got to that... but we didn't betray you Eric. Never. Not yesterday or any day before.'

I paused. Eric was looking at me, breathing fast.

He turned and started to walk towards the middle of the square, where there was a fountain pouring water into a large stone basin. It was surrounded by tables where people were sitting and eating their sandwiches. I followed him.

'This is disgrace. You and Dani, for God's sake... I used to trust you both. Look at you now. V, we were brothers.... How...?'

'You are right... I can't say anything except that I'm so sorry.'

'Why did you come here? What have you been telling me for the last ten minutes? What can you say? What can she say? That she was lonely and I didn't care enough about her...? Fuck off! You and her both! Get the fuck out of my life, for good!'

'Eric... please. I'm begging you. Let's leave it to time. I don't say—'

'V. Enough! That's enough! Leave it to time?! You don't even... you can't even see the shit that you've done.... You can't know how I felt at that moment! Neither can she. But it's not important anymore. You won't be able to hurt me—'

'Cut the crap! Who wants to hurt you?!'

'You couldn't hurt me much. No....' He sat on the stone lip of the basin and stared into the water. 'It was a sign. A revelation. I already knew it. That I wouldn't share a lifetime with Danielle. Now, after what I've seen, I'm clear. You've done me a favour. How does it feel? Are you pleased about that, huh?'

I sat next to him.

'Look, Eric, I know she's pregnant.'

He smiled bitterly.

'Yes, and do you know when she told me? Just minutes after I saw my best friend kissing her! No, not my best friend – my *brother*! Yes, she told me right after that. What a perfect timing.... Don't you think so? Isn't it perfect? She is a very skilful woman, so delicate. But you already know that, right, fuckface?'

'Hey, hey... stop.... After you saw us, you waited for her. I saw you.'

'So what?'

'Well, you didn't leave. Doesn't that mean something? That you care for her? Eric, don't let this anger ruin everybody's lives... I'm begging you, please....'

He turned to me.

'You idiot. I didn't leave because I was too upset. I sat there because at that moment I imagined myself as her husband. I sat there as I was sorry for our baby. You think I will forgive you or that bitch? You can't be such a bonehead. No. No, you are a fox. A hungry and evil fox.'

'No, I am not. Don't exaggerate everything this much—'

'Bullshit.'

'I'm not defending myself, Eric. I am ready to wait. Maybe you won't talk to me for years, or maybe you will punch me again. I'm not obsessed with making up with you. But I want to explain it. I know that our bond, our trust, has been deeply hurt. But anyway, never mind me... what about Dani? She loves you, man. What will happen to her, Eric? Or to the baby? Danielle wants to marry you and give you your baby—'

'Fuck off!'

'I know there were some problems disturbing you, and she knew something was wrong too, but when you and Amy—'

'Shut up!'

'I mean, she must have sensed something from your behaviour. She might have felt lost... she's pregnant and in love with you! She might have felt afraid, lost her balance...'

'So what?! Does losing her balance give her the right to fuck you?!'

'You don't have any right to treat her this way!'

'I can treat anyone in any way I want, okay! You can't fuck with me!'

'You don't understand.... This incident has become an exit for you to step out of the relationship, and you're using it foxily.'

'I don't give a shit what you think. What I've seen is enough for me.'

'You needed an excuse, and this was enough for you. It's your excuse to leave her. You are using this to do something you couldn't face up to doing for your own reasons, and blaming me and Danielle. I accept that what I did is wrong and disgusting, but so is what you are doing.'

'Save your smart-boy shit for yourself. You can't teach me what to do. Who the fuck are you anyway? The best friend with a betrayal in his pocket?'

'What's gonna happen now?'

'It is none of your business!'

'Come on, Eric.... What's she gonna do?'

'We have broken up and she'll have an abortion.'

The pain grew deeper.

'Don't! Please, don't, Eric. Please, I'm begging you. Please...'

'What is this pathetic begging shit? Get the fuck off of me! Leave me alone! It was gonna happen sooner or later, but you helped speed it along, so thank you!'

'Eric..., it shouldn't be this way. You can fix it, fix everything. Please, give her a chance; she loves you so much...'

'Amy will get divorced from Gary, and we'll be together again. We even want to marry. Now what? Are you planning to ambush her in your store, too? But she won't kiss you. Don't get excited in vain...'

I was shocked to hear that Eric had made such a drastic decision, and that Amy would stand beside him. I had been hoping that Eric and Danielle could make it up again, but everything was only getting worse.

'But... what about Danielle? Her baby?'

'She'll continue her life. She should have thought about "her" baby before kissing you. Or maybe she'll ask for some help from you. What do you think?'

How endless his fury was. I couldn't contribute anything positive to Danielle's problem; I was both dismayed and heart-broken. But there was no point wasting any more time trying to connect to an endless anger.

'What you and I had, what we've shared, is very deep,' I said. 'And even though you reject it now, we are bonded. You are within my veins, my blood. When time helps us to overcome these days, when you become calmer one day and begin to think in a more reasonable way, we'll talk again.

'I accept that I did something very wrong, and I've apologised for it countless times. I'm sure you're using my mistake as an excuse for doing something you really want to do but don't have the guts to do under normal conditions. I'm sure you know this in your heart and will admit this truth to me one day. And you will forgive me.

'We will talk again one day, as brothers. But I am disappointed and very upset now. Not for myself, but for Danielle. I will go now, to meet her and try to do my best to help her. I don't want her to live under this wreckage, and I don't give a shit what you think about this.'

He was glaring at me. Without waiting for his response, I walked away, wishing he'd call my name. That somehow he'd take a step towards mending all that we had ruined. That he would support my pledge to help Danielle.

He didn't.

I went to Danielle's apartment and knocked on the door. There was no answer. I knocked again. And again...

At last I heard her footsteps coming. Was she listening to hear the voice of the man she most needed? If so, my voice must have disheartened her.

'Hey, Dani..., it's me... got a minute for me? Please?'

She cracked the door open.

'Thank you. Hey, are you okay? You...'

Her eyes were swollen and red. When she saw me, she started crying again. I stepped inside and hugged her. Her tears evolved into sobbing. I closed the door.

'I won't tell you not to cry. Cry as much you want. I'm here with you; you're not alone, okay?'

'V, this is hell...'

'But you know that it will end. These days will pass... it's so hard now, I know..., but they'll pass.'

'NO! No, they won't pass... nothing's gonna come to an end! This... this will be with me forever!'

'Okay. Calm down. You'll see that it will pass—'

She pulled out of my arms all of a sudden, furious and with tears in her eyes.

'He's going to marry Amy! AMY! He's not even thinking of me anymore... they've already been sleeping together! They fucked! Before all of this, everything! He'd already made his decision even before he saw us there. Son of a bitch! I shouldn't have trusted him from the beginning. I told him about my baby, you know... and what did he say? WHAT?! That he's going to marry Amy. That bitch, and that bastard... oh, God...'

She collapsed to her knees on the floor. She was crying, yelling and swearing continuously. Finally she paused, swiped her eyes with the back of her hands, and looked at me. I thought that she had relaxed, but I was wrong. She started all over again.

'Dani, believe me, these days are gonna pass soon. Believe me. Just try to stay calm and be patient—'

'Be patient about what? WHAT!?' V, it's too much... too much. I mean, what have I done to him to deserve... this?!'

'Look, stop trying to reason this—'

'All I've ever done is to love him. Love him more than he loves me.'

'I know.'

I kneeled down and hugged her.

'I'm sorry,' she said. 'I know that you're here for me. I'm very grateful to you. Sorry for all this yelling and crying bullshit. But... but I couldn't even fight with him, V. He didn't even... didn't even let me shout at him, punch him or anything.... He just left. I'm lonely.'

'Just forget what happened or is happening, okay? Change your focus. Let your life flow somehow. Let me ask you: what now?'

She looked at me. 'What now?!'

'Yes. What now?'

'Are you serious? Don't you see me? I'm a wreck, for God's sake! Fuck your *what now*!'

'But, Dani, look. You have to be more... Danielle, the baby? I mean —'

'I don't know. I haven't decided anything yet. Maybe I'll have her. Or him. Not sure, I-don't-know...'

'Really?'

'Really what? Why not? This is a baby of love. At least, the baby of MY love— not that asshole's.'

She had courageous intentions at that moment. In their burning triangle (or square, if we include Gary), everyone was right from their own perspective, and everyone had the right to wish or demand whatever they wanted for their own lives. But Danielle seemed the most injured soul among them – maybe the only one who was desperate. The one bright thing on her side was that she wanted to have the baby.

We said goodbye. I tried to make sure she knew I'd be near her whenever required, and let her know of my appreciation of her courage. We hugged, then I opened the door and stepped outside. Was she the woman I kissed?

'V,' she said, 'I know it doesn't mean anything... and maybe it's meaningless to say this right now, but... I want you to hear this.'

'What?'

'I wish it was your baby, not Eric's.'

It was a strange truth that anything I said now would be absurd. I smiled.

'Well... I don't know what to say...'

She smiled.

'I just wanted you to know. It's true. I really feel so. Not because Eric has done this to me, or because I'm pregnant and furious. This is something bizarre – a different feeling that is difficult to explain. For instance, you are here now and... Eric isn't.'

I felt both pleased and under a heavy blanket of embarrassment at the same time. Danielle was looking directly into my eyes and speaking with her overly self-confident voice. She knew I was embarrassed and, like a teenage girl, she took pleasure from this – even under such circumstances.

'Well, I think I owe you my thanks,' I said. 'I feel flattered... and I'm sure you can see my red cheeks now....'

She smiled. 'You don't owe me anything. The woman you love should know she's special... to be able to live you.'

I said all I could say with a nod and left there – in order to prevent the flow of unnecessary and irrelevant attraction between us.

It was almost 2 p.m., and I was on my way to the company to accomplish my big mission.

I arrived there ten minutes early, and found Amy and Lori waiting for me in the meeting room. We greeted each other without mentioning any details regarding our complicated lives. Amy didn't ask anything about my purple eye.

'Let's just wait for Gary to get here and then we can start.'

'Gary isn't coming, V,' Amy said. 'We can start.'

'He isn't? Why not?'

Amy looked at the ground and touched her hair. Then she said it all in one burst: 'Actually, it has something to do with me. I wanted Gary to tell you the news himself, but... anyhow you're gonna hear it soon, so... yes, we've decided to break up. The problems between us, along with Mr Kushner's letter, were altogether too much for him. So, he told me to go, and to "take" whatever I wanted with me. Well, I'm here.'

'To take what you want?' Lori said.

Lori might have guessed earlier that Gary wanted to split up with Amy, but judging by her surprised expression, it seemed this was the moment she became sure of it.

'Okay, I'm sorry, Amy,' Lori said and hugged her.

I knew that Amy had been the one to take this step, so I didn't feel any consolation was necessary for her.

'I'm sorry to hear this, Amy,' I said. 'I hope everything will be fine for both of you.'

She didn't reply, but nodded.

'Yes, I wish the same,' Lori said. 'It must be so difficult for you to... I mean, it's all so hard—'

'Can we start?' I said. 'I don't have much time, sorry....'

I needed to change the subject before Lori started to talk about anything that would complicate the split and everything else coming behind it.

We sat around the meeting table.

'Dad's will has at last been disclosed,' I said. 'The letter he wrote for me also contains his will. What he said regarding his house and his shares in the company is very clear. However, he also said that while his decisions are what he thinks most appropriate, they are subject to change if Lori, Gary or I wished it so. In my opinion, as these are his wishes, I don't see any point in arguing over them. He has his reasons. So, what about you, Lori?'

'I agree with you. We should do this as he wanted.'

'I need to say a few words,' I said. 'During the last week, we have experienced many extraordinary events, but now, in the end, we can see that my father made decisions that would please everyone. I hope we can leave everything else behind us from now on – whatever happened in the past should stay in the past. It might be difficult, but we don't have any other choice.

'So now, about the dough – wasn't everything about that? Okay, to be brief, the distribution of the shares used to be 70 percent to Mr Kushner and 10 percent each for Lori, Gary and me. Mr Kushner wishes to distribute his shares as follows: 20 percent to Lori, 17.5 percent each to Gary and me, 10 percent to Amy—'

'What?!' Amy said.

'Just a sec, Amy, I wanna finish this as quickly as I can... 5 percent to Andrew and Nancy. So as of today, Lori owns 30 percent, Gary and I own 27.5 percent each, Amy 10 percent and Andrew and Nancy 5 percent. Is everything clear?'

'I can't believe this,' Amy said. 'Oh my God! Mr Kushner.... V, thank you! I mean, this is amazing news! More than perfect! Oh-my-God! WOW! I mean, Mr Kushner had, you know, told me that one day... but... this is... wow! Ten percent! I am very happy, and more than honoured. I don't know what to say—'

'Congratulations,' Lori said.

'Oh, Lori..., thank you. Thank you so much!' Amy said.

I was sure she wished to be able to mask her surprise and joy, but she couldn't.

'And one last thing,' Amy said. 'I need to thank you both once more. I mean, I heard that Mr Kushner had left the final word to you guys—'

'Indeed, to all three of us. Gary could also... you know...'

'Yes, yes... to him as well – to all three of you. Your respect for me and for Mr Kushner's decision is... way too noble. Thank you very much. This is, oh God, this is so unbelievable....'

'You don't need to thank anybody,' Lori said. 'We've done what my father wanted us to do, nothing more. This is what you deserve for all those years. Enjoy it.'

Amy's hands were trembling from excitement.

'The next issue is related to the house,' I said. 'I don't think this topic will fascinate you as much the other, Amy, but I must do it.'

'What? I'm sorry, V. I... I couldn't... What did you say?'

'It's okay, Amy. The house. It will be given to Andrew and Nancy. Before I came here, I stopped by and told them the news. Lori, we can take anything from inside as a memento.'

'I know, V,' Lori said. 'I have no problem with that.'

It was of course not nice that she already knew it, but I didn't mention it. I wanted the meeting to come to an end at once so I could return to my life.

'Finally, the books,' I said. 'I have all the books. The most valuable items are mine....'

We laughed. Although Amy probably didn't know what she was laughing at.

'And that's a wrap!' I said. 'Mr Elkins and his associates will take care of the legal side of things, all the bureaucratic issues and so on. Gary and I are of course gonna be outsiders to the business – as usual – so all the responsibilities are on your shoulders again, ladies. Oh, I almost forgot: I should also mention that Lori will be the boss from now on. Mr Kushner also mentioned that...'

Business again, and Amy returned to earth.

'Of course, of course, V; you don't even need to mention it.... She's the boss.'

It seemed what she had been given was more than enough for her.

Lori smiled. 'Flattering. I-am-da-boss! Under normal conditions, this would be the news of my life... but I need to say a couple of things before we wrap up this meeting.'

'No! What now, Lori?'

Behind all these calm moments and her accepting attitude, had Lori hidden all her objections until the end? Were we going to start everything all over again? Weren't we going to cease fire?

'My father bequeathed that I should continue as "the boss," but he said this without knowing whether I actually wanted to. And so here's the last news of the day: I'm quitting.'

'WHAT?!' Amy said.

'Calm down, Amy.... I know this is a lot to take in just now, but... yep, the reality is this: I'm leaving the company. I want to stay on as a shareholder only, like my wise brothers. And if you want to know my decision about who should succeed me...'

She paused.

'What?' Amy said.

'Do you want to know or—'

'Of course I wanna know, Lori, for God's sake! I'm just a bit shocked to hear this....'

'Okay. I propose that the person who takes my place is Amy—'

'Oh, JESUS!' Amy screamed.

'Are you high, Lori?' I asked.

'Why, do I look high, V? To be honest, I don't see any other person who would do it better than her...'

Amy stood up and ran to Lori. She hugged her as if Lori was her long-lost mother who had showed up after decades apart.

'Thank you, thank you, thank you, thank you, thank you, thank you, thank you.'

I had known that Lori would give up one day, but I hadn't imagined she'd do it so soon, and on top of that leave her chair to Amy. Some things were changing. For the better? I didn't know.

Amy now seemed to consider herself the luckiest person on the globe. It spread from Amy to the world in the form of happiness, smiles, and shivering out of excitement. She started to cry with happiness, unable to control herself.

'Don't get me wrong,' she said. 'I'm not happy about you leaving, Lori, but your trust in me – it means a lot.... It means so much.'

The kind of finale I could only have imagined in my dreams – peaceful and quiet.

Amy, with a victorious smile on her face, began sending messages via her cell phone – it was not hard to guess that Eric would be one of the first to hear her good news. Her expression showed she still couldn't believe what she'd heard.

I thought of Gary and wondered whether he was sad or starting to enjoy the happiness of becoming a father. If so, I wished his happiness would last longer than Eric's. Then I remembered that Eric had never felt happy about it at all.

Our meeting ended officially at about 5 p.m. I congratulated Amy once more, but her awareness that I knew her secret news kept us a little emotionally distant from each other. I was angry at Eric and Amy for what they were doing, and Eric was angry with me as well, even though he'd done much the same thing to Gary. One side of my mind kept revolving this inconsistency. We always wanted life to be fair only to ourselves.

'Guys, I need to rush now, if you excuse me,' Amy said.

'Well, no one can stop you, now,' I said.

She didn't answer me and ran out of the meeting room.

'Do we both know whom she's running to?' Lori said.

'I suppose, yes...'

'How is Danielle?'

'She says she's considering having the baby...'

'Oh, crazy girl. It'll be difficult to raise a child alone, but not impossible. I wish all strength to her. In fact, I'm gonna need the same strength for myself...'

'Why?'

'I also have my own plans, V.... I'm also "considering" having a baby. Does that surprise you?'

'Well... I mean—'

'One woman is in love with Eric and getting him for good, but two other women who also love him want to have their babies without the "Eric." Someone could make a movie out of this, right?'

'Forget about Eric for now. Tell me about your plans?'

'In brief, I'm getting divorced. But before that, I want to adopt a child. Then, I will go far, far away with my child for a while.'

'Is this plan as simple as you are making out right now?'

'I said "in brief." Of course, the adoption could be a little problematic, but James said he wouldn't create any problems for me. He'll help me with this, but in return he asks me to re-consider the divorce thing. I accepted that. In other words, I lied. I know what I want to do; it's crystal clear.'

Lori is open. Lori is frank. The world is in change.

'So, why all these changes from out of the blue?'

'Out of the blue? Are you fucking out of your mind, boy? Don't you see what we've gone through – no, what we are still going through? How can you say out of the blue? All those fights, ambitious chases... Upon reading Dad's letters, the real desires in my mind, or in my heart, came to the forefront. This week of hell has ended up positively for me. Look, I see that in the end, you're happy too. I can see that. Even Amy is happy. Isn't this all you've been asking for? Now you've got it.'

'Of course. But, now you're going to extremes, aren't you?'

'Don't you worry about me; I'm strong. Nothing's gonna stand in my way.'

'Trust me, I know it. What about the baby thing, the applications and so on—'

'Already prepared. And I've been in contact with some people. I think that, in a very short period of time, I'm gonna be a mother to a baby girl.... Isn't that fantastic? So, you can consider me pregnant as well...'

'Oh, dear God! Another victim of Eric with a baby to deliver. Alone! C'est la vie!'

'Shut up! Yes, alone. What's the difference if I had James with me? Nothing. My little girl's gonna be enough for me. We can grow up together.'

'Dad mentioned a grandchild in my letter – as you know – and already you're talking about adopting, and maybe Gary will have a baby too...'

'I want to talk to Gary and encourage him to do so. Life has drawn a way for him. He must realise it.'

'The management drive in your flesh and bones never vanishes...'

'Doesn't it? Then hear this. I have a couple of words for you too, quoted from the letter: "Don't you lose her, son, blah, blah, blah... and in the end, marry her, blah, blah, blah. Become a father..."'

'Why not? I can say I'm in the mood...'

Later, on my way home, I stopped for a couple of minutes and watched the river. The fight and the struggle had at last come to an end. I was feeling relaxed and even a little happy – burden-free.

Our lives had changed, for better and for worse. That I hadn't been able to prevent all the bitter moments that had happened this past week gnawed away me. It had been a very severe fight we'd experienced, and it wouldn't cease easily – not without leaving scars.

All the lives around that table seven days ago had completely changed. And one of them no longer existed. Lori would adopt a baby and get divorced, and James would lose his wife. Gary would possibly get divorced and have a baby too. Amy would get divorced and then marry the love of her life, and have shares in the company she was devoted to. Eric had reignited his love for an old flame and would share the rest of his life with her rather than with the woman who loved him endlessly and who was carrying his child. Danielle would lose her great love and raise his child, alone. And I would lose my best friend.

Was that the happiness we got at the end of all the hustle?

Every war has its casualties, but could we even say, with the losses we'd experienced, that we'd won anything? Or, does anything gained in life come with its losses?

That evening, the sun was hesitant to go home, as if it was still summer – it shone over the river in an enticing and beautiful way. There were a few white clouds in the sky: the cream-like white clouds that Andrew had told me to draw in my mind and heart. The clouds gave me hope, and, moreover, they became hope itself. I smiled involuntarily. My inner-voice told me to believe in the cream-like clouds instead of grieving for the losses. Nothing could get worse if I believed in hope.

And from then on, I believed that hope could bring heaven to any day we lived in. Everyone has their own dream of heaven – for one person, it might be watching the love of his life looking outside through the window of a train. For another, it could be sitting on an uncomfortable chair and writing without sleeping or eating properly for a week. One person's heaven could be the most interesting thing we could ever think of; another's might be the most ordinary thing – something the rest of us pass by every day and do not recognise.

What matters is, heaven is here, now. We can reach it with our hands, we can shape it, we can make it happen. In our minds, we should harvest the wisdom to deserve it. We should enable our souls not to admit defeat. We should chase truth, we should chase dreams, we should chase happiness – and believe that we can get them. Our inner compass will guide our way towards them.

We should not be defeated. We should work for the good of all humankind in every action we take – big or small. We are all in the same boat. The boat of life.

We all can say, "Heaven must be like this" in a small fragment of time, and feel the uniqueness of that peaceful moment.

When I heard a bird chirping above me, I reconnected to real life and felt that I missed the cosiness of my apartment. I started to drive. I thought I deserved it and so bought a bottle of wine on the way home. I didn't want to think of anything any longer. I wanted only to stare out my window and watch the city in the dark, to get drunk and fall asleep. The war was officially over, and my body was starting to feel the pain of the wounds. I was sure the first person who would see me would pity me. I wouldn't care.

Even though I had taken hits in the war, I hadn't fallen. I had always believed that everything – relationships, work, friendships and problems, even ones that at first seemed unsolvable – would get better one way or the other. With this motivation and strength, I managed to survive. Though I looked like a wreck as I dealt with life's problems, I could also see the "cream-like clouds." I'd carried them inside without knowing it.

At the door of my apartment, in the hallway, while I was trying to find the keys in my pocket, the wine bottle slipped from my hand smashed into pieces on the marble ground. My losses weren't coming to an end after all. But I smiled. Though that bottle of wine had been the most valuable thing for me in the whole universe at that moment, I managed to deal with its loss.

As soon as I entered my apartment, my phone rang. To my amazement, it was M. If I heard any good news from her, the superiority of hope over loss might become official for me.

'How are you?' she said.

'Hey. Not bad.... How are you?'

'Good, good... Umm, what are you doin'?'

'Me? I just come home. And... I bought a bottle of wine, because I thought a few glasses might be a good way to end the day... but it slipped out of my hand and smashed in the ground. Silly me. How about you? What are you doing?'

'I'm just wrapping up my work here, and then I'll be catching the first flight back tomorrow morning. I'll be at the airport around ten. Can you pick me up?'

Could I pick her up?! That was the moment I felt my life changed completely, and for the better. My hell-like days had come to an end. My losses were still in my mind, but hope was growing and growing in my heart. With that question, hope covered all of my life.

Once more I was sure that everything would get better for everyone, for everything and always – if there was hope.

Hope was the anchor of our lives.

'YES! Of course I can. Of course. I'd love to.... Yes.'

'Perfect. I'd like that...'

'I... I've missed you very much.'

'Well... that's really nice to hear. I mean it. Look, I need to hang up now, okay?'

'Hey, just a sec... I wanna ask you something.'

'What?'

'How about going somewhere. On a train. This weekend? Without any plans, just wherever we wanna go. You and me. One backpack and that's all. Just the two of us.'

'Sounds interesting... okay, let's do it.'

'Really?! GREAT! Just like I've been dreaming about!'

'What's that?'

I didn't reveal that it was my heaven. I wanted her to feel it herself.

'Look, I need to go now,' she said. 'Let's talk tomorrow.'

'Okay! Hey, this is gonna be great...'

'I hope so. OK, I gotta go... bye.' She hung up.

I smiled.

I was happy. The smashed bottle of wine crossed my mind – I still had to clean up the mess – but not even the idea of nonsense drudgery could take my joy away. With her cheerful voice still echoing in my ears, I started to look for the mop.

Then, I heard someone was knocking on my door.

ABOUT THE AUTHOR

Kurt Erkan's quest is to walk the narrow streets of the human soul. He explores our triumphs and our weaknesses, our fearless leaps and our hesitations, our attempts to become better people and our submissions to darker desires – and how every choice we make can change the paths of those around us. He is fascinated by the inner compass we all have, and how its needle can swing toward the ultimate truth when it is fed by hope.

Kurt Erkan believes that the best way to explore the inner world is by writing – namely via prose and poetry. The information discovered and riddles solved in these realms must be shared with other people who are on the same quest.

Kurt holds a BS degree in civil engineering and lives in Berlin, Germany, with his wife.

kurterkan.com | @the_taletella | taletella@hetsoff.com

AND FIVE, SIX, SEVEN, EIGHT!
(Poetry)

AND FIVE, SIX, SEVEN, EIGHT!

Kurt
Erkan

HETSOFF